BILLY TABBS

(& The Glorious Darrow)

by Michael Paul Michaud

Published by Bitingduck Press
ISBN 978-1-938463-88-4
© 2014 Michael Paul Michaud
All rights reserved
For information contact
Bitingduck Press, LLC
Montreal • Altadena
notifications@bitingduckpress.com
http://www.bitingduckpress.com
Cover image by Lewis Stephens
Interior art by Leanna TenEycke

Publisher's Cataloging-in-Publication
Michaud, Michael [1975-]

Billy Tabbs (& The Glorious Darrow)/by Michael
Michaud –1st ed.—Altadena, CA: Bitingduck Press,
2014
p. cm.

ISBN 9781938463884

[1. Homelessness—fiction 2. Civil rights movements—fiction 3. Liberation movements (civil
rights)—fiction] I. Title

LCCN 2014948818

"The idea that some lives matter less is the root of all that is wrong with the world."

~Dr. Paul Farmer

Disclaimer

This is a work of fiction. All characters are fictitious, and any resemblance to real persons, living or dead, is purely coincidental.

The Glorious Contents

The Nine Tenets of Darrowism

1. All in this world should be valued equally
2. Whoever lives in decadence is an enemy
3. Whoever supports or abides inequality is an enemy
4. Whoever lives in the street is a friend
5. Food shall be dispersed equally
6. Sleep shall be enjoyed equally
7. Work is to be allotted equally
8. No member shall harm any other
9. Darrow knows

"Y OU SURE THAT WE'RE safe here?"

The two men tread cautiously along the narrow ledge, their footfalls registering faint echoes against the shaft's tight confines.

Meyers looks back and nods something of a response, then turns back around and trudges onward, the second man following nervously in his wake. They've progressed well into the tunnel before Meyers finally speaks, the words tumbling into the chilly darkness around them.

"Dr. Lambert, we want to thank you again for coming on such short notice."

Lambert doesn't respond, trailing several feet behind and abundantly careful with every step. Both men carry flashlights, the beams dancing brightly on the narrow ledge before them.

"We were fortunate that someone of your particular expertise was nearby," continues Meyers, adjusting his wool cap. The temperature had dropped, and their breaths form intermittently before them each time they exhale, Fall having subsided into an early Winter.

Dr. Harold Lambert carries a trim bespectacled six-foot frame. He'd turned fifty just a few days before the police contacted him.

It was a call he half-expected.

Lambert has been keenly following the news over the last few weeks, but the cursory media reports have barely scratched the surface of the true scope of events. The general public has received only bits and pieces of information, perhaps intentionally downplayed to stem panic, though more likely because the media doesn't have complete knowledge of all the information currently known to the police. Lambert himself is now privy to the full account. The police couriered him copies of all the reports connected to this strange crime wave and implored him to help; to try and make sense of it all. He pored over the documents, though many questions remain. The local constabulary is rightfully perplexed.

Lambert trips under the weight of nervous feet, bracing hard against the side of the blackened subway shaft.

"Careful back there!"

Lambert rights himself, inhales deeply, and plods forward.

He met his underground guide—Detective Chester Meyers—not even an hour ago. A lifer, Meyers joined the force nearly twenty years earlier, no doubt when he had a fuller head of hair atop a belt riddled with considerably less notches. As a seasoned police officer he would have experienced just about every form of living misery at one time or another, but the city had never served up anything like this.

Not even close.

"We probably should have consulted someone in your field before it got this far. Truth is, we can't make heads or tails of this mess."

He pushes the words through a local urban twang. Embarrassment coats the twang. Meyers is an old warrior. A cold warrior. From a proud vet like him, his last statement is tantamount to confessional.

A confession, but not hyperbole.

The fact is that Lambert's particular area of expertise made him the perfect man for the job. Years in the field. Years of study and research. There were only a handful of people in the country who could do what he did. Who could hope to process something like this. Analyze offenders like this.

And none, as it turns out, who were less than an hour away by short-haul.

Yet even Lambert was flummoxed. The carnage. The deaths. He had a hard time believing the reports. It was such markedly uncharacteristic behavior from those who normally led reclusive and isolated lives. Something must have happened; there must have been some catalyst to bring them all together. To act as they did.

"It's just up ahead," says Meyers, his tone more serious than before.

After a few more cautious steps, Lambert sees the detective's beam light up a figure in the near distance. The two men soon arrive in front of a young officer standing guard by a length of yellow police tape. It cordons off a dark opening.

"We're here."

Lambert peers over the tape, flashing his light to the other side and illuminating some obvious blood spatter on the rocky surface.

"Looks like there was a fight there," says Meyers, tracking Lambert's gaze.

Lambert bends down for a closer look.

Fresh.

Likely spilled within the last twenty-four hours.

"You'll need to watch your step," warns Meyers. "There's more blood inside."

The detective nods to the guard—who lifts the tape—then motions to Lambert, whose heartbeat starts to quicken. Feelings of dread and hope well inside him. The area beyond may hold clues not only to the truth behind this deadly crime wave, but to revelations that he can't possibly imagine.

"Now, Dr. Lambert…if you would please follow me."

1

THE ASHFUL DODGER

TRY AS HE MIGHT, Billy couldn't remember his mother.

Not anymore, now that so much time had passed, and his being so young when she'd left him.

Or when he'd left her?

The facts, such as they were, had grown muddled with the passage of time. Yet regardless of the precise circumstances that drew them apart, she now traveled with him along the sidewalk. Not with the fear and anxiety that sometimes accompanied these forays into maternal nostalgia, but with a fond remembrance and a simple longing for detail.

How she looked. And sounded. And smelled.

How he felt under her touch.

The security he felt when he knew that she was near. The loneliness, so absent in her presence, that was now so terribly acute.

And though he strained for the images, the results remained murky—phantoms mostly—and the more he struggled for definition, the fuzzier his conjures; so it was that he finally relented, and having now arrived to the marketplace, returned his concentration to the task at hand. To all that presently mattered.

He'd set out in search of his first meal of the day, a task grown markedly difficult in recent months. These days, it seemed as if there were more like him than ever before, with each new face representing unwelcome competition for what little charity remained. Looking had become scavenging. Eating had become devouring. The dynamic being what it was, Billy had been serenaded by the disgruntled roar of his empty stomach with increasing frequency.

He entered the marketplace shortly past noon, a frantic four-block hub of trendy restaurants and cafés, staking his claim to the wall of a red-bricked structure set at the corner of one of the busiest intersections. One-way streets snaked past him on each side; hundreds of people traveling up and down the sidewalks, entranced like zombies on their way to work, dine, shop, or do whatever it is people do in these hectic cosmopolitan regions.

Billy had a nickname for the more polished subset of zombies. "Bigwigs," he called them.

These were the ones with the fancy color-coordinated business suits or lavish dresses, neatly coiffed hair, shiny shoes, gaudy wristwatches, and sweet fragrances wafting from their bodies; each of them a little different, but all of them pretty much the same. They moved about town with an exultant saunter, and of the few who stopped to chat with Billy, or to offer him a bit of charity, rarely, in his experience, was it one of the Bigwigs.

Running directly alongside the sidewalks, just off the curb and encroaching on the roadway below, were a number of people earning their living from behind makeshift stands, carts, and tents. Some sold vegetables and fruits, others wraps and sandwiches, and still others cheeses and syrups. With the area dominated by pedestrians, the smattering of cars brave enough to navigate the area did so at a crawl, and then only single-file.

Of particular interest to Billy was a turkey-and-brie baguette from one of the market vendors who specialized in fancy sandwiches and organic vegetables. The baguette rested on the vendor's middle stand, one of three rectangular tables sitting U-shaped underneath a makeshift white canopy just a few feet off the sidewalk to Billy's right.

He leaned against the cool brick and studied the vendor's actions. The pedestrians streaming by created a flickering effect, as if Billy were watching the events unfold on an antique movie projector.

The man was currently occupied with two sets of customers: an elderly couple on the right, and a younger man picking through some of the produce on the left. Billy tried to focus, but distractions were everywhere.

Kitty-corner to him was a man in his early forties, his blue jeans offset by a bland tan jacket stained at the waist with grime, his dark hair parted neatly to the right and pressed firmly down to his scalp. The man's voice now blanketed the air:

"...Our struggle is not against flesh and blood, but against the rulers, against the authorities, against the powers of this dark world, and against the spiritual forces of evil in the heavenly realms..."

Billy had seen him there before, loitering for hours at a time, his faded garments reeking of urine. Beside him was a two-sided wooden board resting like an upside-down V on the sidewalk near the wall of a parking garage. The sign stood four feet high, with neatly printed words on both sides, which Billy couldn't read:

Romans 2:11
God Shows No Partiality

The man supplemented his placard with scripture, chanting various passages in a deep monotone, his foreboding drone devoid of emotion.

As with most of the people walking by, Billy soon tuned him out. He'd never been involved in any sort of organized religion; never even considered it. Maybe it would have helped his current situation if he believed in the grace of a greater power, but at that moment, all he really believed in was the mouth-watering construct peeking over the side of the vendor's table.

Not just yet...

Competing with the man's droning religiosity was the sweet sound from a Russian immigrant belting out his living on a creatively played clarinet. The musician stood behind an open instrument case as it filled with loose change and dollar bills. The tunes were pleasant enough, but the rumble in Billy's stomach encouraged him to focus his attention away from the melodious busker.

The vendor had just placed the last of several items into a brown paper bag for the elderly couple. They exchanged pleasantries while the woman fished about in her purse, the young customer on the left now poking through a cluster of plump organic tomatoes. Billy continued to loiter. As usual, nobody paid him any mind. Not that he really stood out, being of average height and weight, with short brown hair, and no distinctive features worth mentioning, except perhaps his eyes—a hypnotic shade of blue, the black pupils shifting excitedly to find a seam in the heavy pedestrian foot traffic.

Instinct set him in motion. He stepped from the side of the building and advanced, slowly at first, but deliberately.

Get in. Get out.

His internal pep talk drove him forward, the rest of the city falling dark and mute. Everything but the baguette dropped from view.

The woman extended her arm as the vendor took the bill from her wrinkled hand, nodding as he turned to retrieve her change from the till. Billy amped up his pace for the final strides. He was nearing the stand and ready to make his lift when the young customer suddenly stepped from the table and directly into his path, Billy turning sheepishly away, as if his thieving intentions had been advertised on his forehead.

His pulse now in his throat, Billy slunk back to the corner of the building to await a fresh opportunity.

Then a voice.

"Nice take…almost."

Silence.

"I said, 'Nice take,'" the voice repeated.

Billy turned to his left.

Peeking around the corner was a male, slightly older than himself, his body largely hidden behind the clean brick façade.

"Sorry, are you talking to me?"

"Sure, I'm talking to you," said the stranger. There was a momentary pause before he continued.

"That was a right decent showin'. Came up on the guy's weak side, waited for him to turn his back to you even, and as it was, the shop-keep bein' full on occupied with that old couple. Not too bad, all told, but you gotta be more careful. You saw that other guy, no? Kinda uninterested, he was. Gotta pay attention! He was sure liable to turn out at any moment, either drawin' the old man's attention, or runnin' smack into you, which is damn near what happened."

Billy remained silent as the stranger continued, still half-obscured from sight.

"Now you want my advice, you wait 'til he's got maybe two or three sets of customers, and all of'em stacked up on the same side. You can be right sure he'll focus his complete attention over that way, no? Then you walk up to the other side all nonchalant-like. Wait for your moment. Grab and run. Easy. No muss, no fuss."

"It's that easy, is it?" said Billy, with more than a hint of sarcasm. Then again, though the stranger's statements were disjointed and choppy, what he said made sense.

"Oh yeah, it's as easy as that. People are so damn predictable. Trust me, I've been doin' it a bit longer than you, and by the looks of things, probably with a bit more success. Now don't get me wrong, I like your attitude. Fact is, I've seen you work before. Even seen you manage a couple good pulls. You're quick. We could use someone like you."

The last part hovered, begging for clarification.

We could use someone like you.

It lingered in the air uncomfortably, and though neither party addressed it at that moment, it sat heavily like the proverbial room-loitering pachyderm.

"I'm Ash," said the stranger, finally offering a more formal introduction, then fully turning the corner and sidling up beside Billy. Ash was thin. Wiry. Looking at him more closely, Billy noticed his eyes: sharp, ugly, and beady. He was a bit short for his age, snub-nosed and common-faced enough, and though he didn't appear much older than Billy, his hair was an even mix of salt and pepper.

"Hey, you sit tight just a minute!" he said.

It was more an order than a request, but Billy didn't argue. With his stomach still hollow and his adrenal glands in full retreat, only then did he realize how faint he felt. He shrunk to the ground and leaned against the cool brick, the building providing a small shaded pocket that Billy adopted for his own. People continued to walk by, keeping something of a buffer from the vagrant slouched up against the cool mortar. Billy tucked his feet beneath him to rest his pulsing soles.

The vendor had several new customers scurrying about his stand. A young couple was sifting through the produce on the far left, while a middle-aged lady was choosing between two sandwiches on the middle table, one of them being Billy's turkey baguette. He glowered, and was already devising his next strategy of attack when the stranger re-appeared in front of him, plopping a generous hunk of cheese to Billy's left. He winked at Billy, who quickly tore through the plastic and voraciously sank his teeth into the fresh cheddar. It was only after several bites that his eyes turned up in alarm.

"Don't worry about that, nobody saw me lift it."

Some more hurried chewing.

"Well, thanks," said Billy, swallowing the last bite and looping his tongue over the circumference of his lips.

"Ah, that wasn't nothin' at all. That was right easy, that was."

"Still, thanks…" he said. "Um…"

"Ash."

"Ash, right," said Billy. "That's a different sort of name…"

"Ya maybe. Was called Ashley before, though, so it couldn't be helped really. Shortened it down to Ash first chance I got. Damn stupid name, Ashley, right? Anyway, it's just Ash."

He seemed fidgety and anxious, the words motoring out of his mouth with the same nervous energy that was coursing through his wiry frame.

"OK, well thanks," said Billy, "I can't remember the last time…"

He held back the last of it.

Ash nodded.

It was understood.

There just wasn't a whole lot of giving on the streets these days. Particularly amongst themselves.

"So what's your name anyway? I've told you mine. It's only fair, eh, buddy, right?" He let fly an annoyingly high-pitched laugh.

Billy satisfied the quid pro quo.

"Well, Billy, truth is, we could use someone like you."

Again…

We could use someone like you.

A pit formed in Billy's stomach. It was all very unexpected. Ash. The gifted cheddar. The cryptic statements. He wasn't entirely comfortable with the progression of the conversation, but his curiosity supplanted his better discretion.

"Who could?" he asked.

"Tell ya in a minute, but first things first…who do ya run with?"

"I don't run with anyone."

A nearly indiscernible smirk crept onto Ash's face.

"Well that's good then…that's real good."

He continued on without missing a beat.

"I'll tell you what…I just happen to be, how might you say, middle management. The boss wants us to keep our eyes peeled for new recruits to maybe swell up the ranks. I see one like you…

young, strong, an' ambitious…and I start thinkin' you might fit in nicely with what we got goin' on down below."

Down below?

Billy was intrigued. Even flattered. While he might not be a part of any gang or crew, he'd also never exactly been headhunted. He'd heard of several groups in the area, quickly rattling off the names.

"Nah, nah, none of those," said Ash, practically insulted at the question. "Them's all about small-minded territorial stuff. We don't run that way. There's a new order in town. We follow the teachings and guidance of Darrow."

"Darrow…" repeated Billy.

"You've heard of Him?"

Billy shook his head.

"The Glorious Darrow!" Ash clarified, his tone pitched with reverence.

Billy apologized once again.

Ash shot back an incredulous smile. "Well, you will soon enough!"

"The Glorious Darrow? Sounds like a faith of some kind."

"Darrow is our faith," Ash said, before adding an exuberant, "Darrow knows!"

The last phrase pinged familiar in Billy's mind. He's certain he saw it somewhere recently. *Carved into a fence maybe?*

People continued to stream by them on the sidewalk; Billy hardly noticed, his attention having been commandeered by this wiry stranger with the salt and pepper hair. His hunger had been equally relegated to an afterthought. It had been displaced by curiosity. Curiosity about this group. Curiosity about this one named Darrow. Still, he was circumspect.

"Why me?" said Billy.

"Why not you?" said Ash.

A fair rebuttal.

"Is it close?"

"Oh, not far. Not far at all." His response was coy, the answer intentionally vague. Billy's temptation swelled, but still he hesitated. It was all too much too quickly for a longtime loner, a self-admitted creature of habit. His more cautious side finally intervened and took charge. It reeled him in and told him to leave.

"Well, thanks a lot for the cheese," said Billy. He started to move away.

"Wait now...you haven't heard what we can offer."

"Thanks," he repeated. "Really."

Ash shook his head.

"You're one of them play it safe types, ain'tcha?"

No answer.

"And how's that workin' out for ya, so far?"

Again Billy didn't respond, just stepped from the sidewalk and started into a brisk walk, trying to extricate himself from what had become both an alluring and uncomfortable situation. Trying to outrun his fading willpower.

Tickled all the while by Ash's stubborn gaze.

BILLY TABBS

HIS DAY HAD STARTED inauspiciously: at the base of an eight-story high-rise in the city's pitiable east end in a seedy ground floor apartment. Billy had staked claim to the vacant flat several weeks earlier, having snuck in through the missing alley-side window. It was no great surprise, though, to discover a soulless spot in this depressed structure. The units were only half-inhabited, and the building was in such decrepit condition that even HUD had washed their hands of it several years back, the property lapsing back into the hands of slumlords through private ownership.

A quick survey of the room revealed significant water damage to the kitchen ceiling, including a sizeable area that had flaked off and fallen down to the floor in a miserable brown clump. The majority of the walls were stained sickly yellow from years of cigarette smoke, and the floors were shrouded dull and gray from filth.

In sum, it was worth every penny that Billy was paying.

The last tenant didn't leave much, just a few pieces of outdated furniture, including a paisley green couch that reeked of stale nicotine and mold. Even when originally acquired, it was likely the result of some thrift store purchase, and the passing years had helped neither the style nor the smell.

The apartment door—itself kicked in months ago by either hoodlums or police—dangled open from a single hinge, while various holes in the walls and windows beckoned vacancy to any number of nomadic critters. Should one appear, Billy would sometimes give chase, but only if he noticed, and only then if he found himself so inclined.

This particular day, he'd woken to a violent potpourri of slurred speech and vulgar epithets a few feet past the window. Vagrants, likely still drunk from last night's debauchery. Not such an unusual soundtrack in this neighborhood, though somewhat surprising to hear at such an early morning hour.

He burrowed his head deep into the back corner of the mold-ridden couch and reached across his ears and eyes in a vain attempt to block out the noise and the light.

No use.

The voices continued to fill the graffiti-drenched alleyway. Billy couldn't tell what had them so unsettled, and though he tried his best to block out the abrasive discourse, he was soon wrestled awake.

Not that he was sleep-deprived.

The fact was that Billy slept...A lot.

It was, arguably, his favorite pastime.

Some might label his recurring indolence a symptom of depression. Others would simply peg him as lazy. Billy himself hadn't turned his mind to it, to the root cause of his desire to so often close his eyes to the world and drift contentedly away into slumber. Perhaps it was just loneliness, or some existential malaise that so commonly siphoned away his waking moments. Regardless of the reason, it was from this well-practiced slumber that he'd begrudgingly awoken, only to find that the modest morning hunger swirling in his stomach was threatening to become a squall.

He stretched out, scratched a nagging itch behind his left ear, then lifted himself from the couch, peeling his warm body from the tattered fabric. It was muggy.

So muggy.

With his belly audibly dissident, Billy stepped groggily to the floor, his eyes panning the circumference of the living room.

Notwithstanding its obvious deficiencies, his present accommodations were as good as any he'd ever had. It certainly beat sleeping overtop a foul-smelling sewage grate, or within close proximity to the putrid stench of an alleyway dumpster.

He'd been homeless for as long as he could remember, with no real prospects for change. No job. No friends or family to rely on. None of the standard accoutrements to which so many others had become accustomed, if not utterly dependent upon. Not even a pot or pan to piss in. His entire inventory of worldly possessions was the small collection of abandoned hand-me-downs that he'd found on his arrival to this first-story shithole.

His mother had been knocked up at a very young age. It was a one-night encounter with Billy's father, and though she would never see him again, he did leave her the most wonderful of parting gifts.

Billy was born healthy enough, and though his mother did her best to shelter and feed him, maternal obligations are difficult to fulfill when you live in a large city with no means. She wasn't in his life very long, not nearly as long as he would have liked, and it lingered as a point of sadness. He held her now only in shards and fragments—powerful, if slight—with the thought of her love and kindness having long ago trumped the memory of any negative experiences he might have incurred during his rearing.

As Billy never met his father, it followed that he would never hear the sound of his husky voice, or whiff the distinct muskiness of his skin. Nor would he ever be on the receiving end of his father's marked intemperance, or know that his father would one day walk into an alley and pick a fight with an opponent that he wouldn't walk away from. Maybe he even deserved it, though the streets were equally dangerous for the innocent and the demur. Maybe more so. Want creates need, and need fosters urgency. The two men arguing outside his window were just another example.

"This is all just an illusion, man!"

Billy crept to the sill and peered outside. Just below him were two men. Both middle-aged, unshaven, and dirty. The nearest man was fattish, and a regular neighborhood nuisance. Even six feet away, Billy could practically taste the rye whiskey seeping out of the man's pores and riding his slurred current of speech.

In Billy's experience, there seemed to be three types of people in the world: rich people, poor people, and everything in-between people.

Then there were these two.

Homeless.

They were like Billy.

They didn't even count.

"It's all just an illusion," repeated the man. "Everybody knows it," he added, before looking up to notice the voyeur in the window. "He knows it too!" he said, pointing to Billy.

"He don't know shit!" yelled the second man, who was shirtless and held a nearly suffocated cigarette between his cracked and yellowed nails. Before he could be drawn in, Billy pulled himself back inside and returned to his position on the mildew-infested couch where he lazed about for another hour.

It was only once his hunger sufficiently overpowered his lethargy, and the two men had moved further down the block, that Billy slipped from the building, emerging into the late spring sunshine now pouring generously over the city.

Notwithstanding the humidity, it was turning into a beautiful day. Still, colder times lay ahead. Last winter had been particularly difficult. Whether or not his current squat would yield sufficient warmth would remain to be seen, but that might as well be a million years away. His next meal was as far ahead as his thoughts would venture.

And so it was that his day started out just like all the rest, and there was no reason to feel that this one would be any different.

3

A FLEETING BOUT OF RUMINATION

*W*E COULD USE SOMEONE *like you.*

Billy cut through a city park as the words cycled endlessly through his mind. Someone like *me*! His self-esteem wouldn't accept it. Then he remembered something else Ash had said: *I've seen you work before.*

The thought unsettled him, giving way to rumination, then anxiety. Then the sense he was being watched. Studied.

Water splattered. He spun around, eyeing the small pond off to the side where two ducks splashed about, either fighting or playing. A pocket of teenagers stood a short distance beyond that, but they exhibited no interest beyond their own immature escapades.

Bushes rustled. His neck craned. Nothing but the wind behind him.

Your nerves are just playing tricks on you.

Yet his encounter with Ash wouldn't be dispelled so easily, particularly given recent events. What had been happening around town.

The disappearances.

It was just last week he'd been chatting about it with Ben, a casual neighborhood acquaintance.

"Something strange is happening," said Billy.

"What do you mean?" asked Ben.

"You haven't noticed?"

Ben shook his head. He wasn't, Billy felt, overly perceptive. Billy sometimes even wondered how he'd survived as long as he had.

"Some of the rounders are missing," said Billy. "They've been gone for days. Some even longer."

"Rounders," like "Bigwigs," was another common Billy term. It meant those individuals that always came around. Hung around.

Were just plain *around*.

Except now they weren't. At least, a noticeable swath. And just as it might be disconcerting to wake up to a missing lamppost or mailbox, it was equally so, to Billy, when it was one of the rounders.

"I hadn't noticed," said Ben. "Why do you think they're gone?"

"Because," answered Billy, "they aren't here anymore."

"But how do you know they're missing?" asked Ben. He seemed slow on the uptake. And the downtake, and most takes in-between.

"Because," Billy repeated, "they're not here anymore."

"Well, you can't be sure they're missing at all. Maybe they're just elsewhere."

"Elsewhere is missing," said Billy.

"Missing to you maybe, but not missing to them. I'm sure they know exactly where they are."

Billy had bowed out of the conversation at that point to avoid frustration.

It was something of a paradox. More of them on the streets every day, yet the missing rounders stood out.

It was as if their kind were disappearing from the alleyways and the overpasses—vanishing into thin air. Of course, they were a transient class, so disappearance wasn't unheard of. It could be that some had been taken by the authorities, but such apprehensions were usually public and very noisy. Perhaps they'd died miserable and alone in the alleys and were removed by the state. Or maybe, just maybe, they'd moved on to bigger and better things. Yet beyond his own observations, he'd heard from more than one acquaintance that a friend or partner had up and gone missing overnight, never to be heard from again.

And so it was, urban legend or not, tricks of the nerves or not, that Billy quickened his pace, fast leaving the ducks and the boys behind him, and arriving back to his filthy squat as quickly as his feet could take him.

He remained inside for the remainder of the night, his imagination still locked in combat with nervous thoughts.

Alone. Tired. His eyelids grew heavy.

The heaviness won.

WE COULD USE SOMEONE like you...

Billy shifted in his sleep.

I've seen you work before...

Another shift, then eyes opening to morning sunlight, his mind wildly spinning the same two phrases. Still they begged the question—who would ever want to spy on *him*? A nobody. A vagrant of the smallest variety. But Ash's interest was real. He could feel it.

Billy lazed about for the rest of the morning, stirred finally by the thick smell of grease in the air. He stepped past the dangling front door and into the decrepit hallway. To his immediate left was a stairwell leading upstairs; beyond that a hallway with more vacant units. To his right was the main entrance, a row of rusted mailboxes set into the wall between the outer and inner doors.

Billy climbed the creaky staircase and, as expected, found Doug Winters sitting on the third floor landing, a box of chicken and biscuits between his booted feet. The landing shot off in each direction to apartment units on both sides.

"That sure smells good," said Billy, his movements as debonair as he could muster. It wouldn't be the first time he'd guilted this person into charity. He could be, he felt, incredibly charming when he wanted to be.

The old man smiled and handed him a piece of chicken. "Figured I might see you up here."

A fitting surname. Winters was a portly old man with a thick silver beard, and should Santa Claus himself ever commit a local misdemeanor, Winters stood a fair chance to be mistakenly picked out of the lineup. He was a recent widower, alone and living off a meager pension supplemented by a crummy welfare check. The story went that any money the couple had had, including their home, was siphoned away alongside the wife's deteriorating illness. After all was said and done, this unfortunate building was the only thing the old man could find—or more accurately, the only thing he could afford—given the lengthy waiting lists for government-subsidized housing. So the story went.

The story also went that he'd found some reprieve by meeting with a grief counselor at the neighborhood community center, yet even that modest door had now closed, the grief counselor himself having gone away on stress leave.

"The President says things are looking up." His voice was hopeful but hoarse. He dipped a hunk of golden biscuit into a small side of sausage gravy, the soggy combination finding rest in his waiting mouth.

This old man is just like me, thought Billy. He couldn't trace the exact moment that it had occurred to him: *That nobody really cared about me but me.* That nobody would look after him if he didn't do it himself. That he was, for all intents and purposes, alone.

They quietly devoured their food, serenaded only by the soundtrack of domestic turmoil one floor above them. The angst was transparent, courtesy of weak character and thin architecture. First the woman shouted something sharp, demeaning. Then the man shot back, angry, defensive. She returned it just as quick. Then a hard slap. More yelling. Another strike. Sobbing.

Silence.

It stayed that way until Mrs. Chalmers came clomping up the stairwell, lungs wheezing, laundry basket in hand. The elevator hadn't worked for nearly a year.

Neither had Mrs. Chalmers.

She struck up a friendly conversation with Winters as Billy withdrew, crawling down the dank hallway to step unencumbered into unit 308, the front door long since removed.

This particular apartment epitomized living despair: bent and blackened spoons on the floor, a few stained girly magazines, and several other clichéd trappings of drug-induced squalor.

The only source of light shone in through a screenless open window at the far wall with a view of a rusted fire escape. A cool breeze washed over the five derelicts inside.

To Billy's left was a young Caucasian man slouched against the wall, his eyelids closed to narrow slits, neither fully asleep nor fully conscious. His right arm was slunk over a beanbag chair, the large orange sack in surprisingly good condition given the squalid state of affairs within the flat.

The couch to Billy's right carried two freeloaders: a young woman resting her head on the lap of a man more than twice her age. But for the slow movement of their chests and the occasional twitch of an eye, you'd hardly know they were alive. The rickety wood coffee table in front of them held an empty pizza box, a pack of cigarettes, and a jumbo carton of Frosted Flakes. Backdropped by the rest, Tony the Tiger's upbeat humor and wide smile seemed shockingly out of place.

Finally, straight ahead of Billy and just beneath the open window, were two people juggling an assortment of drug paraphernalia. He watched them struggle with a makeshift tourniquet, the man trying to tie it around his arm. "It's not tight enough," said the woman. She removed it from his arm, then—with the same honest enthusiasm that Martha Stewart might exhibit in a tutorial on folding hospital corners—explained her method for tying it. Billy watched with detached enthusiasm until the solitary man to his left called out for him.

"Hey, buddy."

Billy ignored him. Billy couldn't even say why he was still in the room, or why he'd gone there in the first place. There were surely more pleasant places he could be. Something more productive he could be doing. Then again, nothing came to mind at the moment. Or most moments, for that matter.

"Buddy," repeated the man, and Billy finally looked over. "C'mon over here." He raised a weakened left hand in Billy's direction, his right arm still partially sunk around the orange beanbag, some cocktail of chemicals streaming through his bloodstream. He slurred a number of words that were, to Billy, utterly incomprehensible. Billy sauntered over to the young man, who continued to spew gibberish in Billy's direction, before rolling over on his side and collapsing into some plane of unconsciousness.

Billy seized the opportunity to try out the beanbag. He mucked around a bit, trying to get comfortable, the malleable material mashing down beneath him and conforming around the contours of his body.

Not bad.

Across the room, the quibbling couple had apparently figured out the tourniquet. The male had drooped back, the angsty look on his face washed away, now replaced by a state of utter contentment. The needle rested at his side, though not for long; soon it was in the woman's hand, after she'd finished manipulating the tourniquet herself. In the distance Billy could hear Mrs. Chalmers laughing heartily with Mr. Winters, their conversation seemingly coming to a close.

There are other places I could be.

But he didn't move. He could not, at that moment, reason why he should. And though it was warmer than he'd like, the soft breeze stealing in from the open window helped. It had also turned very quiet. Domestic bliss had temporarily set in on the floor above them, Winters and Chalmers had now gone their separate ways, and the woman sitting below the window had just then discovered that very same look of utter contentment as her partner. The man beside him was still curled up on the ground asleep. The couple on the couch were still asleep. And, before long, both the people underneath the window had also nodded off.

Billy was relaxed, having finally purged Ash's two obscure phrases from his mind. All of the people around him had fallen into a soft slumber, their shallow breaths drawn together in unique harmony.

It was only after a few more minutes of lying on the beanbag, bathed in silence and warmth, and the chicken now settled in his tummy, that Billy joined them.

"Get up."

The request fluttered softly into his right ear, his left sunk tight against the faux leather upholstery. The voice seemed distant. Dreamy. His eyelids held their positions; his sleepy subconscious refusing to yield.

"I said 'get up,' dummy."

A second annoying flutter, a second ignore.

In the next instant, his eyes flashed open to rapid movement all around him. Things had been so calm. So serene. Now turmoil.

He glimpsed the open window past a flurry of rustling limbs. The sun's fading rays still soaked into the seedy apartment floor.

The next wave of activity lurched him off the beanbag and down to the floor below.

"I said 'get up'!"

Billy scrambled to draw his bearings, finally realizing the angry voice wasn't meant for him, a large man having pulled the young

Caucasian man from the floor and slammed him hard against the wall.

The remaining delinquents had all come round by the time he'd been thrown against the wall for the second time. With every hard thud the rickety coffee table shook from the impact, each time sending the colorful cereal box into an impromptu shimmy, and Tony into a raucous bout of giggling.

The attacker yelled the words "Counterfeit bills," then slapped the young man in the mouth. Again. And again.

And again.

The young man began to cry, his mangled lip seeping blood. There was worse violence to come, but Billy wished no part of it, and with Tony smiling on, he slipped out the open window and scampered down the fire escape toward the ground below, hopping from the lowest rung and skirting quickly from the alleyway.

He thought it best to stay away for a while, so he spent the rest of the evening wandering the city, frittering away a small slice of his finite existence in that hazy malaise—acutely unproductive and thoroughly purposeless hours through nameless streets with faceless people—before ultimately arriving back at the same marketplace as yesterday.

It was late.

Same city. Same market. Same street.

Yet now most of the brick and mortar stores were locked up dark and tight. Skeletal remains stood as the sole reminder of the recently lively street merchants, the goods having ridden safely away with the proprietors, the tents tied up over barren tables chained together, or secured in other ingenious ways. They would blossom again in the morning.

Billy stepped off the sidewalk and into the deserted roadway.

The buskers, the oracles, the Bigwigs. Ash. All gone and replaced by a dark, tenuous calm.

By then his stomach had commenced its familiar rumble, urging Billy toward the food to be had in the alleys. Only now things were different: quiet meant danger as much as opportunity. The streets had grown sullen and murky, the shadows more threatening. At nighttime, walking morphed into prowling. Everything felt more adversarial. More territorial.

Billy knew this, knew it was best not to delve too far into blackened alleyways when the sun was down, particularly outside of his own neighborhood. Knew that the daily influx of Bigwigs, however maddening, also attenuated much of the danger.

But he was hungry, his stomach having long ago burned through the fat-soaked calories of the gifted fried chicken. Now his gut whispered encouragement—and confidence—quickly taking over navigation and guiding him to the mouth of the nearest passage.

This particular alleyway housed the rear door of a popular buffet restaurant and was a treasure trove of castaway food items—a fancy feast for even the most impoverished individual who could reach them before the sun or the raccoons had had their way.

Billy spent a cautious look before entering the alley. The street was nearly still; nothing but a lustful couple ravaging one another under a streetlamp and some rummy staggering across the street, a bottle clutched lazily in his left hand. Satisfied as to his immediate security, Billy stepped tentatively into the darkened crevice.

A fire escape straddled the left wall, just a few feet from the dead end. On the right was the rear door of the restaurant and four garbage cans. A vagrant was already hunched over one of the four steel containers.

Not much of a threat.

Old men, Billy had found, particularly those whose life-beaten faces had cracked with chiseled symmetry, tended to leave you alone. This was particularly true when their breath didn't stink of alcohol, or when you kept a safe distance from their "stuff."

This old man was elbow-deep in the bin furthest from the door. Billy watched him as he turned over several items before shaking his head with disdain, just as one might do after looking inside a half-full refrigerator and concluding that there was "nothing to eat."

Beside the vagrant was a rusted shopping cart that he'd liberated from a nearby grocery store. It held all of his worldly possessions. It was an unremarkable array of flotsam and jetsam, yet he jealously guarded the cart and its contents as if it were flush with objets d'art.

Billy drifted in and positioned himself overtop one of the four metal cylinders, a respectful two-can buffer between them. He stole another quick look back up the alley, then rummaged through the contents until discovering an untouched crabmeat sandwich. He gave it a sniff, satisfied himself as to its edibility, then consumed the decadent item right there on the spot. If it were daylight, both he and the old man might have already been run off from the area. After midnight, it was rarely a problem.

Billy stepped back from the can, only then realizing he'd leaned in too far and picked up some gooey substance on his stomach. He spent the next five minutes cleaning it off, the old man having moved lethargically on to a second can.

The long shadow was the first hint of danger.

The shine of a hovering streetlight muddled his view, but Billy could still make out the murky outline. Two shiny orbs ensconced within a black silhouette, both reflecting sharply in the three-quarter moonlight. They were housed in a large individual, statuesque at the edge of the sidewalk. The statue's head tilted into the alley. Then a second tilt of the head, followed by the distinct movement of a mouth. Billy watched a second silhouette join the first. Two heads turned. Four eyes.

By then he'd forgotten about the stickiness, keeping vigil on the two figures that had just stepped into the narrow corridor.

Billy turned and stared at the dead end behind him. He took stock of the fire escape on the left wall, certain it was out of reach. He berated himself for losing track of his surroundings. For getting too comfortable. Too complacent.

He knew better.

The pair walked up to him, stopping just a few feet away. They were just like him, except the first was much larger.

"Hey," the large one said.

"Hey," returned Billy, uneasily. He reflexively licked a small dab of mayo just off the left side of his mouth.

"You lost?" asked the large one.

"No."

"You sure?"

"I'm sure," said Billy.

"Then what are you doing in here?"

Billy didn't respond, only drew back a step.

"I said what are you doing here, in *our* alley?"

"I'm sorry, I didn't know this was *your* alley."

The smaller one chimed in. "I think he's being smart with you, Gus. You bein' smart with us, goof? You think that's gonna be good for your health?"

They advanced several steps, Billy stepping back two more. Again he stole a look to the dead end behind him. The old vagrant continued to sift through a garbage can just a few feet away, seemingly oblivious to the situation.

"Seen ya around here before," said the large one, "but not from this area, are ya? Shouldn't be walking around like ya own the place. Somethin' bad might happen to ya. That'd be a shame."

"Real shame!" echoed his friend. He repeated the same two words and started laughing. By then any moisture that had accrued from Billy's delicious crabmeat meal had been siphoned from his mouth.

"I didn't know this was your alley. If you let me by, I'll leave." Billy tried to step past the large one, but was blocked. Their faces just inches apart, Billy could smell the foul odor of bacteria and decay emanating from his adversary's blackened mouth.

"What do we do with this one, Danny?"

"I dunno, Gus, what're you thinkin'?"

The large one hemmed and hawed, superficially elongating an already-made decision. Billy's throat tightened. For all his years on the street, he'd only been in a dozen serious scrapes, and though he'd faced uneven odds in the past—like the time last month when a few locals were chirping one thing or another —in that instance they were smaller than him, and quick to take flight the moment Billy set in their direction.

"I think maybe he should pay us a toll for trespassing," said the large one.

"Oh ya, Gus. He gonna pay us. He gonna pay us that toll." This was followed by some more wild laughter. Billy would have found it annoying if he weren't so frightened. His panic quickened, and in that instant he was a child again, the memories flooding back to him. He could hear his mother's impassioned screams as she called out for him from below. Saw the gloved hand reaching for him. Smelled the bitterness of the chemicals, so strong that they clouded his present. He fought against them.

"What ya got on ya?" demanded the large one, pulling Billy back to the moment.

"I don't have anything," stammered Billy.

He looked to the fire escape one last time, but before he could move, they were on him. Billy screamed as he tumbled backward into a pile of garbage. They came with several hard blows to his torso. He cried to the vagrant, who looked over, turned for his cart, then slowly drew away over squeaky wheels.

Billy managed to kick one of them back but they were on him again in an instant. He closed his eyes and braced for the next attack. But then, just as quickly as they'd started, the blows stopped. Billy opened his eyes to see that Ash had just sent the large one sprawling face first into the wall.

"You two lookin' for a fight? How 'bout somethin' a bit more even then?" said Ash.

"This don't concern you," spit the small one, quickly squaring up to engage him.

"I beg differ, eh? I'm here, right, so it concerns me now, I take it?" Ash's words jutted out like tiny darts, not entirely eloquent, but more than sufficient to convey his points.

The large one had come about, his nose gashed open. He shot Billy's rescuer an angry look. The attackers stared at Ash for several moments, then turned and started backing out of the alley. In a flash they were gone. Billy's sigh was audible. He'd expected more of a fight.

"Hey bud, how you doing down there?"

Billy was still rolled up in the garbage. It took him a few seconds to right himself, but eventually he stood up, a slight pain in his ribs.

"You all right?"

Billy surveyed the damage, shaking off small bits of garbage and rotten produce. A small cut on his neck trickled blood.

"I think so."

"Well, looks like I got here just in time, eh?"

Billy nodded.

"You get in many of them?"

"Many what?"

"Scrapes," said Ash.

"More than I'd like. More recently…"

"You oughta be more careful about who you pick fights with. Best keep 'em one on one, at least?"

"I didn't start that fight."

"Well, whether you picked it or it picked you, still gotta be more careful. This city sure is dangerous."

Billy winced again at his bruised ribs. Still, he felt lucky.

"Where'd you come from, anyway?" asked Billy.

"Heard you hollerin' all loud like. From out on the street. Came runnin' right quick, I did."

"Ya, but what were you doing out here to begin with?"

Ash curled up a smile. "No point dwellin' on the hows and the whys. Best just be happy I was."

Billy dropped the inquisition. He limped alongside Ash to the edge of the alley and leaned against the cool brick.

"Yer leakin'," said Ash.

Billy pulled himself from the building, leaving behind a noticeable red smear that marked his wounded presence. Again he looked himself over. A few cuts and bumps. Only superficial.

"I'm fine."

"Gonna feel it tomorrow," said Ash.

Billy nodded. By then the sky had drawn his attention. Ash had noticed it too.

"Gonna pour," said Ash.

"Yeah."

Billy looked east, thinking of the long walk home to the decrepit building with the moldy green couch and whatever was left of the Caucasian man on the third floor.

"You say your group isn't far from here?" said Billy.

"Not far," said Ash. "Right close, in fact."

Thunder distorted Ash's next series of words, and by the second clap they'd both set off in a run.

GREETINGS AND
SALUTATIONS

RIGHT CLOSE" WAS A bit farther than Billy had envisioned.
Ash led him through a tangled web of apartment complexes. They skirted through numerous alleyways while darting between parked cars and trespassing upon countless properties before finally arriving at a subway stop near the downtown core, the humidity buckling the sky just as they slipped below ground.

Billy followed Ash's lead in blowing past the turnstiles to emerge onto the eastbound platform. It was late. Nobody seemed to care. Only a handful of sleepy people loitered about, a similar number of people dotting the platform across the tracks.

"Now what?" Billy asked.

Ash smiled. "C'mon, we're almost there..."

"Where exactly are we going?"

"To see Him."

Billy tried to stifle his inquisitiveness. Still on edge from the day's events, he recognized that his nerves had incubated impatience, and that his questions exposed his apprehension.

Ash led him along the edge of the platform, maneuvering past several people until they arrived to the tunnel opening from where the subway cars themselves would soon come thundering out. The dark shaft was dim and narrow, not much wider than the two tracks themselves. It shot straight back into a murky darkness.

Billy watched his wiry guide look over his right shoulder back to the main pedestrian waiting area, seemingly to see if anybody was watching. The few loitering pedestrians were fully absorbed in their own business, utterly uninterested in Billy and Ash's exploits. Some were reading books or newspapers. Others sat on benches, eyes half-closed. None saw Ash slip out of sight and onto a narrow ledge that hugged the left side of the subway shaft, Billy slinking in nervously behind him.

The ledge was just wide enough to allow people to walk single file, and whereas the main platform was well lit, there were sparse lights spaced at wide intervals within the subway shaft itself. The intermittent orange glow from the tunnel roof shed barely enough light for Billy to make his way, and though his eyes were fast adjusting, he could now hardly see Ash, who crept along a dozen feet ahead.

"Tricky, tricky, right?"

"How much farther?" asked Billy. The air seemed thinner, the tunnel growing smaller with each cautious step forward.

"Not so much," called Ash. He'd now paced himself completely out of Billy's sight, his voice wafting back from somewhere in the darkness ahead.

"What does that mean?" called Billy.

No answer from Ash. Just a distant cry from ahead, from something mechanical. It grew louder until the ground started to vibrate. He yelled for Ash, but the approaching rumble washed Billy's voice down to the tracks with the dirt and the scuttling vermin.

The tunnel flashed awake with bright light. He looked around. Nowhere to run but the track. His mind stumbled. The tunnel had collapsed in on him and felt no wider than a pencil. Billy's legs grew weak and his head light. He lowered himself on the ledge and pressed up against the tunnel wall, closing his eyes as the subway car rumbled closer, one hundred feet away, then fifty, then twenty, until finally it roared past him. Car after car. The sound was deafening, the wind drag substantial. He felt he was losing his footing just as the last car sailed past. Moments later, a high-pitched squeal cut through the air, the train arriving at the main platform where they'd started. Billy looked back. He could just make out the train in the far distance. It looked like a mechanical caterpillar. Ants now scurried to the caterpillar.

"What's going on back there? Comin' still, right?" Ash's voice echoed from well up ahead.

Billy composed himself, then hollered a response and continued his now-trembling progress along the narrow ledge. He finally caught up to Ash by a smooth concrete opening in the tunnel wall. The glow of an orange service light revealed a passage extending approximately ten feet back into the wall.

Ash motioned for him to follow, and Billy watched Ash traverse the ten feet before turning sharply to the right. The passageway extended another short distance before opening into some sort of service room. There were pieces of machinery lying about, all caked with oil stains, including two pieces of track lying on the floor to his left. A light fixture hovered above them. It was encased in a protective steel cage, the bulb flickering on and off at random intervals.

"You stay right here," said Ash. "Be back in a jiffy."

So Billy waited in the unsteady light, relaxing his frayed nerves and soothing his wounds as best he could. Some minutes passed before Ash reemerged.

"They're comin' right quick," he said confidently.

Soon came the first. He waddled in through the opening, a look on his face as if his summons was a great imposition that he'd been inclined to ignore. He had strong shoulders and a large gut.

"Fat Henry," Ash whispered into Billy's ear.

Billy watched Henry trudge to the far wall where he plopped himself heavily to the floor, his present obligation seemingly satisfied.

Moments later came two slender creatures with matching eyes and symmetrical steps.

"Jenny an' Helena," said Ash.

"Sisters?" whispered Billy.

"Twins," said Ash.

They appeared thin but strong. Each eyed Billy, then settled down in the far corner of the room. Billy found it strange that none of the three had made any effort toward an introduction, as if they couldn't be bothered, or it wasn't expected of them.

As Ash slunk off to have a word with Henry, Billy set course for the sisters. Neither stirred as Billy approached.

"How's it going?"

Jenny looked up at him with a slightly vacuous expression.

"We're good," she said.

"Ash told us you just got here," added Helena.

Billy nodded.

"That's good for you then," said Jenny. "This is a good place."

It was, Billy felt, an oddly worded response.

"You have any family?" asked Helena.

Billy shook his head.

"None at all?" said Jenny.

"I had a mother once," he answered.

"I think we all did," laughed Helena.

Billy quieted.

"You mean you're all alone now?" asked Jenny.

"It's not so bad."

"Yes it is," said Helena. She began to pick at one of her nails. "Awful thing, to be alone out there. Especially these days."

"People don't appreciate it," she added, "how hard it is to survive on the streets. Especially when you're not used to it. Even worse if you're alone."

"I'm sure your mother wouldn't want that for you," added Jenny. "To be alone like that."

"I suppose not," said Billy. He looked around. The room seemed a decent shelter, but a little small for a group. "You all live down here?"

"Not exactly," said Jenny, who was quickly hushed by her sister. They shared a conversational look, and the issue—whatever it was–sorted out with a couple of nuanced glances, as only sisters can do.

After a moment, Jenny spoke again. "We just came to see," she said. "Won't stay long. It's been a long day of work."

"What sort of work?" asked Billy.

"Oh, this and that," said Jenny. "Sometimes this…"

"…and sometimes that," concluded her sister.

The vagueness tickled his curiosity.

"We don't live very far," said Helena.

"Not too far," repeated Jenny.

Billy took stock of the room again. The service light flickered. "You like it there?"

"Oh yes," answered Jenny. "It's a good place. We follow Darrow. He provides for us."

"Darrow knows!" Helena chimed in.

"How many are there, in the group?" asked Billy.

They looked at each other but didn't answer before Ash swept in beside them. "Getting' to know each other, right? This is my friend Billy, this is. He's gonna be a key addition for us, no doubt about it."

The girls nodded.

"We'll see," said Billy.

A look of shock washed over the sisters. One of incredulity on Ash.

"Oh, you'll stay," Ash said in a tone of absolute confidence. "You're gonna like what we have to offer here. What Darrow Himself has to offer."

"Oh, definitely," Jenny chimed in. "He provides for us. Looks after us and protects us. You'll want to stay."

"Well, who is this Darrow anyway?" Billy asked.

The sisters looked at each other as if taken aback by the question. It was Jenny who spoke first.

"Darrow is our leader. He found this place and brought us together."

"Together we're strong," finished Helena.

Billy had never heard such reverence for one of their kind. What was it that made this individual so special? What set him apart from any of the rest of them? Yet the exaltations continued to flow.

"He is glorious," said Helena.

"Why?" asked Billy.

"Because…" answered Jenny, "we revere Him."

"And why's that?" Billy prodded.

They turned in toward one another and thought for a moment.

"Because He is glorious," answered Helena.

Billy ceased asking questions, annoyed by their stubborn vagueness and circular reasoning. Even slightly unnerved by their creepy calm and their unexplained confidence.

Ash smiled and drew him aside. "You'll see it right quick, Billy. The Darrow is somethin' to behold. Came across us at different points in our lives, He did. At points when things were kinda slippin'. Gathered us up, one by one, He did. Damn sure saved some of us. I was sure in a bad way when I was brought along down below. And I know it may not look like it now, but Fat Henry over there, fat as he is now…"

Henry scoffed, gurgled a retort at the ground, then slumped down a bit further against the wall.

"Fat as he is now," repeated Ash, even louder, "he was damn near starvin' when the Darrow found him. It's a rat's deal livin' in this world, and don't the Darrow know it. All of us owe Him somethin'. That's what I'm thinkin', and…well, I guess I don't have much more to say about it than that."

In short order, several others dropped by to introduce themselves. Except for Fat Henry, all of them chatty, and all with a story to tell.

George was first. He only had half of his eyes, which was to say that he had one good eye, but a deep patch of scar tissue that ran over his right. Sometimes the lid would drift open, revealing something of a crater behind it. What wasn't cratered was opaque and glassy.

George had been one of four siblings born and raised at the Harriot residence. He didn't want for much through his youth and adolescence, but, as was often the case, he grew tired of the suburban malaise. His first great foray into city life resulted in some small thefts and mischiefs that ultimately led to his incarceration. His family bailed him out after several days, but home life didn't stick, and again he took to the street, where he'd drifted for two years before finally finding Darrow.

Soon after George came Jacob and Tommy. Jacob was older than Billy, with good teeth and blonde hair, the thick locks offset by a pair of deep turquoise eyes. Unlike the rest, he'd come from a family of money and education, even suffering through classes for decorum and civility. Ultimately, the establishment was too much for him, so he left it all behind him. Jacob struck Billy as highly intelligent, and though he'd spurned his former life and material possessions, he'd retained one item of value—a fancy silver chain that traced his neck. All in all, Jacob might even make a decent Bigwig, if he ran in those circles.

Tommy was red-haired and unassuming. He, like Billy, was separated from his family at a tender age, though in Tommy's case, he'd had the dubious privilege of adoption into a family of ne'er-do-wells. His guardians hardly paid him any mind. Rarely was he properly fed or cared for, or spared beatings at the whim of a moment's intemperance, and when he finally mustered the courage to run away, he promised himself never to return to that silently abusive household.

One thing common to all of them, from Jacob and Tommy to the sisters, was the high regard in which they held this Darrow. It was unlike anything Billy had seen among street-dwellers. The devotion, the awe—it was inspiring.

And though his curiosity was killing him—about the group and Darrow alike—there remained an inexplicable queasiness in his gut, a feeling he couldn't shake that something about the place wasn't quite right. Billy had come to accept and rely on his instincts. Those instincts had rarely led him astray, and now they urged him to leave. Despite Ash's kindness, despite the seeming good nature of Jacob, George, and Tommy, there existed an oddity in the air that he just couldn't reconcile. His feelings of doubt having finally gained the upper hand on his curiosity, he discreetly pulled Ash aside.

"Hey, Ash. Thanks for what you did for me today, you really helped me out. But I think I'm going to head back now."

"You sure that's what you want?" asked Ash.

Not at all, thought Billy. He nodded his ambivalence, stepped slowly toward the exit, then froze.

Ash stood silently beside him, a smile curling up on his face. He turned his head toward the soft sound of approaching footsteps; Billy followed suit. The remaining members were all standing, their heads cocked toward the door. A lump grew thick in Billy's throat.

Seconds later, emerging from the darkness, Darrow stood before them.

THE GLORIOUS DARROW

THE REVERENCE WAS PALPABLE.

Billy was immediately impressed by Darrow's appearance and physical stature, which were not at all what he'd envisioned. For some reason, he'd expected to see a thin and wiry individual similar to Ash. Instead, Darrow was tall, taller than Billy, with a strong, fit, muscular build. He looked about middle-aged, and had long hair that swayed as he moved. It was an even mix of gray and brown, as if someone had splashed a pail of silver confetti overtop a bed of sand, and his facial growth was uneven and bushy. His eyes were a piercing dark brown, his gait confident. From the moment he entered, all chatter ceased, as if a four-star general had just stepped into an army barracks littered with enlisted men. All of them—Jacob, Tommy, George, Ash, the sisters, even Fat Henry—rose to their feet.

Darrow wasn't alone. With him were two hefty individuals carrying food.

After a moment Darrow strode forward, his steps slow and deliberate.

"He is your chosen?" said Darrow in a deep monotone, his gaze not aimed at anyone in particular, yet his words obviously intended for Ash.

"Yep, the one I told you about. Billy. He's as quick as he's young. Seen him work before. Think he'll make a good one." Ash said it with a curious twinge of relief in his voice, as if he were also saying, "Good help is so hard to find." Billy found it bizarre to hear his merits debated as if he weren't even there.

"I see," said Darrow flatly, followed by a silent glance to Billy.

He then approached from Billy's left and stuck his nose to within an inch of his face. Billy could feel the heat of Darrow's breath rolling past his left ear, so substantive it practically carried words; it tickled his skin and raised goose bumps. Darrow then proceeded to take an unusually deep breath, as if he were inhaling some part of Billy and holding it for analysis. Finally he walked around Billy, circling him fully before stopping eye to eye.

"Yes, he may have some potential."

Ash struck another prideful smile as Darrow stepped away several feet. He then addressed Billy, his back fully turned on the potential recruit. "Are you angry?"

Billy didn't respond. Numerous seconds passed.

"I asked if you are angry?" Darrow repeated.

"I don't understand," stammered Billy.

"Are you ashamed of how you've allowed yourself to be treated? About your place in the world? Or do you bask in the degradation and the oppression?"

Billy replied in much the same way as before.

"I see," said Darrow plainly. "Then I suppose I will save these most difficult questions for another time…"

There were a few chuckles among the crowd. Billy didn't share in the humor. His body felt tight, his mouth parched. He nervously scratched his right leg with his left.

"So, why are you here?" asked Darrow.

More uncomfortable silence.

"Well, has something got your tongue, young Billy? Surely you know better than anyone else why you stand in our chamber?"

Billy mustered a response. "Ash invited me to come."

A slight grin crept onto Darrow's powerful face. "I see, so I take it that you had no choice in the matter. My loyal minion facilitated your attendance by physical coercion or threat, is that correct?"

"Well, no…he…"

"Then I ask you again…why are you here?" pressed Darrow, his back still turned on Billy.

"Well, I suppose…I was curious…interested…to see what this was all about," Billy said meekly.

"Yes, I see," the deep voice rumbled back. "And what you have found so far? Has it met with your approval?"

Billy didn't respond. Apart from the weighty intimidation, he was trying to discern which parts of the inquisition were rhetorical and which parts demanded an intelligent response. He also worried what might happen if he gave an unfavorable answer. Darrow's two escorts stood side by side, still blocking off the doorway, the food still resting at their feet.

"I am told you have no allegiance to any particular group in this city. Is that true?"

"I don't run with anyone," Billy said, perhaps embracing a more defiant tone than he'd intended.

Darrow finally turned around to face him. The service light flickered as he did, turning the room pitch black for just a fraction of a second. Billy figured Darrow to weigh substantially more than he did. His "escorts" were similarly sized—a formidable entourage if Billy had ever seen one.

"That is good. We do not engage in territorial disputes here. No pissing matches to mark our territory. Ours is a loftier purpose. Ash has seen something in you to get you this far. Where you go now is up to you."

At that, Ash sat down. He leaned back against one of the walls and beamed proudly. The others assumed similar positions, as if the general had just set them at ease. Only Billy and Darrow remained standing.

"Our unit is a culmination of all pieces working together seamlessly," said Darrow. "We have rules and we have order. And with that, we have peace and security. If you pass, you may also share in these luxuries."

If I pass? There it was again, a cryptic utterance hanging in the air. Billy mulled it over as Darrow continued.

"I am not here to sell you on anything. You and you alone now have a decision to make. You can go back to your former life if you choose, scavenging for scraps and fending for yourself in this utterly contemptible and cruel society that holds you in no higher regard than a cockroach. Are you a cockroach? Perhaps you hold yourself in no higher regard?"

The psychology was apparent, and apparent to all, but Billy drew to it all the same.

"You are an abomination of their own creation. They feel simultaneous guilt and resentment. They wish you would disappear from their view, do they not?"

Billy remained silent, guessing accurately that this was one of Darrow's rhetoricals.

"If you wish to remain, you will swear your allegiance to us, and it is not a union of whim or convenience, for once you pledge to be with us, then you are with us. You will also commit to certain labors for the cause. They may not be in line with what some might consider a proper moral or ethical code, yet they are necessary for this unit's survival. You will follow the direction you are given without question. But you will also remain safe from those who would wish you wrong. Your belly will not ache or cry out in the night. Your skin will not bristle from the howling cold. Let there be no doubt: My offer is exactly as described. We do not beg help from strangers. We look after one another. We are a family. If we don't look after each other, who will?"

He paused briefly, seemingly to let the question settle in. "You have only come this far because a member has seen something in you. Should you opt for the safety and camaraderie I have described, then you may move to the next phase. Should you opt to leave now you will not be stopped. But you will also never again return here, nor will you speak of this group to any others. Our deeper purpose will only be revealed should you join our ranks."

Billy could read between the lines: should he leave now and speak of their little hideaway, consequences would follow. That veiled threat alone, despite the flattery of recruitment, should have confirmed his suspicions and sent him scurrying away. Yet just as his curiosity had drawn him there, it now held him captive. His mind churned to the possibilities. The offer was overwhelmingly tempting, like the delicious baguette peeking over the vendor's low table. Even so, his caution entered the ring and urged him to leave.

He resisted.

"If I do stay, what happens next?"

Darrow answered, his voice some decibels higher. "I do not deal in hypotheticals. Should you wish to join, the path will be revealed." And then silence.

The others had fallen silent when the conversation began, and they remained so even now, the moment delivering great theater. There was some fidgeting off to the side, another cleared his throat, yet another scratched an imaginary itch.

The trifling sounds only underlined the uncomfortable silence hanging over the situation. Billy stood mute in the center of the oily service room, his brow furrowed and his body tense. His thoughts were unremitting, caution punching hard against temptation.

He looked at Ash and read the look on his face, hearing the unspoken words...*You're one of them play it safe types, ain'tcha?*

Within that silence his thoughts ran the gamut—thoughts of hunger and loneliness and of the missing rounders, thoughts of his mother, and of the tepid existence he'd been living since she'd been gone. Thoughts of his fragile security that grew more fragile each passing day.

But he was tugged all the while by his instinct to leave. To get out of there.

To play it safe.

It was a dizzying battle, and what seemed like a small slice of eternity wasn't likely even a full minute. To that point in his life, he'd always fended for himself. He had never gone hungry for very long, had never received a beating he couldn't walk away from. But he also felt the allure of Darrow's words, and the chance to belong to something, even something unknown—and the close call in the alley made Darrow's proposal all the more appealing.

Billy scanned the room. All eyes were on him. All, that is, but Darrow's, who had stoically turned away and shifted his focus to the rear wall.

Billy again locked eyes with Ash, who shot back a friendly grin. The grin leaked confidence, and Billy watched his head roll into a slow nod, as if anticipating Billy's decision.

So tempting. Yet of all the thoughts swirling inside him, one stood out from the rest: *Play it safe.*

Safe.

Safe.

Safe.

And how's that workin' for ya, so far?

Not so well, thought Billy.

Not so well at all.

"I think I'd like to stay." It was meekly said, but said all the same.

Darrow curled around, mollified yet without celebration. He bore no smile. There was no applause from the peanut gallery; just silence until Darrow's deep voice pierced through.

"You have just opted to no longer be oppressed by a society that deems you inferior. You have opted for redemption. You have opted for a life filled with purpose and meaning. And that new life begins today."

Billy had awoken that morning to the mold and mildew of his east-end squat, to the greasy chicken and the orange beanbag.

Now this sudden change to the course of his life. It had all happened so fast, all clouded by an intense smog of emotion; but one of those emotions was curiosity, and it ran ever strong. So he pushed his caution aside, as he sometimes did in moments of great temptation, even though it often led to his most spectacular failings.

Billy had to know about this group, had to find out what they are all about and see if he could make himself a part of it. And though his gut still screamed for him to leave, the excitement of the moment boomed loudly enough to drown it into silence.

COMPOUND REVELATIONS

BILLY DREAMT.

Dreamt of this and that. This and that.

And of her.

For Billy, these unconscious trips through REM fostered an uncomfortable array of emotions, particularly painful when they set sail on the maternal. It happened when he was insecure and looking for comfort, as was often the case.

As was the case that night.

In part it was wondrous. He could see her clearly in dream, a vivid and spectacular resolution that was unattainable in his waking moments. He could hear her, touch her, embrace her. He could reenact the most precious scenes from his youth, of his mother's fondness and attention. The visions were reminders that she loved him, of the way it was—real, unconditional, secure.

But then, as often happened, the dream ship drifted to choppy waters. To the tree and the screaming. He felt the scratchy bark and his throat grew tight with fear. He turned from the fireman in the yellowy suit that stank of bitter chemicals. The fireman's hand reached and fell short. Then the falling. Always the falling.

It always ended the same way: Billy waking with a start and a tightness in the gut, jerking up from his sleeping position to the dreadful sound of silence. His mother was gone, and so too was the fireman. Before him was Jenny, and the oil-stained floor, and the lingering pieces of track. They were alone. The industrial light gave a flicker. Billy blinked back in defiance, but the exchange only stirred him further awake.

No windows, but it felt like morning. He was stiff, particularly his achy ribs. He cast his eyes to the back corner where Jenny lay huddled against the wall. She was awake, lying on her side, still but for her breathing and what seemed to be a slight bristle of discomfort. Her eyes were wide and staring.

"You OK?" asked Billy.

She averted her gaze and answered perfunctorily, "Time will tend to things."

Billy let it go, then thought back to the previous night's bizarre series of events—the apartment, the alley, the inquisition. He hardly remembered falling asleep—only the exhaustion he'd felt when everyone but Jenny had finally filed out of the room. Then it slowly came back to him. He'd had a conversation with Jacob, one of Darrow's two "generals." The words drifted back into his mind.

Jacob had told him that each candidate for membership must engage in an act of public mischief as part of the initiation process. Billy had asked what that act might entail, but—as was the case with all of Billy's questions that night—no clear answer was given; Jacob said only that it would embody principles core to the clan's values, and that four previous candidates hadn't passed. When Billy pressed for more, Jacob told him that two of them simply got cold feet and ran away. One suffered some grisly mishap. The fourth had deftly executed his assigned task, only to gloat at the scene. He was nabbed and handed over to the authorities, and the group hadn't heard from him since.

Billy lay about pensively for another hour. He was still in the utility room where Ash had deposited him the night before. He'd been told to sit tight, that they would come for him when the time was right.

He watched an ant crawl past him, loaded with some small scrap of carbohydrate. Billy flicked at it and watched the insect topple over underneath its payload. It recovered quickly, hefted the food up onto its back, and slowly crept away. Billy repeated the process twice more before finally allowing the ant to scuttle along its way.

The wait was excruciating, as was the pain in his swollen bladder.

He looked over to Jenny, who had nodded off to sleep, then slipped quietly from the room and onto the narrow subway ledge where he relieved himself against the wall. The subway shaft seemed clearer now, less daunting. The soft glow of the orange service light seemed somehow brighter, his eyes better adjusted, and his senses having acclimatized.

To his right was the faint glow of light from the main subway platform. To his left, only darkness. He looked down at the ledge, then back toward the main platform, then once again up the darkened tunnel. Before he'd given it any more thought, he was stepping deeper up the tracks, slinking carefully along the narrow ledge. After traveling a short distance, the track bent slightly to the right, and when Billy finally turned around, even the pinhole glow of the main platform was completely out of sight. The extinguished glow brought the first pangs of claustrophobia, yet still he trod onward, through a whole lot of nothing, just length after length of track. Trains flashed by him twice, once on the near track and once on the far, neither experience so paralyzing as yesterday.

He wasn't sure what it was when he first saw it, aside from a welcome break in the nothingness—an opening across the tracks, under the soft orange glow of the next service light. It called to him.

A polite mental decline.

Only it didn't give up. Called again to his curiosity, which further eroded his common sense. His better judgment quickly defeated, Billy snuck a peek down both directions of tunnel, then jumped to the ground and skirted across the tracks where he jumped up to the other side.

This gap was unlike the opening to the utility room. The entrance here was uneven and rough, as if it were rudimentarily dug out or drilled into the earth. The ground was dirt and gravel, not smooth concrete, and it led back in a slightly upward slope. There was a faint light emanating from the far side of the tunnel.

Billy stepped inside and made his way cautiously up the craggy incline. It was a fair-sized path, and before long he could make out the soft murmur of voices, growing more pronounced with each step.

The gravelly hollow tapered off at a gaping circle. He slunk down and hugged the wall, then peeked out, struck still in amazement. It took a few moments for him to fully process it. He was staring headlong at an old abandoned subway stop. There was even a string of three outdated train cars parked on a length of rusted track: two standard passenger cars and a caboose at the end. They looked like something from a museum, relics from an era long since passed.

The layout was surprisingly large in scope, with a high, vaulted ceiling. The smooth concrete platform floor ran alongside the interconnected string of streetcars, seemingly waiting for their passengers to embark. They'd been waiting a long time.

The rusted track ran off to the gloom in each direction. Down to his right Billy could see a stretch of wall with something scribbled on it, and beyond that scrawl was a small room with a large window. Up in the rafters, some hundred or more feet above the railcars, were numerous steel ventilation grates spilling weak daylight down onto the area. Billy could just barely make out the pitter-patter of feet clanking on the grates high above from some sort of pedestrian thoroughfare.

Tink.

Tink...tink...tink.

Up against the far wall was a hefty circular clock with large bronze hands frozen in time. Off in one corner was a wilted fedora turned up on its side, the fabric worn and dusty.

There were more than a dozen souls scattered about. Billy recognized a handful of them from the night before: Jacob and Tommy. Helena. Fat Henry. George with one eye. They were milling about like worker bees, tending to this and that. Some were organizing food while others tinkered with supplies. There were clusters of others huddled together in discussion. Everyone moved with purpose, aside from one slight individual who was huddled up and sleeping in the corner. Ash was nowhere in sight.

All of them were just like him.

No, not like him—they weren't alone like him.

He watched intently for several minutes and soaked in every detail. Then a thought popped into his head: *Are these the missing rounders?* Maybe, though he didn't recognize any of them. This quickly segued into a more significant and dangerous question: *What exactly have I gotten myself into?*

Before he could explore that thought any further, he was shaken by a voice from behind.

"Who are you?" The voice was sharp with panic. Billy spun around to find a medium-built individual with ears far too large for his small oval face. His nostrils flared when he spoke.

"I said 'who are you'?"

"I'm Billy."

"Well, what do you think you're doing snooping around here?"

It was a fair question, and Billy wanted to answer, but he was dumbstruck by the situation. He was equally entranced by those ridiculously oversized ears. It was hard to take someone like that seriously. So it was all the more surprising when the interrogator drove him forward, hurtling Billy through the opening and into plain view of those he'd been spying on.

"Intruder!" he screamed as he shoved Billy through the opening. The tunnel let out to more of the same gravelly terrain. It sloped down some feet to the smooth concrete of the platform where the others had been working. Now they all paused, their eyes locked on the scene percolating above.

Billy called for him to stop, but he just kept pushing Billy forward, his feet slipping on the pebbled ground beneath them.

By then Billy had started a slow boil. His teeth were clenched and his gaze hard. His self-doubt bent back under the weight of the frustration of the past twenty-four hours. The hunger, the anxiety, the attack in the alley. He was raw. The stranger's ears were no longer funny.

"Quit doggin' me!" shouted Billy. He widened his stance and dug his feet into the ground, then spun around and offered a push back of his own. The stranger lunged at him, but Billy side-stepped him and kicked him in the side. Somewhere down the gravelly slope were distant shouts of "Stop!" and "Wait!" but the words felt hazy and without meaning.

His attacker rose quickly and struck a blow at Billy's face, just skimming his chin, but exposing himself on the follow-through. In return, Billy struck him in the neck. The stranger fell back and slumped to the ground, gasping for air, ears flared out in defeat.

Before anyone could react, a hearty voice reclaimed the room. It was Darrow.

"That's enough." His voice boomed loudly, but his demeanor was unmistakably laced with pleasure. For that, Billy was thankful. He hadn't remotely considered the consequences of his actions.

"You chose well."

The words were spoken to Ash, who by then was front and center, smirking proudly at Darrow's compliment.

The felled member struggled to his feet, still gasping for air. He glared sharply at Billy, then at Darrow, then to Billy again before skulking away in anger.

Darrow strode to the solitary Billy. The excitement concluded, most of the onlookers had retreated to their original positions and resumed their work.

Darrow's look sunk into him. "It takes confidence to stand your ground as you did, especially in foreign waters."

Billy didn't respond, just nodded, slowly regaining his composure.

"You've just met Ewen," Darrow continued. "He is one of ours. His ego may be hurt, but he will move beyond ego in time, and you will find him to be an ally. You must forgive him. He is... excitable. He was merely protecting what is ours. He did not know that you had been recruited, and very rarely does anyone stumble upon our lair in advance of initiation. This compound is our home, and our privacy is paramount. It is here that we reside, and it is here where we breathe life into our ideology."

Where we breathe life into our ideology? Billy chewed on that for a moment. "Your ideology? I don't understand."

"Soon will come understanding."

"But this place? What is it that you do here, exactly? Who are all of these..."

Darrow cut him off. "Patience, Billy. All good things come in time." He then called for Ash, who sprung forward at the ready. Darrow ordered him to fetch some food for Billy and return him to the "waiting room"—the enclave from which Billy had started, the oily service room with the flickering overhead light where they apparently lodged hopeful recruits. It meant another cross of the tracks, but Billy didn't argue. He immediately stepped into the gravelly tunnel with Ash, who accompanied him back to the waiting room. Jenny was awake. She left with Ash, leaving Billy alone.

There he waited, bloated by thought and by a growing apprehension that had become all too familiar since he first encountered Ash two days ago. He questioned what he was doing. Anxiety pecked its way back in, growing more insistent as he tried to ignore it.

You will commit to certain labors for the cause.

Billy eyed the door, then the ground, then the door once again.

They may not be in line with what some might consider a proper moral or ethical code.

His left ear burned with Darrow's hot breath.

Once you pledge to be with us...

Another look to the door.

...then you are with us.

And with that, Billy slipped back onto the ledge, scampered down the tracks, and skirted past the main turnstiles. Once above ground he started back toward his east end hovel in something of a run. It was drizzling miserably, and even as he ran, he heard the call of the tunnel behind him. He felt more a coward with every step, wondering what they'd think of him when they found the room empty. He pictured it and felt the shame of it, but not enough to turn back. And so he pressed on, through the cold and the wind and the rain.

It wasn't until he saw the alley that his legs seized. He stood motionless on the sidewalk as the thin mist settled uncomfortably on his body, cool beads running off his ears and his nose. Billy stared blankly at the red smudge still caked to the side of the entrance where he'd leaned the night before. It was shaped much like a butterfly. The rain had somehow missed it, left it as a reminder of his attack, and of the purposeless and precarious life that he was now cowardly running back to. A cardboard box sat just inside the mouth of the alley. It was soaked wet and limp, newspapers scrunched inside.

Nobody home.

He stared at the bloody butterfly as people walked by his sopping frame, umbrellas erect in their hands. He gleaned a few pitiful looks from some, obliviousness from the rest. All of them continued on their way without stopping, hustling themselves quickly through the rain. And finally, Billy moved along, too. Only he did not continue on his way eastward.

He reversed course and returned to the subway as quickly as he could manage, slinking down the track and spreading himself on the waiting room floor, hoping that he'd dry sufficiently before they came for him and realized what he'd done. What he'd almost done—and what he was tempted to do yet again.

Still he eyed the door with thoughts of escape, of running back home. At least two dozen times he got up to leave, and at least two dozen times he sat back down.

SOME HAIR-RAISING HAZING TO END THEIR MALAISING

THEY CAME FOR HIM after nightfall.

He was lying on his side, fully dry. They swept in without warning like a three-headed snake. The lead said his name was Marlon. Behind him bopped two more.

"Get up," said the lead head. His face was heavy and serious.

Billy lurched to his feet, giving the three-headed snake a fourth. Marlon led them above ground and guided them to a nondescript alleyway six blocks west. The rain had stopped and the sky had cleared. Safely in the shadows, they peered across the street to a five-star restaurant. Marlon studied the establishment while Billy inspected his co-conspirators.

Marlon, Darrow's second general, was a hefty individual. He bore jet-black hair and talked through a strong jaw. His features were hard and his body shone as battle tested—including a scar of some significance running nearly two inches down the front of his burly neck. An imposing figure, his presence so intimidated some people that they'd actually change direction just to avoid crossing his path.

Marlon spoke sparingly, the others not at all.

Chuck was the skinniest and youngest of the lot. He tried to put on a brave front but his eyes spoke the contrary. And then there was one-eyed George, whom Billy had met the night before. George's temperament was deadpan. He could have been moments from a high-pressure mission, or moments from sitting down to a quiet lunch. He stood beside them kicking at the ground; from lack of interest or anticipation, Billy couldn't tell.

It was just after nine, dark but for the soft white lights peppered across the circumference of the restaurant and the sky-pocked glow of a few overhead streetlamps. Majestic bay windows faced out to the street, offering a tease of what lay inside: the choreographed dance of black-vested waiters over white-cloth tables, the shimmer of candlelight off crystal. Small portions. Large smiles.

Bigwigs.

The main entrance was tucked around the left where two valets stood beneath a red awning; the adjacent parking lot was chock full of luxury automobiles. The valets danced to and fro as the patrons trickled in, some by foot, others by tire. The men were clad in black vests over red button-up shirts, black pants, and black shoes. They even had silly little hats strapped to their heads like you might see on a bellhop. It all screamed pomp and decadence.

The foursome watched the late dinner rush reach its crescendo. Finally, Marlon called Billy to his side.

"Watch."

"Watch what?" asked Billy, confused.

"Everything," said Marlon after a long pause, his gaze held stoically ahead of him.

Another non-answer. More confusion. But Billy watched everything.

For five minutes, then ten.

"This is where it will be," said Marlon, after another lengthy silence.

Billy responded with a nervous nod.

"You're going to be good for us," he said, turning to face him. "You handled yourself well with Ears. You'll fit in well down below. I can see that already."

The praise warmed Billy, easing some of his apprehension.

"We need more soldiers like you," Marlon continued. "And like Chuck." Billy noticed from the corner of his eye that Chuck had crouched in among them. George remained back several feet and continued to kick at the ground, his good eye seeming pensive.

"One day we won't be held back," said Marlon, looking back across the street.

Billy didn't understand the last reference, but nodded anyway.

"Look at how they eat. How they live," said Marlon.

"I'm jealous," said Billy.

"Don't be," he replied coolly. After a lengthy pause, adding, "Jacob steers us from violence."

"I guess that makes sense," said Billy.

An angry look flickered across Marlon's face. "It makes no sense at all."

"No, of course not," said Billy, who then realized the wisdom of not talking.

Pedestrians continued to stream past them, flowing by on the sidewalk not ten feet from their position. None paid them any mind. None saw Marlon lean in and whisper into Billy's ear. Billy bristled. The instructions were simple, but terrifying.

Billy looked at his feet and tried to remain calm. Any moment now—once a crowd of sufficient size had accumulated outside the restaurant—Marlon would give the signal. Then Billy would go forward alone, the others hanging back to bear witness.

Escape would be no easy task, not with the instructions he'd just been provided. There would be dozens of witnesses close by. But, as Marlon whispered, "The public nature of the act is the entire point of the exercise."

Billy's body tingled, then faded numb. His breath was short. By then the confidence born from Marlon's earlier compliment had largely eroded. He wished he'd run away when he had the chance, silently chastising himself that he hadn't.

Several minutes passed—several excruciating minutes—before a large party spilled out of the doorway and lingered beneath the red awning.

Bigwigs, all of them.

They milled about outside while the two eager valets skipped off to fetch their respective vehicles. Marlon tapped Billy's shoulder.

The valets hadn't stepped five feet before Billy set into the street. The traffic was light, and he slipped across without incident, his eyes locked on the pristine Jaguar parked prominently by the front door, its silver ornament floating atop the black enamel finish—a silver jaguar jumping through starless space.

Billy sprinted to the car and jumped onto the vehicle's hood, a clunk emanating from the hard landing on the soft finish. The people gaped at him. He gaped back, then shuffled about, scuffing the paint in a few spots. Two of the onlookers yelled for Billy to get down. Another snickered. He ignored them and readied himself.

Then the trickle of urine.

It pooled on the hood of the car, rolled off the front bumper and dripped to the ground. The ornament had come in from orbit and was now jumping over a murky stream.

One shaken debutante stepped back into her partner's embrace, nearly losing her balance on her shiny pumps. Another gasped something indefinable as she clenched a shiny leather bag tightly to her chest, the sweet scent of her sophisticated perfume no match for the unsophisticated fragrance of Billy's freshly secreted urine. One of the men advanced, shouting Billy down from the car, but careful to keep his wingtips a safe distance from the liquid now dripping intermittently from the front bumper.

Visceral reactions flooded Billy. The numbness was gone. Now he felt everything acutely, his feelings having flowed back on a tidal wave of adrenaline.

The valets ran toward the commotion, Billy still perched on the hood. He stole a glance across the street. The alley was vacant. Marlon and the rest had disappeared.

He spun around to scan the street.

Nothing.

Billy jumped to the ground and set off in a run as the two men closed in on him. He veered left once he reached the sidewalk, running past the restaurant's huge bay windows. The men were close behind, but he had a several-second head start, and was unencumbered by a tight valet uniform or a silly red hat. His feet pounded the city concrete. His ribs still hurt but not enough to slow him down. A popular rock song blared from the open window of a passing sports car, the frenetic music drowning out the voices of his pursuers and his own panicked footsteps. Buoyed by the rush of adrenaline, Billy easily outpaced them, and the two men gave up their chase after less than two city blocks.

He cut left at the next street corner and continued a vigorous pace up the sidewalk.

Within moments he'd caught up to the group, just where Marlon said they'd be waiting. Together all four took off in a run, only stopping to catch their collective breath once they'd put some additional distance between themselves and the scene.

Marlon curled up a smile, the first from him that Billy had seen. "Well, doesn't someone look like he just swallowed the damn canary?"

His assessment was an accurate one, and Billy could hardly hide the smug satisfaction that had welled up inside of him. "You did good," Marlon added, and Billy seized on the compliment, immediately warming to its deliverer. It was a rare bequest of pride, of accomplishment, things he'd so rarely experienced in his lifetime. Such a small gesture; at that moment it meant everything.

They each took turns congratulating him, mussing his hair, pushing him playfully. Billy soaked it in. The praise made him feel self-conscious, but not so much that he wanted it to stop. George even gave him an encouraging pat on the head—as if he were just some dog who'd mindlessly fetched the morning paper—and though even at the height of his indigence he still fancied himself a step or two above even the most achieved canine, he quite relished the attention. His lungs moaned from the running, but it didn't matter. His ribs still complained, but it didn't dampen the moment. All his life's disappointments had slipped into a deep hibernation, and from hibernation came realization.

He'd just committed an obscene and vulgar act, one with no other aim than to show contempt for society. A crime with no other end but to send a message. A crime unlike any he'd ever committed before, a planned and deliberate act of civil disobedience.

In that instant, the purpose of the organization became apparent, as if the blinders had slipped from his eyes. Their goal was to send a message to perpetrators of inequality and superiority, to those who lived ignorant to the needs of others around them. Ignorant to those like Billy.

Simple. Obvious.

Glorious!

It was an emotional high, a rush of power and meaning.

Only minutes had passed, but Billy already knew that he wanted to participate in something like that again.

And soon.

THEY HADN'T LOITERED LONG before a group of people eyed them curiously from across the street.

The focused eyes triggered a silent alarm, and Billy was drawn to them instantly. Marlon saw them too, and immediately ordered their retreat back to the compound, their name for the railway Atlantis Billy had stumbled upon the previous day.

After hiking through the gravelly tunnel, they stepped down the rocky slope to the main platform floor, where he was immediately mobbed by the membership. Ash took the lead, Darrow observing from a short distance.

Billy glimpsed past their congratulatory gestures and immersed himself in the feel of the compound for the first time. It felt incredibly spacious, airy, and welcoming. It smelled of stale oil, sulfur, and the promise of better days to come; the aromas blended rather sweetly.

Tall walls of rock fenced in the area, with the ceiling solid granite, save for the slew of steel grates peeking out to the surface high above. There was a slight chill to the air, perhaps due to the cold slabs of concrete and rock.

The compound floor itself was smooth concrete in fairly good condition. One side held an office, accessed by a short stretch of hallway, while the other side let out to the string of subway cars and the defunct stretch of track that ran off to the darkness in each direction before dead-ending in rubble.

To the immediate right of the lone hallway was a list titled *The Nine Tenets of Darrowism*. These were the scribblings that Billy had noticed yesterday, scratched prominently on the near wall.

He quickly noticed a common theme:

1. **All in this world should be valued equally**
2. **Whoever lives in decadence is an enemy**
3. **Whoever supports or abides inequality is an enemy**
4. **Whoever lives in the street is a friend**
5. **Food shall be dispersed equally**
6. **Sleep shall be enjoyed equally**
7. **Work is to be allotted equally**
8. **No member shall harm any other**
9. **Darrow knows**

Members had to know the tenets by rote and follow them without exception. Furthermore, whenever Darrow invoked the ninth tenet, the individuals engaged in discussion were to immediately show deference and repeat "Darrow knows" aloud. Billy had them memorized within minutes, the concepts rolling easily off his tongue.

It was then that Helena started into one of their anthems. Soon enough the whole group was engaged in unison:

> *You've got the homes, you've got the food*
> *Your selfish actions ever rude*
> *You turn your eye*
> *You skip on by*
> *Our plans for you now rather shrewd*

> *So here we are beneath your feet*
> *And no, our kind will not retreat*
> *We won't fade 'way*
> *We're here to stay*
> *Our will and spirit won't be beat*

They continued that way with playful, hopeful, spirited anthems about homes and food and equality. Billy had never sung before that moment. It was uncomfortable and made him feel vulnerable. But those feelings passed quickly, and they soon gave way to a singular feeling of liberation.

The atmosphere was festive. They had nothing—no power, no property, no accumulation of wealth or hopeless attachment to luxury—yet they were happy. They recognized each other as equals, regardless of size or skill, of ability or intellect, with no one member more important than another. Unified. Indivisible.

By midnight, the initiation ceremony was complete, and Billy was made the twenty-first member of the group. And he was, for the first time in a great while, no longer alone.

THEY SANG AND DANCED deep into the night. And they ate—oh, how they ate.

In anticipation of Billy's induction, they'd collected an impressive array of food. There was ham, beef, a thick salmon steak, a pair of turkey legs, a hunk of marble cheese, and much more. It was, Billy decided, just about the most impressive array of tender vittles he'd ever set his eyes on.

"Where did you find all this?" he asked openly to the forum. Several laughed in response.

"*Find,* I suppose, is a generous way of putting it," said George, who then winked his good left eye at Billy.

Ash also responded, but with a question. "What'd ya usually eat?"

"Whatever was around," said Billy. "Whatever I could find."

"Yep, like most of us before comin' here," said Ash. "But no more settlin'. The Darrow says that since we're equal to the best of 'em, we eat what they eat."

And they did just that, and were boisterous for the next several hours, with three notable exceptions.

Through much of the revelry, Darrow stood alone by the wall of tenets. There he remained, watching from an isolated distance, stoic and thoughtful. He observed those carrying on before him, basking in their basking. Sometimes he'd smile or nod, but mostly he bore silent witness to the congregation of hope splayed out generously on the cool concrete.

Marlon joined him after a time. Like Darrow, he too neither sang nor danced, only ate. Then he sequestered himself beside Darrow, where he also stood. And watched. And digested.

And then there was a scrawny individual named Lyle who, despite the raised decibels, slept blissfully against the side of an old wooden crate resting just in front of the caboose on the compound floor.

The rest, however, were unabashedly raucous. Ash loud, his choppy dialect resonating around the room. George bopping his head to the songs while Chuck strutted around, cocky in self-adulation. Fat Henry lying around grumbling about this thing or that, as surly as he was rotund, yet begrudgingly, unmistakably content. Jenny apparently having recovered from her early-morning discomfort; she and Helena were dancing as one, slinking around each other as if they had shared the same mind and not merely the same womb.

Between bites of food and shouts of song, Billy sponged information. He learned that the clan was born into existence less than a year ago, shortly after Darrow discovered the compound. Soon thereafter he'd met Jacob, and together they started bringing the needy in from the cold. One by one the clan grew, and by the time spring had hatched, so too had their revolution.

Darrow, Billy was told, spent much of his time in the office. Some sort of administrative room, it contained tables, chairs, a gray filing cabinet, and even an old telegraph machine. Now it was Darrow's private chamber. As George explained it, there'd been some debate as to whether this room should be "given" to Darrow, since they were all to be equal. Yet he was their leader, after all, so it was decided that he should have the office to use as he saw fit, and he accepted, after some mild cajoling.

There was so much more that Billy wanted to know, but the hour soon grew late, and the members started disappearing into the lead railcar. Billy remained chatting with Ash and George, with Darrow and Marlon conversing nearby.

"Curfew's midnight, unless there's a mission," said George. "All of us being night owls, and all. Darrow likes to keep some sense of order."

Billy was trying his best not to stare at George's disfigurement. That was when he remembered the rounders.

"Have either of you heard about the disappearances?" asked Billy.

"We've heard," said George.

Ash nodded.

"I wasn't sure if it was just from my neighborhood," said Billy. "At first I thought maybe they'd been coming here."

"Jenny and Helena thought the same thing when they joined," said George.

"What do you think has been happening?" asked Billy.

"We don't know. Darrow says maybe just coincidence," said George.

"Hard to keep track of us all, anyway," blurted Ash. "Especially these days. Missing. Finding. Missing. Finding. Who's to say what's really goin' on. So crazy out there. And nobody cares about us so much."

"But you don't just disappear," said Billy. "Something, or some-one, has to make you disappear."

"Unless maybe you're making *yourself* disappear," said George, though he didn't himself sound convinced.

"Maybe it's the authorities?" proffered Billy.

"Or maybe somethin' else," said Ash. "Anyway, that's just spec-ulation, that is. No point wastin' time wonderin' about it, I say."

"What about here? Has anyone here ever gone missing?"

"Missing?" asked George.

"Ya, missing. I mean, left the group and not returned?"

Ash and George grew quiet.

"Not so much," said Ash, after a tellingly long pause.

"What does *that* mean?"

Ash looked at George, who looked down, so Ash again looked to Billy. "I guess maybe there was one before,"

"Well, was there?"

"Ya. There was one here before," answered Ash. "But it was different. Didn't disappear exactly. But ya, there was one before."

"What happened?" asked Billy.

"Just not here anymore," said Ash, his logic bearing the same evasive tint that Billy had heard yesterday from the twins.

"What was his name?" pressed Billy. He felt two heads cock in his direction. Two heads. Four eyes. Six feet away. Most everyone else had gone to bed.

"What's that?" asked Ash, purporting not to hear him.

"I said 'what was his name?'" repeated Billy.

"So sure it's a 'him,' are ya?" said Ash, followed by a nervous laugh. George stayed mute and kicked at the ground.

"Well, was it?"

"Ya, it was a 'him' all right," said Ash. A pause. Hesitation. Billy held silent, forcing Ash to elaborate. "His name was Derek, but we're not really supposed to talk about him too much, 'cause he's gone now."

"I see," said Billy, who now wanted to talk of nothing else. He saw Marlon approaching from the corner of his eye. "What happened to him?"

"We're not supposed to talk about it," said George. He blinked his good eye and seemed apprehensive.

"Any particular reason?"

"Yes," said George, the monosyllabic response dead-ending to Billy's dissatisfaction.

Another pause. More hesitation. A second kick at the ground by George.

"A lot of information on the first night," said Marlon, his mood suddenly as black as his hair. He looked at Billy and, seemingly with effort, softened his demeanor. "You must be tired. It's been a busy couple of days."

Billy prepared to deny it when a fierce yawn betrayed him. Yet, for Billy, it was as if they'd just placed a large box on a table—a box that growled, trembled, and puffed out small plumes of smoke from several unseen crevices—only to be told he ought not consider what might be inside. The clumsy moratorium on Derek only served to heighten the mystery, making Billy all the more inclined to ask questions; but given his fatigue, and the fact he'd only joined that night, he gave himself over to restraint and toed the party line.

"I'm tired myself," admitted George, and with that, Billy was ushered into the lead railcar, where his spinning mind and unsated curiosity finally gave way to an exhausted, adrenaline-depleted slumber.

8

TOTTER, TENETS & TRUISMS

IT WAS LATE MORNING when Billy woke up. He was refreshed, clear-headed, and alone.

He stepped down to the compound floor, almost immediately coming face-to-face with a member he'd interacted with only sparingly the night before, and if Billy had heard his name, he hadn't listened well enough to remember it. He was older, with perfectly groomed locks of brown hair and, similar to Henry, more than a little extra weight around the belly. It struck Billy that he was surprisingly clean, given their living conditions.

"Oh, hello there. Hello." He was jocular, introduced himself as "Totter," then engaged Billy in friendly conversation. Like Jacob, Totter spoke with a polished tongue that was unfamiliar to Billy.

Ash soon approached from the side. "Was gettin' near ready to come in there after ya," he remarked to Billy, at which point Totter bid them adieu and shuffled further down the platform toward Chuck, as if Ash's presence had somehow steered him away.

"What's his story?" asked Billy.

And so it was that Ash told him about Totter, whose most distinguishing feature was his skillful gift of gab. Some of the group even called him Teeter Totter, for his uncanny ability to spin around his listeners with such gentle persuasion that it would leave them teetering off balance. Convincing in his convincing, Totter apparently deployed this skill to evade unpleasant tasks, or to trade bad meat for good—yet on each and every occasion, he had his counterparts so off-balance that they were satisfied it was in fact *he* who had just done *them* a great and selfless service. Quick to Darrow's side at most events, he was even quicker to nod in agreement with anything Darrow said with any degree of emphasis, and though no one seemed to know exactly what Totter did on a day-to-day basis, he explained how he did it so well that nobody seemed to complain.

"He's harmless enough, I think," said Ash.

Billy looked over to see Totter now chatting with their youngest member. Ash noticed as well. "You see him there with Chuck, now, right?"

Billy nodded.

"Just watch a bit," said Ash.

So Billy watched, as Chuck's face transformed from guarded obstinacy into fierce gratitude. Moments later, Chuck stepped away from Totter, made haste up the slope, and disappeared into the tunnel.

"There he goes," said Ash.

"Goes where?"

"Probably off to some job Totter was supposed to do. Totter'll convince 'em it impresses Darrow to volunteer for stuff when you got spare time. Maybe it does, even. Hard to say. That's why it's so tricky. Stuff he says kinda makes sense. At least, it makes just enough sense when you first hear it. And him bein' so likeable and all. Got *me* once, even. Anyway, enough on ol' Totter. We better get on to the Darrow an' get yer first assignments."

So it was that Billy spent the next several days shadowing various members of the group: He went on patrol around town to locate food sources with Ash, surveilled a potential mischief target with George, and helped Jenny and Ewen—who was appropriately nicknamed 'Ears'—clean out the lead railcar.

In between missions Billy was taught tricks of surveillance, theft, and even sparring. The time commitments were a stark departure from the idle existence he'd previously lived. They were, however, not infinite, and when not assigned to a specific task or function, he was free to come and go from the compound at his leisure. To that end, Billy learned three secret ways of traveling between the subway tunnels and the surface, each of which was accessed by a short walk up the live subway tunnel.

In those first few days, Billy kept his eyes open and his mouth shut. He absorbed the workings of the organization, watching closely as the duty shifts cycled through. He observed the sharing of food and marveled at the mutual respect given and received, Totter's antics aside.

He was most impressed by the group's commitment to equality, having lived his whole life with the realities on the surface, where people so hopelessly embraced inequality and where, almost without fail, the greater the concentration of individuals, the greater the chasm between want and need. Their community of twenty-one had thus far avoided this sad dichotomy.

Jacob—Darrow's fair-haired general—seemed most vocal about it.

"As long as there are people who feel they are better than others," said Jacob, "that their lives are more important than even the humblest neighborhood wanderer, then the world will run askew." Much to Billy's delight, Bigwig types—by far the worst offenders—were targeted above all. "Our own world will never run askew," added Jacob. "The tenets will preclude that."

Billy loved the guidance provided by the tenets, which, he learned, were heavily influenced by Jacob. Some even believed that Jacob had scripted them himself, with Darrow merely giving the final stamp of approval and adding the ninth of his own accord. Yet, regardless of authorship, there they were to guide them all toward a better way of life. Billy had only been there three days, but from his perspective, the culture was clearly working.

In accordance with the seventh tenet, there was a fair division of labor, an equal rotation of tasks and missions, and symmetry in the number of hours worked. One day you'd stay inside cleaning and maintaining the compound, the next you might be assigned outside to gather food and supplies, or to scout for new food sources or potential targets. Morning missions rotated with evening missions. Outside work was much coveted, and the disbursements were always fair.

The same applied to the allocation of food and rest, in keeping with the fifth and sixth tenets respectively.

With regard to sleep, the subway cars themselves served as makeshift hotels. The first car, clearly the newest of the three, had soft, comfortable seats and was a perfect place to stretch out for a peaceful night of slumber. The second car was similar to the first, just older and larger, with the seating slightly worn and not quite as luxurious. The caboose, which was smaller than the second railcar, also had seating; but the seats were not only packed more closely together, they were also rigid and hard. Not surprisingly, all the members streamed into the lead railcar when it came time to sleep. Fortunately, it was large enough to accommodate every member, and with room to spare.

As for food, they'd discovered a variety of good sources from which to steal or obtain high-end cuts of meat and fish. The outside markets were ripe for the taking, but there were also stores and restaurants with lax security or back doors left ajar, and sometimes loosely manned delivery trucks. When these sources were exhausted, the group secured what they could from the street via refuse bins, or unwatched patio or picnic tables. Whatever food was "acquired"—regardless of who acquired it—was set down on the compound floor, and spread, as if ceremoniously, atop freshly laid newsprint directly beneath Darrow's large office window.

The food was equitably consumed. One day a member might walk up and select a piece of chicken and some bread, the next day a piece of beef and some sort of vegetable. It worked on the honor system, and there was always enough of the good stuff to go around that nobody went long without. The preference, as could be expected, was for the best cuts of meat and fish. The sole exception was Helena, who'd long ago rejected all forms of meat and dairy. She would say that "the fruits of anguish taste bitter"—an aberrant philosophy among their kind. They would question why she'd care about such things, and she would question why they didn't. Nevertheless, they respected her unique viewpoint, particularly as it manifested to their benefit with slightly increased portions.

They stole only food, necessities of life, and the tools required to further their schemes of social unrest. Darrow had impressed upon them to take from society only that which society had unfairly secreted away. They didn't steal for greed, to sustain any addictions, or to support any particular vice. Some members did dabble in a bit of the weed now and then, but there weren't too many places to find it. Even when they did manage to locate some, Darrow urged restraint, as it often made the user either too lethargic or too buoyant to work. "Keep off the weed," he admonished them when there was serious work to be done. Yet consumption in leisure time was perfectly acceptable, and even Darrow and his generals would nip a bit of the good stuff from time to time. As with all things, moderation was key, lest they succumb to a taste for overindulgence. "We must never blight ourselves with such an illness," said Darrow, "for it is fiercely resistant to treatment."

"Inclusion in a large community changes you for the worse," trumpeted Jacob. "Greed, ambition, envy, complacency, conflicting agendas, all inevitably give rise to disparity and inequality. One by one, values fall like dominoes. I've seen enough of this world to know that when you put enough individuals together, class trends begin to emerge, including a desire for power, a lust for materialism, and the abiding of inequality. It would appear to be a natural progression."

Darrow himself cringed at society's hopeless commitment to currency and decadence, jesting how "they will most surely be the end of me." He condemned submission to authoritarian oversight, particularly disgusted by insular gated communities and security-laden condominiums that shunned undesirables.

"Just look how they treat each other!" said Darrow. "How quick they are to turn on one another!"

"And us?" he cried. "Humph! Always they move us on from one place to another, shuffled aside like rubbish. Can't stay here. Can't go there. Can't rest an hour on their stoop without being run off of *their* property." He delivered the penultimate word rather derisively, before adding, "And where is *my* property? Where is *yours*? Everywhere, it would seem. Everywhere. And anywhere. But nowhere."

The words and concepts were deeper than anything Billy had previously been exposed to, but he inherently understood it. All of it. In one form or another, he'd seen it every day: selfishness, elitism, the weak and the forgotten being pushed out of sight by the strong and powerful. Some lives valued over others.

"What clever devices could they employ? What propaganda machine could possibly maintain this divide?" begged Darrow, to the receipt of myriad nods. "Why do people so readily accept the way things are? Accept a world that runs that way? We, on the other hand, will not."

"The city is going to burst!" shouted Ash, followed by a hearty belt of the ninth tenet. George followed, then Ears, then the rest. Totter had cozied up to Darrow's side, nodding forcefully with every few words from his leader's mouth.

"I dream of the day we are no longer invisible," cried Darrow. "For the day we are no longer deemed extraneous. I dream of the day that the people of society accept that we are just as important as anyone. That each of us, every single one of us, is as equally deserving of respect, love, and compassion as any person!"

Several more echoed the ninth tenet, their heads nodding in rapid agreement. Billy, like all the others, was enamored with Darrow. He said all the right things, his words flowing into their ears as ice water into the parched mouth of a dying man. He instilled within them a profound belief that if they all worked together as a unit, bit-by-bit, toward a single and unified purpose, they could make a difference. That their campaign would bring an increased awareness to their existence and their suffering—awareness of the overpopulation of their kind and of the societal forces that put them there in the first place. They truly believed that they could force society toward reinvention, given the recognition that their neglect would no longer be ignored or tolerated.

Yet as much as Darrow opened the bloom of their spirits, he was conversely closed about his own origins. None of the members, from what Billy could figure, knew with any degree of certainty from when and where he actually came. Speculation became hearsay became truth, but the truth was varied and clouded.

Some of the members said he was born into a wealthy family but spurned a life of excess and riches; others believed he was of the divine and received his direction from a higher order; others bore still more fanciful ideations. The pervading mystery only served to enhance his mysticism and power.

Whether Darrow was his first name or last was also unknown. It could even have been an alias. As for the "Glorious" moniker, there was some whisper that this was a descriptor Darrow conferred upon himself—though such a suggestion was tantamount to heresy, and the founding members were quick to dispute that Darrow had ever advanced such an arrogance-laden suggestion. Akin to the Immaculate Conception, they would simply state that he had "always" been the Glorious Darrow, and that was that.

There was a Machiavellian charm to Darrow, creating in his followers a unique dichotomy of affection and fear. His personality was equal parts David Koresh and Anthony Robbins. Magnanimous when he spoke, he not only condemned any society that favored some lives over others but also spent significant time extolling his clan's virtues—praising their determination, diligence, and strength in surviving in the face of such obvious inequality. His passionate sermons mesmerized and captivated his subjects with a skill on par with even the most seasoned religious zealot, his eyes full of fire and hope. Yet the tension behind them betrayed an internal battle, a schism of sorts. On occasion his gaze would spontaneously wander, obviously caught up in some other place or memory—though on each occasion his focus would invariably, after a time, return to the present.

Whatever oddness existed, Billy recognized why the group followed Darrow with such unquestioning loyalty. Beyond his inspired and hypnotizing advocacy, he also provided them the security of guidance and leadership, and the structure of community, that most of them never had. He never held himself above any of them. He made himself available to all—frequently strolling around the compound platform and chatting with the members, welcoming their input—and his office door remained ever open.

Darrow imbued the group with the confidence that they were not alone in the world—they had each other, and they had him. That he would never let them go hungry, and would never let them be harmed. Woven into these promises, he'd fostered the conviction that each of them was just as important as any person, worthy of all the same rights, respect, and fundamental dignity that might be shown to any man or woman in the city, and that they each had a real purpose on this often harsh and cruel planet. From what Billy had observed through those first three days, Darrow had been good to his word. Nobody went hungry or wanted for any necessity. Their group was safe and secure; and, perhaps most important of all, they lived with a sense of purpose and pride that none of them had truly believed in before they met him. He frequently assured the group that "I will always place my ambition before your needs," and the immediate cheers always washed away any negative interpretation of that double entendre.

On his third night there, Billy found himself seated alone with Jacob below the wall of tenets.

"Things are different here," said Jacob. "The tenets have changed our thinking. They insulate us from the way most people live their lives. Now if we can just change the thinking of the world, the consciousness of the world, then the rest will fall into place."

"The world is a big place," said Billy, swallowing a bite of cheese.

"Sure it is. But you don't lie down to die just because the scope of a problem appears insurmountable. No evil is insurmountable, social or otherwise. You just have to start with yourself. Then one individual. Then one family. Then one block. Then one borough. Then one city."

"Then one world?" asked Billy.

"Then one world," answered Jacob, confidently. "But let's start with the city first."

Billy nodded, and he adored the sentiment, even if it did sound hopelessly naïve. "And we accomplish this how, exactly?"

"By doing what we've been doing. Reminding them that we're here."

"And once they've been reminded?"

Jacob looked out across the platform floor to the three railcars, his concentration seeming to stray. "They'll know what to do," he said hopefully, "I'm confident that by the end of this they will recognize us as equals to them in every way."

Billy cast a doubtful look.

"Have faith," said Jacob. "As our numbers grow. As our 'reminders' increase in frequency and force. Eventually they will change. Eventually they will understand what must be done to help. That the strong must always look for ways to help the weak."

All of this resonated with Billy. Like most of the others, he'd lived through some very lean times. Yet even in his darkest days, he'd protested internally but suffered in silence. What could a solitary vagrant do to change things? The world was so utterly entrenched in the way that it was, and there was nothing that he or anybody else could do to change that. And so he lived, socially maligned and withering on the vine. Not equally valued, not equally respected.

Not equal.

But why not? And what was to be done about it?

Nothing.

Anything.

Everything!

But what would it take? Of his long line of thoughts, this one forced itself to the front of the line. It was only his third night with the group, but it had been on his mind from the beginning.

"How far will we go?"

"What do you mean?" asked Jacob.

"I mean, how far will we go, with these...reminders?"

"As far as we have to," answered Marlon, who happened to be walking by.

"As far as we have to," agreed Jacob, before adding the modifier..."*within reason.*"

What followed next was hardly a surprise. Billy knew something of their personalities by then. Knew that Marlon was a misanthrope, Jacob an idealist. One brash and mercurial, the other cautious and considerate, their very essences standing in direct opposition to one another.

A terse debate spilled out between the two, each trying to convince the other, as much as Billy, of the rightness of their positions. All the while they hardly looked at one another. Marlon's animosity toward Jacob was palpable, even worse than Billy had imagined; and as he parted from them at the first available opportunity, so too parted Billy's short-lived illusion of a unified shakeup.

But what a shakeup it was.

Several months ago, there had been an epidemic of jammed mailboxes. Turns out that it was them.

The three weeks of nightly urination on the side of the police station? Them.

The dirt smeared on the front windows of some of the fanciest stores? Them.

The nudging of a loose cinder block off a five-story condominium, the block landing tragically below on Ms. Worthington's prize-winning beagle? Them.

The vandals who slipped in the back door of the Ritz and "tampered" with the ratatouille? Them yet again.

They'd been openly and defiantly punching society in the nose; it was a revolutionary mismatch sight unseen since Snowball and Napoleon put Mr. Jones to his heels. Anywhere a large concentration of Bigwigs or authority figures congregated was a preferred target.

These incidents and disturbances had aroused much discussion on the street amongst their kind. Even before he'd met Ash, Billy had heard of a few of the incidents. At the time, he hadn't paid them all that much attention, dismissing the chatter as urban legend. But now he knew the truth, and he was a part of it. He had arrived.

And he belonged.

Doctor Lambert defers to Detective Meyers, and soon enough, they've both crept beneath the stretch of yellow police tape and stepped onto the uneven terrain. The young officer remains dutifully posted behind them at the tunnel entrance, Meyers having ordered that the scene not be disturbed, at least not until Lambert has the opportunity to examine it. From the difficulty in reaching it, Lambert feels there is little chance of that happening, but if they can spare a pair of long underwear and a peach-fuzzed cadet, he knows it isn't his place to argue.

The death count on either side is yet to be finalized, and from what Lambert can tell, it will likely never be known with any degree of certainty, a fact that had been glossed over in the Mayor's speech. He'd listened to it on the flight over, heard the panic in his voice, the platitudes to remain calm as his constituents fled the city or shuttered themselves inside their homes. He assured them that things were now under control, that they had the backing of the nation; that "The event" had passed, and their best people were working it. It had occurred to Lambert in that moment that he was the "best people" the Mayor was counting on, and he felt the stifling pressure of expectation. They were relying on Lambert to explain how it could have happened and, perhaps just as important, how to ensure that it never happened again.

At least not if they could help it.

The two men advance slowly into the darkened tunnel, Lambert traveling directly alongside Detective Meyers, his nerves having equalized since stepping off the narrow ledge. Notwithstanding the assurances of his immediate safety, Lambert had felt more than a little queasy walking so close to an active subway line. He is the kind of person who would never stand too close to the edge when he is waiting for a train or a bus, always keeping a safe buffer until the mode of transportation has arrived and come to a complete stop. Needless to say, the travel arrangements have thus far tested his resolve.

"Watch your head," says Meyers, motioning to some low-hanging rock.

They plod slowly forward, Lambert feeling the rough chunks of rock and stone peppered beneath his Rockports. With the faint glow of orange light now behind them, they would be subsumed in total darkness if not for their flashlights. It wouldn't be so bad, except for the fact that Lambert's has already flickered dark on more than one occasion.

Standard police issue?

The walk is a short one, and before long Lambert can see an opening fifty feet in front of him.

"It's just on the other side," says Meyers.

As they draw nearer, Lambert feels a slight breeze from the circular gap ahead of them. The soft current of air brings with it the hint of a fragrance, and a foul one at that.

Jeezus…That smell.

I know that smell all too well.

Lambert crinkles his nose in a lame attempt to deflect it.

"You better get used to that," says Meyers, "it only gets worse. Just wait until we get inside!"

Great, Lambert thinks. *I can't wait!*

SIGNS AND PORTENTS

THE DREAMS RETURNED THAT night.

Though not of his mother or of the fireman. Not of the falling or the screaming. He dreamt instead of Jacob, and Marlon, and of the irreconcilability of their positions. In slumber mere hours, Billy lived weeks of heated squabbles, months of fierce looks and cutting barbs. He dreamt of the two generals tugging at Darrow from both sides, their heels dug as firmly as their ideologies, pulling Darrow apart around millions of spiders. It shook Billy, not just the macabre imagery or the discord, but the vague manifestations of their future that flitted across his dreamscape.

The visions were fresh in his mind when he woke the next morning, stepping groggily down from the lead railcar, his fourth day among them. It was barely dawn. Weak light spilled in through the overhead steel grates high above. The "tink tink" of pitter-pattering feet was virtually nonexistent at such an early morning hour.

Chuck was the only member in sight, munching some ham in front of Darrow's office, the large window just overhead, acrylic white blinds pulled to the top behind dusty glass. Billy drew in beside him and offered a nondescript morning greeting. Chuck nodded back, his mouth too full for a more substantial response.

"You're up early," said Billy.

"Yep," said Chuck, after several more chews, and only then managing his response through a wad of pork. "Always get up early. No point sleeping half the day away." Bits of ham and spittle launched to the ground as he spoke.

Chuck was a bundle of energy. His jaw moved nonstop. Even while eating he could hardly sit still. Overtop of the smacking, Billy heard the murmur of voices from the open office door just a short stretch down the hallway beside them. Billy could only make out intermittent words, and while no sound seeped through the large glass window directly above them, he could see the occasional bob of a head from someone sitting on the office desk.

"Darrow?" asked Billy.

"Ya," said Chuck, "an' Jacob and Marlon, too." His words were more fully enunciated, his having just swallowed the hunk of meat. Billy peeked down the hallway; then, his curiosity conquered by fear of discovery, he pulled back and returned to Chuck's side.

"What are they talking about?"

"Probably today's work assignments. Every morning it's the same thing." Chuck had already turned his attention back to the floor-laden buffet. "I hope I get something good today. Something exciting."

"You don't worry about getting caught?"

"Nah." He smiled, quickly adding, "My name is Chuck, and I don't give a…"

He capped it as might be expected and then started to laugh. Billy had heard him say the same thing once or twice before. It was his shtick.

Down the hallway, the murmurs grew in vitriol.

"A little early for that?" said Billy.

Chuck nodded. "Marlon gets a plan in his head, Jacob argues it down, Marlon gets angry. Goes like that a lot."

"Jacob doesn't want to see people get hurt. Or us," said Billy.

"None of us is going to get hurt," said Chuck. "And as for the people that might get hurt, serves 'em right. Fact is they've had this coming for a long time!"

Billy shrugged, equivocally.

"Hey, don't just take my word for it," Chuck continued. "Most everyone here feels the same way. Ask Scarface. Ask Ears. Even Fat Henry. Most of us wanna ratchet things up more serious. Well, most everyone else, except maybe Tommy. But then he's just Jacob's lapdog."

This was a fairly sizeable insult, at least from Billy's perspective, and from what he'd seen, not entirely deserved. Up to that point, Billy had spoken to Tommy only a few times, and, as Chuck had intimated, Tommy was particularly tight with Jacob. Still, he didn't seem like anyone's lapdog. Billy's early impression of Tommy was that he was introverted and rarely spoke, opening his mouth only when he had something meaningful to say, which would differentiate him from most of the people in this city. Yet from even their limited conversations and interactions, it seemed that Tommy was, like Jacob, merely a well-meaning pacifist.

Chuck resumed his early-morning meal while Billy continued to strain his ears at the muffled conversations, glimpsing the discord. He'd only managed to corral small bits and pieces before Jacob and Marlon exited Darrow's office and emerged from the short stretch of hallway onto the main compound floor. Marlon stopped beside Billy and Chuck, his jet-black hair seeming more ruffled than usual.

"You're both on food recon today," he said sharply, then walked across the compound floor and up the rocky slope before disappearing into the gravelly tunnel.

With the announcement of their assignments, Billy could practically see Chuck's chest deflate, but in that very exhale he also detected a hint of relief. Billy, on the other hand, was entirely content with his low-risk assignment. His initiation atop the Jaguar had been exhilarating; yet once the fanfare and the adrenaline had faded, and he'd had more time to reflect, the reality of that maneuver had festered retrospective anxiety.

"It's early," said Jacob. "You two rest until the others get up." He seemed deflated from whatever disagreement had just taken place in the office. He set off slowly across the compound floor, Billy following closely behind. He'd been waiting for precisely this opportunity, to explore the reasons behind Jacob's nonviolent ideology. He caught up to him in front of the caboose.

"You certainly aren't the first to ask. Unfortunately, most in our group favor a broad escalation of our methods. We all want reform. We all want to be valued equally in society, but many seek bloodshed as the means."

"I've had those same feelings myself," admitted Billy.

"But anger isn't constructive. Hate isn't constructive. And there are some very good people out there, and shelters governed by kind men and women. The problem is that the kind people are few and far between; and the shelters are just temporary solutions, in any event. They don't address the problems that find so many of us out here in the first place. Neglect. Abuse. Abandonment. People must change their way of thinking. They must relinquish their superiority." Jacob paused, then repeated, as if for emphasis, "They must remember that we're part of this community, too; and they *must* relinquish their superiority."

Jacob painted a bleak picture of humanity, so thoroughly deconstructing the average person's capacity for compassion that it seemed he was making Marlon's case that much stronger.

"But keep in mind," he continued, as if reading Billy's mind, "that for the most part, they're ignorant, not evil. Selfish, not malicious. Most just can't accept that our lives are as important as theirs. Maybe they would act differently if they did, but it's what they've learned, and it's what people are accustomed to. It's the only reasonable explanation for their unequal valuation of life. Just watch their interactions with their own children, and it's obvious—it's taught. There's a hierarchy among the living that

I will never appreciate or understand. See us sick on the street? Keep walking. See us beg for food? Turn the other way. Most people have been raised to believe that they don't have to go out of their way to help us, or to curb what puts us here in the first place. They've been indoctrinated that our lives are less valuable than theirs. And if that's true, we'd be hurting them for something that they don't truly understand. It would be like hurting a child for misbehaving."

"But these aren't children," countered Billy.

"Aren't they?" Jacob submitted, wryly. "Let's just say they are short-sighted. I don't think they really see us for who and what we are. People *must* change their thinking."

"And what we're doing here...you think it will be enough?"

"I do," said Jacob. "From what I've seen, I think most people want to do the right thing...they just need a tremendous amount of encouragement before they actually do it. Silence hasn't worked. Pacifism hasn't worked. The mischief, I think, is the best approach. It reminds them of our suffering and increases awareness. It tells them that we will no longer lurk silently in the shadows. In time, our disobedience will register. As our numbers grow, as our efforts increase, our reminders will be enough. I'm sure of it."

"Marlon seems sure the other way. He says that people will have to get hurt to change. Says the mischief won't be enough." There was a hint of agreement in Billy's voice, but also uncertainty.

"He's angry," said Jacob.

"Seems to be."

"He has the right..." Jacob took a heavy breath before he continued. "His sister was killed. Lived out on the street with him. Died at his side on a slab of dirty pavement."

"What happened to her?"

"Killed," said Jacob, "by some kid with a knife."

"How?"

"By a knife," repeated Jacob, and Billy immediately felt ridiculous.

"That's awful."

"Yes," said Jacob.

Neither spoke for a moment.

"He loved her, I think. As much as he loved anyone."

"Awful," said Billy.

"Awful," repeated Jacob.

"Why'd the kid do it?"

"Why would anyone?" said Jacob.

"But murder?"

"Some people think nothing of it."

It's true, thought Billy. He thought back to last summer when he'd found a local rounder lying still in an alley. At first he'd just appeared to be sleeping against a brick wall—only then Billy had noticed the hand marks, the gaping mouth, the dried spittle marking his chin, and the bulging eyes.

He'd been strangled.

"What did Marlon do?" asked Billy, trying to refocus.

"Went to his sister. Died alongside her, I suspect. At least the best parts of him."

"I see."

"It's sad. She wasn't very old."

"How old?" asked Billy.

"Not very," said Jacob.

"And the boy?"

"Marlon said he was gone when he finally looked up."

"What else?"

"There's not much more to tell. He doesn't talk about it much. Doesn't talk much about anything. Even less these days since…" Jacob halted, tripping clumsily over the silence.

"Since what?"

"Nothing," said Jacob.

Something, thought Billy.

Knew Billy.

"It's nothing," repeated Jacob.

"Did it involve Derek?" Billy was momentarily unable to resist mention of the taboo topic.

Jacob's eyes softened. "We don't speak of it."

"He was your friend?" prodded Billy.

Jacob's silent nod screamed "Yes." It seemed pained. Billy released him.

"Awful," said Billy, "about Marlon's sister."

"Certainly awful," said Jacob.

"You think that's why he is the way he is?"

"Maybe. Could be that he was that way already. None of us really knew him that well before he joined. All I know is he's out for revenge as much as anything."

"But the boy is gone?" said Billy.

"Society is the boy."

"I see," said Billy.

"Revenge won't help his sister, and it won't help us change people's minds about us. It clouds your vision and makes you take unnecessary risks."

Again Billy drew quiet, feeling Jacob's eyes sizing him up.

"You agree with him, don't you? You think violence is the answer?"

"I don't know," said Billy. "I haven't really had too much time to think about it."

A white lie.

He'd not only been thinking of it, but had been thinking, even dreaming of little else since he found himself sandwiched between Darrow's two squabbling generals. He'd been ruminating over their competing ideologies and the realization that their deeds might not rest at mischief. Part of him had known when he joined the group that it was a possibility. They were, after all, insurgents. The surprise, if there was one, was that his first instinct was to accept Marlon's position, particularly when he thought back on his own chaotic life: the separation from his mother, always being moved on from one place to another, the dearth of comfort or permanence, the despair so replete in both borough and belly. It was easy to be angry when he thought of the marked indifference he'd absorbed from all those who'd so callously disregarded him in his lifetime, an anger not mitigated by the fact that he, admittedly, hadn't paid that much mind to them. After all, what could he really do for them that they couldn't do for themselves? But what they could do for him could mean everything. Most people had so much to give.

Jacob had been waiting silently for Billy to continue. The tornado of thought had delayed Billy's response, perhaps inappropriately so, and at the end of this pensive funnel he simply offered the following: "I know that I've been hurt, and I wouldn't mind seeing some people get hurt, too."

Billy heard himself speaking, his own voice supporting the calls for escalation. He wanted not only revolution, but he wanted it to sting.

"As I said, you're not alone," said Jacob. "But you have to ask yourself what you hope to gain. Do you want to see people change, or do you just want to see both sides suffering? I just don't think you ever advance your cause with violence."

"No matter what they do to us?"

"No matter what they do," said Jacob.

"It wasn't your sister killed."

"It wasn't," conceded Jacob. He waited a moment before adding, "Don't think it would be so easy to hurt a person. To kill them, even. Violence gets very ugly very quickly. I don't mean just the physical act itself. I mean what comes after. What you'd have to live with. Have you thought about that?"

"No," Billy confessed. And it was the truth. He hadn't actually considered what it would be like to intentionally wound, maim, or kill a person, even one of those who'd been so indifferent to his existence. Any violence he'd committed to that point was in the name of survival. "What does Darrow think?"

"He's...unsure. But as long as He asks my counsel, I will endorse a more measured approach. One that targets lifestyle over life."

Then how do you account for crushing the beagle with a cinder block?

Billy thought it but didn't say it. He knew it would be too snarky to do so, and in any event, he'd already heard that the dog's death was Marlon's brainchild, not Jacob's. Still, he felt himself already siding with Marlon, and Chuck, and those among them who sought to tug the strings of mayhem. He couldn't help but think of Jacob's notions as hopelessly naïve. Noble—attractive even—but naïve all the same. It must be so easy, Billy thought, to preach nonviolence from the safety of an ideological pedestal.

He stepped like he was going to leave, then held up.

"Something else on your mind?" asked Jacob.

"Darrow..." said Billy, tentatively.

"Mm-hmm?"

"He's like a hero to everyone..."

"He is the Glorious Darrow," said Jacob, as if that answered everything. It nearly did. Billy was just as captivated as the rest whenever he heard Darrow speak. Still, his pause begged for more.

"You need proof," said Jacob, "before you'll believe?"

"I just don't accept things that easily."

"And you think we do?"

"I can't say."

Jacob smiled. "You *are* the suspicious sort, aren't you?"

Tommy had emerged from the lead railcar and had come up beside them, red hair bouncing over green eyes. His presence silenced Billy, until Jacob assuaged him.

"It's OK to question things," he said.

"I just need to know why."

"Why what?"

"Why the devotion?"

"You need things explained?" said Jacob.

Billy's silence nodded for him.

"I'm not sure true faith lends well to explanation."

"There's got to be more to it," said Billy.

"You want something more concrete?" said Jacob, and before Billy could answer, he had set into a story.

"There's a church not far from here. Maybe you've even seen it, all mossy and hemmed in by rows of pine trees? Behind it, on the church property, was a shabby old building. Not much to look at, but it had turned into something of a flophouse for our kind. The people at the church were kind. They'd sometimes bring us food and blankets. I stayed there myself when I first arrived in the city."

"Sounds nice," said Billy.

"It was. And it went like that for some time. The two sides generally left each other alone. Went about our own business, neither side disturbing the other."

"How many of you? In the house, I mean?"

"It changed all the time, but usually close to forty. Old and young. We even had a few newborns. It was a big house."

"I see."

"There weren't any lights, so at night we only had a bit from the church or the moon, but we still made our way. Sometimes I'd visit the church people as they locked up the grounds, or walk around the neighborhood to stretch my legs. Things were much simpler then.

"Then one night I was out on one of those walks. I remember the chill in the air. There'd been a light snowfall and you could smell the chimneys and could see the glow of candles through people's windows. I was making my way back and immediately knew something was wrong…"

Jacob described how he could smell it before he saw it. The angry clouds of smoke choking off the moonlit sky. How he'd set into a panicked sprint and come up on the sidewalk in front of the church, finding the church engulfed by fire.

"It must have started at the back. I saw the flames had spread and caught onto our own building. By then it had already crept up onto the front steps and was climbing toward the second floor. It was an old wood building, practically kindling. It spread so quickly, and the smoke made everything so black, so hard to see."

Billy was fixated.

"Some made it out, but I could hear many more calling from inside. They were trapped and scared. I saw some frantic against the windows. A fire truck pulled up in the street, but they seemed focused on the church…

"I ran in the front door, somehow getting past the flames. It was already so hard to see through the thick clouds of black smoke, so hard to breathe. I pulled out two and laid them safely on the ground. The sounds were terrifying. Not just the screams—the cracking wood, the shattering glass. I can't exactly describe it… but it was as if the house was buckling. But still I went back inside. Maybe I wasn't thinking clearly. Maybe I was. Either way, I moved to the higher floors. So many were paralyzed. Some of the younger ones had hidden in closets. Many had already been overcome by the smoke. I'd been holding my breath as best I could but then the smoke finally got me. I think I passed out somewhere on the third floor."

Billy had been holding his own breath. "But how…"

"How am I alive?"

Billy nodded.

"The next thing I knew I was on the grass. I remember seeing a hazy figure disappear into the front door, through the smoke and the fire. The next part I don't remember so well. I was dizzy. I tried to see through the blur. I remember the figure emerging and re-emerging from various holes in the building. Each time his hair more singed and his face more covered in soot.

"I didn't recognize him and I don't know where he came from. He was just there, carrying young and old alike. It was miraculous. I watched him go in and out at least a dozen times before the building finally crumbled to the ground. I thought for sure he'd been caught inside until he reappeared on the grass beside me, carrying my friend."

"The rescuer was Darrow," said Billy. He knew the end of the story even before Jacob confirmed it.

"He must have saved close to twenty of us. Some he coaxed into movement. Others he carried."

"And the firemen?"

"They didn't reach us until it was all over. They'd been stalled at the church. Maybe they didn't know we were back there. Maybe we weren't a priority."

"I see," said Billy, who then turned to Tommy. "The friend was you?" Tommy shook his head, and Jacob intervened before Billy could prod any further.

"I can't tell you why Darrow is glorious, Billy. I can only tell you why He's glorious to me."

Billy finally left them to chat amongst themselves. He stepped over to the wall of tenets and slouched down to the ground, reflecting on Jacob's story as he watched the morning sunlight seep in ever stronger through the overhead steel grating.

He watched Helena step from the lead railcar. She loitered in front of Darrow's office where she picked briefly through a cluster of granola before slumping down despondently against the wall. Darrow noticed her too, having just stepped out from the hallway. Billy watched their interaction as Darrow moved slowly to her position and tried to console her. At first she appeared reluctant, but eventually he got her talking, with Billy close enough to overhear. Seeing him so soon after the story of the church, Billy could feel himself looking on Darrow with a heightened sense of awe.

"Things will get better," said Darrow, his voice smooth and sure.

Helena didn't answer him; she just let her head fall slightly to the ground.

"Better times lie ahead," he continued. "One day our deliverance will come."

"I just feel so alone sometimes." She almost whispered the last part, as if she wasn't sure she should be saying it. Darrow knelt down beside her.

"You will never be alone. Never. You have your sister. You have this place. And, of course, soon will come The Progeny."

Darrow continued talking to her, only he did so at a whisper, as if alerted to Billy's presence. Billy couldn't hear the rest, but he could see. And he watched, after a time, as Helena noticeably rebounded, even lifting her face to Darrow's and allowing a smile to its surface. It wasn't the first time Billy had seen Darrow restore confidence in a member where it had faltered, his words working like a lathe to winnow away their insecurities. Nor was it the first time he'd heard Darrow mention The Progeny. Though he had no idea what it meant, he was reluctant to ask, not only for fear of sounding foolish, but also for fear of exposing his indiscretion, as he'd only ever heard the phrase through intercepted whispers or eavesdropping.

Over the next two hours, the entire membership emerged from the lead railcar. First after Helena was George. Then Ears. Then Jenny. Then Fat Henry, who waddled out sleepily and beelined straight for the food. A handful of others did the same. And then, seemingly last to awaken, was Ash.

It was late morning before he and Billy finally stepped above ground to scour for fresh food sources, and by mid-afternoon they had discovered a goldmine six blocks north. A large truck had backed into the alley of a busy restaurant. They watched as the driver wheeled dolly after dolly of fresh meat and produce down the steel ramp and into the open kitchen door. Some items were boxed, others rattled loose in milk carts. A lone delivery-man making eight, nine, ten trips. They counted how long he dwelled inside the building and took careful note before moving along. Both doors begged entry, but they held themselves at bay. As Billy had already learned, food *reconnaissance* was something apart from food *acquisition*. One did not turn into the other merely by opportunity or temptation. Darrow mandated their targets be watched, the sequences studied, and the patterns identified, preferably over a period of many days. Expectation minimized risk. Then, when it did come time to *acquire*, they were instructed to pick discreetly. They pulled only enough to make it worthwhile, but not so much to readily expose their treachery, lest that avenue lock down in the future. There was indeed a method to Darrow's madness, and despite the temptation before them, they merely committed the scene to memory and left without interfering.

By late afternoon they'd identified several more promising spots, and had collected as many mental notes as they could manage. By then they were also famished. Finding themselves a fair distance from the compound, they decided to lift a bite of food from a local merchant. Billy did so at the first prime opportunity. He'd always considered himself pretty handy at shoplifts, the baguette incident notwithstanding; and such was the case then, as he returned with enough for the both of them.

"Lunch!" he said, coming up alongside his scouting partner, who'd been watching from a short distance.

"That was real quick like," said Ash, his voice pinched with envy.

It occurred to Billy, as they ate their chicken, that he still knew very little about his new friend. "You have any family?"

Ash's demeanor curdled. "Lived with some people. Wouldn't go so far as to call 'em family, I think. They didn't treat me all too good." Ash paused, as if he were contemplating, then added, "But then maybe I wasn't so good to them either."

Billy sensed a sadness in Ash. A regret mixed with defiance.

"I've been thinking of my own mother a lot lately," said Billy. "Been dreaming about her, even."

"I never met mine," said Ash. "Never gonna, I guess."

"I knew my mother."

"You know where she is now?"

Billy shook his head. "I don't even know if she's still alive."

"Ya, well. All of us just orphans out here," said Ash, puffing out his chest.

"I've been trying to remember her," said Billy, not quite ready to let the subject go.

Ash curled up a smile. "You're kinda sentimental like, ain'tcha?"

Billy clammed up.

"Oh, I ain't judgin'. Just not sure that sorta stuff plays so well out here. Or with what we got goin' on down below."

Billy turned the page. Mentioned Jacob and Marlon.

"What about 'em?"

"They were arguing yesterday."

"They do that."

"I thought they might fight."

"Jacob wouldn't fight, I don't think."

"Still, it got bad."

"Been that way as long as I've been here," said Ash. "Some support Jacob. Probably more go the other way. But the Darrow, He and Jacob been friends a long time. Longer'n Him and Marlon. I think that makes Marlon more angry than anythin'."

"Shame about Marlon's sister," said Billy.

"Them's the breaks out here."

"What do you think? About the two sides?"

"I ain't really lookin' to get killed either, but then I'll go along with whatever the Darrow says."

"It makes me nervous how they fight," said Billy.

"Things gonna be fine. We got the Darrow leadin' us."

"I suppose."

Ash laughed. "You ain't the trustin' type so much?"

"Life hasn't been very good to me."

Again Ash laughed. "Life ain't meetin' your expectations?"

Billy shrugged.

"Think it owes you somethin' maybe?"

"I guess so."

"Ya, well Marlon says ain't nothin' owed can't be taken. Anyway, you just keep on expectin'. Me an' the Darrow're gonna change things for our kind right quick we are. Ain't gonna have to worry no more when we're all through."

No sooner had Ash said this than he began streaming tales of his own past successes, some of which seemed, to Billy, of questionable veracity, or, at the very least, artificially inflated. He'd noticed this overwillingness to impress in many of their conversations. Ash admired Darrow, that much was obvious, but to Billy it seemed like more than that. Ash pained for his approval. Whether this was born from a simple insecurity, or something more nefarious, Billy couldn't say.

Ash chattered on, and Billy's attention steadily waned as he dwelled in possibilities. The possibility that he might indeed have a real purpose in this world beyond one of mere survival, a relevance that he never before could have appreciated. That he might be, as Darrow proclaimed, worthy of just as much respect as any person in society.

IN THE DAYS THAT followed, Billy was tasked with increasingly complex assignments. One day, his task might be demolishing the lavish floral arrangements in front of a fancy department store, the next morning toppling cones and construction markers to create confusion and even some small fender benders.

Despite his familiarity with Ash, Billy quickly grew a preference for working with George. They were close in age, George the elder by a brief margin, and what he gave up in depth perception he more than made up for with good judgment and a strong work ethic. When acquiring food, George would play the distracter, approaching a merchant's goods in an obviously ham-fisted manner to garner the attention of the shopkeeper, while Billy—his skills becoming more refined by the day—slipped from the other side with the bounty. Gold Dust Twins of the strangest variety, they'd honed their lawlessness to a clockwork precision. Occasionally they'd be discovered, sometimes even chased, but never caught. They had the advantage of youth and speed, not to mention an aversion to capture that invariably outweighed the shopkeeper's desire to punish.

By then Billy had heard all the nicknames: Scarface, One-Eyed-George, Cyclops. Billy liked Scarface but thought it mean, so he settled on One-Eyed-George. Only when it came time to say it to George's face, he couldn't quite say it out loud; so he settled on George, which seemed OK, since that was his actual name.

As it was, it was all Billy could do to keep his eyes from George's face. It wasn't so bad when his right eye was shut tight to just a thick patch of reddish scar tissue. But when it cracked opened to reveal the glossy white crater in the middle, Billy found it difficult not to stare.

He'd only been there a week before George called him on it. "You gonna ask or aren't you?"

"Ask?" said Billy.

"The eye," said George.

"Mm-hmm?"

"You've been staring since you joined."

They were lying back on the sidewalk observing a potential target. Billy was mortified he'd been so transparent. "Sorry."

"It's OK," said George, "you can go ahead and ask, I don't mind."

Billy exhaled his mortification. "What happened?"

"I don't want to talk about it," snapped George.

Billy inhaled it right back.

"Just kidding." George winked his good eye.

A second exhale. Then a second, more tentative, "What happened?"

By then George's right eyelid had lolled open halfway. Billy stared straight into it, figuring it was as good a time as any.

"I just looked at someone the wrong way."

"That's all?"

"That's all," said George. "It was at night. We were in an alley. I don't know what his problem was, but he was making an awful racket. Singing and kicking at garbage cans. It was ridiculous. I was trying to sleep. Got up. I remember glarin' at him. Maybe I even yelled something. I don't remember anymore...

"Anyway, it all happened so fast. He was wearing some big overcoat. He pulled a corkscrew out of his pocket, and I remember thinking that was pretty weird, because it wasn't one of them little flip-out things. It was a real big one. So it was surprising. But not as much as when he scraped it down my face. Took my eye out. Not exactly the whole eye, but enough of the important parts, I guess."

Billy's own eyes watered. "That's awful."

George nodded. "I was in a real bad way when Darrow found me and took me in. They took care of me as good as they could."

Billy's mind detoured to Jacob's story of the church, and how Darrow had saved so many.

"Once they patched me up, Darrow wanted to know what happened to me. Asked me who did it..."

Billy shifted on the sidewalk. He felt uncomfortable with where this was going, but only listened all the more intently.

"So I told him. Described the alley and the guy in the brown trench coat. Didn't think nothin' of it. It was an hour or two later when I noticed Darrow was gone. Still didn't think nothin' of it, least not 'til Darrow came to me the next day and told me what

He'd done. Said He'd made it right for me. As right as it could be made, at least."

Billy didn't want to ask.

Absolutely had to ask.

"Made it right?"

George's demeanor turned. Billy saw his face light up. "He found him all right. Said he was passed out drunk somewhere. Said He just watched and watched."

"Then?" said Billy, trying to speed him up.

"He snuck up on the man real slow and silent-like."

"Then?"

"Then He returned the favor."

Billy swallowed hard. "His eye?"

George nodded with a little smile, then offered up a bit of a chuckle. "Yep, but not just the *one!*"

Billy didn't answer. He was too disturbed by the image, too unsure what to make of it or how to process it. This wasn't like the story about the church. This was different.

"I can't explain it," added George. "How it felt to be avenged like that."

Still Billy kept quiet. He figured the man probably deserved it, but it unnerved him all the same. It highlighted what Darrow was capable of, for good or for bad. Finally he asked: "Did you ever see the man again?"

George shook his head, his face glowing with sentiment. "I just can't explain how it felt."

A MUSICAL MARTYR

FOR THE NEXT SEVERAL weeks, Billy solicited no further revelations. Otherwise, the daily routine went on much the same, and by the end of his first month with the group, Billy had carved out a role as a quiet yet capable contributor.

He'd also, in his own mind, mentally sorted the fat from the meat. Whereas George had already proven himself to Billy, he found Jacob and Tommy to be equally capable, Marlon as valuable as he was vicious, and Ears a skilled thief.

Some of the others, however, were remarkably uninspired—or uninspiring. Ash, for example, was reckless and impulsive, skilled enough but overly ambitious. On multiple occasions Billy had watched helplessly as Ash tried to lift more food than time permitted, each time alerting the owner to their presence. His misguided ambition had not only resulted in several panicked retreats, but by exposing their points of attack, those outlets had dried up in the days ahead. When Billy suggested to Ash that he sometimes bit off more than he could chew, Ash responded triumphantly, "Nah, I can chew real good. Look at these chompers!" then had proudly thrust his open mouth to within an inch of Billy's face. It had made Billy think of Ben, his old neighborhood acquaintance who'd always been so slow on the uptake—though in Ash's case there remained a certain savviness about him.

Then there were Neven and Hannah. Neither had a very good grasp of direction. Each could be easily turned around and find themselves right back in the exact position from where they started. Jenny was skittish and frail; Totter usually had a convincing reason for deferring his missions; Lyle seemed beset with an incomparable laziness; and Henry's lungs would draw short, and his gripes conversely long, after even the shortest physical tryst.

Yet as a unit they were a force to be reckoned with; and as the days rolled on, their mischiefs—the *reminders*, as Jacob called them—continued to mount. Sometimes the acts were public, other times secret. All the while they railed against the Man, thrashing hard against a world that saw the inalienable rights of so many far too easily made alienable. Theirs was a holocaust of indifference—yet with each new story of another death in the streets or another unfair apprehension by the authorities, of an unearned eviction or inexplicable beating, Jacob would defend the perpetrators, assuring the clan that people weren't inherently evil, that most people were just too consumed by their own lives to appreciate the suffering of those beyond their own walls.

Even if Jacob was correct, that it was people's ignorance over malevolence, the knowledge was little more than cold comfort to Billy, especially when he would watch Darrow and see how the burden of their liberation weighed on him like an anchor. Billy saw it in every hardened stare that Darrow fixed unfocusedly ahead of him, saw it each time that he would turn that hardened gaze stoically yet beseechingly to the wall of tenets, heard it in his voice each time Darrow assured them of the change that would inevitably come.

But still nothing had changed.

Thus far, their reminders had been small, isolated exhibitions—sufficient to harass or annoy discrete pockets of society, sufficient even to trigger an undercurrent of discussion among their kind—but none so grand as to bring about city-wide attention. Darrow increasingly sought that type of deed, an act of mischief or destruction that would cause the entire city to open its eyes.

To that end, there'd been an increase in reconnaissance and surveillance, at some expense of the simple acts of mischief themselves. Darrow, Jacob, and Marlon had collectively agreed that it was time for a bigger—though, to Marlon's chagrin, nonviolent—splash.

It had been time well spent.

That afternoon, the latest reconnaissance team had returned with pivotal intelligence. As they told it, there was substantial activity at the much-ballyhooed amphitheater; and given the large crews laboring about, there was sure to be an event of some significance that very evening. They'd seen it all before. Loud music, inebriation, general tomfoolery. Darrow regarded this as the opportunity they'd been waiting for: the chance to affect hundreds, if not thousands of zombies in one fell swoop.

Darrow stepped to the area in front of the caboose and jumped atop the large wooden crate. The crate seemed both solid and rickety at the same time, if such a thing were possible, and had uneven slats with darkness tucked inside the off-kilter gaps. "My friends," he declared, "we have a special mission tonight."

The members, Billy included, gathered around the de facto dais, murmurs rumbling excitedly at Darrow's feet.

"Significant time and resources are being used for recreation and hedonism, while our brothers and sisters continue to live and die in squalor!" He then enthusiastically recited the first, second, and ninth tenets.

Immediately upon hearing the ninth tenet, the membership chanted "Darrow knows" in a rousing bout of unity.

Darrow asked for volunteers, and though most—including Ash—were eager to join, he settled on his two generals plus Billy, Chuck, and George. He then announced, to a great roar of approval, that he would lead the mission himself.

As Darrow stepped from the crate, a timid voice rose from the crowd. Barely heard over the pattering footsteps of the dispersing crowd, Billy was almost as surprised as the rest that the voice was his own.

"How will they know it was us?" he asked. He'd kept fairly quiet through his first month with the group, particularly in assembly, but this question had been on his mind for several days.

"What do you mean?" asked Darrow.

"I mean, the people. We're trying to send a message, right? To remind them that we're out here. So how will they know it's us?"

"Because they see us half the time," said Marlon.

"But would they really know one of us from the next?" he pressed. "And what about when our missions aren't public? When we leave them a present overnight or in secret, it could be anyone. A group of kids, a drunk, a pack of dogs even. Who gets the credit?"

"Our message would have no carrier," added Jacob, as if finishing Billy's thought. "It's a fair point. I'm not sure why we haven't considered this before."

"You're talking about a signature," said Darrow.

"Something like that," said Billy.

"There's a risk in identifying yourself," said Darrow.

Billy held uncharacteristically assertive. "Seems to me we want to be identified."

Others in the group had started to mumble quietly amongst themselves.

"He's got a point," said Jacob. "Then they'll know we're organized."

Billy felt Darrow looking at him but averted direct eye contact. The murmurs grew more excited as approval rippled through the group. George. Tommy. Ears. The twins. Several others. All nodding in agreement.

"It might be a good idea," said Marlon, in a rare showing of congruity with his fair-haired counterpart. With both generals on board, Darrow quickly followed, tasking Totter to come up with something "meaningful" before they departed.

As for the mission itself, those selected were told to prepare for departure within the hour. Several of them chose to feast. Others chose to rest.

Billy found his stomach too tied up in knots to do either.

THEY ARRIVED AT THE concert grounds shortly before dusk, the scene just as described by the reconnaissance team.

There were a large number of people filing in like zombies, at first by the dozens, then by the hundreds. They were, for the most part, young and irresponsible, and none looked as if they'd gone more than a few hours since their last meal. These zombies appeared to be mostly offspring of the Bigwigs, though some actual Bigwigs had also joined them. All of them seemed happy, content, not a care in the world. Darrow aimed to throw a wrench into their self-induced state of social obliviousness.

An open-air facility, the concert venue had no roof—only a stage and a large number of seats immediately in front. A grassy hill ascended behind the seats where people placed blankets and folding chairs. A short fence surrounded the entire grounds.

The six impoverished comrades took up a position on an adjacent hill a short distance away. From their vantage point, they couldn't quite see the stage, but they had a good view of the stadium and the surrounding grounds. They watched as some teenagers tried to hop over a shorter portion of the fence to gain access to the grounds, the gate-crashers quickly caught by security and unceremoniously ushered away.

"Amateurs," chortled Darrow.

There were several large vans parked directly behind the stage, and from out their back doors, a series of thick cables flowed into a generator. Billy noticed how the guards paid special attention to that area, and noticed in turn how Darrow paid special attention to the guards.

They continued to watch, the stadium gradually filling to

capacity. All but Jacob, who'd already slipped down the hill and seemed to be digging into the grass. Billy did as he was told, focusing on the movements and patterns of the security force. The guards milled about the area, keenly alert to the flow of pedestrians, though never turning around to look at the generator behind them.

Da dum, dum dum. Someone tested the drums.

Promise glistened from Darrow's careful, probing stare. At last he turned to Marlon and said, "Do you see those guards there going round and round?"

Da dum, dum dum.

"Yes," said Marlon, hanging slightly on the 's.'

"And that box behind them there right on the ground?" Darrow said.

Da dum, dum dum.

"If we manage to sneak past them carefully…"

Da dum, dum dum.

"…they won't know what's hit them…" he paused just long enough to cock his head to the left toward Marlon, "…and then victory!"

Darrow and Marlon shared a mischievous look, the former imparting a rare lift to his lips into something resembling the birth of a smile.

Soon enough, nighttime had fallen and the concert was under way. Multi-colored lights glowed brightly from the stage, leaving much of the surrounding area in darkness, save for a smattering of lights near the confection stands and restrooms.

Darrow waited more than an hour into the show, "To let them get good and liquored." He then sent in Billy, along with Marlon, George, and Chuck. The instructions were simple, though why Darrow selected his two newest members to execute such an important mission was unclear. It could have been because they were both fast and keen to impress—yet the pessimist in Billy thought it might equally be that Darrow considered them the most expendable. As they set off down the hill, Billy coaxed himself into believing the former over the latter.

They were on the grounds in moments. Billy and Chuck remained out of sight, tucked neatly behind a cluster of shrubs, while George and Marlon approached the most isolated of the guards, then launched into a contrived fit of acrimony. They screamed at one another, and George even took a healthy shot to the side of his chops, for authenticity's sake. The fight, like all fights, immediately attracted the attention of all nearby spectators, including several of the closest guards. One yelled at them to stop. The others laughed. The result was exactly as desired: a sizeable gap that allowed Chuck and Billy to slip past unseen to the maze of cables behind. Their diversion a success, George and Marlon backed away and retreated toward the hill, much to the discontent of their audience.

Safely inside the perimeter, Billy and Chuck knelt down and pressed their bodies up against the large metal generator. The box hummed and purred, its outer casing warm to the touch. They quickly located two openings where most of the cables converged. Chuck squeezed in as far as he could. Billy did the same through the second opening. The cables were thick and difficult to manipulate; it was all they could do to pull and dig at the connections, tugging and tearing with reckless abandon. It wasn't long before Billy fell back in pain, hair standing on end, body abuzz and mouth tasting of metal.

Chuck went on undeterred. He continued to indiscriminately rip at the cables. He was grunting and making a great racket, but the pulsing sounds of the nearby concert and the steady drone of crowd noise were sufficient to drown him out. It took time for Billy to regain his composure, and for the feeling to return to his temporarily numbed body. He'd just gotten to his feet and peeked over at Chuck when a flash of blinding light cut through the air, and Billy saw, for just a fraction of a second, his partner tense up violently. The crack of electricity that had just coursed through the unsuspecting fleshy conduit was followed by the foul stench of burnt flesh and hair.

The cascading effect knocked out the power to the immediate area, including the stage itself. The hum and the purr were gone, as was the music, the stadium now cloaked in darkness.

The silence was fleeting. Boos soon descended from several segments of the audience. From some, there was laughter, and shouts from still others.

Billy's eyesight gradually returned. His pupils fully dilated, he could fuzzily make out Chuck, lying on his side. His body was steaming and his eyes bulged out of their sockets. Billy backed away, nauseous, his legs threatening to buckle.

Commotion grew within the concert grounds. Bottles shattered. Some of the attendees grew fearful and tried to exit. Pushes turned to shoves turned to screams. There were shouts for calm and order, but some of the zombies were pushed to the ground amid the fervor. The security guards and paid-duty police tried to bring order to the situation, flashlight beams dancing wildly in the air.

By then Billy had already slipped off the grounds and had rejoined his compatriots, who were waiting on him at the base of the hill.

"Where's Chuck?" asked Jacob, his nails soiled with dirt.

Billy couldn't concentrate. His response was robotic. "Dead."

"Are you sure?" said Jacob.

Billy nodded, though his attention had already moved above them. It was dark, but Billy saw through it well enough. Something had been cut thick into the hillside grass: an upside-down triangle, with three beams shooting off from each side.

It didn't immediately register, but then he realized: It was a symbol.

Their signature!

His mind flashed back to their leaving that night. Just before they stepped into the gravelly tunnel. He'd seen him chatting with Jacob, giving instructions.

Totter!

He'd done well.

Billy didn't have long to admire the design before Darrow urged him forward with the rest. All of them ran through the darkness—all, that is, but Chuck, who lay smoldering on the ground next to the charred and smoking generator, a collateral casualty in pursuit of the greater good.

The concert was over. They knew this from the sights and the sounds they'd left behind them. The grumbles, the boos, the angry calls for refunds. Some of the younger zombies were even in tears. They had themselves become victims of saboteurs.

Saboteurs of the status quo!

Darrow had successfully engineered the group's first great strike to society.

It wouldn't be the last.

FOR WANT OF GRAPEFRUIT

CHUCK WAS DEAD.

He had just died a sudden and violent death, and while it was fortunate that he hadn't suffered at any great length, in those scant last seconds of life, he surely suffered greatly.

Billy could still smell the burnt hair and skin as they made their way back to the compound. Nothing seemed to displace the foul odor, not the cool night air or the swift race through the streets. It festered thick in his nose even as he found a spot on the compound floor and slid down vacantly against the wall.

Billy looked out towards the others, unaware that he was shaking, confused by the lack of remorse on his comrades' faces. Few seemed to care that they'd just lost one of their own. He could tell that Jacob did. And Tommy, and a few of the others. But the rest were too consumed with excitement. By then, most had circled around Darrow and Marlon. Billy sat watching the jubilant cluster.

Darrow rose to the top of the wooden crate to spread the gospel of their mission, his minions splayed out beneath him. "The first significant strike," he proclaimed, "against a significant societal target." People were screaming. People were scared. People were affected.

People took notice!

"Those who ignore our plight have now started to receive their comeuppance," shouted Darrow, "and we will ensure this becomes an increasing reality. You are the ones who can make this happen. *You* have the power. You and you alone!"

The crowd cheered wildly.

"The House of Darrow is strong!" he screamed.

Again the compound roared to life. Several shouted out the ninth tenet. Someone in the rear yelled, "Death to decadence!" It was a furious scene, emotions highly charged. It was also the first time Billy had ever heard the compound referred to as *The House of Darrow*. They loved it. Standing around the crate, faces raised, they consumed every single word, as if Darrow's victory speech was something that could be chewed, swallowed, and digested.

To much whooping and shouting, Darrow lauded Billy for playing such a key role in the mission—even though his actual contribution, as far as Billy himself was concerned, was negligible. He'd told them as much on the way back, as well as he could articulate anything at that point. He'd told them that he'd tried to cause damage but had only fallen back dizzy, and that the next thing he knew Chuck had knocked out the power. It didn't seem to matter. He and Chuck were at ground zero when the generator went out. That was what mattered. But it wasn't him at all. It was Chuck—turned dead by current.

"Do not grieve for our fallen comrade," proclaimed Darrow. "Celebrate his achievement. Indeed, he may be the most fortunate of us all. His was a death of courage. A death of meaning. And now he will live forever! If you are fortunate, perhaps you too will be presented with the opportunity to sacrifice for the good of our cause."

Forever, thought Billy.

Wondered Billy.

The others didn't seem to wonder. They buzzed at Darrow's feet with such hopeful energy that it seemed possible they might raise him into the air on a thick gust of fawning. Except his feet didn't rise. They held root atop the old wooden crate that tilted and creaked with the cadence of the rest, as if it too yearned to hear Darrow continue the tale of Chuck and Billy.

But it wasn't Billy at all.

It was Chuck. Turned dead by current. Turned martyr by current.

Only at that moment Billy wasn't thinking of Chuck as a hero or a martyr, nor was he thinking about how he might also sacrifice himself for the group. All he could think about was Chuck lying on his side, his eyes bulging from their blackened sockets, smoke rising from his charred body. He kept replaying in his head, "My name is Chuck, and I don't give a..." It played overtop the visual of his limp carcass. Same cocky voice. Same upbeat tone. But the words fell flat against the image, and the reality that he could easily have been the one electrocuted instead of Chuck. Would his own death have been dismissed by the group in the same blasé manner?

But despite it all—the shock, the stench, the apprehension, and the misgivings—Billy still appreciated the magnitude of what they'd accomplished, and the hell that they'd raised, complete with Totter's symbol marking it as their own. He recognized that they'd finally struck a substantial blow against society, and that their discontent would surely, finally resonate on a wider scale. People wouldn't change unless they were forced to change. Even as he trembled, Billy believed it.

It wasn't long before Jacob noticed him slouching despondently against the wall. He approached and tried to rouse him. So too did George, then Tommy. Ash looked on from something of a platform purgatory, a conflicted look on his face—not exactly coming to Billy's side, not exactly beneath the crate with the others.

Unlike Billy, Darrow was positively emboldened. He proudly hailed *the Concert Caper*—as it would soon become known—as a watershed moment for the organization.

It wasn't long before they'd broken into a hastily cobbled song.

The selfish ways that you have born
Have turned us rather all forlorn
You made us mad
Our brand new fad
And now your perfect world is torn

The lyrics flowed through confident and excited voices. They sang of Billy and Chuck's immortality and the promise of a changing world. Dancing followed suit, though Billy took part in none of it. He was exhausted on all levels.

His eyes grew heavy, and before long they'd locked him into blackness. The last thing he saw, just before they closed, was a member of the group looking at him strangely. The observer struck a curious pose, the look in his eyes unfamiliar. With Billy's mind so groggy, it took a moment to decipher.

Then the penny dropped.

It was reverence.

THE NEXT MORNING ARRIVED quickly, bringing with it the welcome tandem of fresh sunshine and fresh perspective.

Billy had enjoyed a lengthy slumber, and some of yesterday's apprehension had receded. Chuck was still dead, but the haze had subsided, the shock significantly dulled.

He considered that he might still be dreaming as he rose to his feet. He blinked hard but it was still there: an upside-down triangle, three beams shooting from each side. Overnight it had been scratched prominently into the middle of the compound floor, centered between the three railcars.

Billy hadn't stepped three feet before several members of the group approached to congratulate him. It wasn't the standard array; no playful pushes or mussing of hair. This was something else, the regard more potent, the commentary more earnest. It was an unusual feeling for him, and nearly overwhelming. It not only made him uncomfortable, but also seemed incongruent with the first tenet—that *all in this world should be valued equally*. He was, after all, just one among them. He mentioned it to Darrow, who quickly admonished his humility.

"You've earned this," Darrow said. "Indeed all should be valued equally, as the tenet proclaims, but there's no harm in recognizing individual achievement." He then added, "A bit of kind treatment has never harmed anybody, and it won't harm you, either!"

Billy knew he hadn't done anything special to earn it. Didn't feel—perhaps couldn't feel—that he was worthy of special attention. Yet still it was happening, growing like a weed from a misdiagnosed achievement. It was much like Jerry Doyle's "Grapefruit Mentality": the theory that if you put a simple everyday object on TV—even something as banal as a grapefruit—individuals would suddenly clamor to see it. The bizarre phenomenon of faux importance through attention; the attention of others, somehow serving as a contagion.

Billy himself was now the object of Grapefruit Mentality, just on a smaller scale, the medium not television or radio, but the witnesses themselves and gossip healthily disseminated. It had worked to the same end, the adulation coming from all corners. All, that is, except Ash, who kept his distance, his hue a discernible green.

And so it was, that sometime between shutting his eyelids last night and opening them this morning, Billy had taken on a new stature within the group.

Unknowingly, unexpectedly, even unwillingly, he'd become the grapefruit in front of the lens.

A HEALTHY DOSE OF SYMBOLISM

ILLY PRACTICALLY INHALED A thick slice of ham for breakfast, then set out with Jacob for a day of reconnaissance. Darrow had offered him the day off as a reward for the previous night's contribution, but Billy had declined. He needed to get outside to clear his head and keep his mind occupied. He could use a day's rest, but with it came a day's rumination.

They spent the bulk of the day surveying the west end of the city, identifying several promising targets along the way, including a fancy water fountain that could surely be jammed up with some well-placed clumps of dirt, rock, and brush. They also had considerable time to chat, and by midday, Billy's spirits had rallied.

"I've been thinking…about the message we're sending. Even if people connect us to all this, how're they going to know what we want from them?"

Jacob turned toward him, his look prodding Billy to elaborate.

"I mean, we do these things and then we run away. We wait a few days, then we do some more. Then we just sit back and watch for change that never comes. But how can we expect change without them knowing exactly what we want? I mean, I know we can't exactly give them a list of demands…"

"You think our acts are too random," interrupted Jacob, "and our demands too vague?"

"Maybe a little."

Jacob opened his mouth into something of a smile. "Our demands are obvious if people want to see them. We want homes and shelters. Access to food and clean water. To be safe from violence and neglect. Kindness. People shouldn't need that spelled out."

Billy remained circumspect. "You actually think we can get people to change?" He watched Jacob nod. "You have more faith in people than I do."

"I tend to have more faith in many things than I should," said Jacob, "or so I've been told." It was a rare lightness from Jacob, a mash-up of tongue in cheek and self-deprecation. "I'm not saying it will be easy, Billy. People here are insular. They're driven almost entirely by consumption. Just look at what goes on all around us. Watch where their focus is—they're relentlessly engaged in exchanges for food, products, services. That exchange is consumption. Consumers are valuable, non-consumers are not. We, unfortunately, are the latter. And until people change their views on this, until one's worth isn't measured this way, then our lives will never be valued like theirs."

Billy chewed on everything Jacob had just said. Did people truly believe that he and his kind had less value just because they didn't consume? The logic appeared sound, but could it possibly be that simple? Billy pledged, when the time allowed, to give the matter more thought.

It was late afternoon by then, and they continued home in relative silence, which was only to say that their mouths weren't moving. There remained the unremitting symphony of muffled exhaust, the incessant bleating of horns birthed by impatience, the shrill of technology bouncing off every façade or fixture. An unending line of stores peddling their latest wares. And all the while, the zombies filing in and out. In and out.

"It's not like this everywhere," said Jacob, as if sharing Billy's thoughts. "I came from a place with a lot more field and a lot fewer people. A place with more trees and streams and nature, where the stars hadn't been choked away by the spread of smog and the glare of technology. Things moved a lot slower there." Jacob described where he grew up, a long way from the city. Billy held the image in his mind as they walked. It gave him a sense of calm.

Whenever they could, they'd cut away through greenery. Parks, walking paths, gardens—they were there to be found, if you knew where to look. Jacob steered them through one of those areas on their way back to the compound. Smooth pedestrian walkways with soft grass. Bounds of trees looming overhead—oak, maple, birch—strong and healthy. Their branches were full and heavy, swaying evenly in the steady breeze, rustling soothingly over-head as they blanketed the ground with a generous shade. Small slats of sunlight broke through to the ground as the branches whispered to each other, until it seemed that all of the branches on all of the trees were gossiping wildly amongst themselves, robbed entirely of their discretion.

Billy breathed it all in, letting the air draw into his mouth and sink into his pores. Even back in the east end, he'd slunk off to public parks or fields whenever he could. The freshness and greenery helped to offset the drudgery, if only for a few hours; helped to remind him that the world stood for more than concrete and steel. He sometimes wished he could just live out his days somewhere among the grass and the foliage. He was thinking like this when Jacob's head cocked to the right, his face asking if Billy had heard it. He hadn't. At least not at first. Now he did: a high-pitched weep. Jacob had already started off toward the source, disappearing behind a cluster of dense shrubbery. Billy followed closely behind. He found Jacob loomed over the source of the pleas. It was slunk down in the dirt, close to where the nearest shrub sprouted up from the earth.

"It's a blue jay," said Jacob. "Not much more than a baby."

It squawked twice more, quivered a bit, then squawked again.

"What's wrong with it?" asked Billy. A rabbit had just run off at the sight of them, skittering away into a patch of shrubs.

Jacob leaned down. "Here," he indicated. Its left wing was mangled, the same side split open and soiled red. They watched it try to stand up. It had a frightened look in its eyes. It stopped chirping momentarily, then overcame its fear and started up again, calling for help. For its mother, perhaps. Billy looked to Jacob. His eyes mirrored pain. "It's hurt," said Jacob. He spoke as if it was he who was injured, or Tommy, or any number of his closest colleagues, with his spirit bent to match the creature's broken wing. "It's hurt badly."

Billy kneeled over the pitiful creature. "What do you think happened?"

Jacob looked up to the tall oak above them, then back down, then back up once more. He considered it to himself, his thoughts back-dropped by a fresh chorus of pained chirps. "Could have fallen from the nest. Or been flying and hit up against something. Maybe even been attacked. It's hard to say."

The bird chirped once more from its slender black beak. It tried again to get up but fell down just as quickly. Some of the grass beneath it was stained red.

"It won't last long like this," said Jacob. He reached down, and Billy, stepping back, wondered how Jacob possibly hoped to heal it. There, with only grass and trees and nature and pity. Billy waited for the comforting words that the bird would neither appreciate nor understand, for Jacob to search out some form of sustenance and drop it into the wounded creature's crying mouth. He listened past the whispering branches for the act of kindness that Jacob was now administering.

And so it was all very confusing as he watched Jacob with the bird. Overtop, pressing down. The bird shook its good wing frantically, its lame wing limp at its side, its scraggy talons digging defiantly into the soft brown earth. It fought desperately for life against the unforgiving appendage now pressed up against it. Its right wing beat faster and faster, scuttling plumes of dirt up into the immediate air around him, into the air that would not come. Billy felt his own airways constrict. The branches overhead whispered and thrashed, as if the trees were casting dissent.

Finally, mercifully, the combat concluded. The beating wing drooped gracefully to the ground and fell tenderly to the side atop a short thicket of grass, followed by an awkward stillness.

"Why did you do that?" Billy heard the accusation in his voice. It was just a bird, but something wouldn't reconcile. His view of Jacob, by then, was bound inextricably to compassion. He couldn't bear watching Jacob take the life of another.

"It was too far gone," said Jacob.

"Maybe it would have gotten better," said Billy, doubtfully.

"It was in pain," said Jacob. "Something would have gotten to it. If not today, then tonight. And if not tonight, then tomorrow. Either way it would have suffered. Unable to defend itself. Unable to reach food or water." Jacob paused, then added thoughtfully, "It was my responsibility."

His responsibility?

Billy kept silent, even though he knew that Jacob was right. He knew it but couldn't accept it. At least not sufficiently to displace his misgivings. Jacob didn't take life—that was for the Marlons of the world.

"Sometimes…" said Jacob, now exceptionally careful with his wording, "sometimes when something is too far gone, you have to put it out of its misery." It seemed that he was trying to rationalize his decision as much to himself as to Billy.

"I understand," said Billy. And he truly did. It might have been that his nerves were still raw from the previous night. "It was just a bird," he reminded himself. He'd killed birds himself. But it bothered him all the same. Bothered Billy that the area was suddenly so quiet.

The bird lay still and mute, its eyes now dark and empty. The trees crying softer than before.

"We should get back," said Jacob.

They stepped from behind the shrub, the ruffled feathers bent down behind them, a black beak half-caked in the dirt.

Their walk back to the compound felt morose. Billy imagined the bird flapping both healthy wings down from the sky, perching next to Chuck on the ground. His thoughts flowed in that current all the way back to the compound, even as they trod along the narrow railing of the subway tunnel.

Billy might have gone on this way much longer, but as he and Jacob stepped out through the hollowed out tunnel, they looked down to a surprising sight: more than a dozen fresh faces littered about the compound floor. Male and female, old and young, short and tall, fair and dark, and all variants in-between. Many were waiflike—with frames ranging from noticeably malnourished to dangerously emaciated—their limp shadows splayed ghostly on the compound floor.

Even the shadows looked hungry.

The newcomers scuttled about, wondrously perplexed, the clan's symbol blazoned freshly beneath their dirty feet, and Marlon directing their movements. Billy turned to Jacob, his own puzzled expression mirrored on the face of his fair-haired general.

As it turned out, less than twenty-four hours after the execution of the Concert Caper, a groundswell had swept through the ranks of their underclass. For months there'd been subtle chatter about this new group waging acts of social mayhem against society—Billy had heard the rumors himself—but these latest whispers had ripped through the city with the same speed as the current that ended Chuck's life. The organization was being talked about on the street.

The organization.

Yesterday they were just a ragtag bunch with an enigmatic leader, a small fringe group operating under the cool metropolitan surface. Now, with their newly earned credibility, their popularity had exploded among their kind.

Somehow, information had leaked to reveal the general area of the compound, and the intervening hours had brought a small flock home to roost. Given Darrow's desire to grow the movement, and his impatience with the speed of society's response, Billy suspected that the leak might have been orchestrated internally. Yet however the information was disseminated, sometime before noon Marlon had found six lost souls milling about on the sidewalk near the subway entrance asking questions about *Darrow* and *the movement*. He'd quickly brought them inside through one of the secret paths, lest their presence draw the wrong kind of attention.

After depositing them in the waiting room, Marlon made haste up the tunnel to discuss the situation with Darrow. In short order, they'd determined that the most appropriate course of action was to bring the newcomers immediately into the fold; this represented a smaller risk than turning them away.

And so it was, for the first time in their history, that the melodramatic inquisitions and showy initiations were dispensed with, Billy's having been the last. Instead, Darrow tasked Marlon with the responsibility of quickly training the new recruits, such as showing them the layout of the compound and the three secret paths between the tunnel and the surface. Marlon even developed a crash course on the Nine Tenets of Darrowism, with the new members voraciously gobbling up the culture.

That had been late morning.

By the time Billy and Jacob had returned, there were a total of fifteen new members, with still more collecting on the street with each passing hour. By the end of the day, their group had more than doubled in size. The situation became so intense that Darrow assigned two members to patrol above ground and act as sentries. As soon as would-be loyalists were identified, they were to be discreetly whisked down to the compound to undergo the rapid indoctrination process. None balked at the lifelong pledge or the midnight curfew; they puffed out their chests and wore them like badges of honor. Some had been searching out the group for many weeks, Darrow's having already garnered something of a savior-like status.

Darrow and his clan could only hold their collective breath that their movements wouldn't come to the attention of the authorities. The irony was that the group, so angered by society's lack of respect and attention, now desired invisibility—at least until their message had been disseminated city-wide, and to those in a position to do something about it.

As the down-on-their-luck legions arrived, they recounted some of the stories being spread on the street; and while no two accounts were the same, they were generally consistent on the main points, and those main points were consistently inaccurate. According to the latest version, Billy and Darrow had engineered fire or explosions to targeted vans and equipment, killing hundreds of people and sending thousands of snotty rich kids running and screaming. This was, of course, a far cry from the truth. Even if they had access to bombs—which they did not—they wouldn't know what to do with them. And while there was some pushing at the Concert Caper, and even mild panic, from what Billy had seen, no one sustained any meaningful injury aside from Chuck.

As the pressure from this mass influx mandated inclusion, there wasn't time to select the healthiest and fittest members for their organization, which would have been Darrow's preference. But one of Darrow's many strengths was his ability to adapt as conditions required. The situation before them now required inclusion not only of young, strong, healthy males, but even the aged and infirm, who were plentiful.

Indeed, with so many of them long since abandoned or orphaned, some carried with them myriad untreated maladies. Others were dangerously malnourished. Still others were wild and difficult to integrate. Yet they all arrived with the unmistakable glint of promise in their eyes; for in addition to the inflated perception of the group's concert exploits, there was also a mistaken belief among them that Darrow was a healer. One particular rumor held that a blind member regained his vision in the wake of one of Darrow's crate-top sermons. In reality, only Fat Henry had significant vision problems, in the form of cataracts, and his vision was only getting worse with each passing day; and, of course, Darrow's sermons had done nothing to restore George's excised eye. Yet the rumors persisted, and Jenny unknowingly perpetuated the misconception, telling all newcomers that, "This is a good place," and "A place where you can become whole," with many accepting these as literal rather than spiritual statements. It was a pauper's panacea.

Billy and Jacob stood with Tommy watching the hopeful swarm. Tommy's eyes expressed concern for the sickly newcomers, especially those in an obvious state of distress.

"Just look at them," he whispered.

"This is what we're fighting for," said Jacob. Billy listened, his mind still partly behind the shrub.

"It is," said Tommy. "But how are they going to fit in? Some of them can hardly even move." It was said with no hint of elitism. Billy knew Tommy well enough by that point to know that his views weren't coming from any air of superiority, only from pragmatism.

"They will fit in," said Jacob. "And they will grow stronger in time."

"Of course," Tommy agreed, though the look on his face and his tone revealed the contrary: that some of them, like the bird, might already be too far gone.

Regardless of their pitiable state, they arrived with that glint of promise in their eyes. The organization was, to all of them, much more than a collective of like-minded individuals spearheading an assault against the upper crust. It stood as a promise of better

things to come. It said that their kind wasn't alone or unwanted, that they weren't dirty or dangerous or unloved or without
purpose. That they were valued members of the community and
should be treated with the same kindness and respect as any
person.

That they were *not* second-class citizens!

The organization broadly, and Darrow and Billy specifically,
had become symbols of hope. Indeed, Billy soon found himself
surrounded by eight of the newest members. They called him
"Bill." One reached out to touch his hair with a reverence that
made him feel queer in the belly.

"Amazing," said one.

"Did they really beg for mercy?" asked another.

"Can't believe you pulled it off," said a third.

"It was just one concert," said Billy, but they dismissed this. He
tried to elaborate, to give a true account of the Concert Caper,
but they discounted his explanations over and over, believing him
a humble victor trying to minimize his own heroics. They did
finally accept that he preferred to be called Billy, but beyond that,
their impression of the Concert Caper remained unchanged.

Darrow endured the same type of hero worship, only delivered
more fiercely. He, however, did not attempt to correct them or
to minimize the events, instead allowing the reverence its full
bloom. "They need heroes," he said to Billy, overtop a chant of
song that, with the addition of so many mouths, reverberated
raucously across the compound floor. "They need heroes," Darrow
repeated, "and it would be selfish to deprive them of that."

Totter, standing at Darrow's immediate right, was quick to
agree. "Yes, absolutely, this is very important, we must not be so
selfish," all of which accompanied his requisite fit of nodding.

Darrow and Billy weren't the only group members to have
reaped a rapturous following. The newcomers clamored to see
where Chuck was buried so that they might pay homage. They

were dismayed to hear that there was no such marker, his body having been left behind for the state.

For all of the inaccurate information bandied about, the one truth not lost in this procession of whispery rumors was the root cause of the action. The newcomers had arrived with a precise understanding of what the group represented—as much as it could possibly be defined. This was an organization meant to strike out at society for the furtherance of those lost and forsaken on the street. In their own way, they were Robin Hood fighting against the Sheriff of Nottingham. Willie Stark before the graft. Reverend Reginald Bacon crusading against the Establishment. Terry Malloy pit against the longshoremen. They were the downtrodden united, tilting against class injustice and social tyranny.

As if there wasn't already enough focus on Billy, Darrow capitalized on the fervor surrounding his sudden popularity. He unilaterally created, then immediately conferred upon him, an *Award of Valor*. He did so for Chuck as well, posthumously, of course. Most of the clan received the decision with great aplomb. At Darrow's instruction, one of the newest members, with a marked exuberance, inscribed the honorees' names onto the wall to the immediate right of the nine tenets. Following this ad hoc display, Billy endured nearly twenty more minutes of adulation before he extricated himself from the mob.

The influx continued through the night, and by the next morning their ranks had swelled to a robust sixty.

It wasn't long after this that Billy met Claire. Scrawny and doe-eyed, she ran about the compound floor querying the residents about her missing brother. She repeatedly offered the name "Brian" as she pinballed desperately from member to member. She approached Lyle, unable to rouse him, before finally arriving at Billy.

"He vanished last week," she said, meek but frantic. "It's not like him to disappear for more than a day. When I heard about this group, I thought maybe he'd ended up here."

"No," said Billy, "I don't think I've met anyone here named Brian. But the city's a big place. He could be anywhere. Maybe he got in some trouble and was taken by the authorities?"

"No. He wouldn't do anything bad. Nothing to attract attention."

"Does he have any enemies?"

She shook her head. "Brian is kind. We keep to ourselves and sleep under bridges." Her voice cracked. "He would never have left me like this. Not unless something happened."

She was overcome at that point, her voice muddled to incoherence. Billy tried to settle her down, assuring her that he'd ask around for her brother, not daring to mention what he'd heard about the disappearing rounders. With so much going on, he hadn't thought of it for some time. Only now Claire brought the issue squarely back to the forefront of his mind. It unnerved him the remainder of the morning and into the afternoon, when Ash approached him tentatively on the compound floor.

Things hadn't quite been the same between them since the Concert Caper. Ash, previously so extroverted and buoyant, had grown noticeably sullen.

"You been gettin' hard to locate," said Ash.

Billy nodded.

"Seen you walking' and talkin' with Jacob lots."

"Mm-hmm."

"And been kinda cliquey-like with Scarface, too."

"With George," said Billy.

"Just like I said it. Anyway, that's OK, I guess. To get in good with the group."

Billy knew what he was hinting at—the fact that Ash had recruited him, but Billy had forged his own identity and grown tight with others.

"What'cha think?" said Ash, seemingly quick to change the subject, "'Bout all these newbies?"

"Not sure yet. I guess it's good."

"Still kinda hesitant-like, aint'cha?"

"I suppose."

"There it is again," said Ash. He laughed and started to come out of his shell. "The Darrow's impressed with decisive. Gotta have more confidence!" His eyes then wandered to the Wall of Valor. "But then maybe your ways got some benefit…"

Billy saw the hope in Ash's eyes. Saw it each time Darrow addressed Ash or so much as looked in his direction—saw the way his wiry colleague responded, saw it in his instantly eager posture and from the transformation of every crevice in his face, saw the pained wait for affirmation.

"I didn't ask for that," said Billy.

"Don't bother me none," snapped Ash. Only it did. Obviously. Painfully. "Anyways," he added, "I'll be up there one day."

"Mm-hmm," nodded Billy.

"Sooner'n you can blink. Only a matter of time, really."

Billy nodded again, though his focus was elsewhere. "One of the new members…Claire…she said her brother is missing."

"Ain't nothin' new to that," said Ash.

"It's still happening," said Billy. "The missing rounders."

"Like I said, ain't nothin' new about it. It's a real rat's deal up there."

"Don't you find it strange? That so many of us are disappearing without any explanation?"

"Haven't thought much about it," said Ash. "You worried they might start turnin' up dead soon?"

"Maybe."

"Guess that'd be better'n nothin'."

"I'm not sure it would be better for them," said Billy.

"Well 'least then they'd know for sure they were dead."

"I'm pretty sure they'd know it already," said Billy. He looked intently at his colleague, but couldn't tell for sure if Ash was joking.

Ash changed gears, his demeanor continuing to lighten. "You want maybe we prowl tonight?"

It had been a while, Billy thought, since he'd just walked around under the stars. It would be good. Therapeutic, in many ways. So he agreed, and they chatted for some minutes, with Ash's frosty demeanor now melting away like the last icicle in a warm spring thaw.

They were preparing to leave when Jacob appeared at the mouth of the hallway. He called for Billy, who looked curiously at Ash. "I'll be right back…"

It was an infrequent occurrence, being summoned like that. He stepped into the hallway and then through the opened office door to find Darrow perched atop the desk, Marlon sitting on the side table next to the telegraph machine. Jacob took a spot on one of the chairs. Darrow had a vacuous look on his face. He wasn't looking at Billy so much as looking through him, and he held that way for several seconds. Then, as if he had been alert the whole time, he snapped into speech.

"Turns out the symbol was a good idea," said Darrow. Billy remained quiet, and Darrow finally added, "Could be you have a few more inside you."

Billy drew his eyes to Jacob, who shot him back a wink.

And there it was. The Concert Caper. The Wall of Valor. It made sense as much as it didn't. The newcomers looked up to him. The leadership seemed to believe in him. And, of course, Billy now had to align with Darrow's vision. He was no longer just a common foot soldier. He glanced through the wall to where Ash would be waiting on the other side.

"Please sit," said Darrow.

So Billy did, feeling himself at best unworthy, at worst a fraud, and the meeting commenced.

Over the course of the next two hours they bandied about various ideas to move their initiative forward. Billy offered the occasional nod or monosyllabic contribution. Before long he found himself grumbling or nodding in conjunction with Darrow. His agreement was genuine, but then he thought of Totter; so he made a conscious effort to avoid the appearance of fawning, which turned him largely still for the rest of the meeting.

One potential target was the water supply, but that notion was quickly shelved, as they couldn't figure out a proper method of attack, nor guarantee that they themselves wouldn't be affected.

From there they considered striking at various banks and financial institutions, as Bigwigs often visit such places; but those establishments were nearly impregnable, and they couldn't imagine how to mount an effective assault.

All the while Billy watched the tension mount between Jacob and Marlon, the latter increasingly urging Darrow to take advantage of their growing numbers to push the movement forward with aggressive tactics, the former saying it wouldn't be noble to do so.

"Noble?" Marlon scoffed. "Since when was any of this supposed to be noble?"

"We may be desperate," said Jacob, "but we don't have to act like it."

"And it's worked out really well for us so far, hasn't it?" said Marlon. He then turned to Darrow. "We can be as noble as we want to be, but if we hold ourselves back from doing what truly needs to be done, then we're just going to end up noble failures."

"And where does it end?' challenged Jacob, drawing back Marlon's attention.

"It ends at the end," said Marlon, his face marked with exasperation.

Darrow held silent as his generals continued to squabble. Finally, before the argument could escalate any further, he silenced them with a harsh command. After a moment they again started to bicker, at which point Darrow was moved to quote the ninth tenet, which they immediately repeated. He then ordered them from the room.

Billy followed on their heels, stepping back onto the compound floor, Ash nowhere in sight.

It was a challenging time for the group, and for Darrow in particular.

From what Billy had seen, things had started to wear on him more than ever. There were more gazes lost in time and space, more frequent staring at the wall for minutes on end, and more audible debates with himself. Yet the pressures continued to grow; and a recent event, which had been pending some weeks, compounded matters still further.

It had come suddenly in the dead of night: the shrill wail of arrival, of dissent against violent expulsion from the womb, of eyes shut tight and pink in defiance, followed by the uncontrolled, almost drunken movement of limbs. The members had stepped slowly and groggily from the railcars to find Jenny resting comfortably on the floor, the quivering newborn tight to her breast. Darrow had already ascended to the wooden crate to announce its arrival to the blinking eyes beneath him. An uncommonly white moon spilled its light through the steel grating high above and splashed itself dimly across the compound floor. The brightness behind Darrow made him appear as a living shadow.

"Behold," he said stoically, before momentarily losing his voice. He stood up straighter, then repeated, in a slightly deeper tone, "Behold...The Progeny!"

He said nothing further, just disembarked from the crate and, to Billy's surprise, walked immediately toward his office, his pace brisk and his attention held forward, as if his thoughts had somehow escaped and run ahead of him, and he were trying desperately to catch up.

Helena was soon by her sister's side. Billy moved closer and could hear Jenny speaking weakly to her twin.

"You remember what I told you," she said. "Samuel if a boy..."

"Yes," said Helena softly, "and Samantha if a girl."

They were still completing each other's sentences. Only this time was different. It lacked the usual playfulness.

"You do remember," said Jenny. She seemed relieved, then giggled slightly before falling back to silence. Billy looked through the pale moonlight at the wriggling entity at Jenny's breast, then at the even paler shadow that the newborn cast down to the compound floor, down to where it cloaked an object curled up in submission. Nobody was moving except Helena, who gently stroked her sister's weary head. Jenny finally raised her gaze upward, as if she were wondering, as Billy was now wondering, if it would have made a difference if they'd lived above.

After a period of time, Jacob stepped solemnly over to Jenny and whispered some words that Billy could not hear. She nodded, and a moment later he lifted the shapeless form into the warmth of the moonlight, though even then it looked dark and grey and cold. Billy watched it all sadly, saw Jacob's gentle footsteps as he carried the stillborn tenderly down to the tracks for a moonlight burial.

Billy and Ash were among those who attended the early morning ceremony, along with Helena, George, Tommy, and several others. Marlon was there as well, standing remotely off to the side as the body was softly lowered into the cool dark earth. His face appeared both solemn and relieved.

Jenny remained absent, as did Darrow, each shut away in quiet seclusion.

IN THE DAYS AHEAD, the task of tending to The Progeny fell almost exclusively to Jenny, Darrow citing the need to remain focused on their cause. Though Jenny received some assistance from Helena and a handful of others, she was mainly left to her own with little Sam, who cried and acted out often. It bothered Billy to see this, but Darrow was not to be questioned on such matters, so it was consigned to an uncomfortable silence.

As it was, the arrival of The Progeny wasn't the only significant development that week, as it had become evident that their culture had started to shift since the mass influx.

Aside from a few lazy or skittish individuals, most of the clan desired outside missions of theft, reconnaissance, and mischief. However, with so many able bodies to choose from, the important missions were increasingly being assigned only to the fit and most capable members, and it had become common for simpler and menial tasks to be assigned to the females, elderly, sick, and weak. As the days rolled on, those kept inside started to question whether the seventh tenet, promising equal work, was being honored. In reply, Darrow asserted that any disparity in job allocation was mere coincidence; though as the trend repeated itself day after day, it became harder for him to deny their claims. They found the compound work to be tedious, and they lamented the lack of fresh air and sunshine. Some were more vocal than others, and eventually a handful of frustrated souls attended Darrow's office to complain.

Darrow was quick to respond. "The seventh tenet has not been violated at all," he assured them. "While members may be given different tasks and assignments, all still work the same number of hours."

The tenet, Darrow reminded them, was silent on the exact nature and location of the work to be performed, and merely spoke to duration. He further added that it was his duty to ensure the well-being of his weaker members, and that he was merely looking out for them, particularly since outside work was more taxing. He also reminded them that the tenets were silent on the distribution of fresh air and sunshine.

Yet the protests weren't limited solely to the allocation of work assignments, as the distribution of accommodations had also shifted.

The entire membership, now numbering sixty, could no longer

fit within the cushy comfort of the first subway car. The first time this issue arose, there was heated discussion over who would get to sleep in the lead car, including some pushing and shoving between several frustrated members. It became necessary for Darrow to intervene. Realizing such squabbles would be a recurring issue, he appointed an individual named Chester as the de facto town crier.

From that moment forward, Chester would relay Darrow's rules and regulations—including the assignment of beds—his deep voice carrying throughout the compound for all to hear. The crate would strain beneath his rotund frame. Fat body, fat voice. The fat ones, it seemed, always made the best town criers.

"This is the word of Darrow," he would begin, before serving up their leader's daily pronouncements, and though Darrow assured the group that the assignment of beds would be entirely random, appointments to the first railcar tended to go to the same individuals involved in the most important missions, while those who toiled with the simple labor were sent to sleep in the second railcar.

Those fortunate enough to find themselves assigned spots in the first railcar had found a large number of widgets scattered around inside. The widgets were of all different shapes and sizes and colors, and some members had kept a few of the nicest and prettiest ones for themselves, if not in recognition of their true worth, then at least to retain them as ornaments, or for the fad or novelty of it. However, many saw the widgets as not only unnecessary to their existence, but as impinging on their comfort—this despite the negligible footprint they occupied—and continually pushed the unclaimed objects to the back of the railcar. Once the lead car had finally filled to capacity, they'd moved the unwanted widgets into the second railcar—itself now taking on nocturnal tenants.

As for Darrow, he'd begun to spend increasingly little time in the main compound area, preferring instead to hole up in his office. It was not necessary for him to appear, he said, with Chester's acting as his daily public address announcer. He even started to have his food brought to him, citing the need for solitude, and the need to remain focused on his meetings and his strategies, which would eventually benefit them all.

In time, the sight of Chester being summoned into Darrow's office, and then jumping atop the wooden crate, invariably meant that new rules or procedures were to be announced; and each time the weak among them would cringe, as they were often the most affected.

As might be expected, some were put off by the new work and sleeping arrangements, especially the founding or longer-standing members who now had to sleep in the second, less comfortable railcar, or toil hours on end with menial tasks. Jacob urged Darrow to develop a more equitable system, but was unable to sway him. Darrow said that he didn't have time to coddle the members, maintained that his assignments were fair and random, and was steadfast that the tenets were being honored. Nevertheless, unable to shake the feeling that the current apportionments abided inequality, both Jacob and Tommy voluntarily ceded their positions within the first railcar to sleep out on the compound floor on stacks of old newspapers.

It was the first sign of friction that Billy had observed between Darrow and his pacifist general.

RUFUS: THE FOREIGN ONE

HE'D NEARLY REACHED THE subway shaft when he heard a voice from behind ask where he was going. Billy turned around and watched Tommy negotiate the last of the gravelly floor that separated them.

"Just out for a walk," said Billy, "to clear my head."

"Want some company?"

Not really, but he bit his tongue and nodded instead. He liked Tommy, and though he'd wanted to go alone, he was content enough that it wasn't another newbie looking to ingratiate himself.

It had been nearly two weeks since the Concert Caper. Two weeks since the sheen of that event had gradually faded under the disenchantment of their weaker members, the icy disconnect between Jacob and Marlon, and the weighty pall of unmet expectations. There had been smaller successes above ground, but none quite so grand as they desired, particularly given the sizable workforce now in place.

Still, new members trickled in daily, wide-eyed and hopeful, floating high praise in Darrow's and Billy's direction. Billy wanted to rid himself, at least for a few hours, of the responsibilities that clung to him like fleas on mange. The last two weeks had exacted a toll that he hadn't been prepared for. The attention, the demands for his time, and the invitation into Darrow's inner sanctum all came at him like waves. All because he'd been at ground zero when Chuck knocked out the power.

They waited for the next train to pass, then stepped onto the narrow subway ledge and hurried to the nearest exit point. Once above ground they pointed their noses to the sky and took stock of the dark clouds hovering above.

"Looks like rain," said Billy.

A quick nod from Tommy and they set off at a slow pace, careful not to go too far in case the skies decided to open. It was Sunday evening, not quite dusk, and the streets were quiet. They peeked up every so often, but the rain never came, so they stretched their walk a greater distance. Above them, the grayish clouds streamed steadily across the sky, then broke apart into splotchy patches that hung above in silence, and eventually disappeared into a dark night sky.

"I'm uneasy about things," said Billy.

To that point he'd kept away from the subject, purposely away from what he'd fled. He blurted it out quickly, without really thinking. He eyed his colleague's face. No change. Not a twitch or tremor or tick. Just a very cool "I see."

Another half block went by in silence.

"It's just that things don't seem like they're heading the way they're supposed to be," added Billy. "The way things are around the compound."

A full block of hesitation.

"Even good intentions can become…muddled," said Tommy.

"You mean like you and Jacob sleeping on stacks of newspapers?"

"Things aren't so simple sometimes."

"No. And it doesn't help to have Jacob and Marlon at each other's throats."

"I think it's more like Marlon at Jacob's," said Tommy.

"We need to work together better," said Billy.

"I agree," said Tommy.

"You still think Jacob's right?" asked Billy. "I mean, that we stick with just property damage?"

Tommy smiled at him. "Do you?"

And there it was, spinning it around on him with just two words. Jacob was good at that, too, so it shouldn't have been a surprise that his friend might be the same. The fact was that Billy remained ambivalent about their tactics, Chuck's death notwithstanding. He wasn't sure exactly how to respond, and the thunderclap that buckled his knees rescued him from the moment of indecision. Both he and Tommy looked up, but not a drop fell. Then the crash came again, and his knees gave way all the same, only not so violently.

"What is that?" cried Billy. There were a few people on the opposite sidewalk. They'd flinched as well but kept on their way. Then came a third blast.

"It's not the clouds," said Tommy. "It's coming from back there." He led Billy around the side of the nearest building and into the rear lot to some sort of commercial loading area.

It was the yelp that Billy noticed first. The high-pitched squeal of pain and fear. He saw it curled up overtop a stain of its own blood. A black Lab. He was trembling up against a brick wall. Ribs poked through his sunken chest as if he'd swallowed a xylophone. Three boys had set upon him.

"Why are they doing that?"

Tommy shrugged. "You expect me to explain people to you?"

People indeed. Teenagers. Though what they lacked in maturity they'd topped up with cruelty. Billy and Tommy watched it unfold. Looked on as the tallest one reached into his pocket with his left hand and pulled out a firecracker, his right hand lighting the fuse. He threw the sizzling projectile toward the cowering creature beneath them. It hit the side wall and exploded above his head. The dog cried and shrunk down further to the pavement, as if he were somehow trying to get beneath it. The other two boys laughed and rooted on the tall one. One was short with locks of curly red hair, the other was plump, with a shaved head and a tattoo on the side of his neck. He lit a firecracker of his own and jettisoned it at the shaking figure. It popped violently by the dog's ear, resulting in another frightened yelp. The dog tried in vain to curl up tighter, as if he might make himself smaller and smaller until he disappeared.

"Better they just killed it," whispered Tommy to Billy, "than to torment it as they do."

The boys swarmed the Lab, teasing him, mocking. The pudgy tattooed one was taking pictures as a keepsake of their dominance, their superiority.

The short red-haired boy threw a rock. It cracked violently off the dog's forehead.

"Got it!" yelled the pudgy one.

"Hold on, hold on. Get this!" The tall one reached into his back pocket and pulled out an even larger firecracker. Up went the lighter. He held the silent red flame to the short fuse, igniting an ominous sizzle.

He was pulling his arm back to throw when the attack came. Billy, who'd gotten up a good head of steam, launched himself at the skinny boy's arm, knocking the firecracker out mid-release. It flittered off toward the red haired boy and exploded at his feet.

The tall one screamed. By then Tommy had entered the fray.

The boys were momentarily shocked, but their anger quickly returned full bore and was transferred now to these two interlopers. The pudgy one moved in for Tommy. He kicked at him with a sneakered shoe but caught air when Tommy sidestepped the attack and drew back. Meanwhile, the tall one had come about for Billy. Rather than wait for it, Billy lunged for his neck. The boy pulled to his right. Billy flailed out as he went by, scraping the side of the boy's face and leaving a red smear across his left cheek. He screamed profanity in Billy's direction but kept his distance.

Billy looked up to see Tommy now cornered by both the red haired boy and the pudgy one. He'd drawn himself into a defensive stance but it was no good, and they quickly overpowered him. Billy moved to help, but the tall one blocked him. Billy could see them punching Tommy in his head and side. Again Billy tried to help, but the tall kid grabbed him by the neck and a fierce struggle ensued.

A guttural protestation boomed from behind them as the wounded beast rose to his feet and bound forward. Only then could Billy appreciate how truly massive was this animal. Even with the emaciation, he was, without a doubt, the largest canine Billy had ever laid eyes on.

The Lab drew up on his hind legs and threw himself against the tall kid, knocking him off Billy and face first into the pavement, his pimpled face smeared into the concrete.

The giant left him there, immediately sweeping around to the other two, who instantly released Tommy. The pudgy one grabbed a two-by-four that was lying on the ground. He swung at the beast, who evaded the brunt of the blow. Another swing and another miss. Then a third.

As the boy drew back for the fourth swing, the Lab launched forward, driving the boy's pudgy body into a nearby green dumpster. It crumbled against the unforgiving exterior. The boy slumped to the ground, the back of his head leaking blood. By then both the tall kid and the red-haired kid had taken off in a run.

The emaciated beast loomed over the remaining boy. All his fear was now stripped away to the reveal of unbridled fury, his pain held in abeyance. His chest heaving, he seemed confused about what to do next. He didn't ravage the boy, as Billy expected. Instead he just howled. It was a scream of desperation, of anger. It screamed a question at the boy, demanding an explanation, to know why they'd attacked him. Blood dripped from the giant's open mouth. The boy slunk down further, tears welled up in his eyes. Tears not for his choice, but for his consequence. The giant reared up again, six feet tall on his hind legs, but before he could do any further damage to the boy, Tommy had struggled to his feet and eased himself between them.

"Enough," he said, his own ear bleeding.

The boy extended his bloodied left hand. It quivered before the imposing figure. Billy stepped next to Tommy, at which point the giant howled once more, then relented. The Lab bowed his head, fell back two steps, then limped slowly behind the dumpster where he disappeared from sight. The red-haired boy was already crawling away on his hands and knees. Billy watched him spring to his feet and scamper clumsily from the area.

Billy turned to Tommy, "How do you feel?"

"Dizzy." Tommy's left ear was mangled, and he was clearly favoring his left side. "Might have cracked something taking those shots."

"Sorry I got us into this."

"It's OK," said Tommy. He moved gingerly to a nearby parking bumper and sat down to rest. He'd only just laid down when the skies opened up with a slow drizzle.

"Figures," said Tommy.

"I'm going to see what I can do for our friend here."

"Be careful."

Billy nodded, then followed the trail of blood behind the green dumpster, where he found the Lab laboring to lick his wounds. He growled once he noticed Billy's presence, then bared his teeth until Billy stopped advancing.

"It's all right."

He barked again, then drew back to his mending. He whimpered as he worked, his tail beating hard against the ground. Blood dripped from his mouth to the concrete as he worked. Pockets of fur had been blown from his dull coat, leaving flesh singed and exposed. His breathing was shallow, and he seemed to have used up what little strength he had left when he'd come to their defense. Small droplets of rainwater now peppered his face, blood and black powder rolling down his tattered frame.

Billy edged closer. The dog simply stared back at him, his eyes filled with pain and mistrust. A moment later he'd slumped down further and curled up his swollen body on the pavement. Then he seemed to pass out. From the pain. From the fatigue.

Billy moved cautiously closer until he was standing over the Lab and studying the wounds on his body.

Maybe it was the image of Chuck that did it, or of the blue jay beating his wing hopelessly against the soil. Whatever the reason, Billy decided that he couldn't leave him as he was, and so it was that he and Tommy stayed there through the night, Billy looking after the mammoth creature as best he could. The dog would occasionally wake up, opening his eyes and baring his teeth, but unwilling or unable to move. It went that way through dusk, and it was only at the first crack of daylight that Tommy pressed them to leave.

"They're going to be wondering what happened to us."

"You go," said Billy.

"He's alive," said Tommy. "Pretty beat up, but the bleeding has stopped. He's breathing OK. I'd say he's through the worst of it."

Billy turned toward his patient, who had woken at the sound of their conversation. He bared his teeth again, but only for a moment, then slowly pulled himself up against the dumpster. His eyes studied Billy, this surprising source of kindness, and seemed to satisfy himself of his benevolence. Billy saw it in his eyes. He leaned in and reached out to touch him. The dog allowed it.

"We have to go now," said Billy.

The dog looked back unknowingly, but once Billy started to walk away, the Lab called out for him. He staggered forward two steps, then braced himself once again against the side of the dumpster.

"You're going to be all right now," said Billy. Again he started to leave, and again the Lab called out. He pulled himself from the dumpster and started to follow with slow, labored steps.

"You've got to be kidding me," said Tommy.

Billy looked to his colleague, as if the permission should flow from him.

"We can't bring a dog back with us, Billy."

"Why not? We're taking anyone now." He paused briefly before adding, "I thought that all lives were supposed to be equal."

"Yes," said Tommy, visibly moved by the mention of the first tenet.

"Isn't that why we're doing this in the first place?" pressed Billy.

"It is, but—"

"But what?"

"But this is different," said Tommy.

"Why?"

"I think you know why."

The dog continued to limp toward them, small whimpers magnifying his movements. His wounds glared red and swollen. A noticeable chunk had been blown from his left ear. As he came up to their side, Tommy stared at the pock marks decorating his body.

"If things just weren't so crazy right now..."

"But what about the fourth tenet?" asked Billy.

And that, finally, is where Tommy succumbed. And as they made their way back at a glacial pace—Billy swallowing the smile that had crept up onto his face—he couldn't help but replay the fourth tenet over and over in his mind.

Whoever lives in the street is a friend.

IT WAS EARLY MORNING when they staggered through the gravelly tunnel. Surprisingly, the Lab had gained strength as they went along, and though he had some difficulty traversing the narrow subway ledge, the trip passed without incident.

The anticipated wave of excitement spread through the members. Breakfasts were abandoned. Sleepy members streamed groggily out of the railcars. Any relief in their colleagues' overdue return was immediately trumped by suspicion and fear. The fact is that it wasn't just a dog. It was a stray dog, wounded and leaky, massive in size. Jenny gaped, pulling Sam close to her side. George kicked a couple times at the ground. Fat Henry was the first to step forward, intercepting them as soon as they'd set foot on the cool compound floor.

"You brought a freaking dog down here? Does this place look like a damn kennel to you?" He'd set himself directly in their path.

Billy just stared back. By then all eyes were cocked toward the unassuming trio. Marlon stood beneath the list of tenets, his head obstructing the words "Darrow knows." Ash looked on from in front of Darrow's office, Totter from beside the wooden crate.

"Whether there is a place for him or not will be His decision to make," said Jacob, stepping between Henry and Billy. "Now step aside."

"Or what?"

Henry had bent his head down, his chin disappearing into his plump neck. A small crowd had gathered behind him.

"Or you'll be stepped aside," said Jacob.

The solidarity filled Billy with an unfamiliar emotion. Not just pride. Not just respect. It was something a notch or two more satisfying than that, particularly as the much larger Henry backed away from Jacob, grumbling further bigotry and expletives under his breath. The exchange had not only swelled Billy's chest, but had equally backed off any others contemplating a similar intervention. The small mob that had gathered behind Henry quickly dispersed.

They convened in Darrow's office: Jacob, Tommy, Billy, Marlon. The Lab waited outside, the preponderance of members gawking from a short distance as he slid down to the floor to wait.

"He certainly is…large," said Darrow, reentering the office after stepping out to have a look at their new arrival.

"Be even bigger when he gets healthy," said Tommy.

"It doesn't belong here," blurted Marlon. "Beyond the fact that it's a dog, it's getting crowded enough in here. Our food only goes so far."

"I can find him food above," said Billy.

"What about disease?" pressed Marlon. "Or if he becomes violent?"

"I don't think that's going to happen," said Billy.

"You have a lot of experience tending stray dogs, do you?" said Marlon.

By then Darrow was pacing the floor. He muttered a few frustrated words at his feet, but nothing distinguishable.

"He could be useful," said Tommy. "We patch him up and get him strong. He's massive. He could be good for us."

"And where would he sleep?" asked Darrow. "Our space is already so precious."

"There's lots of room out on the compound floor," said Jacob.

Darrow visibly chafed at the mention of this, at the reminder that Jacob and Tommy had voluntarily moved out of the railcars to sleep on stacks of old newspapers. A public dissent against Darrow's relaxed interpretation of the sixth tenet, which promised equal sleep. Billy recognized the conflict stirring inside him and seized on it.

"The fourth tenet," said Billy. "It says that anyone who lives in the street is a friend."

Darrow turned and faced the rear wall. Nobody else spoke. They waited. First one minute, then two. Finally he curled around and turned to Billy, "He's your responsibility."

And so it was that their newest member was announced to the group. Some were pleased, many skeptical; but in the end, even the dissidents grudgingly accepted Darrow's wisdom to keep the dog, even if they remained suspicious.

By then he was limping along behind Billy wherever he went, so Billy led him to the end of the compound floor where they could be alone.

"I'm going out on a limb for you," said Billy.

The Lab opened his mouth, his tongue lolling out at the words he couldn't possibly understand.

"Not one of my favorite things to do, I can assure you."

The Lab just stared at him.

"First things first, you're going to need a name."

More wagging of the tongue.

"So what are we going to call you?"

To this the dog barked back something indistinguishable. A husky communication that sounded, at least marginally, like "Rufus."

"Well," said Billy, "that's good enough for me."

'14

THE HOUSE OF DARROW

HE DAYS SLIPPED BY, and their mischief started to mount.
Soon after the Concert Caper there was *Deep Divot Dawn*,
with Marlon the vanguard to a fierce early-morning assault
against one of the city's most prestigious golf courses, the troop
laying waste to several of the finest greens before the morning
sun could stir itself from slumber beneath the East's blackened
horizon.

Equally successful was *Construction Corruption*, a Jacob-and-
Tommy-led mission that saw a handful of members sneak into
the worksite of a nearly completed "Apartment Therapy" store.
The overturned paint cans (and other hazardous materials) were
but a small sampling of the damage they would accomplish, with
their destruction creating sufficient havoc that it would force
eager consumers to agonize an additional month before exercis-
ing their right to purchase $300 laundry baskets.

There was *Newsstand Nuisance*, with Billy, George and Rufus
ravaging several newspaper stands, toppling stacks of Lilian
Braun paperbacks, shredding copies of *The Economist*, and committing unspeakable acts to the gum and candy.

And finally there was *Floral Fracas*, when Jenny and Helena
paid a midnight visit to an outdoor garden center, systematically
destroying entire inventories of azaleas, daffodils, and tulips, and
though they showed a modicum of mercy to some of the rest,

none would sufficiently recover to grace even the shoddiest corsage or centerpiece.

On each occasion they would proudly mark their victory—the symbol scratched into a bag of mulch, or a "Darrow Knows" shouted loudly from one of the sand traps. And though all of the missions were deemed successes, they remained—contrary to Marlon's persistent urging—confined to property damage and general mischief.

And still nothing changed.

The stagnation did little to stabilize Darrow's fragile psyche. He'd grown increasingly frustrated by the continued societal indifference, and was now inclined toward severe bouts of irritation, and even lengthier sessions of brooding.

It was late morning. Billy sat on the compound floor, Rufus sleeping by his side. He watched out the corner of his eye as several members returned from a mission of food acquisition. One of them clenched a length of salt pork; the others carried small slabs of cheddar. As was the custom, the food was deposited on the compound floor at the base of Darrow's office, directly in front of the large glass window. Billy salivated at the thought of the meat. It had been several days since he'd sunk his teeth into anything quite so tasty. With all the recent arrivals, the more coveted food items were being consumed at an alarming rate. He noticed Fat Henry and several others eyeing the pork and the cheddar before he was called into Darrow's office.

Billy entered to find Jacob and Marlon sitting rigid and apart. There was a queer tension in the air, Billy's arrival likely interrupting yet another terse discussion.

"We've identified a new target," said Darrow.

"Some sort of art house," said Jacob. "Just opened yesterday, as far as we can tell."

Billy listened to them describe it—Bigwig after Bigwig sipping champagne and staring lovingly at the abstract creations hanging on the walls. Darrow was livid.

"How many of us might find shade and shelter within those very walls? How many might sleep safely on its barren floors? So much space to live. Yet its only overnight tenants are flat inanimate constructs affixed to the walls!"

"Mm-hmm," said Billy.

"The back door will be our way in," continued Darrow. "Our point of attack."

"Attack?" said Billy.

"Jacob wants us to sneak in and destroy the art."

"Mm-hmm."

"Marlon suggests we go in late, attack the last person there."

"I see."

"Do you?" injected Marlon. "Concerts and putting greens are all well and good, but they don't bleed."

"I see," is all Billy said. He could tell that Marlon was in a particularly ornery mood. His body was tense, almost shaking, and his eyes crinkling judgment in Billy's direction.

Billy looked to Jacob, who remained silent.

"And if the choice were yours," said Darrow, drawing Billy's focus, "how would you have it?"

Billy bent his head down. The salivating effect of the salt pork had dried up. He was apprehensive about where the conversation was headed. Up to this point, there hadn't been a single mission aimed at hurting people. Billy couldn't tell if Darrow was sincere; a test, perhaps.

Darrow clearly sensed his equivocation. "You must be willing to take a stand when you feel it is right to do so. Otherwise you are merely an ornament."

"Why would I get to choose?" He knew the answer the instant he asked it.

"Because," said Darrow, "tomorrow you're going to lead it."

His first thought: *Why me?*

Then a flash from his ego: *Because I'm important.*

No, intervened his ample pessimist: *Because I'm expendable.*

Billy's head swirled with contradiction. With excitement. A mission of his own! Not just scouting, not just stealing or sabotage or upending magazines. He couldn't think of what he'd done to earn it. He'd contributed some decent damage around the city: broken into car dealerships to break off antennas, continued to steal at a good clip, a few other smaller exploits. But there hadn't been anything to mark him as a leader. Even Tommy and George hadn't led a mission like this yet. All he could think of was the Concert Caper. The Wall of Valor. Accolades that he still felt were ill gotten. They traced his neck like a noose, and as Marlon continued to stare at him, the noose only grew tighter.

"Our numbers continue to grow," said Darrow, as if highlighting the explanation that Billy himself couldn't identify. "Our missions are destined to become grander and more frequent. This will be a good test for you. If you do well, there will be more opportunities in the coming days."

Important or expendable?

Maybe neither.

Maybe just a test.

But what if it wasn't?

"The art, then," said Billy, and quickly, as if Darrow might lose patience and make the decision for him.

"The art," repeated Darrow, with no affect that would betray any preference for Billy's decision.

Marlon jumped to his feet. "So soft and so sweet," he seethed. Turning his stare on Jacob, he added, "It will only lead us softly and sweetly to our graves."

"The decision has been made," said Jacob sharply. "Now keep a civil tongue in your mouth." He then reminded Marlon of the ninth tenet.

It was all that Marlon could take. He lunged at Jacob, Darrow intercepting him at the last moment, then ordering his intractable general out of the office to cool off as Billy and Jacob shared a glance; they themselves left Darrow's office several minutes later.

Billy had hardly stepped from the hallway before he noticed Marlon standing alone overtop their symbol, his gaze fixed hard to the overhead metal grates, where something sang to him that Billy could not hear.

"He's angry," said Billy softly.

"Yes," said Jacob, who'd come to rest beside him.

"Always so angry," repeated Billy, still with his eye on Marlon.

"Yes."

"Maybe he's right," said Billy. "Maybe someone needs to get hurt."

"You think so?"

"I don't know. I'm just saying maybe."

"Maybe," said Jacob.

"It was a big decision."

"Yes."

"I just don't understand it," said Billy.

"What's that?"

"Why would Darrow do it?"

"Do what, exactly?" said Jacob.

"Take a chance like that."

"What chance?"

"Him leaving it to me. To make such an important decision."

"You think He left it to chance, then?"

"What else?"

By then Jacob was smiling.

"What's so funny?"

Jacob leaned in, lowering his voice to almost a whisper. "Did you consider that He might have already known exactly what your answer would be before He asked you for it?"

Now it was Billy's turn to smile. "You're suggesting Darrow knew my decision before I did?"

"He is the Glorious Darrow," said Jacob, once again as if that answered everything. He still said it confidently, though perhaps not with the same zeal as before his and Tommy's move down to the compound floor.

"I didn't even know until I said it," said Billy.

"I see," said Jacob, "then I suppose He indeed took a chance, then." It was spoken without sarcasm, but still he was smiling. The idea irked Billy. He fought hard against the notion that anyone, Darrow included, might know him better than he knew himself.

"You sure give Darrow a lot of credit," said Billy, with a glance back toward the office.

"And maybe you don't give enough."

Rufus joined them a moment later, bounding to Billy's side and nuzzling him with a wet nose.

"Believe what you will, Billy, but do believe this: It is an important mission, an important target. He's putting a lot of faith in you." Jacob stopped talking, and by then his smile was gone. It had been replaced by a look, as if to add the words, *We all are.*

Billy nodded back, recognizing the solemnity of the occasion, before Jacob left him alone with his canine companion. Darrow had told Billy to pick any two "soldiers" for the mission; indeed, although Darrow had not yet embraced Marlon's violent ideology, his terminology was nevertheless becoming increasingly militaristic.

Billy scanned the area for his would-be accomplices. It made all the sense in the world that he'd call on George, or any of his closer friends, so it came as something of a surprise—perhaps to Billy as much as the others—when he found himself moving in a different direction.

He first approached Cecil, a new recruit who'd arrived shortly after the influx that had brought Claire. Cecil was young and eager but cautious. He had no family to speak of. Billy saw much of himself in the newcomer, and that was good enough for him.

Yet it was his second pick that was the most unexpected. He tracked down Ash, finding him crouched alone halfway down the compound floor. Indeed, if envy truly showed through in green, then Ash's current hue now rested somewhere between myrtle and electric lime, and while there were surely more capable members Billy might have drawn on, there were none so in need of an olive branch.

"I could use your help," said Billy, the branch now fully extended as he outlined the details of the mission. Ash examined it, hanging in the air between them. They'd never gone for that prowl around town. In fact they'd hardly exchanged more than a few words since Billy had abandoned him outside Darrow's office. Not that Billy had made many overtures, always finding himself thrust in this direction or that; and with Ash recently downgraded to sleeping in the second railcar, the opportunity for reconciliation had dwindled that much further.

Ash appeared conflicted by the invitation. Part of him seemed pleased with the offer. But the other part of him—his rawest of emotions—appeared resentful that it was coming in the form of a sympathetic handout from his own would-be protégé.

"You reckon you really need me?" he asked. The branch grew heavy in Billy's clutches, but he nodded, swallowed his pride and, after asking Ash once more, he accepted Billy's invitation.

Billy finally turned to the food—only to find that the cheddar and the salt pork had already disappeared.

MORNING CAME QUICKLY, HIS dreams bombarded by a host of images; his mother, the fireman, Chuck, the blue jay—each of them made an appearance in one way or another, and each still lingered in his mind as he met with Cecil and Ash to sort out the details of the plan. They went over the specifics multiple times, Billy only content once Ash's eyes glossed over from the repetition.

The rest of the day whipped by in an instant, and soon enough the trio had arrived at the art gallery. They studied things from the front before moving to the rear, where they discovered the back door wedged open, just as Darrow promised. Billy stashed Ash and Cecil behind a dumpster, then crept stealthily to the doorway and peeked inside. It was a storage room, filled with boxes, supplies, and reeking of pungent fumes. Billy stepped two feet inside, spotting the door leading into the gallery itself. He could hear people moving around on the other side. The sounds were distant and muffled. Emboldened, he stepped deeper into the room, taking a mental picture of the area before retreating to join his colleagues behind the dumpster out back.

"Gonna be a snap, this is," said Ash.

Cecil peeked around the dumpster. Billy pulled him back. "Remember, no matter how long it takes for them to close. We're going to be statues in there," said Billy.

"Statues," repeated Cecil.

Billy looked at Ash.

"Ya right, statues," said Ash, already fidgeting with excitement.

Billy held them there, slunk back to the door, then waved them in one at a time. Soon all three had taken positions behind large crates in the farthest recesses of the storeroom.

An hour passed, then two. Two gallery staff had stepped briefly into the back room, but none had come close to the three stowaways. By the third hour of waiting, the tense pall in the air had given way to boredom, and on at least two occasions Billy heard Ash expel an impatient sigh. Each time Billy shot him a look.

Statues!

Billy had kept one eye on the back door, watching the wedge of sunlight slowly fade to darkness. Gradually, the murmurs up front descended into silence.

Finally, one of the curators came to the back and fiddled with something on a workbench. Billy and the rest remained still behind their crates. After a couple of minutes, her heels clicked to the back door. The door slammed shut, sealing off their ready means of escape, and with it, Billy's confidence. His anxiety had already started pecking its way back in. The clicking of heels had stopped, but he was certain she was still there. A further moment of silence was broken by a garble of dangling keys, then the clicks recommenced in their direction. Billy looked at Ash, who was mouthing a silent "Tricky, tricky" at his feet.

Click click click…

Billy tensed up and closed his eyes. His anxiety had already discombobulated his senses, and he could no longer tell if she was six feet away or six inches. What he could feel was the bark of the tree pinching his skin, and the frantic echo of his mother's screams down below, and he could hear the crack of the branch as he choked on the stench of chemicals from the fireman's yellowy uniform.

Click click…

He opened his eyes and peeked at Ash, who'd now hunched down and shut his own eyes, each likely craving the return of the mind-numbing boredom of the last several hours.

Click…

More jangling keys.

Billy readied to spring. His inner voice urging him to run.

Run. Run. Run.

Click…

Then a muffled voice, the male curator calling for the clicking lady. She called back to him, then clicked her way from the storage room back to the front gallery. With each step away, Billy's heart slipped down his throat and back into its proper cavity. Minutes later the back room went dark. A few high-pitched beeps echoed up front, followed by the distant closing of a door.

Then…silence, and they were alone.

Billy held them there a short while before finally stepping out from behind the boxes and into the darkness. All three then cautiously made their way to the front of the gallery.

"Careful," whispered Billy. "Not too close to the windows."

He'd hardly finished the words before something else caught his attention: A stairway hugging the far wall, leading up to some type of loft. The others had noticed it too, and the trio immediately crept up the wooden staircase. They emerged onto a second level of art, one completely invisible from any ne'er-do-wells who might be walking by on the sidewalk.

It was perfect.

Billy sent Ash downstairs to stand guard, and to alert them if he heard or saw anything that might signal trouble. He was also tasked to scratch their symbol somewhere noticeable. "Just stay clear of the windows," repeated Billy.

They watched Ash slink silently down the staircase; then, without delay, they became the city's harshest art critics.

Billy slashed wildly at an original Gottfried Mind, reaching up on his tiptoes and jumping when necessary. His body pulsed warm, the fruits of his labor so immediate and satisfying; and it wasn't long before a kaleidoscope of color rained down all around him, the incalculable particles of pigment and fabric reflecting the promise of looming change in his wide blue eyes. With each and every strike, Billy could already see the world changing for the better; could already feel the city's ignorance slipping away; could already envision the dawning of a more responsible society—convinced that each hearty blow to the now-ravaged canvas brought their pitiable clan that much closer to one more meal, one more bed, one more act of kindness—sad dollops of hope, consequent to his unshaken belief in the existence of some yet untapped well of human philanthropy.

After a moment he glanced over to Cecil, who was putting the finishing touches on his own creative masterpiece. By then their nails had grown thick and gummy, a sickly bruised purple. They'd soon enough moved onto subsequent victims, each one rendered as garish as the one before it.

"This is gettin' tiring," said Cecil, himself in the midst of working over his fifth canvas. They'd been going strong for fifteen minutes.

Billy nodded and suggested a short break. "We've got all night, anyway."

He called down to the final third of their triumvirate. The normally chatty Ash had been uncommonly quiet since his descent to the ground, a silence made all the more conspicuous by the nonresponse to Billy's query.

"Ash!" Billy called out again, his tone raised an octave.

Once again he was met with silence, the kind of peculiar and unwelcome quiet that often accompanies the nearly instantaneous discovery of an unwelcome pit planted squarely in the recesses of your stomach.

Billy whispered to Cecil, and they both crawled to the edge of the wooden staircase, looking down into the darkened showroom. The front door remained firmly closed, the gallery still dark and quiet. Ash was nowhere in sight. Billy looked over to Cecil; flecks of dried paint adorned him, but not so many as to disguise his look of consternation.

In the next instant there was a wild noise from below, as if a scrum had broken out in the back room that served as their transient hideaway. They scampered down the stairs and flew to the rear where they found Ash hopelessly trying to fend off two large men. Billy looked left to see the back door wide open, the clicking lady watching nervously from outside.

Without thinking, Billy leapt wildly at one of the men, striking him in the shoulder and knocking him sufficiently off balance so that Ash could shimmy away and bolt out the waiting door. Billy and Cecil followed, only Cecil wasn't so fortunate—the second man grabbed hold of him just a few feet shy of his liberty. Billy scrambled past the lady curator, stopping just beyond the door. He looked back in to see Cecil subdued and pressed hard to the floor, his face twisted in pain. Billy spun around and scanned for Ash, but he was already nowhere in sight. He then saw that the first man had recovered and was starting toward him, the lady curator pointing excitedly in Billy's direction. With that, Billy abandoned any thought of rescue and fled into the street.

His head felt light. It couldn't comprehend what had just happened, how it had all fallen apart so quickly. His feet beat down hard on the ground.

He ran this way until he began to feel pain, one deepening with each passing step. Only it wasn't his feet that cried out—it was his jaw, shut tight, clenched in anger.

HE RETURNED TO THE compound to find Ash safely home. He was standing on the main platform, chatting excitedly with several members.

Billy pierced him with a stare before slinking into the office. He found Darrow inside with Jacob and Marlon. He spit out the news of their failed mission as quickly as possible, as if the speed of its delivery would somehow lessen the impact and curtail Darrow's disappointment.

It didn't.

Darrow immediately called for Ash, who scuttled into the room. He stopped just inside the doorway, his feet fidgeting nervously beneath him. He looked at Billy, who was near at his side, then to Darrow, then back to Billy. Finally he explained that he was merely following Billy's orders when the people arrived without warning. He investigated and they tackled him. "A real rat's deal," he added, "they appeared right quick. Tricky, tricky it was."

Darrow bubbled over. "We stand to them equal in numbers, yet you flee in fear like errant running dogs!"

Billy held silent. He felt their discretion was the better part of valor, and that he had no choice but to run, particularly as Ash had already abandoned them. Still, he opted against voicing that viewpoint. As it was, his reserve of self-esteem had shriveled from exposure to Darrow's berating: "And what have we accomplished? Nothing! A small handful of paintings? They're surely laughing at us right now. Mocking our feeble attempt. Mocking our cause. Mocking me!"

A lamp sat at the desk's edge. Darrow swiped it to the ground, shattering it to countless pieces. It was a temper tantrum unbefitting a seven-year-old, and Billy wondered whether Darrow would have held back if it were Billy's face mounted on the desk corner, instead of merely an outdated light fixture. He also recognized, just as with Chuck, that Darrow's concern was not for a lost comrade but on how the event might affect their cause or result in him losing face.

Billy remained silent throughout the furious tirade. Darrow was yelling partly at Billy, partly at the walls, and partly at his own feet. Jacob attempted to calm him, but the words wouldn't penetrate Darrow's fury. Angrily, he ordered everyone from the office.

On their way out, Marlon uttered, "Weak intentions get weak results." Billy shrugged him off, his mind preoccupied with Ash, his imagination already running wild with suspicion, with thoughts that Ash had been sloppy or lazy; that he'd run away when things were at their worst; that perhaps, consumed by jealousy, he'd even sabotaged them. He confronted Ash just a few feet in front of the office and challenged him to explain what had happened. Ash denied his allegations, showed righteous indignation, then turned to walk away. Billy reached for him.

"Get yer grubby paws…"

Ash didn't finish his sentence before a brief struggle ensued. Rufus had run up by then and was barking wildly behind them. George and Ears managed to separate them, ending it nearly as quickly as it had started.

Billy walked away as unsettled as unsatisfied. Even at the best of times he found it difficult to gauge the truth of Ash's pronouncements; his exaggerations seemed habitual, and on more than one occasion, Billy had caught him talking out both sides of his mouth. Depending on his audience, Ash would sometimes fawn over Marlon, praising his ferocity and denouncing Jacob's timidity, while the next day he'd laud Jacob's temperance while questioning Marlon's aggression. Yet Ash, like Totter, seemed skilled with his sincerity, and on each occasion would purr his praise so affectionately that it was impossible not to believe in his good intentions.

Ultimately, the events only further strained Billy and Ash's relationship, and it equally served to tweak Darrow's growing paranoia. He immediately arranged for two more sentry postings above ground, with sentries now covering each of the four entry and exit points, and a fifth sentry posted by the waiting room. The sentries, who were changed every four hours, would not only continue to identify newcomers looking for "the movement," but would now also serve as security. Darrow was concerned they might have been exposed, even followed. Billy told him that they weren't, but it didn't seem to matter. These additional monitors, he said, were for everyone's safety and protection.

After arranging for the sentries, Darrow kept alone in his office the remainder of the night. It was only before curfew when he finally surfaced, striding slowly across the compound floor, the members curling away from him like the Red Sea receding from Moses. As was customary for his most important speeches, he jumped directly atop the wooden crate in front of the caboose to loom above his waiting minions.

"My friends, my sons and my daughters, my soldiers."

Most of the group was now standing, all very much aware of what had occurred at the gallery. Worry and concern showed on many faces. Darrow, as always, had their undivided attention.

"Today it appears that the House of Darrow sustained a bitter defeat. Our plot was interrupted well before completion, and, even worse, those who wish to repress us have captured one of our own."

Several members muttered audibly in the background.

"Yet appearance can sometimes be an illusion, for after fully contemplating the evening's events, I have come to the realization that this was no defeat at all. The appearance of setback was an illusion. The events of the day have actually advanced our noble cause forward."

This last proclamation was followed by inquisitive murmurs, the group's trepidation giving way to a tentative excitement.

"Our oppressors now recognize the danger that we present, and they are scared to death. They realize they are powerless to stop the movement, and they quake in fear. Their seizing one of our own is proof of that fear. It is a clumsy and desperate attempt to try and regain control, which they now know they have lost. And indeed, fear us they should. For each one of us they capture, five will spring to replace him. For each of us they murder, twenty will rise up to avenge. They have only made us stronger today. Their fear has made us stronger. The House of Darrow is stronger than ever!"

The group erupted in a raucous bout of cheering. Even Rufus joined in, howling with joy at the steel grates above. Everyone was freshly galvanized by Darrow's speech. And so it was that the half-botched mission was artfully spun into an entirely successful one, one that had society running scared. This was the bill of goods that Darrow was publicly selling, and the entire bill was quickly snapped up and devoured. Half-truths had a funny way of becoming full truths when filtered through hopeful ears.

Darrow didn't stop there; Billy was congratulated for his role in leading the successful strike, while Cecil was claimed as a living martyr, with one of the group ordered to scratch his name under Billy's and Chuck's on the Wall of Valor.

The group turned frenetic. A good number of them started to sing and dance as if the Munchkinland coroner had just delivered his findings.

The House of Darrow strong and true
We stand united through and through

They sung of a frightened decadent populace:

For now you clearly show your fear
You kidnap one, five more appear!

There was an edge to their songs that hadn't existed before, along with an unspoken confidence. Billy couldn't believe it: From trepidation to jubilation inside of two minutes. Darrow promised them that their best days were yet to come, that society would change, and if this change required escalation, then escalation it would be. Save for a handful of exceptions, notably Jacob and Tommy, the declaration was gobbled up with voracious approval.

Just before bedtime, Darrow sent out the town crier.

"Listen up…this is the word of Darrow!" Chester bellowed obediently from the top of the wooden crate.

Their home was to be called "*The House of Darrow*" from that point onward, as "the compound" didn't capture the true essence of their abode. The announcement was received with great enthusiasm by most. It made perfect sense—after all, they were only there because of him.

They slept that night on pillows of pride, and though their house eventually turned supremely quiet, their leader's closing words still rang loud in their ears.

"Forward, comrades!…Long live the revolution!
…Long live the House of Darrow!"

L AMBERT BLINKS EXCITEDLY AT the scene laid out before him, his thoughts shifting about as rapidly as the silver flashlight in his right hand.

"What the hell is this place?"

Detective Meyers nods.

"Hard to believe, isn't it? I had no idea this area existed until two days ago. And I've been working this town eighteen years."

They step from the uneven terrain and down to the smooth platform floor, Lambert's imagination running wild.

"I looked into it," says Meyers. "Apparently the city over-hauled the subway system decades ago. For whatever reason, the bean counters decided that it just wasn't worthwhile to remove these cars and fill in the expanse. So they left it here, abandoned. And that was that."

Incredible, Lambert thinks to himself.

"And if the inhabitants here hadn't gone insane, we *still* wouldn't know anything about it. Maybe we should even thank them," Meyers quips sarcastically, before shaking his head and adding, "The stupid animals," under his breath.

The stupid animals?

In the short conversations they've had, Dr. Lambert has pre-sumed through Meyers' tone that he holds little sympathy for their plight, and Lambert's interpretation has obviously been a correct one. This old warrior, so far from enlightened that his knuckles practically scrape the concrete. How many others in the city share the detective's pointed and close-minded views? Lack of compassion is, Lambert believes, the fundamentally wrong approach to this situation, but he keeps his own pointed views bottled up for the time being.

Meyers proceeds to give Lambert the dime tour. Within minutes he's shown him the office and taken him through the three railcars. It's not until Meyers makes another sharply insensitive comment that Lambert excuses himself from the detective's company.

"If you don't mind, I'd like to poke around a bit on my own," he says, and Meyers offers scant resistance. It gives him the opportunity to move off to the side and fire up a Lucky Strike.

Lambert steps quietly away, and soon enough, the smell of burnt tobacco has incorporated itself into the mix of stale air and death.

ILLY WALKS DOWN A posh city sidewalk, tall, upright, and
proud.

He sports a set of designer pants and an argyle sweater bearing
a green alligator over his left breast. He wears shoes with a shine,
and his hair and nails are neatly trimmed. He feels great.

How did I get here? Where did I get these fancy clothes?

Things can sure change quickly!

He stops for dinner at the same fancy restaurant where he'd
performed his initiation. The female maître d' meets him with a
warm smile and seats him at the street-side window. Table for
one.

Soft music plays; a candle is positioned in the center of his
table, red flame dancing sensually over hot wax, its flicker casting small shadows across the freshly pressed napkin lying idle
to Billy's left. Théophile Steinlen's artful nod to Rodolphe Salis
hangs on the wall, along with a series of other retro-chic pieces.
The atmosphere is snobby and pretentious, deliciously decadent.

The waiter arrives to takes his order, a warm and welcoming
smile on his lips, as if Billy is actually welcome.

The food arrives promptly, and he feasts on a thick slab of delicious prime rib.

The best I've had in my life, ever.

And the first he's had in his life, ever.

In short order, he consumes the full lot, then leans back, his belly protruding slightly. He daintily dabs each corner of his mouth with the cloth napkin, just as he's seen the Bigwigs do so many times before through the majestic restaurant windows. He bellows a hearty laugh.

The most perfect meal. Yes indeed, this is what it's all been about. This is what we've been working towards.

They couldn't keep us down forever!

He feels so important. So respected and relevant. So sure now that he belongs in this world.

So equal!

Only then the waiter returns, his smile washed away by a look of concern. A second man soon arrives beside him—the manager, perhaps—and a lump grows full in Billy's throat.

"I'm afraid there's been a mistake," the second man says, gently dabbing his forehead with a handkerchief. He wants to say more but seems embarrassed to do so. He looks to his left and right, guarding against kibitzers, then leans in slowly and whispers four words into Billy's ear: "You don't belong here."

Billy is cut to the core; not just by hearing the words, but also because in his heart of hearts he knows that the man is right. It isn't fair.

It is not fair!

Billy looks out toward the large restaurant window. He sees a blue jay flutter down and come to rest on the sill. He leans forward a few inches and squints his eyes. The bird presses up against the window pane and peers inside. It taps at the glass with its slender black beak before jumping from the window and flying out of Billy's sight.

Billy sets to give chase, but suddenly feels exposed. He looks down to find every scrap of his clothing has vanished, reduced to his natural state. The people sitting at the table next to him start to laugh. Soon the entire restaurant is laughing. Then, without fail, he's right back in that tree, alone, frightened, his movements seized with fear. He can see the yellowy uniform and smell the sweat wafting over from the metal rungs. His throat tightens and he cannot breath. The gloved hand reaches for him, but he yells for it to stay back.

Why did I do that?

The branch cracks and he feels himself starting to slip. His mother screams. The gloved hand is still too far away to reach him.

He looks further down the branch. Jacob sits precariously on the edge next to Chuck. The blue jay flutters down from above, its healthy wings beating gently. It perches next to Jacob and looks at him disapprovingly.

Billy's eyelids lurched open before it went any further.

It wasn't the first time he'd had such vivid dreams. So real he could practically smell the burn of the candle, or taste the delicious meat between his teeth. As always, he found himself right back in the tree, his mother screaming from below, the fireman lingering.

It *was* real.

Only it wasn't.

Billy wondered where they came from, these dreams that so frequently unnerved him. Though he'd never read Dickens, perhaps the root cause was as simple as Scrooge had imagined: an undigested bit of beef, a blot of mustard, a crumb of cheese, or a fragment of an underdone potato. Last night, Billy had consumed none of those items, though it may just be that pink bits of stolen pork yielded the same psychological fermentations.

"THERE'S A MAN IN the tunnels!" screamed Claire.

Billy had tossed and turned nearly two hours before waking to the clamor. He stepped from the lead railcar to find Claire speaking excitedly with Helena and several others. She was panicked. Told them that she'd been out early looking for her brother when she returned to find a man in the subway tunnels. He was clad in blue overalls, a tool belt snug around his waist, a flat cap on his head. He'd harnessed himself to the roof of the tunnel and was changing the orange service lights.

One by one the members gathered around her: Billy, George, Ears. Darrow soon emerged from his office and penetrated the circle. The rest of the members drew quiet to listen.

"Could you have been seen?" he asked.

"I don't think so. I kept out of sight. Watched him from a distance."

"How far did he get?"

"Like I said, he was going real slow. Didn't get more than a short stretch."

"His direction?"

"Toward us," said Claire.

Darrow turned to Jacob, who nodded back and slipped out of sight.

"Describe this man," said Darrow.

Claire shut her eyes and did her best to recall specifics.

"Old, I'd say. Kinda scraggly."

"What else?"

"Blue coveralls. The kinds with the straps up around the shoulders. A blue cap on his head."

"Anything else?"

"His movements were slow. Shaky. Maybe like he was sick. Or drunk maybe."

"Was anyone else with him?"

"None that I saw," said Claire.

"How long," Darrow paused, highlighting the seriousness of the next question, "how long before he passes by our tunnel?"

The members remained quiet. They watched Claire close her eyes again and fidget in place. "Hard to say," she said. "I didn't watch for too long. But the pace he was going. It will take him a while. Probably a week. Maybe two."

"And then…" said Helena.

"…he sees the tunnel," finished Jenny, pinching Sam closer.

"Might be he doesn't bother us," said Claire. "That he just keeps going on his way."

"We can't rely on that," said Marlon.

"Human nature," said Darrow, "is inquisitive."

"This was bound to happen eventually," said George.

"And if he wanders in here?" cried Ears.

"He's got to go!" shouted someone from the rear.

"Bet he could be tripped down into the tracks real easy," heard Billy from the side.

"It's him or us," called yet another.

"There's got to be another way," said Tommy.

Darrow didn't speak. He just stepped quietly from the circle and walked back to his office where he would hold for the remainder of the day.

Jacob returned an hour later and confirmed everything that Claire had just said. He estimated the man would pass by in two weeks, if not sooner, assuming he kept up in their direction and maintained his current pace.

This development unnerved the group. It also re-ignited the ideological struggle between Jacob and Marlon. Jacob said that they should bide their time. See if the old man even makes it to them, and, if so, to weigh their options at that time. Marlon wanted the threat immediately eliminated. The issue had become a tipping point among the membership. Some felt Jacob's approach jeopardized everything that they'd worked so hard to create. Others felt murder wasn't worth it, particularly given the tenuous nature of the threat, and that it would just bring them all the needle if caught.

More than ever before, partisanship tore throughout the House of Darrow. New members were now readily accosted with, "Are you a Jacob or a Marlon?" and, with Marlon's supporters quick to embrace aggressive proselytizing, the preponderance of those polled invariably aligned with the latter. It wasn't just the serviceman. A growing majority were pushing for violence to be introduced into their regular campaigns as well.

Each day of work brought the man closer: the same grease-stained coveralls, same blue cap snug on his head. Billy had snuck out to watch him on more than one occasion; watched him dangling from the tunnel ceiling, the new lights glowing behind him, looking not that much different than the old ones. Billy would watch him secure himself each time a train roared by: tight grip on the rope, cautious with his life. A life that dangled precipitously closer to harm than he could possibly appreciate.

On the fourth day Billy set out for a nearby city park. He passed one of their new members, Chet, who was posted as sentry at checkpoint three. Their open immigration policy had seen all different sorts join their ranks, and Chet was no exception. He was a skittish sort, with skinny legs bent slightly at the knees. And eccentric. Or autistic. Or eccentrically autistic. Chet refused to make eye contact when speaking, instead looking down and to the side, and, due to whatever peculiarity brewed inside him, communicated in short bursts of rhyme. And so it was that some called him Rhyming Chet, while others just called him weird, and still others set their tongues to more pejorative monikers. Billy, however, just called him Chet.

He stated something as Billy passed; but it was mumbled at his feet, so the rhyme, battened down by the silencing effects of insecurity, had evaded Billy's ears. Billy did catch something about "safe" and "strafe," but failing to consecrate its full meaning, merely nodded in return before he traveled to the surface and walked the six blocks to his destination.

A cast iron sign arced over the park entrance like a rainbow. **Eternal Gardens**—a fitting name for this idyllic setting of lush green grass and vibrant perennials. People dotted the area, some on blankets, others on benches, others chasing Frisbees or dogs. The tone was calm and pleasant.

An atmosphere so unlike what he'd left behind.

Rufus would love it here, thought Billy. He'd been asleep when Billy had left, but he vowed to bring him next time.

A paved path circled a fountain in the heart of the park. It was the sort of fountain that, through some undefined magic, caused young children to readily forsake the potential for string licorice or Gummi bears with every wish-accompanied jettison of copper and nickel. A man with a guitar sat on the edge of the fountain and delicately strummed a Yusuf Islam classic.

It was the same sort of fountain that Billy had been cruelly pushed into when he was young, his acute reaction on par with the meanness that dwelled within the boy who'd so thoughtlessly bullied him into the basin of cool water. It was a long time ago. Billy was older now and more mature, more able to defend himself from such treachery. Still, it evoked negative feelings, so he kept back from the frolicking liquid, coming to rest on a grassy hill, and watched the water spurting high into the air and cascading down into the shiny pool at the base. He then watched a boy circle the fountain, a toy plane held as high as his chubby arm would allow. Billy basked in the simplicity of it all and lamented never having a toy like that to play with. His own youthful leisure had always been more modest. Sometimes he would chase bullfrogs, or try to catch a butterfly, or explore the local cemeteries that had grown thick with weed and moss. Peaceful times, thought Billy.

He stretched out. Summer was nearly beyond them, but it remained bright and sunny to the last. There were sparrows in the trees, but the sparrows kept their distance. Billy laid his head down to a warm patch of grass and shut his mind to the world. He could still hear the fountain bubbling menacingly out of sight as he tried to suppress thoughts of the tenets and the serviceman and the discord. The hill curled up around him and drew him into darkness and safety.

He'd hardly closed his eyes before he was engulfed by his mother's scream, cascading up from the base of the tree. Billy had been ascending the inviting lengths of bark. He was young then, but stubborn and cocksure. Slowly he moved up, inch-by-inch, branch-by-branch. The climb was invigorating. The elevation intoxicating. Billy remembered feeling so inspired, so alive.

Then he looked down.

In an instant his invincibility gave way to panic. His pulse raced. The descent looking exponentially longer than the short journey upward. And he remembered calling for help. From his mother, from anyone. He remembered choking tight the dry stretch of bark that dug into his soft flesh. The pain reinforced that he was secure, and for that, he remembered the pain being welcomed. He snuck another frightened glance down the tree and saw his mother at the base of the tree screaming for help; he saw people walking by on the ground. And he remembered nobody helping.

Nobody, that is, until the fireman.

The fireman.

It was so long ago, yet he could still see the ladder's metallic rungs. Could still smell the artificial chemicals emanating from the fireman's yellowy uniform, the sweat balling up and glistening on his stubbled face, and the battered helmet, forever stained black from years of soot and grime. He'd never seen a fireman so close.

Then a gloved hand reached out to collect him. Billy yelled for it to get back, leaning away from the fireman's grasp. Just an inch or so, but it was enough. It had pulled him safely from the fireman's reach. Safely away from the fireman.

Safely away.

He could barely hear the crack of the branch over his mother's cry. He'd never heard her that way before; her voice so raw and frantic. Then the snap of the branch. An innocuous sound. This time it was different. Angry. He remembered how the sound sucked the cool air from his lungs, that which had been so plentiful on his ascent. Remembered how it was suddenly so difficult to breathe. Remembered how he looked for anyone to help him, even the fireman, but how he saw only leaves. They were rustling under his weight: yellow, red, brown. They collaborated in pushing him from the branch. And he remembered how he could feel himself moving—falling from the branch and down to the earth below.

Only he hadn't moved, not an inch. It was the fear playing tricks on his mind. The gentle sway of the branch dizzying him, disorienting him, and he quickly discovered the true source of the sound—the cracking branch—to be some fattish squirrel bounding about recklessly on a thin limb to his left.

And suddenly the fireman was there again. A second reach, and this time Billy would not pull away, and this time the gloved hand would reach him. So it came to be that his rescue was complete.

But the memories, the fireman couldn't save him from those, and he would carry those memories with him forever, often finding himself right back in that tree in his dreams. It came when he was anxious or overtired, or when he allowed his thoughts too much slack.

He heard the fountain again as he opened his eyes, only to find a young girl hovering over him. She wore a blue and white paisley dress, her bare feet clad in sandals, tiny ladybugs painted on her tiny toenails. Her hair was pulled back into a ponytail. One hand held half of a bologna sandwich. The tips of her pale fingers were stained red. She smelled of baby shampoo and strawberries.

Billy looked past her down the hill, where he saw, in all likelihood, her parents laying on a blanket. Her father was on his back reading a book, knees curled up, his feet flat on the grass just an inch or two off the blanket. His son was trying to tie his father's shoes together. Her mother was seated upright, legs folded beneath her. She had one eye on her magazine, the other on her daughter.

"I'm Tracey," she said. By this point Billy had brought himself into something of a seated position. He glanced at her sandwich, then to the ground, then back at the sandwich.

"I know that you're hungry," she said, then tore her half-sandwich in two, handing Billy a triangular portion of bologna, cheese and mayo, all tucked between two slices of Wonder Bread. Billy accepted the sandwich and devoured it there on the spot. He only realized how hungry he was after he'd swallowed his first bite.

"This is great," his mouth half-full of processed meat and starchy bread. "I really like this."

"It's my favorite," said the girl. "Bologna and cheese. I can just eat it without the cheese. Though I do like cheese, too. I just don't need it to like it."

There was something slightly strange about her. She was unlike most little girls. Her affect blunter, more robotic.

Billy wolfed down the rest of the sandwich, then got to his feet, the girl picking up on his look of gratitude. He stole a look back down the hill. Her mother was still seated on the blanket, only now the magazine was at her side, her eyes locked on the situation.

"I'm Tracey," she repeated, as if perhaps he'd missed it the first time. "Do you want to play?"

Before Billy could respond, she'd set off at something of a run, jutting further up the steep-sloped hill. Billy playfully gave chase, keeping a couple feet behind. As soon as he got close, she'd let out a scream and run back down the hill, her quarter sandwich still clutched tightly in her hand. This was repeated, playfully, sometimes in reverse, but effortlessly. No vocal exchanges, just the occasional shriek from the girl as she turned quickly and ran down the hill. Billy relished it, and always slowed down just as he was about to catch her.

From the corner of his eye he'd already seen the mother flicking the back of her hand on her husband's thigh, alerting him to the curious game of no-touch tag that was occurring on the hillside; and by the sixth pass he and the girl had made toward one another, he could see the mother hurriedly mounting the slope of the hill, the husband alert and watching, as were several others, some faces twisted tight in concern, others unalarmed and smiling.

They continued rolling gracefully between chaser and chasee. Fluid, as if rehearsed. As if they'd played together before.

"Tracey!" called a voice. The voice was tight, but the girl continued, undeterred.

"Tracey!" repeated her mother. Billy heard the voice grow closer. It was then that the young girl stopped, and so did Billy, lying back down on the grass, ending nearly in the same spot he'd begun.

She bit into her sandwich, her handprint set deep into the bread. "You're happier now," she said, at which point her mother scooped her up into her arms.

"Leave him be, honey. He's here enjoying himself, too." She carried her daughter back down the hill, and Billy was alone once more.

Billy slept after that, managing a second, more restful nap, then returned to the House of Darrow where he found Rufus not with Tommy, or Jacob, or any of the members who'd taken fondly to him, but with a female he'd never seen before. She was about Billy's age, with a slender face and a small pointy chin. Her hair was dirty blonde, possibly dusted with soot. She was thinner than might be considered healthy, and her nails were in need of a trim, but she was otherwise very attractive.

She sat with Rufus beneath the list of tenets, stroking his fur. Rufus had curled over onto his back. His fattened belly in the air, tail flapping excitedly against the cool concrete below him.

"Hi there," said Billy.

"Hello," she said. She continued grooming Rufus without looking up.

"He likes you."

Rufus had turned his head to acknowledge Billy, too paralyzed by her strokes to offer anything more.

"He's beautiful," she said.

Billy set himself down beside Rufus and watched her continue to work.

"Your pup?" she asked.

"I suppose so."

"I'm Lola," she said, still without lifting her eyes from Rufus.

"Billy."

"Billy?" she said. "This Billy up here?"

She motioned to the Wall of Valor above her. Billy's name at the top. Chuck and Cecil falling in line below.

She read the answer on his face.

"Must have done something really important," she said, looking at him. He noticed her eyes were light brown, with a bright yellow swirl around the circumference. There was something in her voice that Billy found soothing.

"They think so," said Billy.

"I've never done anything all that important," said Lola, continuing with Rufus. By now he'd shut his eyes and drifted halfway to sleep.

"I haven't seen you before," said Billy.

It had been getting harder to keep up with all the new members. What was once twenty-one now numbered close to seventy.

"Just got here today," she said.

Billy looked past her, up to the gravelly tunnel that led to the subway shaft and the man in the tunnel.

"You came at a difficult time," he said.

"I heard."

"We may be in danger."

"Yes," she said, seemingly unfazed, "I heard."

"It doesn't worry you?"

"No more than being out there does."

She had a gentle confidence to her. Billy studied her eyes, her hair, her silky movements.

"Could be he doesn't even make it this far," said Billy.

"Could be."

"But if he does…"

"Let's not talk about it," she said.

He moved on.

"How about you, then. How did you end up out here?"

Lola kept to her grooming.

"My family. They moved here to the city not long ago. Everyone was already so busy. I'd come and go as I pleased. More and more time went by and I got less and less attention. Then one day a baby boy came along, and from then on I was invisible."

"It's not the first time that's happened…"

There was a short pause, before she said, "It was the first time it happened to me."

"So you just left?"

"Not at first. But after a while. At first I just started staying away longer and longer. They didn't seem all that concerned. So one day I just didn't come home."

"They're probably looking for you."

"Could be," she said.

"Is that fair to them?"

She didn't answer.

"Where've you been living?"

"Here and there. There are places to get by, if you know where to look."

"How'd you find us?"

"Look at you with all the questions," she said.

It quieted Billy, but she smiled and answered nonetheless.

"Wasn't so hard, what with all the talk out there. Talked to a friend who talked to a friend who talked to a friend. Next thing I knew I was here."

Lola told him what she'd heard, and Billy found it to be more of the same. Inflated accounts of their exploits juxtaposed with an accurate snapshot of their vision: to upend the status quo, to move society toward a deeper appreciation and respect for all of its inhabitants. It had struck a chord with her, particularly given the precursors that had led to her self-imposed exile.

He spent the next two days by her side, their minutes together flowing imperceptibly into hours. He taught her their culture, warned her of the divisions and idiosyncrasies, and introduced her to most of the members. She was an instant boon for the group, exhibiting the same carefree spirit that had been so replete when Billy first joined, and so lacking now. She was really quite a beauty, and garnered interest from all corners of the House of Darrow, including Fat Henry, who would stare lewdly from afar, his chin having again disappeared into the fat of his neck. Yet it became evident very early that Billy was hers and she was his.

She immediately forged friendships with Helena and Claire, and bonded equally with Jenny and little Sam. She also spent time with the weak and the sick, listening to their lamentations and commiserating their disappointments, and all the while growing closer and closer to Billy. For him it was something beyond mere infatuation. It was love, in all likelihood, or the next closest equivalent.

16

FAMILY, FAIRNESS & THE FAIRER SEX

THE WEEKEND BROUGHT WITH it two significant develop-
ments.

First was the much-celebrated absence of the serviceman. It
was the first day in six that he hadn't reported for duty; and
while the group couldn't be sure his absence was a permanent
development, hopes blossomed confidently, even irresponsibly,
that they'd seen the last of this unwelcome interloper.

Unfortunately, any goodwill generated by this first occurrence
was dashed by a second, more puzzling development: Overnight,
the food supply, normally sprawled out before Darrow's office
window for all members to partake, had conspicuously been
moved down the hallway, just past Darrow's office, and was now
guarded by one of the members.

Only once a critical mass had emerged from the three railcars
did Darrow send Chester to make the announcement.

"Listen up…this is the word of Darrow!"

Billy had already suspected what was coming. With only so
many good cuts of meat to go around, Darrow had decided that
the communal cupboard that was once possible with twenty-one
members was no longer manageable with seventy. As such,
meals would now be distributed by a member assigned to food
distribution.

This development, in and of itself, wasn't any cause for alarm. That is, not until Chester announced a tweak to the food allotments themselves.

Going forward, the food would be rationed as follows: Darrow, his generals, and the more important or "favored" members would receive the better cuts of meat. Those of average talent and contribution would receive average or slightly dated meats; and those who tended to the compound, toiled with menial labor, or were too unhealthy to work altogether would be left with the least desirable bits, such as stale bread, starchy vegetables, and any castoff or spoiled bits of meat. Darrow believed this to be necessary, as his best soldiers must be well nourished and strong in order to execute their tasks effectively. The new disbursements, he reassured them, would ultimately be to everyone's benefit.

Many were off-put by this new development, and several individuals approached Darrow shortly after the announcement. They questioned whether the fifth tenet—which promised equal food—had been violated.

In response, Darrow assured them that the tenets were still very much being complied with, that no rule had been broken, and that no exception had been made. Each member, he said, would still receive equal servings of food. It was only the type of food that would differ. Since the actual portions would remain equal, Darrow was proud to tell them, the equality guaranteed by the tenets was still very much a reality.

"But today I've only received two pieces of stale bread, while he got two pieces of fresh chicken," lamented one of the sick.

"And I only got one piece of potato and some gristle," bemoaned one of the general laborers.

"Yes," Darrow said, "but as you both have now conceded, just like everybody else here, you have each received two pieces."

The tenet, Darrow reminded them, was silent on the exact nature and quality of the food they were to receive. From his interpretation, it merely commanded equal portions, which, he reminded them, they continued to garner.

"Death to decadence!" Darrow shouted, which most of the rest—especially those with the strongest voices—immediately shouted back in unison. Darrow looked down at one of the weaker members. "And you, young one. Surely you wish to see the end of decadence? Surely you wish to see our best soldiers strong?"

The young member responded in a trembling voice, his breath stained thick from scrapple: "Well, sir, of course to both of those I would say 'yes,' but couldn't we... "

"Excellent!" Darrow shouted over the remainder of his sentence.

The food was but one source of concern.

Angst among the lesser lights was further exacerbated by a recent shift in accommodations, their membership having grown so large that even the middle subway car was completely filled at nighttime. As a result, some of the less fortunate tenants had been downgraded to sleeping in the rigid caboose, where most of the widgets had already been stashed ahead of their arrival, the tenants of the second car holding onto a select few, as had the tenants of the first.

When pressed by some members to explain the apparent inequity, Darrow responded much as he had before, saying that it was paramount that his most important members and soldiers sleep comfortably and be well rested. This, he said, was for the betterment of all. When asked if this accorded with the sixth tenet of equal sleep, Darrow responded that it quite clearly did. The sixth tenet, of course, spoke only to duration of sleep, not location. As each member continued to enjoy at least eight hours of slumber, the sixth tenet stood unblemished.

Though many of the members soon resigned themselves to the new order of things, there were several pockets of dissent.

Billy watched Totter attend Darrow's office, then emerge after a short period of time, his movements less walk than saunter, a sort of airy glide that soared with confidence. He approached three individuals who'd been publicly bemoaning the quality of their rations.

"My friends, my friends," said Totter, slowly moving his stocky figure up alongside them, readying to douse the malignancy. "It has come to my attention that you've expressed some displeasure with the current state of things."

All three concurred, and explained the source of their frustration.

"I see, yes, you are unhappy with your food. Yes, food is certainly important, isn't it? Yes, I see in your faces that you agree with me. Of course, you do. Though how you could not be happy is a puzzle to me. This can only mean that the three of you have yet to embrace the power of Joy Transference. Ah, what is Joy Transference, you ask? Well, certainly, I can explain. You see, we are all friends here, correct? Yes, of course we are, there can be no disagreement about that. Otherwise why would you be here? And certainly you wish to see your friends well fed, isn't that true? Well, of course it is. Why would you ever wish to see your friends starve? You wouldn't, of course. That would make no sense. So then, if you wish to see your friends well fed, and would be unhappy to see the contrary, then it follows that you can only be happy if you see them contented by their meals. It would make no sense otherwise, would it? So, when you see so many of your friends happy, you yourself can't also help but be happy, can you? No, of course not. And this, quite simply, is Joy Transference."

The three appeared somewhat confused. One of them asked if this came from Darrow himself.

"Does this manifesto come from Darrow? What a peculiar question to ask. When you see the sun in the sky, do you challenge it to explain from where it started its journey before you accept its warmth? When you see the water in a stream, do you demand to know from which great lake, or river, or ocean it was born before you drink on a hot day? Of course not, that would be absurd. The fact of the sun and the stream, being now what they are, is just that—and it would seem an odd question to ask if the manifesto comes from Darrow, when it is, as we have now just determined, a reality already before us. We've been talking about it for some time now, haven't we? Certainly you wouldn't talk about nothing, would you? You have asked questions about Joy Transference as well, and certainly you wouldn't ask questions of nothing, would you? No, of course not. That wouldn't make any sense. So then obviously we can all agree it is real, and if that is the case, then where it comes from doesn't matter at all, now does it?"

Though he already had them teeter-tottering, they still weren't convinced. They agreed now that the origin of Joy Transference was no longer an issue. They also admitted that they did wish to see their friends happy, but asked why they must be deprived of sharing in the better food.

Totter sighed.

"Really, I'm surprised that I even need to explain this, but very well. Tonight, you surely saw your good friend Marlon with his steak? Yes, of course you did. And you saw how happy it made him to eat that steak? Yes, I can see you all nodding. Well then, let me ask: Don't you wish to see Marlon happy, given that he is your friend?"

They agreed that they wish to see Marlon happy.

"And," continued Totter, "someone must eat that delicious cut of meat, or else it would not be eaten. Surely you wouldn't want to see the meat wasted, or cast aside to turn rancid?"

They agreed that they would not want to see it wasted or cast aside to turn rancid.

"And you three, of course, had never had the meat in your clutches, you can't rightly disagree, since that is a point of fact. If this is true, and you never had the meat, then you have not been deprived at all, only your comrade has gained, correct?"

Yes, they had to admit that their comrade had gained. They could not rightly say that Marlon had not gained.

"So then, given that you never had the meat to lose, and your friend had merely gained it, and was so happy to savor the delicious beast between his teeth, then you can certainly only find happiness from this simple series of events, which, we have all agreed, are facts. You are therefore no worse off than you were before, whereas your friend is well fed and happy from what he's gained. Since your friend is now happy—and you desire to see your friend happy—then seeing him happy, must, of course, make you happy. This, my friends, is the wonder of Joy Transference. Embrace it and make it your own."

They stood in stunned silence as Totter leaned in for the finishing blow.

"And let me add, out of an abundance of caution, that if you'd somehow come into possession of that meat, wresting it away from your hard working comrade—and I don't know why you would attempt such a treacherous act—but if you did, then at the moment of the first bite, you would feel such guilt that any joy you might have derived from that meal would be canceled out by the self-loathing you would inherit by your selfish act. Clearly, you would not feel good if you deprived your friend now, would you?"

They agreed, with some reluctance, that they would not feel good about depriving their friend.

"No, of course you wouldn't, because then you would feel so guilty, so miserable, and what would be the point of that? Nothing, of course. Then you see now, when you consider everything, that you are happier—clearly happier—if it is your colleague who eats that meat, instead of you? Don't you see it now? How much happier you are than you originally thought? Why yes, of course you do!"

Unable to offer a counter-argument, the group dispersed, two of them thoroughly confused, and the third having convinced himself that he was indeed happier now than he originally thought.

Jacob, however, was unconvinced that any of this was for the better. He approached Darrow and implored him to reconsider the apportionments.

"How can we justify this?"

"I must ensure the well-being of this organization," said Darrow. "All of us lose if the House of Darrow gets shuttered."

"But some are hungry," said Jacob.

"And, no doubt, so are you. I've seen you handing them your own food."

"My appetite isn't what it once was."

"For a great many things, it seems."

Darrow stepped up onto his desk. He looked out his window toward the membership.

"I am responsible for them," said Darrow.

"Yes," said Jacob. "And we are all responsible for each other."

"I am responsible for this cause."

"I don't dispute that."

"Our task is a difficult one."

"It is."

"And now, what with a man in the tunnels."

"There will always be a man in the tunnels," said Jacob.

Darrow fell silent.

"Things aren't the way they should be anymore. We've grown too large too quickly," said Jacob.

"You'd have me turn some away?"

"Not at all. But we've reached the point that these decisions should have input from our membership. Not be so unilateral."

"You wish to see us more democratic?" Darrow said.

Jacob nodded, and though it took some time, he finally convinced Darrow to establish an Equality Committee. This committee would analyze the distribution of food, beds, and labor, and decide whether or not the current arrangements were truly consistent with the tenets, and, if not, forge a plan to bring about equilibrium. Jacob felt that the members would more readily accept such decrees if they came from a collection of their peers.

In short order, Darrow selected a panel of six: five members from the first railcar and one member from the second railcar. Though many had expressed a desire to sit on the committee—including Jacob, Lola, Tommy, and several of their underclass—Darrow felt his appointments the most qualified for the jobs.

The first committee meeting lasted only forty-five minutes, ultimately deadlocking 3-3 over the precise definition of "consistent with." They did consider several other issues, even finding a quorum of votes to pass one resolution, only to realize that seven votes had been cast, as one of the committee members had apparently voted on both sides of the issue. Finding no true consensus, the committee adjourned and agreed to meet again in several weeks.

THE SERVICEMAN RETURNED AFTER a two-day respite. The same tool belt strapped around greasy denim, the same flat cap fit loose on his head, the same thermos of coffee left on the ledge by his equipment. He'd continue to work morning to evening, stopping only for lunch, cigarettes, or the occasional sip from the thermos, which he'd spice up with tips from a flask. By then he'd bridged more than half the distance to the tunnel, and the group had temporarily abandoned use of the waiting room.

Billy approached Darrow's office, slowing as he drew near. Marlon's was the first voice he recognized.

"I've heard it myself," Marlon said.

"From who?" said Darrow.

"Mostly just the rabble. The complainers."

Billy slunk up beside the door, remaining out of sight as he listened.

"They want to know what I've done for them?" seethed Darrow.

"Some have started to question it."

"I found this facility."

"Yes."

"Brought us together. Grew this organization from nothing."

"Many haven't seen your glory in action. They've only heard the tales. Seen the tenets. Sung the songs."

"Ingrates."

"I nearly ran them off," said Marlon.

"What else did they say?"

"They wonder how you will lead us to victory if you can't even deal with one shaky old man."

"Who said this?"

"Several," said Marlon. "They want you to act."

"I do not give myself over to whims."

"They're losing patience. They need a reminder of your greatness. It's been too long since our last victory."

"These things don't come easy."

"Still, they could use a demonstration," said Marlon.

"I could make a demonstration of them," said Darrow, before cocking his head to the door. "Enter!" he screamed.

Billy revealed himself.

"If you're going to listen," said Darrow, "you might as well come in so you can hear everything clearly."

Billy was flummoxed.

"And have you heard these same things, young Billy?" said Darrow.

"Some," Billy replied tentatively. "I think maybe they're just worried. Frustrated."

"Reassurance," said Darrow, "I see. And is that what you've come for? Reassurance?"

Billy's mind drew a blank, then he remembered.

"My assignment," he blurted.

"Yes?"

"I'd like Lola to join me."

"I see."

"She's good. Quick," said Billy.

Marlon turned to him. "Quicker than Cecil, hopefully."

Billy clenched his teeth.

"Very well, take her with you," said Darrow.

Marlon laughed.

"Next thing he'll be asking to bring the dog."

Billy backed away, refusing to be goaded by Marlon. He stepped to the exit, holding up just inside the doorframe.

"Have you decided?" asked Billy. "What you will do with the man?"

Darrow stared at him, then turned to face the window.

"Best not to waste your daylight."

IT HAD BEEN, AS Marlon said, some time since they'd accomplished anything worthy of celebrating. Even the artificially successful Arthouse Annihilation was now a full month behind them. Darrow had grown increasingly frustrated and indecisive.

And all the while the serviceman inched up the tunnel. He was, by all accounts, no more than a day from passing their location.

Lola had been one of the few bright spots. She'd transcended the cliques and held dialogue with the Jacobs and the Marlons alike. She listened patiently to the gripes of the downtrodden. Even Ash had grown fond of her, despite her manifest closeness to Billy.

"The man will probably pass us tomorrow," said Billy.

"And then what?" said Lola.

Rufus was panting by their side. They'd just been above scouting for food. It hadn't been fruitful.

"And then he finds us," said Billy.

"Or maybe he doesn't," said Lola.

"Maybe."

"This isn't going to end well, is it?"

"Let's get out of here," said Billy.

Their duties complete for the day, they gathered Rufus and slipped from the compound. They weren't walking for long before Lola fell behind. Billy turned around and saw her stopped and peering up at a sign that had been taped to a lamppost.

Billy drew in and discovered that it was a picture of her.

"It's me," said Lola.

"Mm-hmm."

It was a close-up. She was younger then. Her features softer than they were now.

"The old days," she said. A smile had strayed onto her lips.

"What's that in your hair?"

"I think it's tinsel," she said.

"Tinsel?"

"I love shiny things."

"I see," said Billy.

"Don't you?"

"Sure I do," said Billy.

She continued to stare at the picture, looking dreamily at the sun-worn paper.

"I was beautiful then…"

"Yes," said Billy, immediately unsure if his response was a good one.

"They're looking for me."

"Seems that way."

"I don't care."

"Don't you?"

"I'm not an object," said Lola.

"They're probably scared," said Billy.

"They know I left because I wanted to."

"Maybe they do. Maybe they don't."

"This isn't even my neighborhood," she said.

"There must be more of these around," said Billy. He stared at Lola until she looked back at him.

"Do you want me to go back?"

Her tone seemed more test than genuine inquiry, and Billy left the question loaded. The fact was that he very much did not want her to go back, but felt it would be selfish to voice it.

"I've just never been wanted like that," said Billy.

"Never?"

"Not since my mom," he clarified.

"Where is she now?"

"I couldn't say."

"You must have been so lonely."

"Sometimes," said Billy.

"Don't be brave."

"Yes, I was lonely," said Billy.

"Is that why you joined?"

"Maybe that was part of it."

Billy fell silent, drawing into himself.

"Well, you're not alone anymore," said Lola.

He wasn't.

And they weren't.

Billy looked up the sidewalk and saw Rufus rooting in a set of bushes, then he drew his eyes closer and noticed a woman staring at Lola.

He tracked her eyes and watched her look at the poster, then to Lola, then back to the poster. By the time she'd stepped forward Billy had already whisked them off down the sidewalk. They ended up at the Eternal Gardens.

It was evening then, and the sun had set on the park.

They made their way to the top of the grassy hill, not far from where Billy had met the girl with the ladybugged toes. They spread out on the grass and looked at the stars, Rufus sprawled out beside them. They talked of home and of family, of good times and of bad. Lola had a way of absorbing his words that made him feel so tremendously important.

"You don't know what became of her?" she asked, after Billy had again mentioned his mother.

Billy shook his head.

"The life we lived…"

"You don't have to explain," said Lola.

"I just remember bits and pieces."

"Like what?"

Billy looked thoughtfully toward the stars, as if they'd somehow assist his memory. Instead he told her of his dreams, of being comfortable and safe with his mother, then a moment later high in the tree, his mother screaming from below as the fireman tried to reach him.

"Do you dream it often?"

"More than I'd like. The bad part, I mean."

"What do you think it means?"

Billy shrugged.

Lola started to laugh.

"What's so funny?"

"Just thinking of you…stuck up in a tree!"

Billy chafed at first but eventually she coaxed him into a smile.

"Didn't you ever climb trees when you were young?"

"Sure I did, but I just never needed rescuing."

Again Billy smiled, but his thoughts quickly trailed off.

"You miss her a lot, don't you?"

Yes, thought Billy.

Said Billy.

"I remember my own mom when I was real little, she told me that no one ever leaves you until they know for sure you'll be OK."

"Your mom said that?"

"When I was little," said Lola.

"Do you believe it?"

At first she didn't answer. Finally she smiled and said, "Don't you?"

The grass around them darkened, a hazy cloud having slipped in front of the moon.

"Your mother wouldn't have gone from your life unless it meant you'd be OK," said Lola.

"I guess. She raised me good. Good as she could."

"Mm-hmm."

The cloud released the moon and again Billy looked to the stars, this time holding his gaze there as he spoke.

"She hated goodbyes. That's one thing I do remember. I used to say goodbye anytime I went ten feet from her. And she would tell me, 'Goodbyes are only for when you won't see someone again.' Or something like that."

"She's right," said Lola.

"You think?"

"Oh, for sure. Goodbyes are too final. It's better if you don't say it and then it will never be final."

"I'm not sure it works like that," said Billy, though the idea warmed him.

Rufus suddenly sprang to his feet and cocked his ears back. A moment later he set off down the hill to chase a squirrel.

"See?" she said. "See how easy that was for him?"

Billy grinned, then watched as Lola stretched to her feet. She took two steps away before winking at him.

"Goodbye!" she laughed, then set off in a run up the hill. Billy pursued her to the top where they sheltered themselves behind a trembling clique of gossiping bushes, the soft dewed grass beneath them, a looming oak having crusted the ground with a variety of lust and crimson with its most recent wind-assisted ejaculation. The rest of the world disappeared. It was only the two of them now, all alone in the moonlight, the stars looking down from a polite distance.

Billy broke a settled silence.

"I don't want you to go..." he said, answering Lola's earlier question, "...to go back to them."

Lola didn't respond, only turned from him, playfully, a sultriness woven through her lips. The look said "come hither."

He did.

Dense concentrations of pheromones permeated the air. His face to hers. Tongue grazing her cheek. Within moments, he was behind her, inside her. The union was brief, powerful. At the conclusion they rolled exhausted onto the grass, relieved and peaceful.

She was so happy. He could hear it. Could feel it.

Nothing, he felt, could ruin this moment.

Only then the thought crept back into Billy's head. They would soon have to return to what passed for their reality: to the man in the tunnel, the factions, Darrow's fragile psyche and shifting ideologies.

Rufus burst through a clump of bushes, the squirrel having eluded him. He curled up beside them, his own chest heaving along with theirs. And in that moment—in that perfect moment—Billy considered not returning, instead leaving with Lola and Rufus that very night.

But where would we go?

Easy...*Anywhere.*

There was, it seemed, an unintended luxury to being homeless. When you're not tied to one physical address, or weighted down by unnecessary stockpiles of various and sundry material possessions, you are free. Liberated by your very lack of social integration. Billy had never set an alarm clock, or governed his comings and goings by the rigid parameters of any calendar or day timer. Indeed, there was a certain amount of freedom that came with destitution.

Billy recalled something that Marlon once told him. Back when they were getting along better, when Billy even admired him.

"I could never live my life trapped inside walls like these

people," said Marlon. "A lot of us would be perfectly content living that way. Not me, I'd rather die first."

He was right, though. At least about one thing. True immersion into society, into its homes and its shelters, brought unbending rules and curtailed independence just as much as it delivered warm beds and square meals. Marlon, for one, seemed uninterested.

It begged Billy's question: "Then why'd you join in the first place?"

It was, as it turned out, the closest they'd ever come to a heart-to-heart.

"I may not be after the same result, but that doesn't make it OK for us to be dismissed the way we are, as objects. To value our lives any less than they value their own. We are not an inferior class. I am inferior to no man. None of us are. It is a myth. A manmade creation. It can be unmade, and it should be, and it will be."

Billy had been nodding along at a feverish pace.

"After all," said Marlon, "we're the same as them, aren't we?"

The look on Billy's face must have telegraphed his doubts.

"I mean it," pressed Marlon. "No matter how big their homes or how fancy their clothes. They may think they're better than us, but they're wrong. They bleed out just like the rest of us. Cut the best one open and you'll see it, flowing just as fast and as wet and as red as ours. Blood doesn't recognize superiority."

Still Billy had waffled, maybe not even believing it himself. After an inordinate pause, he'd finally produced a weak nod; but was he really just as important as a tall, dark, and handsome Bigwig living in a cushy penthouse? Or a primped and perfumed starlet stepping daintily out from her shiny stretch limousine? Were any of them? And if *he* had trouble believing it, how could they hope to convince others? Was it Marlon's sureness in their equality that allowed him to go farther than Jacob? Was it that his beliefs were simply more fundamental?

After a short hibernation, the thought returned...

We could go anywhere!

But as Lola nestled up beside him, he pushed it from his mind. He'd pledged his allegiance to the group, as they all had. He had friends there, and still believed in the overarching cause. Felt a sense of loyalty and belonging. Felt he owed the group something more than slipping away like a coward in the night.

And so it was that they cleaned themselves up and set back for the House. They stepped past the sentry, waited for the next train to pass, then slipped quietly up the subway shaft and into the large opening that now left them so vulnerable.

Billy felt it the moment they stepped from the tunnel—that strange vibe of assembly set with undulating silence, the tightness in the air.

Darrow stood high atop the wooden crate. Eyes opened wide below him. Nearly the whole of their membership was packed tightly around his makeshift dais, the masses uncommonly, even eerily still. There were no sounds to be heard except for the silent cry of displaced doubt and the faint overhead hum of the city.

Darrow stared out ahead of him. Billy caught his gaze. Tried to decode it. It wasn't exactly contempt. Wasn't exactly satisfaction. It was some unfamiliar hybrid of emotion, and had Darrow himself been able to put it into words, he'd chosen to remain silent.

It took some time before Billy could penetrate the masses.

That was when he saw it. Limp at Darrow's feet.

The flat cap.

Blue.

Soiled.

It had progressed as far up the tunnel as it ever would.

Darrow eventually dismounted the crate. There was no victory speech. No recalcitrant rant. He merely waded through his subjects and maneuvered to his office. Nobody tried to approach him; none would ever ask him how he managed it.

The hawks didn't cheer. The doves didn't cry. And, at least for one more night, he was irrefutably, unapologetically, and unmistakably the Glorious Darrow.

"If the misery of the poor be caused not by the laws of nature, but by our institutions, great is our sin."

~Charles Darwin

OH, THE HUMANITY; THESE ACTS IN BRUTALITY

— Act I —

IN SHORT ORDER, SUMMER gave way to the start of fall. New members continued to trickle in, and their ranks had now swelled to over a hundred. The House of Darrow had become, unto itself, a small civilization.

It wasn't all addition, however, as they'd recently lost two of their own. One of the sick, Gary, had passed away amid little fanfare, his withered body disposed of in perfunctory fashion well away from the living area. No speeches, no flowers. After all, he'd contributed very little to their community.

Poor Jenny had also met an untimely end. Some undesirable people, loitering just beyond one of the sentry points, had dropped a small packet of dope. Hard stuff. She was curious and consumed its contents. Within seconds she was convulsing. The sentry ran to assist, but there was nothing that could be done—another soul lost to excessive drugs meeting excessive curiosity—and so it was that, at not even eight weeks old, Sam was left without a mother.

Darrow seemed to accept the news with remarkable indifference. He'd never been emotionally attached to Jenny, her being merely an outlet for his physical gratification and a necessary vessel for The Progeny. Even after her death, he remained paternally aloof, leaving Sam's rearing to the House of Darrow at large.

Helena, on the other hand, despaired at her sister's passing, and though Billy had often sensed a sadness within her, this was, from what Billy could see, an entirely new level of pain. Given the depth of Helena's nearly paralyzing despondence, it was Lola who stepped up and took Sam under her wing, herself pained by the half-hearted attempts toward her breast for milk that would not come.

Meanwhile, Jacob and Marlon continued to debate every course of action; and as most members had grown restless with the pace of their revolution, an overwhelming majority now pushed for the tactics espoused by Marlon. At one office meeting, Marlon seized on this. He outlined a plan to sneak into a facility that housed bungee jumping equipment commonly rented by the tourists. Sabotaging the lines, said Marlon, would surely lead to a gruesome, if not fatal, "accident."

As could be expected, Jacob vehemently opposed this scheme. He pressed Darrow to authorize only the theft of equipment that would render the leisure activities unplayable; and though he wavered briefly, Darrow ultimately sided with Jacob, still clearly encumbered by his fair-haired general's temperance.

The debate over violence was just one source of tension among the membership, as Darrow had recently put forth more rules, "To keep things running orderly," as he liked to say. Spooked by Gary's death, and fearing that their sick might be contagious and threaten the movement from within, he relayed, through Chester, his newest pronouncement: All outwardly sick or infirm individuals must either move down into the tracks, or else move down the live subway tunnel and stay in the waiting room. The same applied to members of advancing age, those who seemed particularly weak, or, as Darrow described it, "those who are quizzical in the head." They should also not eat with the healthy members or get too close to them for any stretch of time.

As it was, both subway cars, and now even the caboose, had swelled past capacity. Those who'd taken refuge in the caboose had already swept the majority of the remaining widgets down into the tracks, yet even with this extra space there was no longer enough room in the three cars for everyone. The superfluous members had been loitering on the platform floor or sleeping in the rocky tunnel until Darrow's latest pronouncement evicted them down into the tracks.

Totter approached the few defiant stragglers and, following a spirited discussion in which he reminded them of the magnificent power of Joy Transference, they made their teeter-tottering way down to the tracks below.

Without delay, Jacob visited Darrow's office and argued vigorously against these new policies. Totter had arrived just ahead of him, followed by Billy, who remained outside the open office door to eavesdrop. Jacob insisted that the tenets weren't being complied with, and that their once homogeneous community was turning sickly incongruent, with a growing number of members caring only so much about equality as to what they could achieve for themselves. He also considered the benefits of Joy Transference to be speculative, at best.

"I am surprised," offered Totter, "to hear you speak in this way. Perhaps, Jacob, you misunderstand the merits of this wondrous manifesto? A manifesto, I might add, that the others seem to accept. Surely you do not speak for the others? Surely others can speak for themselves, no? Yes, we all have mouths; I'm sure this is the case. You, of course, no doubt agree, that each of us has his own mouth to speak with? You cannot deny this!"

Jacob responded, unruffled, "I understand the merits as you state them, but I do not accept them. And as for the others, they are certainly free to speak as they wish, but most don't have experience speaking with someone whose tongue is so forked."

Totter exuded surprise. "Now really, Jacob, I don't know what you mean by that."

"I mean that I wonder how you expect to benefit from all this."

"Benefit? What a peculiar suggestion. Is the sincere look of gratitude on the faces of those that I've helped not benefit enough? It is the most any of us could ask for, is it not? Of course you can see that?"

"What I see is that you'd argue day is night if it somehow served your interests."

"*Interests?*" exclaimed Totter. "Again, I don't know what you could possibly mean. *Interests?* This is certainly a foreign concept to me. I am just His simple servant, and don't pretend to understand such things." With that, Totter excused himself from the office and stepped past Billy, who still lingered by the office door, trying and failing to look inconspicuous.

Jacob turned his focus to Darrow, resolute that these schemes were unjust and untenable. He also pointed out that the Equality Committee had done nothing to safeguard the rights of those who most desperately needed it, believing the committee to be clouded by self-interest, unnecessarily complicated, increasingly slow to act, and wholly ineffective.

"I walked by their last meeting," said Jacob, "and two of the six members were sleeping."

Darrow defended the integrity of the Equality Committee. As for the sleeping committee members, he reasoned that "safeguarding equality must be a tiring job." He added that, in his opinion, all members of the House of Darrow continued to be equal; "they are merely being equal in different places." He then quoted the ninth tenet and said that his decision was final.

"My friend," Jacob said, "I'm afraid you can't see, or don't wish to see, what is happening here. Our culture has changed. We've veered from our original ideals and the true spirit of the tenets.

So focused is your gaze upon the treetop that you've lost all sight of the bushes."

"But the treetop is our ultimate goal. It's of the utmost importance."

"It most definitely is important," replied Jacob, "yet so too are the bushes."

"I believe you overstate things."

"I think not. Each day we become more like those we fight. I'm begging you to realize this before it's too late."

Darrow again disagreed, the discussion abruptly ended, and Billy slunk quietly away from the door.

Billy had witnessed a slow but steady regression in Darrow. Their leader's blank stares into nothingness were becoming more frequent, his paranoia more overt, and his dialogue increasingly militant. He'd also become noticeably insular. He'd spend hours buried in the darkest shadows of his office, leaving only to make a speech, visit briefly with The Progeny, or, as Billy sometimes perceived it, to grace the populace with his presence. The remainder of his day was either spent meeting with his generals, meditating, sleeping, or, with increasing frequency, hitting the weed, the effects of which only served to exacerbate his erratic behavior. Billy would see Darrow engaged in heated, passionate dialogue—only to discover, in a growing number of instances, that the office was quite clearly empty.

Beyond the ideological rifts in their hierarchy, tensions were also high, and patience low, among a shocking number of the general citizenry. Although the House of Darrow was originally quite spacious, it was now difficult to take three steps without bumping into another, with the air increasingly thin and stifling. Privacy and personal space had become casualties of the movement's popularity, and this was exacerbated each time Darrow sent Chester to the crate to put a new interpretive spin on the tenets. By then, and perhaps predictably, there were constant squabbles over whose achievements most benefited the community. Those who'd registered more showy contributions, or had been deemed by Darrow to have accomplished more, felt they had earned preferential treatment—while those opposite on the spectrum felt they weren't being treated fairly or given full value for their work.

Fat Henry had become one of the more vocal objectors. Far from convivial at the best of times, and still chafed by the presence of the dog, his zest for collegiality continued to ebb. He'd not only dropped two slots in the residential pecking order—finding himself now firmly situated in the caboose—but had also been relegated to consuming the grimier fare, the transitions no doubt born from his continually failing eyesight, his ever-widening girth, and his increasingly limited contributions. On several occasions Totter had attempted to explain to Henry how lucky he actually was, given a full appreciation of the facts, but as unwilling as Henry was to embrace Totter's rhetoric—no matter how eloquently sculpted—he was equally incapable of articulating a cogent rebuttal, and always walked away from the conversations grumbling incoherently at the compound floor.

Beyond the complaints of inequity, it had also been some time since the organization managed a significant victory. There'd been smaller exploits here or there, including a group of them running through freshly laid cement in front of a luxury hotel, but nothing of such significance that might bring about new song and dance. And to top it all off, the response from the community had been virtually nonexistent; their efforts in social disobedience had been a collective request for more thin gruel, with society's continued indifference the ladle applied sharply to their collective noggins.

They'd racked their brains to come up with some grand idea that would finally shock the masses into true social reform, but any such scheme usually carried with it the intent or risk of violence. Such schemes were vigorously opposed by Jacob and ultimately kiboshed, albeit with reluctance, by Darrow.

"It is wrong to harm innocent people. And," warned Jacob, "we must avoid any action that might bring us the needle. We must only use force as a last result, and only then to defend ourselves."

"That's exactly what we'd be doing!" Marlon replied.

Their positions, Billy felt, were two sides of the same coin, and though they both viewed an identical situation, they did so through their own personal prisms, rendering consensus impossible.

The current stagnation and competing visions had nearly dead-locked the House. The group was in dire need of some significant action that would cut away their differences and re-unify them. And while the House of Darrow continued its struggles, there remained intermittent rumblings about homeless individuals, those just like them, vanishing into thin air. If the stories were to be believed, it was as if a large hand had been reaching out of the sky and plucking them away to oblivion. Still, there had been no witnesses—at least none willing to come forward—and none of their own members had yet disappeared in such fashion.

If it was a problem, it wasn't one that had been brought to their doorstep.

At least not yet.

— Act II —

A MISERABLE ROTTEN DAY.

It was the thought that had run through Billy's mind a dozen times since sunrise. He was sitting on the platform floor, Lola leaning on him, Sam tucked neatly in-between, Rufus curled up in front of them.

Billy saw Lola staring at something. He tracked her line of sight up the gravelly incline to the tunnel opening. George was standing at the end of it, his head crooked to the side, his good eye staring blankly at the flat cap at his feet. It had been propped up against the wall to the right of the opening as a trophy.

"You think they'll send someone?" she asked, noticing Billy looking along with her. "Send someone to find the man?"

"They haven't yet," said Billy.

"But they might."

"They might," he said, before looking up to the steel grates. It was raining hard.

The soggy interruption had seen all missions canceled, the torrential rain having continued more on than off throughout the last thirty-six hours. The fall air was damp and cold. This was particularly difficult for their weaker members, who were prone to illness at even the best of times.

Virtually all of them were now sequestered inside, though Darrow continued to direct a handful of members outside to find food, with the unlucky volunteered always coming back soaking wet, moaning and carrying on as if they shared the same genetic frailty as the Wicked Witch of the West.

There was almost no pitter-patter of overhead feet, and while the grates served a valuable purpose in allowing fresh air and daylight to seep in, they also allowed for an influx of water, which now trickled in past the slatted steel. The result was a soaked and muddied track. Most of those on the tracks had temporarily moved up onto the main platform, which had become dense with misery. Only Darrow and Marlon had any real space and comfort, holing themselves up in the office. Jacob had been invited to join them, but declined.

Their collective spirit had dwindled as low as Billy had ever seen it. There was no singing or dancing. Most were sleeping or lazing around. The movement was essentially on hold.

Morale had been further diminished by an unfortunate event a day prior.

It seemed that the pulsing rain had gradually pecked its way through some miniscule imperfections in the second railcar's structural integrity, resulting in a section of its roof crumbling down to the ruin of numerous cushions. Fortunately, the inhabitants beneath scrambled away in the nick of time so that none were caught in the debris.

Notwithstanding their good fortune, the affected inhabitants of the second railcar were left dismayed, as they'd now been displaced from their shelter.

After discovering that the decay had started at the front corner of their roof, many of the refugees immediately blamed those living in the lead railcar, believing they would have seen the damage developing through the large glass windows of their own car, but sat idly by and did nothing.

Those in the lead railcar would neither confirm nor deny the accusations hurled at them, saying only that the welfare of those living outside of their own railcar was not their responsibility. A few of them even went so far as to blame the aggrieved occupants themselves, stating that they would have noticed the leak and done something about it had they not grown so comfortable and complacent with their surroundings.

Darrow and his generals were also not immune from criticism. Some of the displaced members directed blame at their leaders for failing to protect their welfare as, they felt, it was their duty to do.

Darrow sent Chester atop the wooden crate to explain, quite candidly, that Mother Nature was responsible for the production of the weather and, obviously, such free-running forces could not be disturbed. Chester capped this impromptu oratory with a hearty bellow of "Death to Decadence!"—the phrase instantly repeated with stunning force, particularly so from those within the first railcar, and those unaffected from the second.

The few beleaguered transplants eventually accepted their new reality in the caboose, but only after one had violently kicked at some of the widgets in protest. Of course, it was a smattering of unfortunate souls in the caboose who were most acutely affected, as they'd now been pushed down to the tracks to make room for the influx of displaced members. Naturally, they too also complained about the recent turn of events, but given the depth and the distance from which their voices now had to travel, their pitiful bleatings petered out indistinguishably.

And so it went…and such was the inclemency, for nearly three days straight, and directly up to the present evening. The house was stagnant and uncommonly quiet.

Then there came a faint stir of movement from the tunnel.

Billy heard someone shout "move aside," then saw one of the sentries whisking in yet another new member, a sense of urgency in their footsteps.

"Darrow...Darrow!" screamed the sentry.

Darrow emerged from his office, Marlon closely behind. The membership stirred to their feet.

"Darrow, I'm sorry I left my post," said the sentry, "but this one just arrived, and you've got to hear what he has to say!"

Billy stared at this new arrival, as did the rest of the group.

"What is it, my child? What has happened?" said Darrow.

The soggy stranger loped forward. Scrawny, clearly malnourished, he looked as if he hadn't had a decent meal in weeks.

"Oh Glorious Darrow, I've been looking for you for days." After blurting out the words, he offered up something of a genuflect. Small beads of rainwater intermittently dripped from the tip of his pinkish nose and down to the chilly platform floor that propped up his bony legs.

"What is your name, child?"

"They call me Bing." His voice was deferential but shaky.

"Yes, then. What is it? What's happened?"

"I don't know how to say it, exactly, but they got him...they got him!" He started to hyperventilate.

"Calm down. Take your time and explain," Darrow said softly.

Bing forced himself to slow down. He inhaled deeply before he continued. "Three days back. Maybe two. I dunno anymore. I was with my buddy Daniel. We were under a bridge. I left for just a bit, then I saw the van. It was weird, because we don't ever see vehicles down there, so I ran back to see what was going on. At first nothing looked wrong. Just two men talking with him real casual. It looked like they may have been offering him something, I can't really be sure, but Daniel let his guard down. And that's when it happened..." Again he started to break down.

"Calm, now...what was it? What did you see?"

Bing composed himself as best he could. "They took him! They took Daniel. Grabbed him all rough like and forced him into the back of a black van. Daniel screamed, but it was too late. The back door shut tight and drove off. I haven't seen him since."

Gasps washed over the group as Bing shivered—from his exposure to the elements or from fear, Billy couldn't tell.

"I'd heard the rumors, ya know?" said Bing.

"We've heard them, too," replied Darrow.

"I never believed it though…until now. But it's true. Someone out there is taking us!" He screamed the last words, having amped himself back to hysterics. He was much in need of a tranquilizer, or, at the very least, a generous nip of the weed.

A chill ran down Billy's spine.

Then it's true. This is no coincidence. There's no innocent explanation. There are people out there abducting us.

The words echoed in his mind. *Abducting us.*

A wave of fear broke evenly over the group. George kicked at the ground several times, clearly disturbed by the news; Ash fidgeted about on the left, then uttered an anxious "tricky, tricky" under his breath, more to his own feet than to anyone's waiting ears; and Chet did fret that "their end may soon rend." There were other expressions of doomsday sentiment. Some started to panic. Billy even saw a glint of fear in Marlon's eye, however brief. Even Lyle, sound asleep on the platform floor beneath the list of tenets, exhibited some mild displeasure with a slumbery grunt and a spasm of his right leg.

Darrow himself remained unshaken. He managed to calm the group with a command to silence before cross-examining Bing for further information. "Who else knows of this?"

"No one. I've told no one else."

"Who did it? Was it the authorities?"

"No, I'm certain it wasn't them."

"Were the people known to you, or perhaps to Daniel? Maybe his guardians?"

Bing dispelled this without hesitation. "No, we've both been on the streets for a long time, neither of us woulda had anyone lookin' for us. I'm sure it wasn't anyone we knew. Pretty sure we knew all the same people. Not that we knew too many."

Darrow pondered this further. "Was there anything about this black van? Anything distinctive that you can recall?"

There was a hushed silence as everyone waited on the answer. Bing thought hard. It was so quiet that one could almost hear his synapses firing. Then…a spark of recognition.

"Yes…" it came to him slowly, "there was something…yes. It wasn't very big, some smallish symbol on the back of the van. I got a decent look at it. Pretty decent, I think."

He described the symbol as best he could: a logo with some blue lettering, with a distinct reddish swoosh through the top, and two interconnected blue squiggles just above. All listened and took note, the image burned into their minds.

Suddenly they heard something high above them.

Tink…tink.

Footsteps!

Tink…tink…tink.

The rain had finally started to subside.

Bing provided the direction the van was heading when he lost sight of it. It was all the information he had.

It was all they would need.

Darrow retired to his office with Marlon and Jacob. They emerged soon after to address the community.

For perhaps the first time since Billy's arrival, Darrow, Jacob, and Marlon were in complete and passionate agreement. The missions were to be placed on hold, and every capable member was ordered to scour the city in search of this sinister van with the peculiar markings.

Tink tink tink.

The city came alive for the first time in two days. Mother Nature had relented, her timing impeccable.

To Billy, even confronted with the fully credible account of an eyewitness, it still hardly seemed real. None of their own had gone missing.

Lola stared into Billy's eyes. "What do these people want with us?"

Billy couldn't answer. He couldn't truly conceive it: Dark agents abducting them for some unknown purpose? His fear was briefly supplanted by rage before it swung back to fear. His emotions ebbed and flowed wildly this way for several hours before finally equalizing at general unease.

IT WAS, OVER THE next two weeks, a total team effort.

It was incredible what a true emergency could do to effect unity among a splintered base. Egos were checked, partisanship shelved. There was less bickering in the House of Darrow, less bemoaning the obvious inequalities that had surfaced in recent weeks and months. This newest mission, to find a clue to their missing brethren, had galvanized the membership.

It took just two weeks before their collaborative efforts paid off with the discovery of a facility in the heart of the industrial district.

Billy and Lola had been readying to start their next shift when a scouting tandem came scampering through the gravelly tunnel: two very large ears and two small ones, and three eyes bearing similar promise.

"We found it!" screamed Ears.

The members, those few who were still present, clamored around the duo. Darrow emerged from his office.

Ears described a spooky nest of nondescript buildings. "It's half a day's walk from here."

"Not many people around," added George. "The odd truck or car. Real industrial."

"Isolated?" asked Darrow.

They nodded. "Some of the buildings don't even look like they're being used anymore," added Ears.

"Describe them."

So they did. Bland, square, and mostly windowless structures. Purely functional. Their purposes cryptic.

"The one we're looking for," said Ears, "was the last at the end of the road. Up on a hill."

"We saw a vehicle parked in front," said George. "It had the symbol."

"We went around back, hid in the tall grass," added Ears. "It looks like a large brick box, five or six stories high. Not many windows. Some vans parked out back, all with the same symbol. There's a fire escape running down the back of the building."

"I think we can get onto it," said George.

"Security?" asked Darrow.

"None that we saw," said Ears. "Must not expect any threat."

"Tell them," said George.

"I was about to."

"Tell us what?" asked Billy.

"You won't believe it," said Ears. "We watched for a while, to sort of get the lay of the land. Watched back far enough so we could see the front and the back. Hardly anything happened. One car was parked at the front lot. The driver was wearing all blue. She went in through the front door."

"Then?" asked Darrow.

"Then maybe an hour later, one of those vans showed up. It pulled to the rear of the building, then backed up to some sort of loading dock. The driver and passenger got out. Big guys, rough-looking. One went to the building and lifted up a steel door. We could see inside. It was lit pretty well. Plenty of places to hide, if we could get in."

"Tell them the rest," prodded George as he kicked at the ground.

"The driver opened the back of the van," said Ears. "That's when we heard them."

"Heard what?" asked Darrow.

"Screams," answered George. "They were back there. I saw four or five. The men dragged them inside."

Lola shivered.

"What did the men do?" asked Darrow, his tone somber, his eyes tilted downward, "when they cried out like that?"

"Nothing," answered Ears. "They didn't care. Just went on dragging 'em inside. Dragged 'em in screaming…"

Ears bristled and paused his narrative. Darrow's calm had been steadily eroding. Billy saw it in his eyes: the anger, the hatred. He could see Darrow struggling to keep them contained.

By then several others had returned from scouting, Jacob and Tommy included. They'd drawn in around the circle.

"Ears an' me wanted to go in, you know," said George. "To help."

"It was good that you didn't," said Darrow. "Not yet, at least."

"They went in," continued Ears, "then the screams stopped. It was silent."

"But the back door…" said George.

"Open?" said Darrow.

"Open," he affirmed.

"How long?"

"Long enough for us to get inside, I think." His good eye beaming. "Definitely long enough."

It was hours before all members had returned, and the news was cause for both celebration and concern.

The duo saw their names etched into the Wall of Valor—Ears going up more formally as Ewen—with a song of tribute no doubt to follow. They both convened in Darrow's office with Jacob, Marlon, and Billy.

Darrow was muttering profanity under his breath, and if there had been a second lamp on his desk, it might already have been swept to the floor with its dismembered counterpart.

"Barbarians!" seethed Marlon, and in a rare occurrence, Jacob did not disagree.

"It just doesn't make sense," said George. "Doesn't make sense this could be happening."

"Sure it does," said Darrow. "We should all know people well enough by now. If there's an advantage to be had, some benefit, people will find a way to exploit it."

"Bad people," added Jacob.

"People all the same," said Marlon.

"What advantage could we possibly give them?"

Billy was thinking the same thing before Ears voiced it. Maybe they all were. Darrow coaxed them away from speculation.

They considered various options. Should they try to alert the authorities? Should they infiltrate the facility in an effort to discover the true nature of events? Should they launch an all-out attack? Marlon pushed for the latter while Jacob, as usual, warned against violence.

"We can't let this discovery displace our values and taint our cause red. No matter the horror inside those walls, it's surely only a small group of evildoers behind it. Our priority must not be vengeance. We must focus on what can be done for our brothers and sisters trapped inside, and to expose this vile organization."

Darrow was again caught in-between, but finally agreed to employ tactics of espionage rather than violence. "At least," he said, "until we know what we're dealing with."

They named the mission *Focus: Facility*.

"We'll need an infiltrator," said Marlon.

Darrow turned to Billy, and it was a great relief when he spoke the next two words: *Fetch Kinsly*.

Kinsly was one of their newest members, and had quickly demonstrated a stealth and speed that was second to none. He was young, likely not much older than Chuck was at the time of his death, and had grown a healthy hatred for society ever since his mother perished prematurely in a fire. As Kinsly told it, they'd lived together on the second floor of a dilapidated apartment with several people. Fire broke out in the dead of night. Soon enough, the building was ablaze. Amid the chaos, Kinsly managed to escape, along with a flood of people. Emergency workers arrived on scene, and Kinsly watched from the sidewalk as they pulled numerous people to safety. One of them even came out carrying, as he described it, "some mangy dog." The vision chaffed him. His mother was not so fortunate, and in one fell swoop, he'd lost both home and parent. He'd joined the House of Darrow soon after.

Kinsly entered the office and was told the nature of the assignment.

"It will be a dangerous mission," warned Jacob. "All may not return."

"I understand," said Kinsly, without so much as a batted eyelash. Billy wondered if he would have been so brave in Kinsly's place. Before Kinsly's arrival three weeks ago, the task of infiltrating the facility might well have fallen to him.

"Then it's agreed," said Darrow. "You must breach their security, be it from above or through the rear door that Ewen has described. Discover whatever information you can, then escape. We will give you a certain amount of time to reappear. Otherwise, we will assume that you yourself have been taken hostage."

"I understand," Kinsly said, once again without a tremor in his voice.

Darrow would stay behind, leaving leadership of the mission to his two generals.

It would be a mission of five. Marlon and Jacob were to take up a vantage point on the roof, if possible; Ears and Billy on the ground. When the opportunity arose, Kinsly would infiltrate the building. Subterfuge and invisibility would be key.

They got what little sleep they could, rising early the next morning. Billy turned to Lola as the others prepared to leave.

"I don't like this," she said. "It's crazy."

"None of us like it."

"You don't have to do this," she said.

"There are people taking us!" he cried.

"Let them take someone else. Someone older. Why does it have to be you?"

"Who then, instead of me?"

To this she quieted down, looked down to Sam who squirmed beside her.

"I'll be fine," he said.

Rufus ran up to them, his tail wagging fervently behind. He drew in close to Billy's face, pushing his wet nose against Billy's. Billy leaned in, kissed him, then turned to kiss Lola. Each tried to hide their worry from the other with brave faces. Each failed.

Finally he departed with the others. They were sent off like heroes, with songs of courage and bravery sung at their backs.

And why not?

For as correct as Jacob was in assessing the risk, he was equally prophetic in the end result…

Not all five would return.

— Act III —

THEY ARRIVED TO THE complex by early afternoon, having taken only brief breaks for food and rest, immediately spreading out among the high weeds. All was quiet as Billy studied the back parking lot. He could see the fire escape that Ears had mentioned. The area around the fire escape was something of a dumping ground, with broken wooden skids and sharp piles of scrap metal growing up from the pavement like so many rusted stalagmites.

"It doesn't seem so bad from out here," Billy whispered. "Looks sort of calm, even."

"Don't be fooled," said Jacob. "Something can appear to be one thing on the surface, but in fact be something entirely different when you look a little closer."

Billy accepted this wisdom, and his anxiety rose accordingly. Each of them looked apphrehensively toward the oppressive structure, perhaps, like Billy, contemplating what dark secrets might lay inside.

"Ah, this world," said Jacob after an extended pause. He said it to himself more than the others, in a solemn tone and with a heavy countenance. The thought seemed to occupy him for a great while, so Billy left him to his own silent vigil.

There was little movement through the rest of the day. A few people came and went through the front door. Later in the afternoon, one of the black vans exited the rear lot. Beyond that, nothing of significance.

They waited out the daylight, then set into motion the first phase of their plan. Fortunate to find one of the vans parked directly beneath the fire escape, Jacob and Marlon ran in tandem to the vehicle and hid by the front bumper. One at a time, they sneaked up onto the hood, then to the roof of the van. Then, with a hearty jump, Jacob launched his body onto the lowest rung of the fire escape. His landing resulted in a loud clang, and he immediately looked over to Billy, still hiding in the brush. Billy looked around, nodding back that they were still clear, at which point Jacob scampered up to the rooftop. Marlon quickly followed suit, the two generals now in position above.

They searched in vain for some way to access the facility from the roof. Finding it impregnable, they motioned down to Billy and Kinsly that they would remain above as lookouts.

There they waited. First one hour, then two. It was quiet.

So quiet.

Billy and Kinsly remained hidden in the thick brush by the back parking lot. Ears was stationed near the front. Billy felt tight. He looked over at Kinsly, who sat casually in the nearby weeds. He appeared, by all indications, to be calm, even stoic. It was a virtue with which Billy couldn't identify. The anticipation of the moment had already called on his anxiety; he couldn't help think that if he were in Kinsly's position, he'd already be halfway up his tree. His limbs numbed, the crack of the branch having choked away the cool air from his lungs. Even now it was all he could to do control his breathing.

He remembered the gallery, how quickly the calm had turned to bedlam. He'd survived that encounter. Had survived the concert and the attack in the alley. And as he thought back on how he'd survived everything so far, he wondered how many lives he had left—and the more he thought back on his luck the more he felt certain to jinx it.

It was midnight when the van came, the hour when curfew would have been called. When he would have been curled up with Lola, safe and warm. The van rumbled slowly to the rear of the facility, then reversed itself to the large steel door. Billy peeked past the tall green blades that masked him, his eyes wandering up to Jacob, who'd scrunched up against the edge of the roof and was discreetly looking over the side. Marlon, from his position, was doing the same.

Both the driver and his passenger exited the vehicle. The driver, a burly man, lumbered to the loading dock. He fiddled with the lock, snapping it open with a violent tug downward, then rolled the door up and into the building, a steely clang and a rusty squeal echoing into the silent night air. He pulled out a steel ramp and fixed it at an angle against the opening.

The second man opened the van's rear door and stepped inside. Billy immediately heard the protestations. There were calls for help, then some small commotion before the man gave a yell. Then a thump, as if someone had just been punched or kicked. The driver lumbered to assist, and soon enough the captives were being forced up the steel ramp and into the rear of the building. Rage stirred inside Billy: five of them, just like him, trafficked inside like chattel.

A rustle drew Billy's attention, shifting his rage back to fear. There was a sound of footsteps to his right. He spun rapidly around to see Ears arrive through a thicket of shrubs.

"Do you see?" whispered Billy, momentarily relieved.

A whisper back said that he had.

Then more movement directly ahead...

...Kinsly. Billy watched him step from the brush and signal up to Jacob and Marlon. Kinsly suggested he advance and the generals motioned back their agreement. Kinsly snuck forward out of the brush, then darted quickly to the building, positioning himself just under the loading dock. He peered back toward Billy, who'd stepped halfway from the brush.

Billy looked into the loading room, watching as the two men carried their prisoners deeper into the building. Then he looked beneath the opening and saw Kinsly huddled down next to the steel ramp. Billy couldn't help but marvel at how small Kinsly looked against the van, against the opening—against what he was about to attempt.

The men were now nearly out of sight, their backs to the opening. Billy gave Kinsly the signal and watched him leap up and start to follow. Kinsly slunk slowly behind the men, ducking behind boxes, bins, and other large objects; and then he, too, vanished from sight. Silence took root once again.

And then they waited…and they waited.

And they waited.

For Billy, this wait was even more unbearable than the first.

How long had they been there?

It seemed like hours.

Seemed like seconds.

The area fell eerily quiet, save for the creepy soundtrack of stridulating crickets, and the occasional rustle of a bush or snap of a twig that nearly caused Billy to jump from his skin. All the while he wondered what horror Kinsly might find inside—wondered how many of their kind might be trapped and what their condition might be.

He looked up to the roof, where Jacob waited patiently near the fire escape, Marlon on the other side pacing anxiously back and forth. They were to wait only so long, then assume that Kinsly had been discovered.

And then what?

Only it didn't come to that. In the next instant Billy heard frantic footsteps and looked up to see Kinsly run toward the unmanned opening, then leap from the building to the ground. Billy and Ears rushed from the straggly weeds to meet him.

"We have to get out of here," screamed Kinsly. "I was discovered! They're right behind me!"

"Where?" asked Billy. "How many?" Billy looked through the opening but still didn't see anyone. It was both still and silent.

"They're not far behind," he gasped. "Come on, we've got to get out of here!"

Billy signaled retreat to Marlon and Jacob, then turned back to his frightened colleague.

"How many?" Billy asked again.

Kinsly didn't respond.

"What was in there?" cried Billy. "What did you see?"

"Oh, it's horrible…horrible."

It was Kinsly's sole response. His thoughts then slipped somewhere far, far away—to some dark place Billy was fortunate not to visit. He wondered what could possibly have thrust his colleague, previously so calm and cool, into his present state.

Now is probably not the best time to discuss things, he thought. "Let's get out of here!"

They had turned to run when Billy's attention was pulled to a loud scream from above—an awful sound born of fear and surprise. Billy drew his eyes skyward just in time to see Jacob tumbling over the side of the building. The fall seemed eternal, but it was, in all likelihood, not even a few seconds.

He can survive this…

Down he plummeted. Mercilessly down to the parking lot below, his limbs searching for solid ground.

He can survive this…

An odd sound rang through the air as Jacob touched down.

SHUNKT!

Billy hurried to where Jacob had landed and found him flat on his stomach, limp atop a short pile of rusted scrap.

"Jacob…"

His eyes rolled up and found Billy's, but his head hardly moved. He twitched and tried to speak, but no words came out, just a thin stream of blood out the left side of his mouth and a sad gurgle.

Only then did Billy notice the slash across Jacob's throat and the blood that poured freely from the gaping wound, his eyes wide and moist as his gaze held Billy's.

"Jacob…"

Just another sad gurgle, another attempt to move, but in the next moment he was gone, his wide eyes beseeching Billy with sadness and panic.

Billy fumbled back a step, then looked up to see from where Jacob had fallen, finding Marlon peering intently over the edge of the building. Their eyes connected for a fraction of a second before Marlon pulled his head back and out of sight.

"Come on, Billy, let's go!" screamed Ears, who'd already pushed Kinsly into motion at the sound of footsteps within the facility. Ears screamed again, snapping Billy sufficiently back to reality to get his legs moving. In his peripheral vision he saw Marlon scurrying down the fire escape.

A moment later two men had leapt from the loading dock to give chase, one of them wielding some sort of wooden club.

Billy had never run so fast in his life. Fear, adrenaline, and anger fueled his steps like thunderclaps. He ran with his colleagues through a field and over a small brook. By then the skies had released a slight drizzle, the ground growing slow and muddy beneath their feet. They ran until they could run no longer, stopping for a reprieve beneath a thicket of tall trees, the facility safely behind them, their pursuers out of sight.

Billy immediately approached Marlon, his feet caked with mud, his chest heaving. "What happened?" he said, the vision of his bloodied friend still seared into his mind.

There was no response. Marlon didn't look up, keeping his face tilted slightly toward the ground. Billy inched closer.

"I said, what happened?" he demanded.

Marlon, still looking down, replied plainly, "He got too close to the ledge, some loose cinder gave way and he lost his footing."

"I didn't see any loose cinder," said Billy.

"There was loose cinder," replied Marlon, again without affect.

"His throat was cut," said Billy.

No answer.

"Did you hear me?" pressed Billy. "I said 'his throat was cut.'"

"Must have been cut by some scrap," said Marlon.

Heard Billy.

Doubted Billy.

He tried to play the scene back in his mind. To Jacob's limp form. Tried to see through the flood of red and to the area around him. Where had he fallen? What had he hit? The effort was useless. He saw only red.

"Very unfortunate," added Marlon, his stare downward.

"Come on," said Ears, before Billy could say anything more. "We have to get back."

And so they did, starting their long journey home. All the while, Kinsly moved robotically. The light that was in his eyes before entering the facility had been extinguished, and he wouldn't utter a single word their entire trip home.

Kinsley's muteness wasn't the only silence among them. Billy and Marlon were equally quiet.

THEY ARRIVED TO A hero's welcome.

Rufus was the first to greet Billy, wagging and carrying on and nearly knocking over his weary frame, one in desperate need of food and rest.

He saw Lola wash up in front of him, watched her lean in, felt her forehead against his own. When he heard Ears call his name, he separated from her and convened in Darrow's office with what was left of the others.

By the time Billy entered the room, Darrow was turning away from them, a tear welling up in his eye. "My good friend is dead."

Billy had never seen Darrow get upset, certainly never cry. He didn't think it was even possible. They sat in silence for some time before Darrow turned back to face them; by then the nascent tear was absent.

"How?"

"Slipped," said Marlon, as Billy percolated.

"Must have leaned out over the ledge too far," Marlon added, and the percolation increased to a boil.

"Liar!" screamed Billy. "You're a damned liar and a murderer!"

Only he screamed it in his mind, where the same words had been crashing about for hours. He kept them bottled up under a nugget of uncertainty, and more than a nugget of intimidation. Marlon, quite simply, scared him.

"A damn shame," capped Marlon.

Billy looked to Ears; saw his expression was flat and resigned. He hadn't seen, thought Billy, and so the burden fell squarely on him to expose it.

Only then Billy looked at Darrow, caught his glance to Marlon and Marlon's glance back; saw something in Darrow's eyes— some vague level of recognition. Billy couldn't tell for sure, not at that moment, his exhaustion being what it was. Either way it turned him mute, and before Billy could consider it further, Darrow had asked for Kinsly's report.

"Speak, my child."

Kinsly, nearly catatonic since the facility, had not yet spoken of his findings. His stare held blankly forward until Ears tapped his shoulder. It stirred Kinsly from his trance. Slowly, the words started to tumble out. "It was horrible," he muttered, "…horrible…"

"Take your time," Darrow said. His voice was calm and reassuring. "Now tell us," he said. "Tell us what's in that facility. For them…for Jacob…for all of us."

Kinsly's pupils slowly dilated. His focus returned just enough. Again he started to speak, and the words droned out. "I followed them to the back of the building," he said. "Stayed out of sight and followed them into a large room. There…"

They briefly lost him again. It took a few moments but he managed to find his tongue.

"They were...there. Some strapped down to tables...others locked up. I even recognized someone I used to hang out with. Things had been done to him...things. Maybe tests, or experiments. I don't really know..." He stopped again to collect himself, clearly replaying the scene in his mind. They left him alone now. To work through it. He did, after a short pause. "One had no foot. One had no eyes. Some looked like they'd been burned. Many had been cut. I think there were a few that were dead..."

Billy couldn't tell how long he'd been holding his breath. He looked over to Ears, whose mouth gaped open.

"...I watched...from a distance, as the new ones got locked up in big cages...like rats...just like bloody rats..." He was sobbing now, but struggled onward. "There was moaning...so much moaning...and screaming...loud screaming as they locked up the new ones. It wasn't just us. There were others. I can still hear the screams. They're everywhere. Can you hear them?" he asked, trembling.

Again Billy glanced to Ears, who returned his look of concern. There was little doubt Kinsly meant what he said. They had, thought Billy, lost more than just Jacob at the facility.

"I hear them," Darrow said softly, trying his best to nudge Kinsly along. "Now go on. Tell us what else you could see." It worked, and like a record, Kinsly's needle shifted mechanically forward to the next track in his memory.

"There was a woman in blue scrubs, she was ordering them around. They...they sort of repositioned some of the others. I managed to reach the far side of the room and whisper to one of the captives through the bars. He told me what's being done to them. The torture. The experiments. I can't repeat it, and some of it made no sense to me. He'd been operated on. They had injected something inside him...drugged him maybe, and I think now that he'd been blinded..." Kinsly's voice trailed off again softly, as if he was speaking as much to himself as to any of the rest, "Yes...blind, I think. The way his eyes looked at me...or didn't, as it was. He saw enough through his ears, though…knew the sort of things that were going on. Going on all around him. He was confused and in pain. Great, great pain…"

"And then?" Darrow prodded.

"Then…then I told him I had to keep gathering information. He…he must have thought I was there to rescue him, because he started to scream when I moved away. I told him to be quiet, but he was out of his mind. Why wouldn't he stay quiet? Why wouldn't he…I…I was discovered, and they chased me. I got a good head start. I was lucky they'd left the doors open."

"It's unfortunate you were discovered. Any element of surprise that we had is gone," said Marlon. "No doubt they'll raise their security. It's going to be harder to mount a rescue or attack the facility."

"Rescue?" Kinsly scoffed, his voice trembling. "There can't be any rescue for them. The condition they're in. Just let 'em die, and hope they die quickly." He collapsed again, this time to a place from which he wouldn't be so easily roused. Darrow didn't push him, only stood in apparent disbelief with the rest.

It was Ears who spoke next. "How could this happen? In a civilized society?"

"*Civilized?*" screamed Darrow. He repeated the word even louder, his long hair bouncing angrily around him. "And what makes you think this society is civilized? The presence of decadent structures? The laying of long roads and wide bridges? Civilization doesn't flow from these things. It flows from a kindness of the soul, from empathy, from looking after your weakest constituents and facilitating their prosperity. Only then do you have a civilized society, and not one moment before."

They all saw it: the fire in his eyes, the hate, the righteousness.

The truth, thought Billy, before adding, "What are we going to do?"

"I can't believe it," said Ears. "Can't believe this is happening." As far as suggestions went, it was wanting.

"Believe it," said Marlon, flatly.

Ears tried again. "Maybe we should try and find some people to help us?"

"Help from society, is that what you're suggesting?" said Marlon sharply. "They're why we're in this position in the first place. I'd rather die in that facility than beg for their damned help!"

After a moment, Darrow nodded his silent concurrence.

Billy thought about all the rounders locked up inside. Knew they should do something for them. But knew equally that he didn't want to be the one to do it.

They sat in silence until Darrow excused them from the room. Before they left, Darrow tasked Marlon to ensure Jacob's name was etched prominently onto the Wall of Valor. Billy bristled, wondering, as he stepped away, at the depth of Darrow's complicity. He thought back on Jacob's fall, and of the fear and surprise that he saw in his face. It had all happened so quickly.

The scream. The fall. The jarring sound of twisted metal.

SHUNKT!

His eyes open wide and moist. His throat slashed. His golden locks stained red.

And the gurgle. The sad gurgle.

What had he tried to say?

Billy quietly reunited with Lola and Sam. He watched as Jacob's name was added to the Wall of Valor, then burrowed his head into Lola's shoulder.

As news of the events cycled through the House of Darrow, the members buzzed with anticipation. Billy himself toggled hopelessly through the possibilities.

"What are you thinking?" asked Lola.

SHUNKT!

"Nothing," said Billy.

"Nothing?"

No response.

"Talk to me."

The sad gurgle.

"I'm just tired."

She didn't press.

Frightened whispers continued to simmer, and nervous discussions dominated the compound. Billy himself was soon engaged in one, as George approached from the side.

"What's going on?" There was an excited tremor in his voice. "Did you see anything? There's a lot of talk."

"I didn't see anything. Only Kinsly went inside."

"He's just curled himself up in a far corner," said George. "He won't talk to any of us. Did he say anything to you?"

Billy looked into Lola's eyes. "He told us enough," then reluctantly outlined what Kinsly had seen in the facility.

"I can't believe it," said George.

Billy didn't answer.

"Who are these people?" said George. "And why are they doing this?"

"How could they," cried Lola, more expression than question. Her voice had unsettled Sam, who was now crying out from below. The look in Lola's eyes said more than what she'd spoken. It asked, "How can we be worth so little to some people? How can any person think it justifiable, for any reason, to force or coerce us, to torture or kill another living soul?"

"What else did he tell you?" asked George. By then he'd kicked several times at the ground.

"We don't know any more than that," said Billy. "Kinsly doesn't seem to know either."

"Couldn't he do anything while he was inside?" George asked.

Again Billy didn't answer. By then his thoughts had wandered off and set upon something else Kinsly had said.

It wasn't just us.

What had he meant by that?

Not just rounders like us? Who else then?

Who else was in there?!

A voice interrupted his thoughts before they could run too far amok.

"If I'd've gotten inside, I would have ripped their freaking throats out."

It was Marlon, his voice sharp. Billy tightened, turning his eyes to the floor as Marlon stepped into the circle.

"Then it's too bad you weren't," George replied coolly. Single eye or not, he was more than an able fighter, and was one of the few members not intimidated by Marlon's pronounced rancor.

"Do you think they'll come for us?" asked Lola. "I mean, they know we're out here, right? They know we saw them!"

"They won't come here," said Marlon. "Those people are just a bunch of cowards. They target the weak. Those who can't fight back."

"But were you followed?" asked George.

Billy answered, his head still tilted downward: "I think we got away. Pretty sure. It was a long way home, and I think we would have noticed being followed."

"If they want to come after us, let them," said Marlon, who then departed just as quickly as he'd arrived. He was immediately replaced in the circle by Ash, who'd been loitering a few feet away.

"How long do you think it's been going on?" George's question was lobbed up for anyone to answer, as much introspection as inquisition.

"I couldn't say," said Billy. There were so many questions and so few answers.

"You think it could be happening elsewhere? Maybe in other towns?" asked Lola.

Nothing seemed impossible anymore, thought Billy.

Said Billy.

Lola persisted, "Do you think many people know this is happening?"

"I wouldn't think so. Even Bigwigs would be shocked by this, I think," said Billy.

Ash finally chimed in from the side: "You're presumin' they ain't the ones behind it all in the first place."

A sobering thought indeed, and one Billy hadn't truly considered until Ash drove the possibility to the forefront. From what Billy had seen, the Bigwigs held obscenely disproportionate levels of influence and power in the world. If they had any involvement in the facility, even incurred a residual benefit from it, it would be that much harder to crack.

The members continued frightened chats among themselves. Before long, Billy noticed Marlon re-enter Darrow's office. Several minutes later Darrow stormed from the hallway, Marlon close behind him.

"It's the only way!" shouted Marlon at his heels.

Darrow didn't respond or turn around, just vanished up the tunnel. He did so infrequently, usually only with a heavy heart or a troubled mind.

Alone. No security attachment. Like Nixon sauntering out to visit with Lincoln; he was the leader of the movement...who was going to stop him?

And though only one soul had left, the House of Darrow now felt surprisingly empty.

— Act IV —

THEY WERE ON PINS and needles waiting for Darrow's return, though it was a mixed feeling for Billy: frightened at the possibility that Darrow might not return; almost equally apprehensive that he would.

He'd seen the increasingly aberrant behavior. There was more talking at the walls, more blank stares into nothingness. His decisions were increasingly arbitrary and unequal. Yet Billy was torn. He still felt a security in Darrow's presence that he hadn't felt for so long; still felt inspired whenever Darrow would cry havoc against the lack of respect for their kind; and still found solace in Darrow's ability to articulate the loneliness, angst, and lack of self-worth that they'd all always felt but were unable to put into words.

Darrow was a father to some of them; to others, a priest; to others still, a savior. Only tonight, when all was said and done, Billy would first entertain the possibility that he may, in fact, have turned truly mad.

Darrow had been gone for hours, and there was a collective sigh of relief when he finally returned, shortly before midnight, striding onto the crowded platform and immediately assuming his position atop the old wooden crate. The entire membership swelled around him.

Once they were settled, he wasted little time. "My friends, my children, my soldiers," he said. "Today is a day of great sadness, for we have lost a good and dear friend."

There was a pause, as if Darrow had just demanded, and received, a moment of silence for Jacob. Had the old clock hanging on the wall still been ticking, it would have lapsed a full fifteen seconds before he found his voice to continue, adding a solemn, "And now he shall live forever."

"Forever!" echoed someone from the rear, as several others murmured "Darrow Knows" in something of a hypnotic cadence.

Darrow continued, his voice raised, "Yet as much as this is a day of sadness, it is equally a day of revelation, for our great cause has come to a crossroads. We have toiled toward reformation—to shake this city into realization, to shake its citizens from blindness and ignorance, to show them that we will not sit idly by and accept life as second-class citizens. To teach them that all life should be valued equally! So we steal from them, and nothing changes. We deface their property, and nothing changes. We interrupt their leisure, and nothing changes. We sabotage their lifestyle...and nothing changes! Our efforts have not brought about any substantial change. They do not bring us food, they do not bring us clean water, they do not bring us blankets. They remain, to this day, largely unmoved by our suffering."

The hamlet was transfixed, Billy included, as Darrow's soliloquy rolled onward...

"Now we discover people harvesting us and experimenting on us for reasons unknown, and though it would be easy to focus the blame solely on those evildoers in the facility, those ravaging our bodies even at this very moment, that would be most short-sighted. I want all of you to understand—understand clearly—that society at large is responsible for every cut, prod, poke, and injection that occurs within that building. Every single person in this city is responsible."

"Yes, of course," muttered Totter, having positioned himself as close by the wooden crate as he could manage, and already given to pronounced fits of nodding. The rest of the group was deathly quiet, the silence complemented only by the blank stares of those who didn't seem to understand how the workings of a fringe handful could be the fault of all. But as Darrow continued, their blank stares slowly turned to understanding.

"Those that commit these heinous acts are the sons and daughters and brothers and sisters of society. They no doubt commit these acts to further the wants and needs of the many, not just their own."

The heads in the gallery started bobbing up and down.

"Yet beyond that, there is a deeper and simpler reality here. We are being selected intentionally, not for what we truly are, but for what they say we are. Or, perhaps more accurately, what they say we are *not*. And why not capture and torture us? Society has clearly dictated that our lives, like so many others like us, are less valuable than theirs. We have been deemed inferior, and we have been deemed expendable. Our misery and suffering is not only tolerated, but quite widely and publicly accepted. It happens every day, and right before their very eyes. So then why not take us? Why not do with us as they please? Yes, indeed, what is now happening at that facility should come as no surprise at all. So let there be no doubt, this atrocity isn't just on those select evildoers in that facility…the blame lies with every single person that turns a blind eye to our plight. And that means virtually every one of them is to blame!"

By the time Darrow arrived at the final few words, he was screaming. He'd veered into a path of anger and rage that Billy hadn't seen before. A tidal wave of agreement washed over the crowd. He was right. It was now so clear to everyone. He was absolutely right.

Darrow lowered his voice to a simmering seethe, further drawing in his subjects. "I have seen things, my children. I have seen things that some of you could not possibly imagine. Not just our kind being picked on and laughed at—not just ignored and stepped around when we lie on a steaming sewage grate for warmth, as if that wasn't bad enough. I have seen a young one spat on while huddled up asleep, another shot in the eye, blinded for all eternity; yet another beaten to death with a metal pipe, seemingly for no reason, aside from his attackers' wanting to see what the inside of his head looked like. Even an elder lying dead on the side of the road for nearly half a day, person after person stepping by him without breaking stride. Oh, my children, indeed I have seen things…"

The gallery bristled with approval, and the fervor continued to build as Darrow stood merchant to truth.

"Though some show kindness and compassion, for far too many, our lives do not hold the same value as theirs. But why? Have we not eyes? Have we not organs, dimensions, senses, affections, and passions? Can we not eat the same food? Are we not hurt by the same weapons? Are we not subject to disease just as they are, and healed by similar means? Are we not warmed and cooled by the same summer and winter? Still, there are many who see us as no better than objects, and we are made to understand that each and every day. Each time a well-nourished person walks by one of our hungry, we are made to understand. Each time a healthy person skips blindly past one of our sick, we are made to understand. Over and over, we have tolerated the abuse and the negligence, but no longer. If we are like them in most things, shall we not be like them in contempt? Long have we watched, and we have waited, and we have learned. This cruelty they have shown us we will now adopt as our own, and we will execute, and we will better the destruction."

As Darrow continued to preach, the group expelled a guttural moan of approval. One yelled, *"Down with the man!"* and the energy level rose still further. Billy, like everyone, was absolutely captivated.

It all made perfect sense!

But before Billy could reflect on this wisdom, Darrow, still standing erect upon the crate, froze mid-sentence, then jumped to the ground and ran quickly through his parting minions, past his office and to the far left of the platform. Hurried footsteps followed his path. Billy was one of the unlucky spectators to lose sight of their leader, though he could still hear—a blood-curdling squeal, then silence.

"We are seen not much differently than they view this rat," yelled Darrow. The crowd continued to buzz a communal murmur, something indistinguishable but distinguished in their agreement, and though Billy still couldn't see him, Darrow's voice had sufficiently filled in the blanks as to what was occurring.

"This is you," he cried overtop another impassioned squeal. "We have not much more value than this vile rat, do we? An annoyance. A distraction. Unclean! At least, that is what many in society would have us believe. That is what many in society would have us accept."

The mob hissed their contempt for society as Billy finally managed to push his way to the front. Just as he envisioned, Darrow now towered over a large rat, his foot clamped down firmly on its tailbone. The eyes of the frightened rodent, small beady black orbs, expressed some emotion a level or two beyond terror.

"But I say they are wrong," he continued. "I say that we are not the rats beneath their feet, the soiled vermin that dirties the world. Quite the opposite—I say that *they* are the rats, with their dirty morality, their tainted ethics, their filthy principles and prejudices, their selfishness and greed. Their disgracefully accepted standard to value some lives over others. They are the rats, are they not?" The crowd roared again.

"Yeah, them's the rats, no doubt about it!" yelled Ash from the rear, Totter still nodding along feverishly.

Billy had never seen them this worked up. Darrow embraced the frenzy and fueled it with his own shriek skyward. Madness took flight. Suddenly, Marlon yelled out for Darrow to kill the rat. Others joined in, their thoughts turned bloody.

"Kill it, kill it."

Three were chanting, then five, and then seven.

"Kill it. Kill it. Kill it."

The mob was relentless. In just a few moments, virtually the entire room was chanting for Darrow to kill the pitiful rodent beneath his heel, a creature that now embodied the society which had long mistreated and subjugated the very individuals now calling for its execution. Their bloodlust was overwhelming. It was what so many of them had been waiting for.

Billy looked into the eyes of the poor creature and watched its fear give way to a sad and hopeless resignation. It was a look that Billy knew well.

Darrow basked in the goading of the crowd for a moment longer, but Billy knew exactly where this was heading. Darrow had no knife, no weapon or object to do the deed, but it didn't matter. Billy watched in horror as he reached down, pulled the rat to his mouth, and bit into the frantic vermin as any right-thinking person might bite casually into a ripe Granny Smith. The creature squealed and flailed in agony, and as Darrow pulled his head away, he ripped off a chunk of the animal's flesh. Blood spurted to the ground and blotted down both sides of Darrow's face. He spat the piece of flesh onto the wall with a muted thud as the crowd roared with approval. Billy had never heard them so loud; he even worried they might expose themselves to those walking high above on the steel grates.

Darrow dropped the poor maimed creature to the ground. The rat had served its purpose, and though it was able to make its way over the ledge and into the tracks, the wound would prove to be a fatal one, and it would die before the conclusion of the meeting. All the while Billy stood in stunned silence, mouth gaping open.

Darrow ran to the crate. This time Billy remained behind, watching from afar as Darrow jumped back atop the wooden structure, his minions again swarming beneath him.

And so it was decided. The fallout from Focus: Facility had led to an irrevocable shift in the organization. There would be no rescue attempt at the facility. "Now is not the time, my children. The time will come, I promise you that, but now is not that time."

Bing and Claire seemed dismayed, but most of the rest were in full agreement. There were scattered shouts of "Darrow knows" as the crowd grew still more electric.

There would be no further acts of simple mischief, vandalism, and social disobedience; no more attacks that merely disrupted people's leisure or trifled with their property. The time had come to embrace violence. The people of this city continued to show no mercy for their plight, so no mercy would be shown in return.

"Violent indifference earns indifferent violence!" exhorted Darrow. They would either change their ways or suffer the direst of consequences.

They were quickly taught a new song, and soon the majority of the House was singing in unison.

> *The House of Darrow strong and true*
> *We stand united through and through*
> *Let go your pride*
> *Run off and hide*
> *When next we come, we come for you!*
>
> *The time has come to hit you back,*
> *With vicious, bloody, cruel attack*
> *You're all to blame,*
> *Embrace your shame,*
> *We will derail your selfish track*

For the first time ever, they sang of anger and bloodshed and retribution, of the suffering that was to come, the words eerily framed by the cool tone of the masses. No longer playful or spirited, there was a cruelty to the verses that had never been present in their other songs.

The singing went on for hours.

Darrow assured them that their kind would be oppressed no longer, and they believed him. He promised them strength and security, and they loved him. They would follow him anywhere. That night, Darrow formally declared war on society.

ONCE MORE TO THE GATES OF HELL

BILLY SLEPT ONLY INTERMITTENTLY through the night, unsettled by both Darrow's declaration of war and the fervor with which most members had gobbled up the announcement.

Even the preponderance of downtrodden continued to support him, notwithstanding their ever-growing frustrations, as Darrow had convinced them—with some assistance from Totter—that he was merely looking out for their long-term interests.

The next morning, Billy and Lola picked up their breakfasts from Chet, who'd been assigned to food distribution. He kept repeating, "War at our door," as he doled out the food, all the while looking nervously down at the floor. Marlon was ahead of them in line, and Billy watched as Chet issued him a delicious pepperoni stick.

"You have any more of those?" asked Billy. Chet said, through nervous rhyme, that there had only been the one. "The ham, then."

They took their food, and something for Sam, then sequestered themselves by Rufus, who was sleeping on the stack of old newspapers vacated by Jacob, refusing to budge from that spot, waiting for Jacob to return.

"I don't like him," said Billy, between bites.

"Who?" said Lola.

"Marlon."

"You never talk about it," said Lola.

"No," said Billy.

"Why don't you like him?"

"I don't trust him."

"Must be more to it."

Billy checked around him. It took some time before she drew it out of him: that he didn't believe Jacob had slipped from the roof.

Lola stopped eating. "You think…"

"I don't believe he slipped," repeated Billy.

An uncommon look washed over her face. "Then why don't you say something?" She'd dulled her voice to a whisper. Billy could barely hear her over the sound of Lyle's nearby snoring.

"I suspect it," he said. "I don't know it."

"What's the difference?"

"Probably no difference," said Billy. He wouldn't go so far as to implicate Darrow. His leader's glance at Marlon had been too slight to be anything definitive.

Lola's demeanor hardened into something unfamiliar. "Jacob was your friend."

Billy nodded.

"We should fix him."

He waited for a laugh that didn't come. "You don't mean that."

"I mean it. In his sleep."

"I'm not sure that would work so well."

Billy's thoughts drifted to what George had told him about Darrow's blinding the man with the corkscrew. Thought about how George appreciated it beyond words. To be fought for.

Avenged.

But Marlon?

Billy dismissed it. He wasn't the revenge-seeking sort. The mere thought of it made him queasy.

"Well I don't like him much either," said Lola, curling the conversation back around to where it had started. "I think most are scared of him."

"Mm-hmm."

"Are you?"

"Am I what?"

"Are you scared of him?"

"Yes," said Billy, unflinchingly.

"I don't think I like it here anymore," said Lola.

"No," said Billy.

By then she was stroking Rufus, who'd set his leg into something of a kicking motion.

"Rufus thinks there's still hope for us," she said.

"He has no clue," said Billy.

"Don't be so sure," said Lola. "My family had a dog. Dogs are smart. They know things."

Her voice was still so very comforting, even when it dangled revenge. There was just something about it. A soothing confidence.

As they were finishing their breakfast, Billy saw Totter exit Darrow's office and intercept a member who was waiting near the tracks. They were just close enough for Billy to overhear the interaction.

"I'm told you have a complaint regarding the sixth tenet?" said Totter.

"I do," said the member. He was slight in frame, with a lazy left eye and a chin pocked with blackheads. "I haven't been enjoying my sleep down in the tracks."

"Yes, well I can see how that could be a problem," said Totter. "Sleep is most definitely important, isn't it? Yes, of course it is, I see you nodding your head. It is one of life's great pleasures, of course! There is no disputing that. You wouldn't have brought it up if it weren't important."

"But it's not a pleasure. Not anymore."

"Well, I don't see how that's possible," said Totter, through something of faint surprise.

"I'm not enjoying my sleep anymore," he said, "ever since I was sent down into the tracks." His lazy left eye lolled down toward the bottom of its socket, then made a slight recovery.

"I'm confused," said Totter, despite the fact that he clearly wasn't. Billy had come to understand that when Totter purported to be confused about something, it surely meant the opposite.

"I don't see what's so confusing about it," said the other.

"Well frankly, I cannot possibly imagine how you can claim to not enjoy your sleep, when, at the point of slumber, you would be in no position to be aware of the level of enjoyment one way or the other."

The challenger appeared confused.

"Surely," pressed Totter, "you cannot be awake and asleep at the same time?"

He admitted that he could not be awake and asleep at the same time.

"Then I say it is impossible for you to tell whether you enjoy your sleep or not, if you are, as you have just conceded, quite unconscious at the precise time that you claim you do not enjoy it. Clearly you can see that?"

"But I wake up often," he said.

"Ah yes, I see, I see," said Totter. Billy could see, by the twitch of Totter's brow, the machinations making their usual rounds. "So the issue then is not as you had initially reported it—that you do not enjoy your sleep—the fact is that you enjoy your sleep very much, as we all do, and as the sixth tenet guarantees! Your issue is, in fact, one of insomnia. It is now perfectly obvious."

The member remained defiant. "I don't believe it's insomnia."

"No?"

"No. I believe it is the rocks and the rats that are the problem."

"But the rocks and the rats," cried Totter, "certainly they were always in the tracks, even when you fell asleep in the first place, were they not? I defy you to say that the rocks and the rats appeared suddenly overnight, as if by magic. Certainly you don't believe in magic!"

He admitted that the rocks and the rats were always there. He further admitted that he did not believe in magic.

"Well then," said Totter, "if the rocks and the rats have always been there, and you were able to fall asleep despite their presence, and enjoy that sleep, I might add, then your subsequent waking up can only be from insomnia. It is perfectly obvious."

When the complainer said nothing further, Totter offered up some basic home remedies, which the member reluctantly agreed to try. "But I still don't like this," he said.

"Nobody likes insomnia," said Totter.

By THE END OF the morning they were assigned their duties. Nothing violent yet, to Billy's relief. He was to spend the day with George acquiring food and supplies. Many others were to do the same. Lola, as had become the custom, was left free from assignment so she could look after The Progeny.

Billy had seen Marlon attend Darrow's office earlier in the morning, no doubt strategizing their first wartime campaign. It wasn't lost on Billy that he hadn't been invited, nor was it lost on him, when he saw Claire approach Tommy, what was in the wind. Her frantic plea followed by Tommy's calm, understanding nods. Billy couldn't hear what was being said, but he didn't need to. He was certain of the topic, and equally certain what was coming when Tommy approached shortly after.

"I've just talked with Claire," he said.

"She wants to go back," said Billy, intercepting Tommy's thought. "To the facility."

"She hopes to find her brother," said Tommy.

"If her brother was in there, he's dead by now."

"We don't know that," said Tommy.

"We know it well enough," said Billy. "Anyway, Darrow already said we're not going back there."

"Darrow has said a lot of things," said Tommy, his tone low.

"We should go," said Lola.

"No way," said Billy.

They briefly fell into an argument before Sam cried out beneath them, forcing their voices to cool.

"If Lola was inside, you'd go," said Tommy.

"She's not," answered Billy.

"I'm going either way," said Tommy. "Bing and I talked last night. The three of us are going for sure. You can come if you wish." And with that Tommy stepped quietly away.

Lola stared at Billy, imploring him.

"There's no way in," said Billy.

"Kinsly got in."

"And look at him now." Billy's mind wandered to Kinsly's deterioration. It hadn't helped that both Bing and Claire had approached Kinsly last night. They had been accusatory, demanding to know why he hadn't done more for their loved ones. Billy had intervened when he saw it and chased them off. Kinsly was huddled in the corner, eyes welling, a delayed "I'm sorry" tumbling from his mouth.

"It's not your fault," Billy had told him.

"Not my fault," echoed Kinsly.

"There was nothing you could do," said Billy.

Kinsly had closed his eyes by then. "If only I hadn't been caught..." he stammered. "Hadn't made Jacob scramble..."

"That wasn't your fault," said Billy, but there was no convincing him.

Yes. Kinsly got in.

He just didn't get out.

"It's foolish to even think about it," said Billy, returning his focus to Lola.

"So we just leave them there?" When Billy said nothing, she pressed, "Leave them in there to die?"

"I didn't put them there!" he shouted. Others looked over. The attention embarrassed him and hemmed in his demeanor. "We can't save everyone. So far we can't even save ourselves."

"Not if we don't stick together," she persisted.

Billy rose to his feet as if he were readying to leave, only he didn't move from his spot. Instead he looked out across the compound floor and said solemnly, "Ah, this world."

"What's that?"

"Just something Jacob said. The last thing I ever heard him say: 'Ah, this world.'"

"What did he mean by it?"

Billy had an idea but instead just shrugged. Neither said anything further. Finally he nodded goodbye to Lola, then set off to find George for an afternoon of food acquisition.

On his way across the compound floor he noticed a female huddled up below the Wall of Valor. She was a newcomer to the House of Darrow, having arrived sometime within the previous week. She was small and thin and, to Billy's surprise, was gnawing happily on a pepperoni stick. She didn't appear very old.

▼

THEY RETURNED LATER THAT afternoon. Billy and George each clenched a thick rib eye, lifted from a nearby merchant with a good eye for beef but a lazy one for security.

They'd found other good spots in the immediate area, having kept their minds on the task at hand. Neither talked much about Darrow's declaration of war, only that it was unexpected. Billy hadn't wanted to discuss any of it: the war, or the facility, or the man in the blue hat. He wanted it all left behind him. More and more Billy longed for the old days. Before red butterflies and electrocuted flesh and blue flat caps. He longed for his old apartment building, for the old man with the fried chicken and the room with the dancing cereal box. Frantic, desolate, happier times.

Only he hadn't known Lola then. She was one of the few bright spots to have endured as the rest had decayed around him. He still felt bad for how he'd left things—how he'd snapped at her, when all she wanted to do was help others, as she always did.

When they got back he looked for her to apologize, not finding her in the usual spots. Then he heard Sam squeal and tracked the noise up by the caboose. It led him to Sam and Jenny's sister.

To Sam, and to Jenny's sister.

It didn't immediately register, at least not until he'd repeated the same two names in his head. Then came the first pangs of alarm. "Where is she?"

Helena didn't reply, just looked down at her feet.

"Where?" he demanded. Only he already knew. He shot his eyes to the stack of newspapers, to where Rufus would normally be sprawled out in slumber.

Vacant.

He spun around and scanned the area. Tommy. Claire. Bing. All gone.

"They left right after you did," she said. "You know how she gets. Real stubborn."

By then she was talking to his back. He'd already turned away from her to run up the rocky slope, quickly skipping past the soiled flat cap and into the gravelly tunnel.

They'd had all day, thought Billy.

They would have reached it already.

HE FELT A COWARD, but also betrayed. He felt he should have gone with them. He should have anticipated this. He should have been there with her.

He should have been there *for* her.

He felt a great many things as his feet beat down on the pavement, following the others' most likely route. The sky had darkened by then, the sun setting to a bloody reddish mess. The slight chill in the air kept him cool, his pace brisk. He could have gone faster if he hadn't been out all day with George, running in short bursts when they stole the food. Now he tapped into whatever reserve that he had left. The facility was on the other side of town, hours by foot, so he had hours to juggle his emotions—to love her, and to hate her, and to love her once again.

He crested through myriad neighborhoods, past Bigwigs and junkies and everything in-between, all of them as equally hurried as they were unequal in station.

He was nearly halfway there when he saw them, rising like ants over the bloody horizon. The ants morphed gradually into three figures and a giant.

Three figures.

Billy started into a run, and though he'd quickened his pace, it somehow seemed as if he were moving more slowly, as if he were stepping in sand with de-boned legs. He listened for his breath but could no longer hear it. Still, he managed to traverse the distance. He saw Rufus first. The dog walked with a noticeable limp. Then Lola, which returned his breath, and Tommy, and one he didn't recognize.

By the time Billy reached them he'd traded his panic and anger for relief. He saw that Rufus' front left paw was swollen and oozing blood. Tommy seemed fine. Lola looked worn and tired. The stranger looked angry.

There were no pleasantries. "You were right," said Tommy, the "we shouldn't have gone back" left unsaid.

Outwardly, they seemed no worse for wear. That is, all but Rufus, who could hardly put any weight on his swollen paw.

"It was like they were waiting for us," added Lola, her breath shallow.

"What happened?"

"We got there," said Tommy. "Did like the rest of you did. Hid in the grass. Waited for a van to leave. Lola kept Rufus back a bit, so he wouldn't run out and expose us."

"And then?"

"Then it wasn't long before the van came back. The doors got opened. They were taking a few in. Bing went in to follow, only it didn't work. Maybe he went in too fast, or maybe they were watching for it, I don't know. They were on him quick, just inside the building. I ran in and tried to free him, then Rufus got away from Lola and ran up, too."

"Things went crazy then," said Lola, again through shallow breaths.

"It was awful," said Tommy. "One of them grabbed a bat and swung at Rufus. We all helped distract the other man while Bing got outside."

"Where is he?" asked Billy.

"Gone," hissed the stranger. "Ran off like a little coward!"

"This is Sherman," said Tommy. "He was one of the new ones they were bringing in. He managed to get loose in the scuffle."

"Took both of 'em to get me down," he said proudly, defiantly. Billy ignored him.

"What then?"

"The man with the bat, he came up on me. Was ready to clobber me when Rufus jumped up and buried him against a crate." Tommy paused, his voice briefly supplanted by the memory. "The man fell back hard and hit his head on the corner. It gashed clear open. He didn't move after that. Least not that I saw…"

Billy heard the sounds and imagined the man, his head split open and dead on the ground. Then he thought of the man in the flat cap, thought how sooner or later they'd all get the needle, as Jacob feared.

No. None of them would be going to the authorities. Surely they couldn't expose themselves any more than Billy could—their sadistic operation, their sick and twisted facility.

"I thought we'd be OK then," resumed Tommy, "but then two more men appeared from within the facility. One picked up the bat from the ground and the other one grabbed Lola hard around her throat. She couldn't breathe. I saw it in her eyes, they were bulging. Next thing Rufus has his jaws clamped around the man's wrist. The man dropped Lola to the ground but Rufus didn't let up. I could hear the crunch of the bones over his scream.

Finally Rufus let go and I could see the man's hand half hanging from his wrist, tendons and everything spilling out of it. Then the other man came in and got Rufus on his paw with the bat. By then we were all scrambling. Somehow we got outside—I don't even know how. There was so much blood, so much yelling."

"Claire was with us. In there," cried Lola. "Only she didn't run when we had the chance. She'd been going on and on about Brian the whole way there. She became too hopeful. She wasn't thinking straight…"

"What happened to her?"

"I called for her," said Lola. "But she didn't run. She looked straight at me, then slipped into the facility through the opened door. Just walked right inside…"

Billy just listened. He pictured Claire—meek little doe-eyed Claire—stepping hopefully and willingly back toward her death. He hung onto the words, not just for the images they held, but for the way they were delivered. Short. Choppy. Labored breaths.

"We ran," said Tommy. "Rufus ran too. Hobbled is more like it. Whimpered as he did. But he still ran."

Billy looked at Rufus and saw that his paw had morphed into a lumpy, soggy mess. Dried blood still caked the edges of his mouth.

"We wouldn't have gotten out of there without him," said Lola. "He saved us more than once." Billy noticed she wasn't looking at him.

"We ran," continued Tommy. "And then Lola couldn't run anymore. Couldn't catch her breath. Said her heart was beating too fast."

"It's OK now," she said, her gaze still averted. "Better."

A lie, thought Billy.

Knew Billy.

"Has it happened before?"

She pinched her teeth and shook her head. He believed her grimace.

"It's late," said Billy.

They moved along at a slow pace, stopping often for breaks. For Rufus, said Billy, which the others seemed to accept.

IT WAS NEARLY CURFEW by the time they returned. By then Darrow had become privy to their defiance, and the participants were called into his office the moment they returned.

Darrow sat on the desk looking down at them, his stare icy cool.

"You leave as four members and one dog," said Darrow.

The group held silent.

"You return as three members and half a dog."

Again the group held silent.

The meeting wasn't a long one. His anger was transparent, so few words were necessary. Tommy, who bore the brunt of the blame, was to have his rations cut. Lola, given the emergence of a heart malady, was from that moment forward restricted solely to labor within the House of Darrow and tending to The Progeny. As for the Lab, they would heal him as best they could, but it would be largely left to nature and time.

The reproaches seemed to end there. Billy was left unscathed, benefiting either from a reserve of goodwill, or Darrow's appreciation of his limited role in the affair.

They would never see Bing or Claire again, nor would they ever visit the facility again. "They will pay in other ways," said Darrow, "they all will."

Billy believed him, his thoughts turning inescapably to the man who'd maimed George; the man with one corkscrew and no eyes.

They were preparing to leave when Darrow spoke once more, his final words of the evening, uttered beneath his breath and as much to the wall as to anyone. "And further treason will be dealt with harshly."

Billy believed those words, too.

THE CROSSROADS LESS TRAVELED

PERHAPS IT WAS A result of the previous night's actions, or perhaps it had been coming all the same. Whichever the case, Chester announced the following morning that the sentries would not only rotate twice per day, but they would now carry a password. The password would be known only to Darrow and to those to whom it was distributed, which meant, effectively, that members could no longer leave the House of Darrow without his blessing.

When a few individuals bemoaned the loss of their freedom, Darrow told them that it was now a time of war and, as such, individual liberties must be curtailed for the greater good. He also reminded them of the ninth tenet, and any voices of disaffection were squelched as soon as they were raised.

Billy and Lola had talked through the night, whispering, for the first time, of desertion. Neither could predict what the consequences might be if they were caught, yet Lola was undeterred.

"It's not safe here anymore," she'd said.

"No," agreed Billy.

"Not for us. And not for Sam."

"No," said Billy. He tried to blind himself to what she was alluding to, but Lola quickly removed any doubt.

"I won't leave here without Sam."

Billy hadn't immediately answered. She'd whispered it directly into his ear but still it was far too loud. He'd perked his ears up and listened to the healthy snores all around him, responding only once he was satisfied everyone around him was quite surely asleep.

"It's not our child to take."

"Sam doesn't belong here."

"You mean 'The Progeny.'" Billy corrected.

"I don't like that name," she said.

"No," said Billy.

It was all they'd say on the subject that night, but it would weigh on Billy from that moment onward. The fact was that the walls were crumbling all around them, but Billy wouldn't leave without Lola, and she without Sam—a simple but untenable calculation.

As it was, Sam was likely even less safe than Lola realized. Billy had seen the look in Marlon's eyes each time he looked at Darrow's child—a slight shift of brows and mouth, the embryonic stage of the scorn that he once held for Jacob. The look sharpened each time Darrow publicly trumpeted Sam as his heir; a plotting telling look that could never be exposed or proven.

Still, Billy couldn't fathom abducting The Progeny. Nor could he imagine how far they would get if they tried. As it was, it was all he could do to keep his mind from the looming bloodshed.

It was those same doubts that spurred him into Darrow's office the following morning, where he tentatively expressed his hesitation about committing acts of violence.

"I have some reservations," admitted Billy. His head was cloudy after very little sleep.

"I'm surprised to hear this," said Darrow. "With all that we've been through, how can your blood not boil?"

"This time is long overdue," added Marlon, also in the room. "So long we've sat back, meek like sheep. I've assured Him that if Jacob had been aware of the horror taking place in the facility, he too would finally have embraced this path."

Billy didn't believe that. Not for one second.

"Maybe you're right," he said, queasily.

With Marlon's help, Darrow had constructed Jacob's posthumous blessing to proceed to war. But to what end? Did they really hope to "defeat" the city? What would that even mean? What would it even look like? Billy then noticed Marlon staring at him. Jacob's fatal plummet arced through his mind, and he decided not to voice any further objection.

He had started for the door when Darrow stopped him. "Don't worry yourself, young Billy. You'll rise to the occasion when the moment is at hand. All individuals merely need the proper motivation. Once you discover yours, the desire for retribution will come naturally."

"I understand," said Billy. "I guess I just haven't found mine yet."

"Nevertheless," added Darrow, "I am counting on you to perform ably in the missions ahead of us."

"I understand," Billy said once more, then excused himself from the room.

Darrow and Marlon remained. They met at length that day before emerging to announce the organization's first wartime campaign: *Operation Overpass.*

A simple plan: They would position themselves atop highway overpasses around the city to drop stones and rocks—the largest they could collect—onto the roadways below. This would hopefully throw the drivers off course, crash in their windshields, and cause all manner of accidents. They were told to aim for the newest, shiniest, and most luxurious looking cars.

Chester announced ten teams of four, with each group assigned to a major overpass. They were to act quickly, cause whatever havoc they could, then immediately make their escape.

All chosen members seemed genuinely excited about being selected for the mission—except for Billy, who faked his enthusiasm, and Tommy, who asked to be excused by reason of illness. Darrow acceded to his request, but had good reason to doubt Tommy's candor. It wasn't just his defiance in taking Bing and Claire to the facility; Tommy had recently been put in charge of meal distribution, and it wasn't long into his shift before one of the well-to-do members caught him providing equal food shares to Gerry, a very likable member, but one hobbled by both a limped step and stuttered tongue. Tommy was also seen doing the same for some of the sick, and a few of the lowly riff-raff.

The information had quickly gone to Darrow. When called into the office and charged with the allegation, Tommy apparently hadn't denied it. "The problem," he'd said, "is that all food looks the same to me."

Tommy was immediately pulled from the position and replaced with another. This didn't dissuade Tommy from doing what he could to help those less fortunate, such as donating portions of his own food, or swapping a high-end cut of meat for a piece of cheap bologna, as he'd seen Jacob himself do many times. And while a handful of other privileged members had also taken to sharing their food with the downtrodden, unlike Jacob and Tommy, they seemingly did so only in return of favor—be it labor, sexual, or whatever sacrifice of energy or dignity the subject was willing to offer.

For this first wartime mission, Billy was assigned to lead a foursome composed of himself, Ash, and two newcomers named Carl and Trevor. Darrow was either unaware of the icy disconnect between Billy and Ash, or else he simply didn't care. All forty mission participants, armed with the current password, immediately filtered out onto the streets through the various sentry points.

Billy's team soon found their intended destination: a downtown overpass that cut across a major eight-lane highway. They arrived shortly before rush hour, the time during which they could expect heavy, yet free-flowing traffic.

The overpass road itself was fairly wide: two lanes running in each direction, with a median in between and a sidewalk on each side. The stretch of highway below them had four lanes running in each direction. Billy and Carl took up a position on one side of the overpass directly over the eastbound lanes; Ash and Trevor on the opposite sidewalk, overlooking the westbound lanes. They waited some time, to allow the other teams to take up their respective positions, the attacks to be as synchronized as possible. In the meantime, Trevor stepped to a nearby hill to cut their symbol into the grass. The others loitered, trying their best to look inconspicuous.

Each had now gathered a pile of rocks and stones. Ash and Trevor were particularly fortunate, finding some larger pieces of debris lying about on the sidewalk, including a few clumps of brick and an empty beer bottle that someone had set down precipitously close to the ledge. By then Trevor had finished marking the grass. He and Ash were already looking anxiously to Billy for the signal.

Billy looked down at the cars roaring by, hoping for some sort of congestion or gridlock, but the traffic ran quick and smooth. He looked into the car windows fifteen feet below him. They whizzed by one by one, but not so fast that he couldn't make out some of the faces in the windows. Men. Women. Children. Elderly.

Happy. Alive. Blissfully unaware of the cruel intent from above.

By then Carl had also turned to him. "Billy?"

He didn't answer. Instead he reached out and touched one of the stones, almost petting it. His sweat dampened the rock as he turned to see all three staring at him, looking for the signal.

He heard Darrow's voice. *Further treason will be dealt with harshly...*

Lola.

Harshly…

He gave it.

Carl immediately pushed a large stone from the overpass ledge. It narrowly missed the head of a motorcycle driver and ticked harmlessly off the pavement below.

Billy studied the stream of traffic, watching car after car fly past. He too pushed several rocks off the overpass, but only off to the side, or when there was a sizeable gap in the procession.

On the other side of the road, Ash and Trevor tossed whatever debris they had at their disposal. Ash managed to hit the windshield of one car, and though the rock cracked the front glass into something of a spider web, it did no more damage than that. Trevor only hit the top of a minivan, the effect negligible. However, their actions hadn't gone unnoticed. Some of the drivers were changing lanes. Others honked their horns.

Billy flung his last stone. He saw Carl do the same, a clear miss to the left of a speeding yellow coupe.

"I didn't hit anything," said Billy.

"Me neither," said Carl, genuine in his lament.

Once there was a sufficient break in the traffic, they crossed the street and joined their two colleagues, arriving just as Trevor pushed the bottle over the ledge, lining it up perfectly with an oncoming vehicle.

It happened so fast. The driver appeared not to notice the tumbling object until the last moment, when he instinctively veered into the right lane. His vehicle clipped the front left bumper of the second vehicle, which sent the target vehicle hurtling off to the right. Billy lost sight of it, then heard the piercing sound of crushed metal and shattered glass.

"We got one!" yelled Ash. He jumped into the air.

They could no longer see the car from their position, its having crashed almost directly beneath them into one of the concrete pillars.

Just then Ash turned to him and cheered, "Billy, we did it!"

As Ash stood there, his mouth gaping open, Billy instantly knew that the "we" wasn't just meant for him and Trevor, but he was sharing the praise among all of them, those who he'd so often failed to impress. And Billy knew in that look, that look of pure and honest joy, and of indescribable relief, that Ash had not sabotaged him at the gallery. From the light in Ash's eyes it was clear that it was not a lack of being earnest that had resulted in the mayhem or Cecil's capture, but at most a failing of courage or ability. His role in that evening's failure had likely cut him as much as it did Billy; the reason behind his increasingly surly nature being his raw desperation to be liked, respected, and valued. And Billy could tell, by his quick turn to him, and by the unbridled elation in his voice, that it may have been Billy's opinion that he had valued above all, and any hardness that Billy had felt for his salt-and-pepper-haired colleague fell instantly away with that return of brightness that had so faded with the seasons. It had always been there, blotted out behind a black hole of self-doubt. Only now he'd been released, as if he'd been holding his breath the entirety of these last months, and the instant before he was set to burst, was finally permitted to exhale. To be liked. And in that moment Billy did like him, very much, but pitied him all the more.

Ash was waiting for a response much in the same way that Rufus awaited the delivery of his next meal. Finally Billy obliged him. "Yes, Ash," he said softly, "we did it."

The affirmation on Ash's face was electric. Yet at what price had it come? Billy could already smell the stench of burnt rubber, could see the thick billows of smoke wafting past the overpass and navigating their way toward the clouds above them.

Ash and the others had quickly made their way to the end of the overpass. "C'mon Billy, c'mon!" called Ash.

Billy followed, reluctantly, and they tumbled partway down the hill to get a better look at the carnage.

It was a pitiful scene. Various liquids dripped from the twisted metal carcass, smoke billowed from the crumpled hood. Billy watched the frantic movements—cars pulling over, people rushing to assist. A small plush toy lay miserably on its side, soaked now with oil and carburetor fluid. There was no sound or movement from the wrecked vehicle.

"The city is going to burst!" screamed Ash.

Billy, already exhausted, now felt nauseous. "We have to leave," he said, trying to hold his breath against the smoke and chemicals permeating the air.

"Look at 'em scramble," said Ash.

"Ash, we need to leave," repeated Billy, having already taken several steps back.

Still Ash didn't budge, not even when several police cruisers pulled up to the scene. Not even as a witness approached one of the officers, first pointing up at the overpass, then emphatically to the foursome on the hill. The officer had taken only a single step in their direction before Billy commanded them to run, and run they did—all but Ash—back up the hill and onto the overpass sidewalk. All three darted across the road, weaving their way through a stream of cars, and several times coming within a whisker of being pummeled by the oncoming traffic. Only Ash remained behind. Staring down the police officer. Taunting him. Goading him.

Finally, once the man got too close, he absconded. He ran up the side of the hill and, seeing his friends already across the street, jumped immediately from the curb in an effort to join them.

"Tricky tri—" His sentence was cut short by a passing minivan. It launched him nearly a dozen feet through the air where he landed crumpled on the side of the road. The minivan slammed on its brakes and was in turn rear-ended by a sports car.

The driver of the minivan jumped from her car and ran to check on Ash's condition.

The driver of the sports car also jumped from his car and ran to Ash, but only after he first glanced over his shoulder, seemingly to survey the damage to his bumper.

Billy and the others looked on from the side of the road.

Ash was still, exhibiting that same peculiar stillness that Billy had seen in Chuck, and Jacob, and the blue jay. And though they couldn't say for certain that he was dead, they ran at the first arriving siren.

IT WAS A HEAVY walk back to the House of Darrow, Billy's mind shifting back and forth between the limp carcasses they'd left behind them: both steel and flesh. All horribly shattered. But mostly he thought of Ash, of how he'd gained him and lost him and, in the course of the last hour, had gained him and lost him once again.

Things were unraveling, Billy thought—if they'd ever been raveled at all—and they were unraveling quickly. They learned, upon returning, that Ash wasn't the only member who'd failed to return. They'd also lost Christian who, leaning too far over the right ledge, had slipped and fallen to the highway. If the impact of falling thirty feet to concrete hadn't immediately killed him, the tractor-trailer that "picked him up" certainly had. Yet in all, their casualties were viewed as unexceptional.

"I'd actually expected more losses," Darrow said plainly.

And what did it matter? In the hours that followed their latest strike, twenty more came forward to join.

Operation Overpass was something of a tepid success. One of them had struck the driver of a convertible squarely in the forehead with a stone, surely resulting in a nasty goose egg, if not a concussion. There were also a smattering of fender bend-ers, likely resulting in assorted bumps and bruises, as well as lengthy backups and delays. Yet it was only Billy's group that had engineered the type of truly spectacular crash that Darrow had envisioned. Nevertheless, never to be dissuaded by the facts, Darrow declared their first wartime campaign to be a "resounding victory." He immediately tasked a member to add Trevor's name to the Wall of Valor, he who had launched the lucky bottle. It was only after a solemn walk across the compound floor, and a spirited urging from Billy, that Darrow directed Ash's name be immortalized as well.

As was customary after their victories, there was instant celebration, the House's joy unimpeded by the loss of two members or the pain of their victims. They'd recaptured their swagger, their mirth manifesting in song and dance.

With the commencement of the war, Darrow had even requisitioned the creation of a battle hymn. It now rang jubilantly from the members:

> *Fight fight, make it right*
> *Darrow's guile will win the war*
> *Fight fight, make it right*
> *Darrow lifts us evermore*

Darrow took to the crate, lauding Billy and the rest for their contributions to a victorious mission. Billy accepted the praise, shuttling off to the side as soon as he could tear himself from the congratulatory gestures that swarmed him.

Despite this success, not everyone was happy. Gerry, he of the limped step and stuttered tongue, had attended Darrow's office shortly after his victory speech to complain about the state of affairs down in the tracks, where the conditions continued to worsen by the hour. Billy came upon him as he was hobbling angrily away.

"You OK?"

"N...n...not so much."

"The leg?" asked Billy.

"It's n...not just that. The t...t...tracks."

"Mm-hmm?"

Billy realized that Gerry had recently lost his spot in the caboose and been demoted down to the tracks. He guessed it the moment Gerry got within two feet of him, from the potpourri of filth and urine and desperation that now clung to him as it did to so many of their disadvantaged members. As Gerry told it, the problem wasn't just the dirt and the dampness. Rats had become a growing problem.

"C…c…can't k…kill 'em fast enough. We k…k…kill one, th… three more pop up in its p…place."

"I'm sorry," said Billy, through a modicum of embarrassment. He, of course, had always enjoyed a spot in the lead car.

Just then a member firmly entrenched in the lead railcar sauntered into the conversation to congratulate Billy on the mission. Billy thanked him, then filled him in on Gerry's problem, the member keeping back a noticeable distance.

"Have you talked to Darrow?" he asked.

Gerry rolled his eyes, then explained to them both how he'd gone to see Darrow, but had been quickly turned away. Apparently two members of the lead railcar had arrived just ahead of him. They were complaining about the previous night's serving of prime rib.

"I c…could hear one s…saying his p…portion wasn't quite as b…big as th…the other's," said Gerry. "It's just n…not fair."

"You're right," said the other, "that doesn't seem fair at all," only Billy couldn't tell if they were, in fact, agreeing about the same thing.

Billy extricated himself from the conversation, only to be immediately intercepted by Tommy, who asked to speak to him in private. His red hair appeared ruffled, his green eyes frustrated.

Given how congested it was on the platform floor, they stepped down into the tracks and walked toward the end of the defunct shaft in order to secure some small modicum of privacy. As they made their way, they were forced to step around some of the members who'd been banished to live there, in what had become openly known among the members as "the ghetto."

It was dirty and smelly down on the tracks, so they hastened their pace, clambering over some of the loosely scattered widgets that had been ground into the rocky surface. Some had been recently discarded from the three railcars, their previous owners having grown bored with them, or weary of their presence, or both.

As they walked, Billy noted resentful looks from a handful of the perpetually downtrodden, including Fat Henry, who had by then lost even his modest accommodation within the caboose. It was something of a rarity for those above to descend freely into the ghetto. Lola sometimes did, to assist the needy as she could, as did Helena, who'd rebounded slightly from the loss of her sister, in part by passing her time sifting through the dirt and rescuing some of the abandoned widgets, and even encouraging others to do the same, though only to limited success.

Billy also noticed Kinsly, slunk down on the ground near the billet of fresh earth that entombed The Progeny's defective sibling, a rat poking around near his feet, to which Kinsly seemed indifferent. He'd never recovered from what he'd seen at the facility. Billy had even pinched him some of the good stuff, but it hadn't helped, and Kinsly had finally evicted himself down into the tracks, to wallow in perpetuity.

Billy and Tommy finally arrived to the end of the defunct track, where it dead-ended into rubble. It was dark and quiet. Billy sat down on a large piece of rock.

"I'm gravely concerned…" said Tommy.

Billy remained silent. He'd seen this coming ever since Jacob died. Tommy had become increasingly vocal and defiant.

"…and I believe you are, too," he added.

Took too many chances.

Billy angled his head down.

"He's changed," said Tommy.

"It's dangerous to be saying this stuff."

"Maybe, but I'm sure you feel the same way. I'm sure that I can trust you."

"Trust me?" asked Billy. "What are you saying?"

"I'm saying that Darrow has things all twisted up. It's bad enough that he tolerates horrid unfairness..." Billy watched Tommy's eyes move past him and travel down the tracks, where he stared thoughtfully for several seconds before continuing. "...Now the violence. He's lost focus. The trajectory we're on can't be sustained. We're putting out fire with gasoline. This is only the first day of this so-called war, and already we've lost two of our own. Many more are likely to die, and on both sides."

Billy had entertained these same thoughts. Had started to chafe against the hypocrisy of it all. They were trampling on the sanctity of life in order to convince people that the sanctity of life should go untrampled; their means and ends were fundamentally incompatible. Yet somehow it made sense to them, or at least didn't sufficiently lack sense to dissuade them. Billy himself lived in something of a glass house. Maybe not with respect to the violence—he abhorred it as Tommy did—but with respect to the growing inequality amongst them. Billy continued to rest his own head in the lead railcar and feast on the better fare. He'd even secured some of these same benefits for Lola, notwithstanding her physical limitations, and that her contributions were perceived as slight, beyond tending to Sam. Yet any feelings of hypocrisy and self-loathing he might have felt hadn't inspired Billy to forsake those luxuries.

"It's madness," continued Tommy. "I don't believe this is just about change anymore. He's lost all sight of right and wrong, and has become just as dangerous as the people who oppress us. With each new member to our community, his head grows further from his feet. Something must be done about him."

Just hearing those words sent a shiver down Billy's spine.

Something must be done about him.

Billy instinctively looked over his shoulder to ensure that nobody had wandered close enough to hear.

They were alone. And safe—for now.

He turned back to Tommy. Steeling himself, he whispered, "What are you saying? That we should try to overthrow him?"

Tommy sidestepped directness. "I don't know what I'm saying. Not exactly. I just know that it can't go on this way much longer. I know things wouldn't have gone this way had Derek and Jacob still been with us. He's going to ruin everything that we've worked for."

Tommy's voice was trembling, and Billy's mood was such that he hardly noticed the mention of Derek, the member that none were to speak of. It had been so long since he'd heard the name that he'd finally resigned himself to the secrecy of it. "What are you suggesting?"

Tommy's voice softened in response. "Again, I don't exactly know, but I'm sure there's more than one way to skin him. He's been challenged once before."

"By you?"

"No, not me. But the right time will surface, eventually, and when it does we have to act."

Billy remained noncommittal. "Why don't we just leave?"

"If we have to, but even that carries risk," said Tommy. "But we also helped create this. We're responsible as much as he is. If we cut and run now, what does that say about us? What do we stand for?"

Self-preservation? thought Billy.

A sad, almost tortured look swept across Tommy's face. "We had only the best intentions…"

I know, thought Billy.

Said Billy.

Tommy's look changed again. His lips poured out the unexpected. "How did Jacob really die?"

The question came out of nowhere, and it hurt Billy to even hear it. To hear Tommy's voice crack under the weight of it. To crack under the weight of suspicion.

Billy knew exactly how Jacob died, and he knew exactly why he died. He was killed for his beliefs, for his stubborn commitment to equality and to peace. He was killed in that sick and twisted paradox.

"He lost his footing on loose cinder," replied Billy, weakly, to which Tommy nodded, before setting heavily back down the tracks.

It took remarkable courage for Tommy to suggest what he did, and more than a pinch of recklessness. But Billy felt he was right—believed now more than ever that violence wasn't the answer. Darrow had to go, or else they did.

And then the most terrifying thought of all flashed into Billy's mind, one that he hadn't truly allowed himself to consider. At least not since he'd said it to Jacob all those days ago. That perhaps they were the naïve ones; that perhaps he and Jacob and Tommy had it all wrong.

That maybe, just maybe, Marlon's way had been the right way all along.

20

WITH BURROWED VOWS AND FURROWED BROWS

THREE WEEKS HAD PASSED since the execution of Operation Overpass. Three weeks since Tommy had drawn Billy down the tunnel and bared his soul to insurrection. They'd met several times since, their meetings always short and secretive. They'd debated how they might turn things around and steer the House of Darrow back to a path of sanity. Each meeting saw Billy on edge, apprehensive that they were being watched, terrified of having their true motives decoded from afar.

"The right moment will come," promised Tommy.

What that would entail—be it words or wounds—he wouldn't or couldn't say. Neither Billy nor Tommy, in any of their meetings, had explicitly suggested violence. And if either was thinking it, neither would let it out of the bag. Each knew Jacob wouldn't have approved of force and understood, without saying it, the hypocrisy of such means. Still, each time they met, the specter of violence always waltzed between them. It reached out its hand to Billy: Forward, right. Step. Step. Step. Darrow's words echoed out of the quarter turn: Further treason will be dealt with harshly.

Tandem disengaged. Dance over.

So their meetings always concluded the same way: with no concrete plan to move against him. For now, they'd simply agreed to manipulate what they could from within, to sabotage

Darrow's designs where possible. With that commitment alone, Billy was frantic. He no longer knew what Darrow was capable of. Had no clear vision of his limits. The unpredictability froze him and begged him to conform.

Tommy wasn't the only danger. If the waltz of insurrection had Billy's right ear, abduction whispered in his left. Lola had become increasingly vocal about stealing away with The Progeny, so much so that on at least two occasions Billy had spoken over the remainder of her sentence to drown out her words, fearing that others were listening.

And so it was some relief, several weeks later, that Darrow had ordered no further violence. All the while Billy had been hoping for some change from society that would sate Darrow's fury and render treason or escape unnecessary.

"Surely," Darrow had said, "our message has been clear."

"Surely," he'd said, "society now knows what we are capable of!"

Yet still, even three weeks later, nothing had changed.

It was Friday. Billy was out with Ears when they passed by Molly Clowder's, a popular Irish pub. A generous wooden patio encased the restaurant, Harry Chapin washing softly over the customers from several discreetly placed speakers.

"You smell that?" asked Ears. Billy nodded, having already detected the sweet fragrance of beef potpie baked in Guinness gravy.

The lyrics waxed poetic about Little Boy Blue and the Man in the Moon as Ears veered from Billy and stepped onto the sidewalk.

"Where are you going?"

He didn't answer. As Ears was sometimes prone to do, as he did when he first caught Billy peeking in on their hideout, he acted on impulse. The front door of the pub was wedged open, the hostess occupied.

"I'll be right back."

Billy called after him, but it made no difference, and soon

enough Ears had made his way through the door and toward the smell of his lunch.

It was the briefest of visits. The publican, a broom clenched in his meaty right hand, soon cast him out, as if Ears were no better than some verminous critter one might find scurrying about in the kitchen pantry. He even made a little joke of it for the patrons, bowing to mild applause. The indignity of it.

The utter indignity.

Ears, a proud individual, tried vainly to slough it off. "It was too stuffy in there anyway," he said, yet Billy could see through his thin façade.

They were still standing on the sidewalk when one of the female patrons exited the restaurant. She was clad in some sort of leather ensemble, like something Julie Newmar would have worn cavorting with Batman. She fiddled with some electronic gadget before tossing it nonchalantly into her svelte leather handbag, then hailed an approaching taxi. Billy looked to her, then, subconsciously channeling Marlon, offered a heartfelt: "I am the same as you."

Of course, he knew that wasn't the case—at least not literally—but the words tumbled out naturally, and before he could give them much thought. Though in reality, he was more right than he was wrong. While all lives might be like snowflakes, each harboring its own unique set of traits and eccentricities, they were, Billy increasingly felt, fundamentally all the same.

I can think, and feel, and hurt, just like you.

But the woman didn't notice him, at least not until he repeated himself, at which point she looked over and offered a slight curl of the lips. The lazy gesture mixed pity with compassion, but it was all she was prepared to offer, quickly stepping into the waiting cab and peeling away.

And so it was, with the stench of unleaded exhaust and beef potpie in their faces, that they slowly made their way back to the House of Darrow.

"Tonight we are going to kill someone!"

They were the first words Billy heard after stepping through the gravelly tunnel. Marlon was standing high atop the wooden crate, Darrow on the ground beside him, Totter planted at his side like a sycophantic gargoyle. Nearly a hundred members splayed out on the floor in rapt attention.

Applause blossomed at Marlon's feet. He trumpeted the phrase once more, eliciting several chants of the battle hymn.

By then Billy and Ears had filtered into the crowd. As they listened to Marlon's speech, it became evident that there'd been no break in the war effort, Darrow and Marlon having merely used the time to conduct surveillance. Dozens of members had been scouting for "indignities," then compiling and analyzing the information in an effort to identify something flagrant.

"Then we saw it!" yelled Marlon.

They listened as he described a homeless war veteran, a gaunt, shivering man begging helplessly for change. Person after person walked past him, dismissing him. Some even teased him or gestured rudely.

With so many of their own kind in distress, Billy found it strange that Marlon would take such a distinct interest in this person—his only proffered explanation being "we are the same as him," before reciting the fourth tenet.

Perhaps Marlon saw something in the veteran's plight with which he identified. Perhaps the stale smell of death that cloaked him was pleasing to Marlon's nostrils. Whatever the reason, the dishonor he'd identified had sufficiently infuriated him that it had spawned their second wartime mission: *Alleyway Attack*.

Billy eyed Lola in the crowd and saw a stunned silence on her face. He quickly scanned for Tommy.

Nowhere.

Rufus had snaked through the mob to rub up against him.

Billy hardly felt it. His ears had commandeered him, detached him from his body. He hung onto the continuing details.

Marlon would lead seven others on the mission, including Little Lizzy—the baby-faced arrival who'd been gnawing on the pepperoni stick. Only she wasn't as young as she appeared. It was something rarely seen in their kind, as street hardship tended to accelerate the aging process. Billy had learned that she was older than he, but she appeared significantly younger, as if she might have snuck into Dorian Gray's attic and absconded with his magic canvas.

Her behavior was erratic. Sometimes she'd float about the platform, twirling and singing to herself, particularly after nipping a generous dose of the weed. Other times she'd isolate herself in silence or tears. Still other times she'd seek out Darrow to show her gratitude, which had manifested in a series of brief nocturnal visits to his office.

There was also a marked cruelty about her. On two occasions Billy had watched her mechanically pulling the wings off a fly as it tried desperately to escape, releasing it only once it was fully defrocked. She would then watch the fly crawl frantically around, hopelessly confused to its newfound reality. She'd laugh, even bat it around and giggle. On both occasions Billy had come forward to step on the maimed creatures.

"Why'd you do that?" she'd asked the first time.

"To put it out of its misery."

"It was just a fly," she'd said.

"Why were you doing that to it?"

"Because it was fun," said Lizzy.

"Not so much fun for the fly," said Billy.

"Get over yourself."

"Tell me why it was fun," pressed Billy, but by then she'd simply walked away.

The fact was that Billy knew why she did it, why the strong harmed the weak. There was a sick sense of empowerment, a feeling of control over another entity, an act of weak self-esteem that only reinforced that weakness. A weakness of the soul. Jacob had told him that. And he was right; he had always been right.

Marlon concluded the announcement; and for the first time he could recall, Billy was left off a significant assignment. He joined Lola as the crowd dispersed. Again he looked for Tommy, trying to remember the last time he saw him.

"Have you seen Tommy?"

Lola shook her head. "Maybe he's out?"

"Maybe," said Billy, though he was already considering the worst; was thinking of Jacob's frantic plunge from the rooftop and of Derek's unexplained disappearance.

"We can't lose him, too," said Billy. He noticed some true be-lievers passing by and didn't say anything further. Lola matched his silence and waited for the others to pass before motioning with her eyes toward the exit, the serviceman's flat cap still lean-ing limp against the side.

"We can't leave," he answered.

"Why not?"

"It's broad daylight. Even if we got past the sentry..."

Lola just stared at him.

"They're going to murder someone," said Billy.

"*We...*" said Lola. "...you mean *we* are going to murder someone."

Billy tried to concentrate, begging his mind to reveal options. Nothing came to him. He thought of Jacob and Tommy and tried to envision what they would do in his place.

He'd only just posed the question when he abandoned Lola where she stood and sprinted to Darrow's office, where he begged to be included in such an important mission.

Darrow applauded his motivation, immediately making him the ninth member of the mission.

THEY ARRIVED WITHIN THE hour.

It was a shopping district, with this waif of a man decorating the sidewalk, just as Marlon had described. He was draped in weather-beaten clothes, with a mutt sleeping at his side and an upside down baseball cap next to a cardboard sign that read: **Veteran—Please Help** in thick black marker. Some change lay strewn in or about his cap, maybe enough for a tuna sandwich and a can of Alpo.

Billy walked to within a few feet of him. The man smelled even worse than his canine companion, and though it was obvious he could use some money, Billy himself had none to give, so it was an impasse.

Gray stubble backdropped the man's bushy Jim-Hunter-style mustache, and despite the fall chill in the air, he wore just a raggedy green T-shirt exposing two bare arms littered with tattoos. One inked creation showed the face of a soldier, perhaps himself, sporting a shit-eating Cheshire grin—though any such smile had long since departed his actual face, and his tattoos were now as faded and worn as his humor.

The man looked up as Billy walked past him. His stare was blank and cold.

Once he was a soldier. Now he was a vagrant.

Billy was a vagrant. Now he was a soldier.

So went the ebb and flow of things, and Billy couldn't help but think of how his own contributions had led to his being there in that moment. Not the formation of the group—that ship had sailed long before he met Ash—but for his role in its uncharted expansion. He thought of his initiation, and how some of the windswept urine flicked back onto his leg, an acceptable side dish to his own birth from the womb of isolated irrelevance. He thought of the shattered car glass, and the art house paint that stained his nails purple, and of the smell of electrocuted flesh.

And he thought of how he originally appraised Marlon's tenacity, so admiring him in the beginning, so wishing that he himself could harvest just a fraction of Marlon's fiery courage. And he thought of how he now loathed him, and everything that he represented.

Marlon led Billy and Sherman into an alley across the street. The other six, including Lizzy, he'd already deposited in the alley where the deed would be done.

Billy followed Marlon into the passage to discover a "Darrow Knows" etched prominently inside. He'd been seeing it everywhere by then—on the sides of buildings, in doorways, on the side of a dumpster. Their symbol, too—carved with flair and determination, was turning up in all shapes and sizes on every surface imaginable.

They looked across the street, where a bank snuggled between an ice cream shop on the left and a shoe store on the right. The homeless man was slumped down against the corner of the shoe store.

Immediately next to the ice cream shop was the alleyway, full of boxes, garbage cans and other indefinable clutter. The others had already taken up veiled positions, as if they were playing a game of hide and seek. Only two members were visible from their position: Little Lizzy, who was loitering nonchalantly at the mouth of the alley picking at her nails, and a second member who could be seen feverishly scratching their symbol onto the wall.

"Look how they all walk by him," said Marlon, his gaze fixed on the homeless veteran. "Disgusting."

Yes, thought Billy.

Said Billy.

"Disgusting," Sherman parroted. He had a way of gnashing his teeth together when he got excited, as he was doing now. Sherman, who'd been rescued during Tommy's doomed return to the facility, had turned out just as Billy had feared: every bit as angry as Marlon, and with a cruelty to match. The composition of their team was no accident. Marlon had selected the most ambitious and merciless members, those who would have no qualms about participating in what was to come.

Marlon had told them what they would see if the pattern held true: a cocky Bigwig would appear, walking hand in hand with his young daughter. Fancy suit, soft leather shoes, a shiny briefcase that looked worthy of carrying the king's papers. He would wave dismissively at the homeless man, or increase his pace as he passed by him. Only that wasn't the end of it. He'd stop, not ten feet from the man, to hand his daughter some money. He'd see her safely inside the ice cream shop before whisking himself into the bank, where he'd exit five minutes later stuffing a fresh wad of cash into his billfold.

Each Friday it was the same. Only this time, the man in the suit would have a chance to do what was right. He would be the master of his own fate, said Marlon. For if on this day he finally chose to contribute something to the man's overturned cap, or even passed him a smile or a kind word, he would be spared the great torment that was to come. But if he walked past the man with the same cruel indifference, the same dismissive gestures, or simply ignored him altogether, then he would suffer the consequences.

Such nonsense, thought Billy; such sick and twisted self-righteous arrogance.

But they meant it. Every single word.

Then they saw him. Billy could tell by the glint in Marlon's eyes and the slow rising gnash of Sherman's teeth.

"He's big…" said Billy.

"Yes," said Marlon.

"He'll give us all we can handle…"

"Yes," repeated Marlon.

"How will we get him into the alley?" asked Billy.

No answer.

He'd spoken briefly with Lola in the minutes before he left. Neither had a clue how he might disrupt it, Lola half-occupied with her anger at Billy for volunteering. As much as she understood his reasons, maybe even knew he was right, much like Billy knew Jacob was right when he killed the blue jay.

"C'mon…" said Marlon. "C'mon…c'mon…"

Billy watched as the man and his daughter approached the soiled vagrant. The girl was smiling, her blonde hair bouncing in pigtails behind her, a small cartoon pin of Thing 1 and Thing 2 affixed to her fashionable blue-striped dress. She couldn't have been much older than the strawberry-smelling girl in the park with the bologna sandwich and the ladybugged toes.

Drop something in the hat!

Billy held his breath as he watched the exchange. The cap was extended, shaken.

Then the Bigwig—head extended, head shaken.

The gnash of Sherman's teeth grating in Billy's ears.

It happened just as they expected. The man watched his daughter safely inside the ice cream shop before he sauntered into the bank, his perfectly manicured fingers cradling his billfold.

It had even riled Billy by that point. Not sufficiently to endorse what was about to be done, but sufficient enough to scuff the original sheen of sympathy he'd held for the man.

"He'll come out in five minutes," said Marlon.

"Mm-hmm," said Billy, preparing for the wait, and relieved that he'd have at least five more minutes to consider his options.

He wondered what they would do once the man exited the bank, wondered how they possibly hoped to cajole him into the alley. He also wondered why Lizzy had just walked to the front of the ice cream shop with a predatory look on her face. "What is she doing?"

Marlon didn't answer.

They watched the young girl take a seat by the window, ice cream in hand. As the girl looked out, she saw Lizzy looking up at her. Gone was the predatory look as she reached up and playfully tapped the glass that separated them. It was only once the girl smiled that the horror of what was about to happen truly registered with Billy. It was almost too wild to comprehend.

"The girl..." said Billy, to no one in particular.

Again no answer. Just the gnash of Sherman's teeth and the familiar glint in Marlon's eye, only now it held a depth of sorrow. It had half-displaced Marlon from the present, and Billy knew instantly that he was thinking of his sister—of her cold body on cold pavement. And even in that moment, in that horrifying revenge-fueled moment, Billy found a place of sympathy for his black-haired general that he never could have imagined existed.

Lizzy tapped the glass separating her from the girl, then danced playfully from view. Billy watched the girl press her face up to the window. Then, as they'd hoped, she exited the store with waffle cone in hand, velvety pistachio brimming over the top.

"She's just a baby," managed Billy, but again Marlon didn't respond, just watched Lizzy linger at the entrance of the alleyway, no more than a dozen feet from the front door of the ice cream shop. She made eye contact with the curious young girl and called out in her most innocent voice. Billy could barely hear it from his position across the street. But he heard enough: It was light, playful. The same voice she'd used with the flies.

The girl smiled, then watched as Lizzy sauntered out of sight and into the alley. Only the girl didn't follow. Instead she looked over to the bank, then back to where Lizzy had disappeared.

Lizzy waited a few seconds, peeked her head out, called to the girl, then fell back inside. The girl didn't move, but she watched as Lizzy poked her head out a second time. The girl could no longer resist. She trotted over to the entrance and saw Lizzy now ten feet inside the alleyway, calling for her. The girl looked back toward the bank for her father. Billy watched from across the street, imagining the gears clicking and whirring in the girl's mind. She was curious. She wanted to make a new friend. And Lizzy. So inviting. So harmless.

Lizzy backed up playfully. And then, finally, the girl stepped into the alley.

The city is going to burst!

"Don't go in there!"

Billy wanted to shout it but the words wouldn't come. He berated himself for being such a coward. He didn't know how to disrupt Marlon's plan, at least not without exposing himself. All he knew was that it was about to happen.

It was happening right now!

The girl giggled and wandered inside. By then the ice cream had started to melt and was dripping over her small bony knuckles, Lizzy just a few feet away.

Turn around, you stupid girl!

Children. So trusting. So naïve.

Leave her alone.

Billy looked hopefully at the bank doors for her father—to holler for their retreat—but there was no sign of him. He considered shouting anyway, making something up. Only Marlon and Sherman held the same vantage point and would surely expose such an obvious lie.

The child stepped deeper into the alley.

LEAVE HER ALONE!! Billy's internal scream was deafening.

She'd made it fifteen feet—offered her ice cream cone to Lizzy for a bite—and they were on her. She didn't cry out immediately, just dropped to the ground and curled up in the fetal position. She tried to scream as the blows descended upon her, but one of the attackers reached for her mouth, so she clamped it shut.

Billy could no longer see her, the attackers' having pushed her behind a large garbage can. He looked for anyone walking by who might be able to see or hear what was going on. Nobody noticed. Each second felt an eternity.

"I'm going in," said Marlon. "You two stay here. Watch for the father."

The sympathy of a moment ago was gone. The scar on Marlon's neck called to Billy; he wanted to lunge for it, to open it full and red, then scream for help in the alley. Instead Billy just nodded, trying desperately to conceal the horror on his face as he watched Marlon set off across the street, leaving Billy alone with Sherman. There they waited, Billy's body numb, his mind murky.

They'd be beating down on her. Clothing ripped. Flesh torn.

The city...

She will not survive this, thought Billy.

...*going to burst.*

Still no sign of her father.

She won't survive.

No authority figure.

She will absolutely not survive!

"We're all clear here," said Billy. "Let's go get a piece of this."

He tried his best to sound brazen, not confident that his tone hid his true intent, or even that the words had all come out. Still Billy had no plan—just to move.

Sherman was ecstatic as they set out to join their colleagues, following close at Billy's side as they ran across the street, narrowly missing cars that honked their displeasure.

Think!...*So many mindless zombies...*

Think!...*That bumper barely missed me...*

Think!...*Sherman right beside me...*

Thi...

It came to him just as they ran into the alley. Billy maneuvered sharply in front of Sherman, tripping him into the large steel garbage can that blocked the brutal attack from the street. He fell into the can with most of his body weight. It rocked to the left, then back to the right...slowly...slowly tipping. The refuse inside the can shifted, and it finally tumbled over with an incredible racket. The lid flew off and saucered on the ground, the can rolling meekly to the side. Sherman leapt up, shooting daggers in Billy's direction.

The clamor was enough. A woman on the street looked in toward the source of commotion and saw the swarm. By then it was difficult to make out the victim—at first just an indistinguishable lump, then the outline of a girl. She was motionless, her hair disheveled, her dress torn and stained red. Directly in front of her was a fallen ice cream cone, cool milky green melting into a warm pool of blood.

The sidewalk scream was bloodcurdling. It brought several pedestrians running into the alley, Marlon and the rest already retreating out the rear through the planned escape route. The people did their best to catch them, but all nine were able to skirt away to freedom.

They ran for blocks, most of them with unabashedly joyous looks plastered on their faces. As they ran, Marlon quipped how "the fabric looks better that way." It triggered Billy's memory. Something that Jacob had once told him; Marlon's savage comment the impetus for its sudden recall…

The fabric of our society needs mending.

It was one of the first things Jacob had ever said to him, always as fancifully announced as it was accurate. But what they'd done wasn't an alteration Jacob ever would have condoned.

Billy couldn't be sure if the girl was alive, but he thought he saw her move, just slightly, before they ran. He'd given her a chance, at least.

Big freaking hero.

They stopped to catch their breath at the base of a multi-level parking garage. It was the end of the workday, the lot still littered with cars, the attendant too far away to notice the small gathering on level one.

Billy looked at Marlon, at the blood on his face that wasn't his own. He seemed set to talk when Billy preempted him. In a loud whisper he laid into Sherman, castigating him for his negligence. Sherman was dumbstruck but stood there and took it. After a while Marlon joined in berating his young protégé. Finally Sherman forced a half-hearted apology, one eye drawn on Billy.

"Why were you two even there?" demanded Marlon.

"We were just about out of time," said Billy.

We weren't.

"And," he added, "I was hoping to get a shot or two in for myself."

I wasn't.

Marlon seemed to accept this. "You two nearly blew the plan, but I like your initiative." He looked at Billy and smiled. "And you...I really didn't think you had it in you."

I didn't.

Despite being cut short, their mission was deemed a success. The girl did not move, Billy assured them, which meant that she was quite surely dead. Since he was the last to see her, they were satisfied that she'd been slain.

Upon their return to the House of Darrow, news of their success spread like wildfire.

It was a small comfort for Billy to find Tommy alive and well upon his return. He'd merely been out on a mission, just as Lola had suggested.

Darrow jumped upon the wooden crate to laud the victory. This assault upon innocence, Darrow said, would send their clearest message yet. That nobody in society was safe from their wrath. That they were all collaborators!

Darrow promised a more complete victory speech later that evening, then ordered Marlon and Lizzy's names to be etched immediately into the Wall of Valor.

The few who questioned the morality of what they'd done were quickly booed back to silence by the lustful majority—all, that is, but Tommy, who was horrified by what they'd done and stubbornly professed the young girl's innocence.

288| M. P. Michaud

Darrow responded fiercely: "Innocence and guilt are never absolute; they're always just a matter of degree," then added, "and don't forget, once fully bloomed, she would have become just like all the rest. We merely caught her at an early stage of her development." Most of the group agreed, and Tommy, with reluctance, sank back into silence.

Billy watched the attackers clean the blood from their bodies. Listened as Lizzy griped about a broken nail, bemoaning how it disfigured her appearance. She then quipped, to no one in particular, that "Eating ice cream can be dangerous to your health." Billy gritted his teeth. He stepped toward her before he heard his name called aloud, careening his neck to the left.

Darrow and Marlon, just in front of the hallway.

They stood firm as they beckoned him over, and as Billy stepped tentatively toward them he noticed Sherman gossiping with several others. He was too far away to make out the words, but close enough to see Sherman eyeing his movements, tracking him intently.

"Enter," said Darrow. He and Marlon stopped at the doorway, waiting for Billy to enter ahead of them. He stepped slowly inside and they followed suit, with Marlon planting himself between Billy and the doorway. Darrow stood off to the side of the desk in silence.

Billy glanced right and saw Marlon staring back at him. His features appeared even harder than when they first met, the thick scar running down the front of his neck somehow more sinister.

"I was just told about what happened in the alley," said Darrow.

Billy looked forward and swallowed hard. Wondered if he could make it to the tunnel if he ran. Wondered if he could even get past Marlon.

Maybe.

If I surprised him.

Bolted.

Abandoned Lola. Abandoned everyone, like he should have done all those days ago when he had the chance.

Billy looked right again, to Marlon, a wall between Billy and his freedom—an angry, vicious, scar-adorned wall. On his way in he'd scanned the immediate area for any allies. There were none. Only Lyle, slunk over on his side asleep in front of Darrow's office.

Billy swallowed again. Looked Darrow in the eyes, then finally said, "I can explain…"

He blurted it out before thinking, immediately regretting his choice of words.

I can explain? Explain WHAT exactly?

He watched Darrow's mouth, his jaw climbing up and down, only Billy couldn't hear the words. His fear had risen up from his belly through his neck and swelled into his head where it had plugged his ears.

He could feel Marlon shifting behind him. Stepping closer.

Further treason will be dealt with harshly.

He felt the walls closing in around him.

Harshly.

Billy curled his toes and readied himself.

"That won't be necessary," Darrow responded. "Marlon has already explained things to me."

Darrow asked him to clarify what Sherman had done.

What *Sherman* had done.

Of the negligence that exposed them. The lump dwindled away, ran and hid behind his good fortune. The situation as originally misdiagnosed as his launch from the beanbag.

Only a debriefing.

Billy swallowed a third time, this time the saliva flooding back to his mouth. He then described how Sherman had clumsily run into the garbage can and alerted the public. He didn't care what punishment might befall Sherman, felt no regret, only the searing rush of self-preservation.

"Very good," said Darrow. "Then he will be dealt with accordingly. We cannot let negligence go unpunished." He nodded Billy away.

As it turned out, Sherman's punishment was some additional work and a loss of rations.

It was no small thing.

Rations among the House had become an increasingly valuable commodity. Billy had just left Darrow's office when he overheard two of the downtrodden debating the subject.

"I've heard that Darrow plans to sh…shrink our allotments again," said Gerry.

"That can't be right, I can't believe He would do that," responded the other, a recent arrival to the group.

"It's t…true, I overheard him myself," persisted Gerry. "I heard it's only a matter of t…time now."

"I see," said the other, his tone now dour with acceptance. "I didn't think he would do that."

Two others, mainstays of the caboose, could be heard lamenting the unequal distribution of labor. "Darrow has been working me like a dog lately," said the first, showing his blistered feet.

"Me too," nodded the second. "It's not becoming."

Hearing these exchanges, Billy desperately missed Jacob—their advocate, his friend. The pin to Darrow's grenade. It made Billy think of their conversations, of the time he'd asked Jacob how people could possibly be content with so much suffering in the world.

"Look at all these people that could help us," said Billy.

"Yes," responded Jacob.

"They could help us so easily."

"They could."

"But they don't."

"Most don't," agreed Jacob.

"It makes me so angry."

"Try not to be," said Jacob. "Most people think we're equipped to help ourselves if we choose to."

"Or else they just don't care," said Billy.

"Or that," said Jacob. "Only they might finally care, if they truly understood the scope of the problem. Recognized that it's their neglect, their customs and habits that put us here."

"And until they do?"

"We disturb the soil," said Jacob.

And disturb it they had—with most of the clan, it seemed, content even with their present form of cultivation. Content still with Darrow himself, the madness and the hypocrisy notwithstanding.

Particularly faithful to their leader were the inhabitants assigned to the first two railcars, as they increasingly credited him with forging the comfortable life they now enjoyed—although occupancy within the second car had shrunk once again, after another hard rainfall had caused further structural damage. Some of the residents in the first two cars even exhibited a slight malaise toward the cause, perhaps having become too comfortable, and having lost a few shards of their original motivation.

As for the embattled underprivileged, they still clung to the faint hope that this was all just a temporary transitional period, especially as Darrow continued to print verbal currency of imminent social change, with most too desperate for him to be right to acknowledge the scrip may be counterfeit. They were also cautiously bolstered by the latest results from the Equality Committee, the announcement recently delivered following the panel's two-hour luncheon.

Though they remained spectacularly inconclusive, the committee had finally agreed on what was meant by the phrase "consistent with," then spent the rest of their meeting trying to lock down precise definitions for "dispersed" and "allotted." After coming to something of a consensus on the definition of those two words, a quorum put it all together and concluded that there *may* be discrepancies that cannot be accounted for in the tenets;

however, they couldn't agree on the extent of any unfairness, should there in fact be any, and they adjourned several more weeks to further consider the issue.

In the meantime, songs were sung about the girl in the blue-striped dress—her being a symbol for their imminent victory. They also shouted the battle hymn at every available opportunity:

> *Fight fight, make it right*
> *Darrow's guile will win the war*
> *Fight fight, make it right*
> *Darrow lifts us evermore*

Billy hardly involved himself in the festivities, only going through the motions so as not to arouse suspicion. The House of Darrow seemed despotic to him now, the cries of The Progeny just shrill reminders of newly created life juxtaposed with an organization hell-bent on taking it.

He, like Tommy, couldn't fathom what had just been done to the young girl. The image of her battered and bloodied body was now burned in his memory beside that of Chuck's smoldering corpse and Jacob's frantic plunge from the rooftop. He'd had enough pain, enough death. Enough ill-gotten glory.

He'd simply had enough.

As promised, Darrow addressed the group with a formal victory speech that evening. From atop his wooden crate, he proudly trumpeted their recent victories in both Operation Overpass and Alleyway Attack, confidently proclaiming they were winning their war against society.

Most cheered. Some started chanting the battle hymn while others danced. Darrow stood back and absorbed it, letting them run through the hymn a full three times. Finally, he resumed his oratory, and their singing faded to listening.

"We have now given them two opportunities to do what is

right. How many more die is entirely up to them!" His demeanor was charged and erratic. He seemed high as a kite, likely having just nipped a generous portion of the weed.

Once more they started into the battle hymn. The atmosphere was frenetic, and they repeated four full verses before he managed to quiet them.

"Again we will wait and look for signs of improvement, some indication that our lives are valued and respected equally to their own. Should they remain complacent, they will suffer the direst of consequences. The next mission will be extreme in nature, it will be all-out warfare, and there will be blood and char on the floor. Some of us will face capture, some will be injured, some may not survive, yet the cause will remain ever strong. That time will come very soon, and when it does, are you with me?"

The marionettes expressed their raucous approval, whipping themselves into a frenzy—screaming, cheering, and applauding his every word. Darrow could announce his intention to stuff them into a cannon and most would not only agree, but would fight to be the first stuffed down the barrel. Their loyalty had gone far beyond what Billy could ever have envisioned. Ironically, even most of the downtrodden rallied exuberantly to Darrow, despite his wretched treatment of them, thoroughly convinced that the present machinery represented their only real chance for change.

Darrow continued to incite them. "Kill or be killed!" he challenged. "It is us against them. Do you want to be killed? Do you want your brothers and sisters to be killed? The Progeny? Should we lie down and choose death?"

The crowd roared a communal, "No!"

Billy looked over to Lola, wishing that she'd never come. That she'd never become mixed up in the quagmire they were now forced to navigate. Then he noticed Tommy out of the corner of his eye. His gaze was desperate. Billy stared sharply back.

Not yet…

294| M. P. Michaud

In those few seconds, they seemingly had a full conversation with only their eyes and some slightly nuanced gestures. Billy could see it plastered all over Tommy's face. The thought of the girl weighed heavily on him. It had compromised his judgment.

The timing isn't right, insisted Billy.

Tommy turned away, his face swelled by disappointment.

Darrow thundered on, the mob transfixed beneath his feet, their wounded souls the blank canvas upon which he would paint his desired scene of retribution. He assured them that their next attack would involve mass casualties and damage. That it would affect dozens, if not hundreds, of Bigwigs.

"And soon!" he shouted. "Very soon, the people will know *my* glory!"

His speech had reached a fever pitch when it was suddenly interrupted by a shout from the gallery. One of the minions had dared to speak up…in opposition.

It was Tommy.

"Stop, everyone, please," he begged.

Celebration spun into confusion. Fervor bent to puzzlement. Darrow, briefly stunned into silence, quickly recovered his voice…

"Who interrupts Darrow?" he screamed. It was the first time Billy had heard Darrow refer to himself in the third person.

"This is wrong," howled Tommy, walking forward to the front of the mob, stopping at the base of the wooden crate. He turned to face them, his back to Darrow. "This is wrong. If we follow this path, we're only sealing our own fates. As it stands, we may have already gone too far."

Some of the group started to hiss and jeer. Tommy fought through their discontent, past Darrow's simmering umbrage.

"No, no, listen to me. Listen to me!" he yelled. "If we continue this way, then we will surely lose. If we continue to shed blood to force their awareness, we'll lose all sympathy. Then what will we have? We won't be pitied, but feared. We won't be helped, but hunted. We won't be lauded, but denounced. We won't receive aid, but scorn. This madness won't help our cause. Remember the teachings of Jacob!"

The hisses and jeers gave way to silence. Billy held his breath at the stillness. They seemed to be thinking of Jacob and considering Tommy's words. Billy looked hard to Lola, as if asking for permission. He watched her struggle with it, before rolling her head into a reluctant nod.

Billy inhaled deeply, trying to think what he could say that could move the masses. He took a nervous step forward, preparing to add his voice to Tommy's, but lost his nerve as the room was reclaimed by a thunderous voice.

"Insolent fool!" screamed Darrow, his thick jowls pinched by rancor. "It's that very belief that has us where we are today—that silent pacifism and naïve acquiescence. So blood is not the answer, my brothers and sisters? Then should we again take to the streets? Sit on corners and beg for scraps while the people around us live and dine in luxury? As our own lives are dismissed with such ease? Is that what you want?"

A soft murmur rose in the crowd.

"We've survived this far," pressed Tommy, "without the need to resort to bloodshed. Our small acts were enough. We just need to maintain that course. Things will start to change. In time, they will start to understand. I promise you. What we are doing now is wrong. Ask yourselves what, and who, you are fighting for. It's not too late to correct ourselves. With this path, we're just begging for the needle!"

"They'd give us the damn needle anyway!" yelled someone from the gallery. Several others shrieked their agreement.

Tommy looked out toward the stunned populace. "Look at what we've become! Is this the life that you want? To live and die for him? Please listen to me, before it's too late!"

Pockets of silence crept into the group, particularly among their weakest subjects. There were looks of confusion on many faces.

Gerry began to nod in agreement with Tommy, as did several others. Billy just watched.

"No!" screamed Darrow, his voice flush with anger. "You listen to *me*. The needle, you say? It is but one mechanism they might use to silence us. They'd just as soon run us down like dogs in the streets, only then they'd have to clean our blood from their tires! We have tried being conscientious objectors. Stay meek and invisible, and they will allow us just enough space to live and die in squalor. They'll allow us only those scraps of food they don't covet. They will endure trifling annoyance and crime just so long as we remain invisible and don't interfere with their decadence. It is our complacency that they want. It is our complacency that they *need!* It keeps them from having to embrace real and substantive change. I know that now more than ever!"

"But change *will* come. It has to. We just need to continue to press our message, but without violence. The change will come." Tommy turned back to the group. "I'm begging you…"

"He begs you toward death, my children," countered Darrow. "He begs you to lie down and die!"

More confused mutters. They grew louder and louder, and before long, even most of their weaker members had been herded back toward the majority, their voices raised but trembling. Marlon started into the battle hymn. Others joined, softly at first.

"Yes, my soldiers," Darrow continued, overtop the growing chant, "change will come. Change will come because we are going to make it come. We are going to shake them out of their ignorance. We are going to dismember their sick social structure, and through their pain, they will find an awakening."

He turned to Tommy, bloodlust in his eyes. "This one…he is not one of us. He is a traitor, sent here to trick us and to divide us. He's no doubt receiving a warm blanket and some fresh cuts of meat in return for this betrayal. They are more scared than ever, and this agent they've sent is proof of that fear. He is an imposter, aligned with those who seek to bind us in despair. Darrow will not allow that to happen!"

Billy watched Darrow jump from the crate and kick Tommy in his side, the dissenter sent sprawling. He watched as Tommy was attacked, as Marlon looked on with delight, as Sherman gnashed his teeth. Watched without stir as Rufus whimpered beside him, his eyes swollen and fixed on Billy, imploring him to stop it. But by then Billy was already back in his tree—frozen, throat tightened. He tried to move but his legs wouldn't allow it, tried to speak but his mouth wouldn't cooperate.

"I'm a coward," said Billy, to muteness.

"Yes, you are," said the fireman.

He stood frozen. On the branch, on the compound floor. His eyes stuck wide in fear as Darrow landed a blow to the side of Tommy's head, bursting open his ear. Tommy struggled to his feet and backed up, dazed. Somehow he managed to stay on his feet and tried again to address the mob, but the crowd angrily drowned him out.

"Imposter!" proclaimed Darrow. "He was sent to destroy us. To destroy everything we've worked for and stand for! To undo all that we have created! He is an agent of decadence! He must himself be destroyed. Destroy him, my children. Destroy him!"

Billy saw the eyes of those around him: empty, cold, desperate, afraid. Saw the others swarm around Tommy as terror enveloped him. Heard Lola scream from somewhere behind him as Tommy spun around to find some avenue of escape.

Surrounded.

Tommy beseeched them to get back, but they herded around him. He screamed for them to stay back as they descended upon him, Rufus barking wildly in the background. Tommy shrieked like a wounded animal—a shriek of stark and primal horror. It didn't last long, and he was swiftly torn apart by the mob. His bloody corpse, barely recognizable once they'd finished, was dragged through the tunnel and dumped at the end of the defunct tracks. The rats would dispose of what was left.

Billy had closed his eyes for the last of it, shutting himself away into darkness, yet his other senses wouldn't surrender so easily. He heard it—softly at first, then with increasing volume. It was the battle hymn ringing out.

Virtually all were chanting in unison:

> *Fight fight, make it right*
> *Darrow's guile will win the war*
> *Fight fight, make it right*
> *Darrow lifts us evermore*

He heard his mother's voice denouncing him. Shaming him for his cowardice, for bending again to his fear, for not adding his voice to Tommy's, as Jacob surely would have done. Even Gerry had hobbled over to intervene, but others had held him back.

He finally opened his eyes and watched several females clean up the bloody mess on the ground. There were tufts of red hair made redder still by blood. He recalled Tommy's words: *Things wouldn't have gone this way had Derek and Jacob still been with us.* And so he pained for Jacob, and Tommy, and even Derek, though he'd never met him. Then he immediately abandoned all thought of insurrection, Tommy's ill-fated overtures dutifully serving as his canary in the coal mine, and surely serving to stifle even the bravest conscientious objectors.

Rufus had slunk off to the side and was now baying hopelessly at the grates above. Billy remained where he was until Lola cried out and stirred him to movement. He floated to her position and buried his head in her side. Sam wailed, though most of the mob was dancing, singing of the war and the defeat of the traitor Tommy.

Billy listened to the macabre stanzas and agonized over his cowardice. He begged Lola's forgiveness.

She gave it. "We'll get out of this," she said. Short. Simple. Confident, misplaced or not. It was exactly what he needed to hear. He loved her for that.

Slowly he regained his composure and felt the blood return to his extremities. Thoughts and emotions swirled in his mind, but he came quickly and gently to a decision. He leaned in toward Lola and whispered softly in her ear.

She listened intently, quickly nodding in agreement.

THREE CHARACTERS IN
SEARCH OF AN EXIT

THEY SANG AND DANCED deep into the night, united in fear and frenzy. Their individuality disintegrated under the hope of imminent emancipation.˙

As usual, the unity was short lived. Discord began the following morning, when a small segment of confused members gathered outside Darrow's office…for had they not just harmed one of their own?

Darrow eased their minds by reminding them that Tommy was, in fact, a spy and a traitor. Since Tommy had merely been posing as a member, the eighth tenet had not been broken at all. As always, Darrow also reminded them of the ninth tenet. Most of the naysayers seemed not only satisfied with this explanation, but positively relieved. They apologized for burdening him with their confusion, repeated the ninth tenet aloud, and thanked him for his clarity.

There was, however, an increased misery among their weak, particularly those subject to the crudest and harshest conditions. Another of their sick passed away that day, and several inhabitants of the ghetto alleged that his death was directly linked to a lack of proper sustenance, and to sleeping every night down in the cold, drafty tracks. There was even a small uprising, which was put down fiercely by Sherman and several others. The rest of the ghetto quickly fell back in line, though some only through clenched teeth.

And so went their wretched masses, riddled with discontent, their patience atrophied by a creeping awareness that their lot might not, in fact, ever take a turn for the better; so they remained toiling in the muck, where even the widgets seemed restless.

In an effort to stem similar revolts, Darrow sent Totter into the ghetto to placate their disenchanted demographic. Totter quickly reminded them that their friends above were doing their very best to win this war. In the meantime, he suggested they embrace the wonderful power of Joy Transference.

One member of the ghetto stepped forward. "So you say that we should be happy because we are all friends, and we should be happy to see our friends happy, is that right?"

"Yes, of course that is the case. You do understand now, don't you? Of course you do," responded Totter. "That is the simple beauty of Joy Transference. Embrace it and make it your own!"

"Then what about Misery Transference?" asked the questioner, trying his best to outwit Totter. "Since we're all friends here, and joy is transferred to us when our friends are happy, then I suppose all of you must be miserable, seeing all of us so miserable down here?"

"Well that is certainly a peculiar question," answered Totter. "Misery Transference? I'm sure I've never heard of it, but yes, of course we would feel sadness and misery if we were to see our friends in the tracks unhappy, if, in fact, there was any unhappiness there. But then, of course, we are all friends. Don't you agree? Of course you do! You had just said we are all friends. Admitted it, hadn't you? Yes, I see you don't deny this. And clearly, you wish to see your friends persevere, do you not?"

The would-be rebel admitted, with some hesitation, that he did indeed wish to see his friends persevere.

"So then, if any of you are unhappy—which I can't understand myself—but if any of you are, in fact, unhappy, and noticeably so, then this will be obvious to the those above, do you agree?"

He agreed. It should be obvious to the others that they were unhappy.

"Well then, there you have it. If you say it is so obvious that some of you are unhappy, then I agree that the others must feel some level of misery, in seeing their friends in such an unhappy state. Yet they clearly persevere through this misery, and this perseverance, which would be as obvious to you as your original misery was to them, can only lift your spirits, can it not? Of course! And on seeing your friends persevere, through such pain and misery, clearly, you must take some joy from this? You said it yourself, just moments ago, that you wish to see your friends persevere. Surely you mean what you say, do you not? Yes, I see you nodding, of course you do. And then, in turn, seeing you joyful once more, from finding joy in their perseverance, your comrades above would in turn regain their own joy, seeing you happy once again. So then, this device of Misery Transference, as you call it—which is something I have never heard of, myself— is really just another form of Joy Transference, when properly broken down."

He had the member teeter-tottering about, along with several other members of the ghetto who'd been listening in on the conversation.

"And, of course," Totter concluded, "if you'd embraced Joy Transference from the start, and had not been so selfish with your thoughts, then you would have avoided becoming miserable in the first place."

Having convinced, confused, or simply worn down his counterpart in the conversation, the matter had concluded, and the ghetto went quiet once again.

Billy and Lola held no discussion of transference, or committees, or any other aspect of the House of Darrow, aside from the best avenue of escape. It was, they decided, the only palatable option. Tommy was right—they were all on a path to the needle.

They'd made their decision the previous night, whispering back and forth in cool, unfittingly calm conversations.

It would be no small task. Part of their compliance was having to live under the watchful eye of the sentries, whom Darrow relied on not only for protection, but also to control the members' movements. In fact, Darrow had recently expanded the number of sentries, which now included three new posts within the confines of the House of Darrow itself.

One sentry was now positioned at the door of Darrow's office, in order to regulate access, Darrow feeling it increasingly important he not be unnecessarily disturbed.

This was followed closely by the posting of sentries in front of two of the three railcars.

Apparently one of the downtrodden had, out of a momentary curiosity, stuck his head into the lead railcar—an act that had put off some of those inside, including several members of the Equality Committee. Soon enough, there was a sentry posted at the door to the first railcar to ensure entry only by those properly assigned.

Those in the second railcar soon asked for the same treatment, and though they felt slightly inferior to those in the first railcar, they felt sufficiently important to garner some level of security, and Darrow agreed.

Naturally, those in the caboose also decided they should have a sentry posted at their door, and though they felt themselves by then sufficiently inferior to those living in the first rail car, they felt not so far removed from those in the second. However, no sentry for the caboose had yet been granted, as on each occasion that members of the caboose waited at Darrow's office to plead their case, the office sentry told them that Darrow was busy, and to come back another day. Such had been the case now for several days.

The role of the sentries had also expanded, as the outer sentries, those posted above ground at all exit/entry points, were now under orders to turn away undesirables looking to join the movement. Where they'd previously allowed entry to all who wished to join, Darrow now sought to exclude any more riff-raff, their underclass already oversized. This could become awkward if two individuals arrived at the same time, as happened recently at sentry-point four.

"Hello, there," stated the first, a strong yet down-on-his-luck young male. "I hear this is the home of Darrow, and I've come to pledge my allegiance."

"You may proceed inside," responded the sentry, stepping aside as he entered.

"And I've come to do the same," said the second, hung with a shabby cough and even shabbier coat.

The sentry looked him up and down. "You may not proceed."

"I don't understand, isn't this the House of Darrow? You just told him that it was!"

"Whether it is or isn't is no longer your concern," responded the unflinching sentinel; and though the individual ultimately left of his own volition, the sentries had been told to use force if necessary.

Notwithstanding fear of reprisal, a small minority questioned whether this new approach was congruent with the tenets, for didn't the fourth tenet proudly proclaim that whoever lived in the street was a friend?

Darrow acted quickly to clear up any potential confusion, stating that he was indeed happy to hear they had so many friends in the city. "And they will continue to be our friends. Only they will be our friends...from a distance." He suggested that the House of Darrow could only accommodate so many, *and*, he pointed out, "there's simply no requirement that all friends need live together."

The doubters turned their eyes to the list of tenets, ultimately agreeing with Darrow that the tenets were silent on whether or not all friends need live together, and though most of them accepted his good wisdom and dropped the issue, there were still one or two puzzled stares.

The sentries, Billy thought, *would be a problem.*

"I could do it, I think, if it were just us," he said.

"We're taking Sam with us," said Lola.

"But if it were just the two of us…"

"We're taking Sam with us," she repeated.

By then Lola had developed a rather maternal commitment to her surrogate, lavishing Sam with the praise and affection that she'd seen dissipate in her own household. She hadn't transferred resentment—quite the opposite. She'd pledged to raise her de facto offspring the right way, not to be tempted away by a lure or cut bait when times got tough or inconvenient.

That Sam was "The Progeny" didn't seem to matter to her. Billy felt it was a mistake. Not only would the youngster slow them down, but Billy knew that the moment they were discovered, Sam's disappearance would bring Darrow's wrath unlike anything they'd seen. It would significantly undermine their chances of getting safely out of the city.

Still, she would hear none of it, and pressed him until he promised to get them all safely away, and promise he did. Only now they would have to wait for the perfect window of opportunity, hoping it would present itself soon, before they could be associated with any further violence.

They'd agreed, with some reluctance, not to inform any of the others, even those who might be allies such as George, Ears, or Helena. Billy wouldn't risk seeing them undone, as Tommy had been, or risk getting turned in for treason, if the others' loyalty to Darrow were to supersede their friendship to him.

In the meantime they went about their duties, trying their best to blend in and function as normal. Lola always inside, tending to Sam. Billy above ground to scour for food or supplies—the latter, in recent days, focusing on all things flammable.

By then, the House of Darrow was more crowded than ever, and though an accurate tally was nearly impossible, word was that membership had now swelled past two hundred. The streetcars were full. The ghetto was full. The platform was crowded. The odor from the tracks was undeniable. The air had grown unbearably thin, the feeling claustrophobic. The House of Darrow was bursting at the seams, this despite continuing to turn away unsavory hopefuls, a policy that continued to chafe not only the turned out refugees, but some of their own. In fact, on that very day, one of the members was heard lamenting the unfairness of it all: "Death to decadence!" he shouted, before retiring to his spot in the lead railcar to feast on a steak dinner.

Always sensitive to the plight of the downtrodden, and reconsidering the true spirit of the fourth tenet—that whoever lives in the street is a friend—Darrow finally warmed to the idea that more could be done for their homeless comrades. Through Chester, he announced the formation of a new committee: the Relocation Committee, which would scout for and choose a location for a second residence, one for all of their homeless friends still out on the street.

When asked by some why it was to be called the "Relocation" Committee rather than simply the "New" Location Committee, Darrow wasn't immediately forthcoming. Nevertheless, someone close to Darrow soon leaked that his primary intention was, in fact, to relocate many of their existing underclass to this second residence.

It didn't take long for the Relocation Committee to spring into action, showing a zest for speedy resolution that had so far eluded the Equality Committee. They quickly located several promising possibilities, though none were within close proximity to the House of Darrow; in fact, the three potential residences were as far away from the House of Darrow as the city limits allowed.

A member from the ghetto had many questions. "Those locations are really far away, don't you think?"

"Yes, I'm truly sorry that we couldn't find anything closer," sympathized one member of the Relocation Committee.

"Well, where else did you look?"

"Nowhere."

After a stunned pause, the ghetto-dweller abandoned his remaining questions.

In the meantime, they continued with the same type of assignments. Groups were sent to look for open flames, loose candles, unattended lanterns, casually lit fire pits, open BBQs, and smoke from chimneys. Others were sent out to gather sticks and brush—whatever might be used as kindling, the dryer the better.

Then the day finally arrived. It was evening. Almost the entirety of their membership was present as Darrow stepped from his office. This time, rather than taking his normal position atop the wooden crate, Darrow stepped onto the rear of the caboose and scaled to the top. It wasn't such an easy ascension as it might have been in the past, and he visibly labored to reach its rusted rooftop.

Once above, he turned out to face his legions, allowing them time to murmur excitedly amongst themselves, with Darrow basking in the energy. After a few moments he started to speak, and the murmurs dissolved into silence.

"My friends, my children, my soldiers!" he proclaimed from atop his makeshift pulpit.

Again they cheered. He let them simmer a short while before continuing.

"As you are all aware, the House of Darrow has decisively won the first two campaigns in this war. This was only made possible by your bravery, your loyalty, your devotion to the cause…and your love of Darrow!"

Again they erupted at his burlesque display as savior.

"The time has now arrived for our next mission, our largest and most significant to date. It came to Darrow in a vision… and how fitting was this vision? For as we now start to feel a chill in the wind, and with colder times still ahead, I cannot help but wonder how so many of us freeze and shiver in the open air every year. Meanwhile, they have fire for light, and for warmth, and even for decoration. But do they share those flames with us? Do they consider how they might help us to stay warm? To keep us from freezing to death in the bitter cold?"

An emphatic "NO!" exploded from the mob below. They were riled up and boisterous.

Darrow joined them, his pitch rising, "No they do not, they most certainly do not!"

They started to cheer once more, and again he was forced to rein them in.

"And so, my children, it is time that we turn their minds to sharing. It is time that we teach these selfish people yet another hard lesson in selflessness. They hoard the heat and the warmth? Very well, then we will teach them to share those flames. And since they don't seem to understand how, we'll show them a few ways…won't we?"

He smiled with menace, his bravado smug and cocksure. The fanfare was nearly deafening as Darrow revealed his latest plan. It was exactly what Billy had been expecting—and dreading.

It would be called *Project Pyromania*. The Bigwigs hoard the warmth, so they will be tortured with that warmth. As usual, Darrow reveled in the poignancy. Somehow, it all made perfect sense to Darrow. Maybe it even made some small sense to Billy, though he felt there was a significant difference between failing to share your fire with a cold individual and starting a fire to exact revenge. It was action versus inaction, the subtle distinction seemingly lost on Darrow and his devotees.

Darrow outlined the details of Project Pyromania: They would wait for a cold dark night, when they could expect the most flames. Then, quite simply, they were to become fire starters. If they saw a flame, they were to tip it over. Knock it into something…*or onto someone!* Or throw something dry on top of it.

See candles in a restaurant window? Break into that restaurant and turn the candles over onto the table or patron, or fling them into the curtains. See lanterns hanging somewhere? Knock them down or tip a nearby tree branch into them. Black smoke bellowing from a chimney stack? Invade that home or business and share the blaze.

It would be an all-out blitz of the city, using their own flames against them. If society wasn't going to play fair, then Darrow was going to burn it down. If the people didn't respect all life, then neither would the members of the House of Darrow. And there was no doubt they could do it; in committing to violence, you require neither bomb nor dynamite—you need merely a limitless imagination and sufficient anger to override your scruples.

Again Billy heard Ash: *The city is going to burst!*

Giant plumes of smoke bellowing in the streets. People running and screaming. Pure and absolute mayhem.

Fall was well under way by then, and the attack could be launched at any time. Though most were wild with excitement, there were also a few looks of concern. Ears was the sole member brave enough to publicly voice his reservations, couching his words as deferentially as he could: "But Darrow, if our goal is to live among them as equals, where will we live after we've set the city on fire?"

Darrow chewed on that for a moment. He glanced to Marlon, then back to Ears, then briefly to Totter, and then again back to Ears. Finally he responded, quite calmly, "It does little good to get distracted by the minutiae."

This dismissive non-answer seemed to satisfy most, and the pre-pyro celebration roared onward.

Darrow had even commissioned a song in advance. It was immediately taught to the entire group, and they burst into the lyrics:

Seek flame, seek smoke, seek embers blue,

Billy watched, and he listened.

His vision's told us what to do.

To the songs. To the celebrations.

So here we come, To have some fun,
And kindly share your heat with you!

And he wondered what response from society might satisfy them. What concession or acknowledgment would be sufficient to give Darrow pause? He'd never actually defined any concrete objective, aside from ever-vague hyperbole, such as "ripping off the pestilent scab to allow a sick society to heal back healthy."

To Billy, Darrow had lost focus, just as Jacob and Tommy had feared. He had turned things ignobly personal. This either didn't occur to most of the members, or they simply didn't care. Perhaps all that mattered to them was the notion that change was afoot, and that they could truly assert themselves against high society. Even Chet—their nervous savant—had settled into a confident strut, droning repeatedly "by hook or by crook, they'll be shook 'til they look."

With most members chanting the battle hymn, Billy sequestered himself with Lola. "Tonight," he said softly into her ear. Lola acknowledged this with a nod, then squeezed Sam tight to her body.

Whether the group's actions were madness, necessary, or some hybrid of the two, Billy would no longer be involved. He would no longer be a willing party, participant, or conspirator to the pain and suffering that was to come.

"Don't worry," Lola whispered to Sam, "you're too young to ever get the needle."

They sat back and watched the members hop, skip, and carry on as though they weren't about to turn the city into a makeshift funeral pyre.

Billy wanted out. He wanted his old life back, the beautiful crippling loneliness that he'd left behind all those months ago.

No. Not that.

But not this. Definitely not this.

They continued to watch the celebrations, and in that moment, Billy couldn't help but feel pity for them. Not the truly evil ones like Marlon and Sherman and Lizzy, though even they were no doubt victims on some level, but for those beleaguered members that had turned to Darrow and vested in him their hopes of a better life. They were vulnerable and wounded. He'd promised them purpose and meaning, and they'd believed in him. Just as Billy had. And somewhere along the way of finding themselves, Billy felt they'd become more lost than ever before.

THE FESTIVITIES TAPERED OFF when Chester took to the crate and bellowed out the hierarchy for that evening's accommodations. The four outer sentry points (as well as the one posted at the waiting room) were up for a shift change; one by one, each fresh sentry was called into the office for his assigned post and the current password. Billy took a walk, examining who was posted where. He found a newbie named Felix at sentry point three, then returned and nestled up on the floor beside Lola, her trembling just slightly more pronounced than his own. "We'll leave from the third sentry point," he whispered.

"I understand."

"Do you remember what you have to do?"

She nodded.

"We can get through this," he said.

She didn't stir.

"We *will* get through this," he said.

She nodded again.

"What about Rufus?" she asked.

Billy looked over. Rufus was sleeping on Jacob's old bed, still holding vigil. His paw was only marginally healed. They hadn't discussed it. "We can't take him with us. Not how he is now with his paw."

"Will he be OK here?"

"He'll have to be," said Billy.

Hoped Billy.

"I see," she said, before adding, "it's almost curfew."

Billy nodded, the "it's time" unspoken but understood.

By then most of the membership had filtered into the subway cars or down onto the tracks for the night. Billy drew himself from Lola's side and headed toward Darrow's office, too focused to hear her "good luck."

He waited by the office door, face-to-face with the sentry governing access. He could hear Darrow talking with Gerry, the latter urging him to increase rations for those in the ghetto.

Gerry stood just a step or two inside the office door, as Darrow had recently enacted a policy whereby office visitors were to keep a healthy distance back from his desk. The basis for this, he claimed, was a superior conversational vantage point—though it was curious, from what Billy had seen, that Darrow seemed to only enforce this policy when the visitors were inhabitants of the ghetto or the caboose.

In Jacob's and Tommy's absence, Gerry had become the chief advocate for their weakest members, many of whom had re-signed themselves to the inequities of their community, content with their dissatisfaction, and were just happy not to have been relocated. Still, an undercurrent was fermenting in the ghetto, and it seemed that Joy Transference—despite Totter's passionate advocacy—failed to adequately lift their spirits for any sustained duration. Indeed, Totter—always seen to be purring this thing or that into Darrow's ear, or simply cozying up to Darrow's side—had garnered something of a mixed prestige among the membership. Their higher circles had come to embrace him as the unofficial ambassador of enlightenment, while the lesser lights seemed to hold him in a much different regard.

Hoping to avert another internal uprising, Gerry begged Darrow to reconsider their rations. However, the meeting ended with Gerry's limping away while regurgitating the ninth tenet.

"I... g... guess he'll see you now," Gerry muttered through a clenched jaw, and Billy immediately entered the office in his place, walked up to the desk, and hopped into one of the chairs. Darrow remained seated on top of the desk.

"Yes, my son?"

Darrow had since shifted away from using their actual names. Everyone was now merely "son," "daughter," "child," or "soldier."

"I'm excited about our next campaign," Billy said. His lies had started to sound, even to himself, quite convincing.

"It pleases me. You've served Darrow well."

Billy quickly spun a tale of how he'd observed some sort of public ceremony in a park this time last year. It involved many lanterns and torches, and he believed it would make a wonderful target for Project Pyromania. Truth be told, he had once observed such a ceremony, but he couldn't recall exactly when or where it occurred. Yet the fact that he had, in fact, seen something like this, lent a tone of credibility to his story. "I'd like to scout this target for you," he concluded.

Darrow considered this. "It's late."

"I'm wide awake," said Billy.

"Your devotion to Darrow reflects well on you."

"It keeps me going," said Billy.

"You may scout this target," said Darrow.

"Thank you."

"Just find a soldier to accompany you."

Billy froze, not having expecting this. He tried not to look alarmed. For a moment he stared straight ahead, thinking.

Nothing coming.

Well, not nothing, exactly. A thought: *Further treason will be dealt with harshly.*

"Yes, my child?"

Darrow's eyes bore through Billy, adding to the nervous glut in his mind, so Billy spit out the first thing that came to him. "If you let me do this on my own, it would be...an honor." Billy held his breath, feeling it was lame the moment he said it, then nervously watched as Darrow considered the matter.

"You may have that honor, my child."

Darrow gave him the current password. Billy stifled his relief, thanked him, and turned to exit.

"When next you return to the House of Darrow," he said, "come directly to see me."

I won't be coming back.

"I certainly will," said Billy, having cleared the first hurdle. The first of many.

He stepped from Darrow's office and past the sentry, nodding slightly to Lola as he did. Then, after a last long look toward the sleeping Rufus, made his way into the tunnel and up the tracks toward sentry point three.

Lola would immediately seek out Helena and tell her one of the newcomers was sick and confined to the waiting room, and that she was going to see what she could do to help. That Sam would be with her and it might be all night.

She can handle herself, thought Billy, as he made haste along the narrow ledge of the subway shaft.

He waited out of sight. There was Felix, dutifully standing guard at his assigned post, quite properly erect and taking his role very seriously. Billy held firm in the shadows. Waited. Waited. Waited.

Finally he heard the faint fall of footsteps behind him.

Billy spun around, his eyes too wide and with far too much alarm on his face.

Lola.

A deep exhale, then he motioned for her to stay back, and quickly stepped out from the darkness.

"Hey you," Billy yelled. Felix curled around, seemingly spooked. "You're Felix, right?" They had, in fact, met at least once before.

"Yeah."

"What in the world are you doing *here?*"

"I've been assigned to this sentry point," Felix replied, hesitantly.

"No, no, no," Billy exclaimed, as if one "no" would have been entirely insufficient. "You're supposed to be at sentry point *five*. I'm looking after sentry point three. I've just been a bit up the tunnel. It's lucky I wandered closer and noticed you. Actually, you're the lucky one—lucky *I* found you, and not Darrow or Marlon."

Felix appeared confused. "I don't understand. I'm sure He assigned me to this post. I've never even heard of a sentry point five."

Billy shook his head and muttered "Incredible" at his feet, purposely loud enough for Felix to hear. "The current password is *ignoranza*. Didn't Darrow give you that?"

"Yes, He did," Felix responded quickly.

"Well, I'm not going to report this to Darrow, but you have to get to sentry point five right now. This can't happen again. When you receive instructions, you must pay attention!"

Felix was deferential. Not any old member could have fooled him so completely, but this was Billy Tabbs, he of the Wall of Valor. With this built-in credibility, and the correct password to boot, Billy had Felix's head bobbing and nodding with his every word.

"I'm really sorry," he lamented yet again. "Please don't tell Darrow."

Billy nodded, then explained that the fifth sentry point, which had only recently been added to the rotation, was a spot four blocks up the street. He convinced Felix that it covered an important strategic intersection for this reason or that, and that he was to head there immediately to watch out for anything suspicious.

As Felix hurriedly left for his "proper" sentry point, he apologized once more, thanking Billy for his promise of discretion. Once he was sufficiently out of sight, Billy motioned Lola and Sam from the darkness—and with that, they were off.

They trod a path away from the sentries, their eyes peeled for any members they might come across. This seemed unlikely, considering the night's celebration had just finished, that it was now past curfew, and that night missions were rare. Of course, they had a plan if it happened. They would explain that Darrow wanted The Progeny taken to a neutral location, given the volatility of the current situation. Billy hoped that story, if necessary, would be sufficient.

It could work, thought Billy.

Doubted Billy.

A recent rainfall had left puddles strewn about the roadways; and only five minutes into their journey, Billy and Sam were splashed with muddy water by the inconsiderate tire of a passing car. Half-drenched, they moved off the road, and Billy took a few minutes to clean himself up. Lola did the same for Sam, before they plodded onward. And so they did, through the usual cacophony—those unremitting waves of bleating horns and purring electricity that now sounded almost musical, blending together in exquisite harmony, as if they'd been scored for this very moment, to announce their glorious departure.

Billy had hoped that the air would be a tonic for Lola; but she was still quick to tire, so they proceeded slowly, with Billy carrying Sam as much as possible to lighten her burden, despite her protestations. It wasn't long before he felt the tug of the tunnel behind him, the guilt of running out on his friends and shame for abandoning Rufus. Even shame for leaving the organization as it was, so sick and dysfunctional.

Billy's eyes then drifted to Sam, to this innocent cargo that weighted down already heavy footsteps. A self-imposed albatross set tight around their hearts and their necks, highlighting and flaunting their desertion. An act, above all else, that begged for them to be chased, caught, and punished. And for the first time in months, Billy could once again feel the paralyzing surge of Darrow's hot breath curling up over his left shoulder.

All it would take is the wrong member to notice Lola's or Sam's absence and to make the wrong inquiries. Lola's alibi to Helena might buy them some time if anyone came looking for them, but eventually it would become clear that Lola was no longer on the premises. That Sam was no longer on the premises. The same type of landmine would explode the moment the third sentry point was discovered vacant. Billy chastised himself for his inability to devise a better plan, something that would have returned Felix to his original post. Eventually the young sentry would be found and would reveal that it was Billy who misled him. Two and two would be put together.

Then the hunt.

The city was going to burst!

What was left of it, that is. Whatever hadn't been gouged out or spit on or shattered or set on fire. What was left would burst, and Billy and Lola along with it.

Lola?

He suddenly noticed she wasn't beside him, turned and saw her lagging behind, nearly immobile.

"I'm sorry," she said.

"It's beating fast again?"

She didn't answer.

"Let's take a break."

And they did. Only thirty minutes into their trip, tucking themselves into the mouth of a nearby alley.

It was as good a time as any. Queasiness had dogged Billy the last several blocks. It came upon him fully as soon as he stopped moving. He turned against the wall of the alley, his body tensed. A moment later he was violently retching phlegm and bile at the base of graffiti-stained brick. The nausea passed quickly, and

Billy heaved several relieved breaths, bile dripping from the side of his mouth, as he raised his head to the wall, coming face-to-face with a recently carved "Darrow Knows." It was somehow apropos to the moment, symbolic of their desperation, and he knew it was vital they press on. Yet one look at Lola and he immediately knew that they couldn't.

They rested for nearly twenty minutes before continuing.

TWO HOURS HAD PASSED, and the breaks for Lola had started to pile up.

Billy had considered sneaking them into the back of a truck and riding away to safety, only he couldn't be sure which truck, if any, would take them out of the city. It might just circle around and deposit them right back in the heart of the storm. They couldn't chance it. Only they weren't nearly far enough away.

They'd just passed a bus shelter, the glass partition defaced with an upside-down triangle and three beams shooting off from each side. Shortly before that, Billy had seen a city bus drive by with "Darrow Knows" scratched sloppily into its side panel. It emphasized Darrow's reach, the precariousness of their situation—and though each reminder gave strength to their legs, Lola would soon falter, forcing them to slow or stop altogether. It was worse than Billy had expected. Each time they stopped she apologized, and each time he assured her that it was fine, that they could break as often as she needed to; but even his finest performance didn't dupe her. He could tell on her face that she knew full well that she was jeopardizing their escape.

They sat in an alley, having still not traversed a third of the city.

Lola apologized between short breaths.

"We're doing fine," said Billy.

Lied Billy.

She smiled weakly, leaning back against the cool wall of an old brick building.

"You're not a good liar."

Billy didn't answer.

"It's OK. It's a good lie, as far as lies go," she said.

Again Billy didn't respond.

"I'm sorry," she said. "I didn't know it was this bad."

"No," said Billy.

"Maybe you could go on with Sam?"

"I'm not going to leave you behind."

"I don't feel very good."

"Then we wait," said Billy. "As long as you need."

"We're not far enough," said Lola.

"Do you want to go to your home, maybe?"

"We're too far from there."

"We don't have many options." He sorted through them in his mind, thinking that if they could only hide somewhere and rest for the night, she might be OK come morning.

Lola wouldn't allow it. Both knew Darrow well enough.

Darrow would put everything on hold to find them and recover The Progeny. Food, sleep, Project Pyromania, everything would take a backseat to finding the traitors who had affronted Darrow's greatness.

And so they rested, shorter than was safe for Lola but longer than was safe for all three. As soon as she felt marginally well enough, they set out at a slow but deliberate pace.

It was nearly dawn when they reached Chinatown, not much more than halfway through the city. Just beyond was a stretch of residential sprawl, then some industrial territory. Then freedom.

Lola hadn't had an attack in some time, Billy having carried Sam a good portion of their trip. She even seemed to be gaining strength as they went along. The pre-dawn streets were dark and quiet, and for the first time in their journey, Billy started to believe that their plan might actually work. The group rarely ventured out this far.

Lola looked stronger now. There was a stillness in the air, a soothing calmness in the first crack of morning light. It was then, for the first time, that he let the thought sink into his head: *We might just get through this, after all.*

His body now buzzed with a euphoria that he hadn't felt since his feet danced over urine and black enamel. He turned to smile at Lola, then glanced behind him; and there they were, as if waiting to spring forward the instant he let his guard down.

Two blocks back, running toward them, was Sherman.

"They've found us," he whispered. There was no need to whisper, only somehow he couldn't manage more volume, the moment having neutered his vocal cords. Lola screamed when she saw them. Sherman was flanked by two others. Their names didn't matter. Their intent mattered: pounding feet now earmarked for their throats.

Billy handed Sam to Lola, as if he were a sprinter handing off a slippery baton. He rediscovered his voice and yelled for her to run, which she did, but only after he repeated the command.

A wider crack of daylight slipped out from the horizon. Dawn creeping in to watch the spectacle.

Billy turned to face their pursuers, knowing it was a battle he couldn't win. Sherman alone would give him all that he could handle, and he'd be looking for payback.

Billy detected movement to his side—an Asian man.

"Please, help us!" begged Billy, but the man just stepped around him.

Billy braced himself, the trio just half a block away.

The first arrived. Billy sidestepped his swing and pushed him into a parked car, knocking the wind out of him and triggering the sedan's security alarm, the pulsing racket breathing life into several early-morning windows.

Sherman was immediately on him. They rolled around on the ground, grabbing and kicking at each other. Sherman tried for his eyes, but Billy was able to push him aside, then regained his footing and kicked Sherman in the ribs. It went that way for nearly a minute before they broke apart from one another, as if a ringside bell has just chimed out to signal a break in the action.

They prepared to square off again when Billy's concentration was broken by a scream from behind him. He stole a look up the street to see that Lola had been knocked to the ground; Sam was sprawled on the sidewalk crying. More heads bopped up in more lighted windows.

The distraction blinded Billy to the hard right that connected to his head. A cut opened above his left eye, blood streaming down his cheek. He managed to recover from the blow and pushed Sherman back, then turned and looked up the sidewalk toward Lola. An elderly woman had stepped from her front door. She took two brave steps toward the commotion, a broom in her shaky hand.

Billy had hardly taken a step before he was tackled from behind by Sherman. They jostled back and forth for what seemed to Billy like an eternity. He finally succeeded in pushing Sherman face-first into a pane of glass lying haphazardly among some garbage at the edge of a driveway. It shattered about him, and when Sherman emerged from the garbage, there was a long gash running down the left side of his face, bleeding profusely.

Billy managed another look up the sidewalk and saw Sherman's two soldiers forcing Lola away. She'd clawed one of them pretty well, evidenced by twin streams of blood running horizontally down his cheek. The old lady was screaming from the sidewalk, waving the broom over her head.

Billy heard the crunch of broken glass behind him, where Sherman stood angry and swollen.

"You caused this!" spat Sherman, a steady stream of blood seeping down his face from his unclotted wound, some flowing into his mouth and dripping from his chin, his plasma-coated words forming red bubbles at the seal of his lips.

Maybe he's right.

Sherman's words hit their mark, and in that frantic moment the blame game flashed through Billy's mind. Was this episode their fault for abducting The Progeny and reneging on their oath of allegiance? Was it Darrow and Marlon's fault for embracing the path of social Armageddon that had spurred their desertion? Or might all of this be the fault of society? A society that had long ago laid the seeds of discontent that had now blossomed ripe with desperation.

Then again, maybe there was enough blame for everyone.

Billy prepared to re-engage Sherman, confident now that he could subdue him, the large gash having already swelled up and closed off his left eye. Then, unexpectedly, Sherman's posture folded into fear and desperation. Billy hadn't seen that look on his face before. Sherman, who'd always exhibited an air of angry invincibility, suddenly turned and ran away—not toward his colleagues, but directly between the two nearest houses, drops of blood trailing behind him. He dashed swiftly into suburbia and was gone.

For a brief moment Billy thought fate had finally decided to cooperate. Only it wasn't to be. Billy had failed to appreciate the true cause of Sherman's flight until his own movements were halted by the firm hand of the state, grabbing his shoulder in a death grip. He'd been oblivious to the arrival of the two men who now dragged him to a waiting van.

"Get off me," Billy screamed. "They've got her!"

"Shut up."

He resisted with what little strength he had left. Useless.

He was manhandled into the back of the truck.

THWUMP!

The last thing he saw just before the door slammed shut was the old woman yelling for help, but he could already tell that it was too late.

Lola. Sam.

Already gone and out of sight.
He had failed them.
And he had failed himself.

THE MINUTES DRIP AWAY like raindrops, and Lambert finally pulls himself away from the scribblings beside the office wall. He inhales deeply, as if it will help him to better absorb them, then steps heavily across the platform floor.

One last place to explore.

After what he'd read in the report, his stomach turns at the mere thought of stepping down to the tracks below, but he can't put it off any longer.

Lambert dissects the smooth concrete, his steps filled with trepidation, his mind trying to digest everything he's seen so far.

He arrives at the edge of the platform where his sweeping flashlight catches a red splotch on the side of his right shoe. He's been exceedingly careful not to contaminate the scene, but must have inadvertently encroached on some of the evidence when he passed near the wooden crate.

Lambert draws a handkerchief from his pocket and wipes the shoe clean, then re-folds the cloth and furtively tucks it away.

No need to make Meyers aware of this slight indiscretion!

He steps to the edge of the platform, just to the rear of the caboose. He then crouches low, placing his left knee on the ground, and lowers himself carefully down to the tracks below. His feet barely touch down when he's nearly thrown off balance by the stench. He shines his flashlight up the tracks and again reaches for his handkerchief, placing the clean side over his mouth, sickened by what's on the ground before him. The disease, the filth, the misery.

What in the hell happened here?

He takes two steps forward when the flashlight dies off in his hand, subsuming him in total darkness. He smacks it a few times, and by the third whack it begrudgingly lurches back to life. He draws it back to the rough terrain before him, the batteries weak and hanging on for their last breath.

Then an odd feeling embraces him.

Detective Meyers aside, Dr. Lambert suddenly feels as if he's not alone.

FULSOME PRISON BLUES

THE FIVE-MINUTE RIDE WAS a bumpy one, though Billy's mind was so thoroughly elsewhere that he hardly noticed.

At first he thought he might be on his way to the facility, that house of misery and torture and pain. Part of him didn't even care, the self-pitying part of him that had already commandeered his spirit.

Only it wasn't the case, and he was soon booked into custody at a small, centrally located detention center. The authority was one Ernie Judson, a portly and gruff-looking man who looked up from his desk just long enough to hand over a key and point lethargically to one of the cells. Billy was processed within minutes, then lodged in a chilly cell with numerous others, the guard slamming the door with a loud metal clank.

Lost in thought, Billy didn't notice the large individual in the opposite cell smacking his lips and yelling out some sort of crass threat. Another yelled, "Well look at what got dragged in." Billy heard them as echoes, distant and surreal.

He sat down carefully on the cool concrete floor. His left eye, still raw and red, had finally stopped bleeding. There were two long rows of cells with a walkway between for the guards and staff. At the end of the hallway was a single door with the word **RANGE** painted black on steel. Everything felt cold and hard.

Billy sat stone-faced. In one of the adjacent cells, an inmate sung the blues in tune to the music now emanating from Judson's radio:

> *I guess I've done some bad things,*
> *but you don't get to judge.*
> *Can tell you've led a good life,*
> *by all that stomach pudge.*
> *And though I've been a tryin'*
> *to straighten myself out…*
> *I guess I'm damn well set now,*
> *as an eternal lout.*
>
> *They tell me to hang in there,*
> *say things can't get no worse.*
> *And though life might get better,*
> *right now it's just a curse.*
> *Yes, I am just a vagrant,*
> *no reason and no rhyme.*
> *But please don't go and blame me…*
> *I blame myself full time.*

Billy stared blankly ahead. He couldn't imagine the terror that Lola must be feeling or imagine what might have already become of her. He remembered Tommy's screams—and poor Tommy's crime was, at worst, oral sedition.

He might have gone on that way for much longer, despondently catatonic, but for a voice from the adjacent cell.

"Billy."

At first he didn't answer. After a short pause, his name was repeated, this time a touch louder. "Billy!"

Finally he turned his head and saw, to his surprise, a familiar face: Cecil, the flecks of dried paint from their botched art house mission long since washed from his body.

"C'm over here," urged Cecil, his face pressed up against the cool steel partition that separated their two cells.

328| M. P. Michaud

"Cecil," Billy acknowledged, drifting over.

"It's good to see you."

"It's been a long time…" said Billy, still not entirely in tune with the conversation, but slowly starting to regain his focus.

"Yeah, I can't imagine. I can't even believe I've lasted this long."

"You been through the process?" asked Billy.

Cecil nodded. "I've seen people. They've seen me. I'm still here's all I know."

"Mm-hmm."

"They're never gonna let me outta here," said Cecil.

"You didn't do anything that bad."

"You think that matters?"

Billy winced and reached for his wound. The workers had slathered some sort of antiseptic cream on it when he first came in. Once Billy looked back to Cecil there was a triumphant grin on his face.

"You see it?"

"See what?"

"Up there." Cecil motioned to the wall behind Billy. It was hovering just above his head—an upside-down triangle; three lines shooting off from each side.

"You put that there?"

Cecil shook his head. "Never been in that cell. We got followers everywhere now."

Billy looked at the symbol again.

"Everywhere!" trumpeted Cecil, as if reading Billy's thoughts. "The movement is spreading!"

Spreading, thought Billy.

Like wildfire.

No, not like wildfire. Like a virus. Replicating and insidious and mutated beyond recognition.

"I see," is all Billy actually said before resting his forehead against the bars. The cool steel felt soothing against his weary head.

"How'd they get you, anyway?"

Billy downplayed the true nature of his capture. He suspected his former colleague might still be a true believer and didn't want to risk creating an enemy. "Maybe it's best we not talk about the details," he whispered back.

"Yes, you're right. Absolutely."

There it was, that quick turn to deference to which he'd become so accustomed. From Cecil's point of view, Billy was still an honored member of the organization, one to be revered. For now, it worked to his benefit, and he would milk that faux reality as long as possible.

"Anyway," said Cecil, picking up on an earlier point, "you'll find it OK in here. They treat us well enough, least as long as they got a spot for you. Warmth, shelter, square meals. A lot of us are actually better off in here than we were out on the streets."

Billy looked around his own cell, then into the cells across the way. What Cecil said seemed true. Nobody was suffering from hypothermia or heat exhaustion. They didn't have to quench their thirst with dirty water leaked from taps or fountains or collected rainwater. Everyone seemed moderately well fed.

It was a diverse mix: short and tall, fat and trim, black, white, brown, yellow—different dialects and cultures. Billy stepped back from Cecil and took stock of the five other residents in his own cell, whose names he would soon know like his own.

There was Tim, who sat silently in the corner and was eminently forgettable. Lucius loitered near the front of the cell, peering stoically to the other side. Keith, the largest, lay on a bed against the back wall, fast asleep. The other two had more absurd names. There was Dash, a slight individual who might have been fleet of foot, if not hobbled by something of a club foot. And finally there was Scarecrow, an obnoxious runt who frightened no one. They were packed in tight, with not much room for privacy, and not enough beds for all six. All in all, the living conditions weren't terribly dissimilar to those in the House of Darrow.

Lucius, at first glance, reminded him of George. This was good enough for Billy. He sidled up beside him, Lucius still peering out the front of their cell.

"Hey."

Lucius turned, cautiously. After a pause he said, "So...you know Cecil?"

Billy confirmed with a nod.

"Well, that counts. Cecil's a friend. Both of us been in here fer a while now."

"How long?"

Lucius thought it over. "I dunno. A while."

"What did you do?" asked Billy.

"Not much. Nothin' that deserves bein' held like this, I think. But I don't mind all that much. I wasn't doin' so good out there."

They chatted quietly amongst themselves. Billy learned that Lucius had been homeless since being separated from his mother. It struck a chord with Billy and helped him forge an immediate affinity for his new cellmate.

Throughout their discussion, the large individual across the aisle continued to show a dogged interest in Billy, smacking his lips, curling his tongue out of his mouth and sliding it across his upper lip.

"Who is that?"

Lucius glanced over to the opposite cell, averting his eyes as much as possible.

"That's the Duke. You wanna stay away from him. He's crazy. They keep him locked up away from the rest of us, mostly. But every once in a while, there's a chance we'll cross paths."

"He keeps staring at me," said Billy, looking directly at the Duke. "He's been doing it since I got here."

The Duke again flicked his tongue over his top lip and proceeded to make an obscene smacking sound. With all that had happened, and his patience raw to the bone, Billy shelved his normally cool demeanor.

"What are you looking at?" challenged Billy.

The Duke barked back something indistinguishable in response, and before long they were engaged in a verbal back and forth across the concrete aisle. Lucius yelled at Billy to keep quiet, that he was just going to bring trouble. He could hear the same sentiment echoed by Cecil in the next cell, but Billy went on undeterred. The two of them went back and forth, their decibels increasing. Soon enough the office door swung open and Judson marched in, his black steel-toed boots treading heavily beneath him, his light blue uniform stretched tight over his large gut. He clomped his way to the front of the Duke's cell.

"Shut the hell up," he shouted. The Duke continued yelling until he saw Judson reach for something on his belt, then quickly ceased and desisted.

Billy, however, didn't quit, at least not until Judson walked across the aisle to kick his cell door. Billy pulled back at just the last moment.

"I said shut the hell up," Judson repeated. He clanged some sort of club against the top of the cell, then turned and marched back through the main door, closing it with a bang. Members of nearby cells had a laugh at Billy's expense.

"That stuff ain't gonna help anything," said Lucius. "And we don't provoke the Bossman. Most of them treat us OK, but not the Bossman. You're both lucky that's all you got. He probably had somethin' more important to do, but he won't think twice about layin' a beatin' on any of us. Just 'cause we're in here doesn't make us any more important than we are on the outside. Remember that."

Billy fumed silently, the Duke still staring at him from across the way.

"You wouldn't believe how they treat some of us," said Lucius, "just wouldn't believe it. Bad enough we get locked up for prac'ly nothin'."

"There's got to be a way out of here," said Billy, as much to himself as to others. Scarecrow started to laugh.

"You find it you let me know!" chortled someone from a nearby cell.

"Ain't only two ways outta here," said another despondently, though he clearly meant the reverse.

"Sometimes we get bailed out," said Lucius. "You have anyone out there who might come get ya? No offense, but I take one look at you and figure yer not from that sorta family, so maybe people won't be linin' up to spring you outta here. Don't get me wrong, same goes for me. That's maybe why we're here in the first place."

Billy had nobody. At least nobody who'd be in a position to do anything about his dilemma. Still, there had to be a way out of there. "What about escape?"

Lucius shook his head. "Not a chance."

"But they have to cut me loose soon, right?"

Again Scarecrow laughed. Keith made some sort of gurgling noise in his sleep, rustled his sizeable frame, then lapsed back to snoring.

Billy withdrew to the side of the room. *Got to be a way out of here!* He leaned against the concrete wall separating his cell from the Bossman's office. Slowly, imperceptibly, he started sliding down to the ground, his thoughts darting back and forth between Lola and his own captivity as he slumped lower, then lower again, until he was finally lying on his side with his head on the concrete floor. His wound throbbed from the swelling and stung from the disinfectant, but exhaustion had dulled the pain. *Got to be a way out...*

He hadn't slept in nearly a day, given their escape from the House of Darrow, his journey with Lola and Sam, his fight and subsequent arrest. Only then did the exhaustion truly hit him.

Got to be...

And just as he recognized his true level of fatigue, his eyes closed, and, with the Duke still watching him from across the aisle, Billy succumbed to deep slumber.

HE WOKE SOME HOURS later. It was dinnertime, Lucius having rocked him awake lest he miss his meal. Billy had sized him up correctly—he was an honorable soul.

Billy felt significantly better by then; his tired body could use more sleep, and he was still terribly sore from his fight with Sherman, but at least his muscles were able to relax, his strained nerves noticeably less raw.

One of the staff was distributing the meals. The inmates called him Keys for the large ring attached to his belt and the dozen keys dangling busily from his waist. The door to the office was propped open as Keys made his rounds. Billy could see the Bossman fidgeting with some paperwork. A black and white television on his desk played a Tom and Jerry cartoon. Next to the TV was a rotating fan that caressed the large beads of sweat on the Bossman's brow. Despite the cool temperature outside, the air inside was stifling.

Once all six cellmates were given their shares, Billy sat down near a side wall to consume his dinner. He got one bite in before he noticed the looming shadow. He looked up to find the size-able Keith staring down on him.

"I think you got my food."

Billy looked over to the opposite end of the cell and saw Keith's portion untouched.

Billy stepped back. Deferential.

"Sorry," he said. "Then I guess that must be mine over there."

Keith disagreed. "Nope. That's mine too."

An albino from somewhere across the aisle let loose a high-pitched laugh. Scarecrow started laughing, too.

"So they're both yours?" said Billy.

Keith nodded.

"Fine," said Billy, conceding the point and stepping to the side.

Keith didn't even wait for him to get fully out of his path, swaggering forward and brushing him to the side with his right shoulder. Lucius just watched. Scarecrow smirked. Dash ate his own dinner, not paying heed to what had likely occurred on countless occasions.

The moment Keith reached down for his bullied apportionment, Billy drove him headlong into the concrete wall. Keith's face mashed into the unforgiving concrete, opening a gash above the bridge of his nose. Keith turned around, dazed and enraged. He spit out one of his teeth, the orphaned fragment landing softly to the floor awash in blood and saliva.

Keith swept his tongue past the gap in his mouth, then lunged at Billy, who sidestepped the attack and delivered a hard strike to Keith's abdomen. Then, before Keith could recover, Billy landed another sharp blow to his throat. Keith stumbled back just as the Bossman arrived to strike the cell with his club.

"What the hell is going on in there?"

The parties remained silent.

The dispute had ended, and though Billy was loath to admit it, his training and experience in the House of Darrow had made the difference in the outcome. Lucius gave him an approving wink while Cecil shouted encouragement from the next cell; both the Scarecrow and the albino were now noticeably silent.

Billy returned to his dinner, and though it might not have been much better than slop, somehow, at that moment, it tasted just a notch short of delectable.

DAYS SLIPPED BY AND nothing changed, aside from Keith maintaining a respectful distance. Billy had been through something of a perfunctory administrative process by then, and had met with various people to plead his case and beg his freedom. After all of it, he remained firmly detained.

Meanwhile, fall crept ever closer to winter, and the temperature outside continued to plummet.

Over the course of that first week Billy did what he could to keep his mind occupied, trying his best not to obsess over Lola, or the helplessness of his situation. He got to know Lucius better than anyone else in the detention center, though his cellmate remained tight-lipped about his past, and of the precise circumstances that drew him to his current predicament. He would only comment, "You wouldn't believe what I've been through," and Billy wouldn't push for more.

He also chatted with Cecil, relaying in whispers between their two cells all that had transpired since Cecil's capture—save for the glaring omissions of his subterfuge with Tommy and his failed attempt at desertion. Cecil was thrilled to hear of his ascension to the Wall of Valor, and was, to Billy's disappointment, equally happy to hear about all the group had accomplished. He relished the news of the devastating car crash, the brutalized little girl, and even the spontaneous killing of the traitor Tommy. Still, Billy realized, a true believer.

It was late in the week when he was first let out into the range—a small grassy common area out back. Two dozen inmates walked about in the chilly fall air, including all of those from Billy's cell, Cecil's cell, and the inmates from the third cell in his row. To Billy's relief he'd yet to be placed anywhere in the general population with the Duke.

Billy took the opportunity to survey the landscape, finding it completely surrounded by tall fencing. He poked around for any weakness that might be exploited.

As if reading his mind, Lucius intercepted him. "Give it up. Don't you think we've looked over every inch of this place for some way out?"

Billy kept on undeterred, stopping only once he'd personally resigned himself to the accuracy of Lucius's assessment.

No way out.

He tried to relax and make the most of his time outside. He walked the circumference of the range. It was the most exercise he'd had in days, and it helped to smooth his frazzled nerves. By then his body had largely healed from his skirmish with Sherman, and physically, he felt strong.

The blues singer sat off against the side wall nursing his left thigh, which had recently became acquainted with the underside of the Bossman's steel-toed boot. Billy listened as he crooned another tune, his voice in sync with the melody that had been playing on the radio just before they were set out into the range:

> *Hey Bossman, why don't you just let me be?*
> *Been so awful since I kicked you in the knee!*
> *And I sure regret my malcontented way...*
> *but must you make me pay, oh, every day?*
>
> *Hey Bossman, I hope you choke on your food.*
> *You're such a damn intemp'rate kind of dude!*
> *And though I may not live a worthy life,*
> *at least my soul with hate ain't near so rife.*

A splash of black smoke cut an otherwise crystal skyline, protruding up from a stout metal chimney atop an eastern wing of the detention center. Billy watched the smoke climb higher and lighter into the sky before it disintegrated into nothingness some distance short of the clouds.

After two more laps around the circumference, Cecil called Billy to join him in the center. There he was introduced to Gabriel, a friend of Cecil's. Gabriel was quick to mention his Egyptian heritage and point out that his ancestors were something of royalty.

"Just look at me now," said Gabriel.

"Look at all of us," said Billy.

"I coulda been a prince maybe," said Gabriel, through the stench of decayed calcium. He was much too young, Billy felt, to be missing so many teeth.

"I understand," said Billy.

"No, I mean it. Just born too late is all it was."

Maybe we all were, thought Billy.

Said Billy.

He learned that Gabriel had been held in custody since he was caught for a break and enter. "I was hungry," said Gabriel. "Just went into someone's storm cellar lookin' for food. They coulda just let me go. I didn't hurt anyone."

Billy nodded, having no reason to doubt him.

"I told him about the group," whispered Cecil. "He can be trusted. He hopes to join if we can ever get out of here."

"I'm pretty good in a scrape," said Gabriel. "And I swear this is the first time I've ever been caught stealin'."

"I believe He would be happy to have Gabriel," added Cecil.

Billy nodded again, as if he'd accepted the credentials and would vouch for Gabriel, readily promoting the false expectation. There could be no harm, he thought, to have more allies on the inside. He then turned his attention to the area with the rising smoke. "What's that?"

"E-Wing," said Cecil. "But the inmates have lots of other names for it."

"Who do they keep in there?"

Neither answered immediately. Finally Gabriel spoke up. "Them's the one's waitin' for the needle," he said.

"I see," said Billy, looking again in that direction.

"Poor bastards," added Cecil.

The smoke continued to rise, to vanish imperceptibly into the chilly skyline.

"They must have done something pretty bad," said Billy, now thinking of the girl in the blue-striped dress and the bloodcurdling scream from the sidewalk.

Cecil shrugged, "They done enough, I guess."

Gabriel raised his eyes and said something under his breath.

"You don't agree?" said Billy.

"I don't trust nothin' about this place," said Gabriel, before leaving them to circle the range.

Billy stared at Cecil, as if to ask what that was all about. Cecil explained how one of Gabriel's cellmates recently came down with something fierce; explained how the presiding authority took him to the infirmary, but that he never returned.

"And he wasn't the first," said Cecil, "to go and not come back."

Billy hoped they were exaggerating. Perhaps the sick inmates had just been transferred somewhere else for fancy treatment?

Then again, perhaps that view was overly optimistic, as he'd seen a genuine look of concern in more than a few eyes of his fellow inmates, especially those who'd been there for a while, or those who were old and sickly.

THE DAYS SOON FLIPPED to weeks, and Billy had settled in as best he could. He'd maintained an uneasy détente with Keith, consciously avoided eye contact with the Duke, forged a closer friendship with Lucius, and continued to regale Cecil with heroic tales from the House of Darrow.

His eye had healed by then, after he was transported to the infirmary for some follow-up treatment. It had been the first and only time he'd passed by the prisoners of E-Wing and, to Billy's considerable relief, the first and only time he'd been subjected to the holocaust of emotions on their doomed faces.

It wasn't long before Billy noticed the first flakes of the season fluttering like dust motes past the filth of the nearest window. The inmates had just received their dinner, the same indefinable hash slopped with the same mystery gravy that sung equally off-key to his taste buds as to his nostrils. Yet it was sustenance, so Billy consumed it without protest.

Once again, the door leading to the office had been left open. Billy walked to the front of his cell and pressed his face against the bars. He watched the Bossman behind the desk swiveling in his chair, mesmerized by the black and white television. The man took the occasional sip from a soda can, gave an occasional belly laugh. The inmates were on their best behavior.

Billy heard a door open out of sight. He saw Keys enter the office, the cluster of metal jangling intensely from his waist. "Man, you gotta hear this," said Keys. He fiddled with the Bossman's television until it landed on a local news station. The reporter was in the middle of a special news bulletin, telling of how Billy's former comrades had been spotted throughout the city causing fire after fire.

The Bossman sent an inquisitive glare toward the inmates before turning back to his desk and huddling with Keys around the television. The reporter detailed how there'd been countless raids on restaurants and cafés, while others had sneaked into apartments and houses. Billy heard all of it. Heard none of it. Only rested his forehead despondently against the cool steel bars.

"We've managed to capture a sound bite," said the woman, "but the audio is weak."

The Bossman ratcheted up the volume, and Billy's ears perked up as the anthem crept hauntingly into their cellblock:

> *Fight fight, make it right*
> *Darrow's guile will win the war*
> *Fight fight, make it right*
> *Darrow lifts us evermore*

Not only had property been affected, said the woman, but numerous people had been caught up in the fires, many suffering from smoke inhalation and burns. There'd even been a number of deaths, including several of the arsonists themselves, trapped in a symphony of their own destruction. One report spoke of some type of symbol being dug into the grass. Small sticks and shrubs had been set into the soil before being lit on fire, the symbol blazing proudly against a black skyline.

"People are warned to move about the streets with caution,"

said the woman, "until the authorities have a better grasp of the situation."

The Bossman scoffed. He shut off the television and flicked on his radio, spiking the volume, the frenzied lyrics pounding into the acoustically inviting cellblock.

Billy looked around his cell and to others across the aisle. They had no idea what was going on, but the war chant had Billy spooked. The whine of the radio poured from the office. Billy just listened; to the pulsing music that hurt his ears and frayed his nerves.

He wondered how long he'd been there. By then he'd lost track of the days and weeks. He turned his mind again to escape, but he knew it was impossible, and finally sequestered himself in contemplation.

An hour slid by, then two. They were preparing for lights out when the main door clanged open. Two guards escorted a new set of prisoners into the cellblock.

Seven. And Billy knew them all. All of them members of the House of Darrow.

Loyal. Vile. Members.

Billy faded as far back as he could and tilted his head to the ground, then watched, through the slits of his eyes, as all seven were ushered down the block and placed in several cells at the end of the wing.

Lucius approached him. "Everything OK?"

Billy wasn't prepared to discuss it. He provided a queasy acknowledgment that everything was fine, then watched intently as the two guards returned up the aisle and exited the cellblock. One of them handed a sheet to the Bossman. He scribbled something on the document before lazily handing the clipboard back to the now-departing guards.

In the following hours, things only got worse. The wing gradually filled with new prisoners, and there was much gossip and discussion slipping between the cells. The new arrivals rolled in hour after hour, bringing stories of society's pending collapse. On each occasion they were paraded down the main aisle and shoved into one of the units—some cells having now swelled to twice their intended capacity—and on each occasion Billy would slink back to the farthest corner of his own cell, hoping that his door wouldn't open.

Then, inevitably, it happened.

The guards stopped at Billy's cell. He hugged tight against the back corner, tilting his head down and speculating wildly about who might be coming through the door. *Sherman? Marlon?*

Maybe even Darrow himself?

He heard the door slide open and a rustle of footsteps. His adrenal glands started pumping as his body readied for a fight.

They will know, thought Billy. All of them will know what I did. What I'd tried to do.

What I'd do again.

The footsteps shuffled closer, now coming from inside his cell. He heard them moving in his direction, his muscles taut. He lifted his head and drew himself into a defensive stance. Then… immense relief.

The two arrivals were unknown to him. Perhaps even unrelated to the organization.

Safe.

At least for now.

But with new prisoners regularly flowing in, Billy wondered how long it would be before he found himself face-to-face with a handful of his former colleagues. And when that happened, would he be able to defend himself? It would surely depend on which members, the odds, and whether or not he received any help from Lucius. He couldn't count on help from any of the other inmates in his cell—not from Scarecrow, and certainly not from Keith, who would likely be more inclined to join an attack on Billy than to defend him, what with his dented nose and crooked smile.

By then many had started into the battle hymn, a chant that ceased to reverberate only when the Bossman entered the cell-block and rattled his club against cold steel.

For the rest of the night Billy remained curled up in the corner and out of sight. He knew he wouldn't be able to hide forever. Eventually they'd be in his cell, or he'd be sent out to the range, where security was lax. He could be thoroughly worked over before the closest staff could intervene, assuming they would even care to. He wondered if he might feign illness when the time came, then pushed the idea away, remembering Cecil's words: *And he wasn't the first…to go and not come back.*

It is said that every dark cloud has a silver lining, though Billy had yet to identify any benefit to his steadily eroding predicament. One day they would get him—if not that night, then the next. If not the next, then the day after that. Eventually the time would come when he would be badly outnumbered by those seeking retribution.

But then, just as quickly as the panic had set in, he found some semblance of calm, some semblance of relief, as he realized that one good thing might come from this reunion. Certainly they would know what had become of Lola and little Sam. And if they told him that Lola had been spared, that she was safe and well, then his anguish would relent. And within the shadow of that fiercely dark cloud, he would at last have found a silver lining.

One that to him would be golden.

THE GREAT ESCAPE

THE NIGHT PASSED WITHOUT incident, though Billy was exhausted come morning. What little slumber he managed had been spent on the branch of his tree. The fireman reaching for him and his mother screaming from below. Each time he heard footsteps he'd awoken and readied for a fight, only to eventually return to his nightmares.

Now it was morning. He'd made it through the night intact.

One down, countless to go.

"It's not normally this packed in here," said Lucius, having just arrived by Billy's side.

Billy didn't respond. He knew exactly what was going on, but kept his tongue still and his gaze fixed on the main door. It had been shut for hours, but soon enough swung open to reveal Keys and an unknown person. And, to Billy's relief, no new prisoners.

But it was also too early for breakfast. Far too early, thought Billy, as he blinked sleep and concern from his eyes. He and Lucius watched the two men walk slowly down the corridor and stop between the first two cells. The unknown man looked at his clipboard and scribbled something in blue pen.

"Start with these two?" he asked, pointing to Billy's cell and the one beside it, where Cecil had also roused to his feet.

Keys unlocked Billy's cell and stepped inside. "C'mon, guys…"

"Where are you taking us?" asked Billy, as one by one they were escorted out.

No answer.

"I said, 'Where are you taking us?'" demanded Billy.

"Be quiet," said the second man harshly.

Without delay, all the inmates from the first two cells were transferred to a nearby truck and locked into the rear.

THWUMP!

A reprieve, thought Billy.

Doubted Billy.

The unknown man assumed occupancy of the driver's seat. Keys took the passenger seat, and the truck roared to life as the driver turned over the ignition. They immediately set out onto the road.

The trip was a loud and bumpy one, the shocks in dire need of repair, the exhaust growling and spitting just inches beneath their feet. Stingy beams of morning light oozed in from thin slats in the two rear doors. Billy looked across the aisle; Cecil was bouncing up and down each time they hit a pothole or fumbled over uneven terrain. He could see that Cecil was nervous. Scarecrow was to Cecil's left, Lucius to his right. On Billy's side of the truck, Gabriel was to his immediate left, offering up some sort of prayer to whatever deity currently bound his conscience.

Billy saw a marked resignation in their faces. They looked demoralized and beaten. Most of them had been trapped in the system longer than he had, and he expected the same forlorn look to eventually wash over his own face once his already waning hopes had sufficiently frittered away.

They rode in silence, speaking only through puzzled eyes and worried faces.

Then a hard jerk to the right and the squeal of tires as the truck came to a violent halt. The roadway calamity sent several of them careening forward, including Billy, whose rusted metal restraint buckled under the pressure and broke loose. A quick glance told him that Gabriel had equally benefited from the crash.

The other prisoners started to clamor, begging Billy and Gabriel to help them get loose. Many, including Billy, were bleeding, the soft tissue of his thigh no match for hard steel.

Gabriel ignored their cries. He immediately huddled by the two rear doors and tried to figure some way to the other side.

Billy looked over at the door, to the slats of light now splayed across Gabriel's fidgeting feet. Freedom just inches away.

Then he looked over at Cecil and Lucius, both screaming for him to help them. Billy hurried to their side, his thigh trickling blood to the floor below. He sized up their restraints and shook his head, seeing no apparent way to free them.

Billy could hear people's voices outside. There was some sort of clamor and loud accusations, muffled and uneven. Again he looked at the restraints. No way to free them. No way to…

The faint rattle of keys drew his attention. "Get over here," whispered Gabriel, excitedly. "They're gonna open it! They're gonna open it!"

Billy looked at Cecil and Lucius, both struggling against their restraints and pleading for help. Both had been kind and loyal. He owed them.

But then he imagined the doors swinging open and the thin slats of light spreading open and full across his face, and he could practically taste the cool autumn air passing into his waiting lungs—could practically feel the brittle leaves crunching beneath his hurried feet. And with those irresistible images, he buried his sense of loyalty somewhere deep down inside him, turned away from his two friends, and hurried to the door. He knew they deserved better.

But then, he figured, so did he.

"Get ready," whispered Gabriel.

More muffled jangling.

A key grooved into its home, then the lock clicked and turned. They could make out Keys' muted voice on the other side. Billy lined up immediately behind Gabriel, who was centered at the rear, ready to bolt regardless of which door swung open.

It was the van's right door that fell away, bringing an influx of light and a look of astonishment on Keys' face as Gabriel launched himself out of the van toward the pavement. Keys' reaction was quick; he grabbed hold of Gabriel and they struggled on the sidewalk.

The flood of the sun was nearly blinding as Billy himself sprung to the concrete. The landing sent a bolt of pain through his thigh and buckled his leg, holding him captive long enough for the driver to turn the corner. He reached for Billy, who darted quickly into the street, shutting out the pain, oblivious to the traffic that flowed undeterred by the roadside spectacle. The man chased closely behind.

Tires squealed, cars honked, people yelled, the city groaning its general displeasure through this impromptu chorus. Billy ducked into the first alley he saw, ran halfway down, then stopped.

Dead-end.

Should have kept to the sidewalk.

He spun around, spying the driver at the entrance.

Billy turned back toward the alley, scanned frantically for something, anything.

Then he spotted the dumpster, and with the man's closing footsteps in his ears he ran as fast as he could toward the large green structure.

The man yelled for him to stop. His thigh screamed its concurrence.

He ignored them both and launched himself onto the bin, clamoring to pull himself up. Before the man even reached the dumpster, Billy had jumped to a rusted fire escape and started his frantic ascent skyward. He arrived at the top of the ladder, turning just before he slipped up onto the roof to see the guard already walking out of the alley.

The roof was covered with steel plating, the surface oddly hot despite the cool fall air. Billy ran across to the other side, his feet pounding hard and ringing tinny pings into the morning air. He could hear the approach of a fire engine down below as he slowly started to digest his new liberty. Only he didn't dare stop to appreciate it. He kept going, to the edge of the first building, where there was a second within reach. A hearty jump took him across. It brought him to a third building, with some sort of metal duct connecting them. He stepped gingerly on it, ensured it would hold his weight, then slipped over to the other side. This third building also had a fire escape. He peered over, found the alleyway clear, then descended to the ground and slunk away. The commotion, along with Cecil's and Lucius's chance for freedom, was left behind in a hazy fog of chaos.

A short distance from the scene, he pulled himself up against a tree in front of Azrael's Attic, a local dessert shop specializing in frozen yogurt. He inspected his wound—the cut wasn't deep. The bruise was another matter, but he was still in decent shape, all things considered.

Billy shut his eyes, replaying his escape in his mind, the events as fresh as the wound on his thigh. Regret had already brewed inside him—and though he surely would have doomed himself if he'd remained to help his friends, he expected their ghosts would eventually creep into his dreams, or into his waking hours, once he had a fuller opportunity to ruminate.

For now he pushed it all aside and managed to his feet, then started into labored steps toward the House of Darrow, not the slightest idea what he'd find once he got there.

24

THE PRODIGAL TABBS

OVER THE COURSE OF the next two hours, Billy cautiously made his way, the bite of the wind and the state both nipping at his heels. Everywhere he looked was the symbol: next to a bus stop, by a park entrance, outside the train station.

Scratched into light poles. Carved in the grass.

He'd been diligent to stay in the shadows and avoid anyone who might know him. He got as close as he dared, then holed up in an alley four blocks from the closest sentry point, sifting his mind for some sort of plan. Nothing came.

Hours passed, the bulk of which Billy spent peeking out from behind a large cardboard box, fighting back the pain in his thigh and the call for sleep as he studied the comings and goings at sentry point four.

Morning turned to day turned to afternoon. Then the first sense of hope was born at the sight of a familiar face walking in his direction. It wasn't Lola, but it was close.

It was George, and he was alone.

He'd been as good a friend as any.

Billy rose to his feet and nearly fell down, his limbs numbed from his prolonged crouch. The wound in his thigh had tightened. He shook out his legs and held his breath as George came slowly in his direction.

Same side of the street.

Billy stole a look at sentry point four and saw the guard looking his way, so he stayed hidden—only George was getting closer. He was about to pass when Billy called his name in a loud whisper, knowing he was taking a chance, equally knowing there was no time for discretion.

George's head cocked toward the sound of his name. Billy called again. This time George caught it, identified the source, and stepped into the alley. He saw Billy.

Then a look. Alarm? Surprise.

Relief.

It was emphatic. Required no translation. Clearly, he still considered Billy a friend. George entered the alleyway and walked with Billy deeper into the narrow passage, finding some privacy behind a collection of garbage bins.

"It's good to see you," said George, his good eye alight. "We were told you ran away."

Billy's thoughts were too single-minded to return the gesture. He looked to his friend, prepared to say her name. He didn't get the word out before George gave him a look. It, too, required no translation. "Lola," said Billy. It was more declaration than question.

George's silence…excruciating confirmation. "I'm sorry, Billy."

Billy's legs buckled. He dropped to the ground, his head lolling to the side as if it was suddenly much too heavy for his flimsy neck. He would have cried if he could. He could not.

George waited patiently, watching Billy's grieving through his good eye. He was momentarily inconsolable, but soon managed a foggy, "What happened?"

George explained how Lola died. That she passed away shortly after her return. Darrow had ordered Marlon to punish her for her "transgression." He said a message had to be sent to all who might ponder such treachery. He'd even offered up some explanation as to how this order complied with the eighth tenet—that no member shall harm any other—one that George couldn't readily remember, but remembered how the explanation had been accepted by most. "He was enraged by what you did. I hadn't seen him that way in a long time. Not since the facility. Maybe not since..." He stopped himself. "They'd barely started. Me an' Ears tried to stop it, along with some others, but we were outnumbered. She cried out, and then..."

"And then she stopped breathing," said Billy.

"Yes."

Billy closed his eyes. He tried not to imagine it but succeeded only in the opposite.

"Rufus went wild," said George. "He nearly tore the place apart. It took so many of us to hold him back from Darrow, and those who'd done it."

"I don't want to hear any more." Billy slunk back against the wall, seething anger intermixed with massive anguish. Only then did he think of Sam. Thought of how much Darrow's child had meant to Lola. Knew, too, that Marlon felt threatened by the existence of The Progeny. "And Sam?"

Billy choked out the words, and George informed him that Sam had been returned safe and sound, and was now being tended to by Helena. Billy expelled a short breath of relief, then fell silent again, hemming himself in desolation. Something from the street had caught his attention. Something shiny.

"Are you listening, Billy?"

A weak nod, and George slowly began to fill him in on the weeks he'd missed.

"We set the city on fire. Good parts of it, at least." He forged ahead, his affect flat. "It was awful. The things we did. The things *I* did."

Billy stared ahead blankly.

"We did some good, though." His voice lightened. "The promise. You remember Darrow's promise?"

"Darrow promised a lot of things."

"But the part about the facility. About going back. Well they got it. Burned it down to the ground."

Billy briefly pictured the facility razed to ash, brutes and blue scrubs alike running frantically from its charred and smoking carcass. But the elation soon slipped free like the air from a carelessly tied balloon. "How was it done?"

"I don't know. I didn't go."

"Who went?"

"I don't know. Darrow, for one."

"Did you see it yourself?" asked Billy.

"See it?"

"The facility."

"No," said George. He paused, before adding, "But I saw smoke. Far off in the distance. In that direction."

Billy kept quiet.

"There was a lot of smoke...." He started to say more, but when Billy didn't comment further, George moved on.

George said that with Project Pyromania behind them, the House of Darrow was preparing to unleash its fourth wartime campaign, one that would center around home invasions of the largest and most decadent residences. Get inside, attack whoever was home—man, woman, old, young...it didn't matter. They wouldn't discriminate, since *the man* didn't discriminate in his systemic subjugation of their kind. It was a maniacal plan called *Homicidal Housecall*, and though there was surely poignancy in it somewhere, Billy wasn't currently inclined to consider it.

As George told it, the announcement of Homicidal Housecall hadn't stirred the usual fervor among the base. Divisions had widened. A greater percentage of membership, particularly those beholden to the niceties of the first railcar, had exhibited increased malingering, and a diminished urgency for social reform, while those in the second railcar and caboose remained the most motivated, keen not only to maintain their current positioning, but with an eye toward upward mobility. And none of the three, it seemed, had shed any tears for their growing mass of unfortunate comrades scuttling in the dirt below.

Darrow and Marlon were apparently unfazed by the malaise of the privileged minority, especially after a recent decision to tap further into the labor of their still sizeable underclass.

As it turned out, none of their downtrodden had yet been relocated, as several members of the Relocation Committee had second thoughts about passing the resolution that would evict them. Realizing that it was these very individuals who toiled with the dirtiest and most degrading tasks—jobs that might fall to them instead—they'd ultimately concluded that the House of Darrow might not be as crowded as they'd originally thought.

It had apparently worked out for the best.

In revealing Homicidal Housecall, Darrow announced that, after reconsidering the true spirit of the seventh tenet—which promised equal work—the weak and the sick would finally be considered for outside missions. The downtrodden were thrilled with this decision. Coupled with the fact that they'd yet to be relocated, many thought that they might, at last, be equally valued by their community. However, their glee dissipated as soon as Chester took to the crate to announce their proposed assignments. It became apparent that they were earmarked for only the riskiest and most insanely dangerous missions, those tantamount to suicide with little chance of success, and they were suddenly less thrilled than they had been.

On the heels of this announcement followed further changes to their accommodations and to the distribution of meals. As George told it, the individuals assigned to the first railcar were no longer satisfied with their arrangements, as they desired more privacy, and more space to stretch out. Darrow acceded to their request to reduce the occupancy within their car, which bumped numerous members down the residential food chain, and thus pushed even more of their membership down into the ghetto.

Accommodations were further challenged by the continually

shrinking middle car, and though several of its inhabitants had ascended to the roof in an attempt to stem the water damage—even jamming a number of their remaining widgets into the leaky crevices—they found the damage to be irreparable and the deterioration irreversible. This circumstance had only exacerbated their feelings of resentment toward those in the lead railcar who, they felt, being deemed the strongest and fittest among them, were most able to help, had they desired to do so.

Resentment equally swelled amongst those living within the caboose. Its fittings rigid and hard, the caboose was now physically larger than the ever-shrinking middle car, and though it remained half the size of the lead railcar, it now teemed with nearly twice as many occupants.

As for those living in the ghetto itself, the conditions were generally understood to be deplorable, and though George didn't seem proud to admit it, he acknowledged, "I haven't stepped foot there in weeks, what with the filth and the lice."

The strife wasn't restricted to quarters, as the sharing of food had also been revisited. Some of the favored members had not only grown increased appetites, but were now prone to squirreling away extra helpings for a late-night snack; and though the less fortunate members still received an "equal" number of pieces, the size of their morsels were continually shrinking, and were of increasingly putrid quality.

Darrow, of course, maintained that all of these distributions accorded with a strict construction of the tenets, and that if there was any real unfairness, which was not evident to him, it would be addressed in due course by the Equality Committee.

As could be expected, none of the new pronouncements sat well with their underclass, the disenfranchised members having finally turned a deaf ear to Totter's propaganda. Their patience with the Equality Committee had also been exhausted. The committee convened even less frequently than before, and continued to spend significant portions of their meetings arguing over the firmness of their language, with the final words shrouded in hopelessly ambiguous phrases such as "doesn't considerably demonstrate the contrary" and "not unreasonably inconsistent"—and their conclusions relayed back to the masses in equally mealy-mouthed fashion. Even when they conceded there was a problem, they would always adjourn several weeks to consider a solution, only to reconvene to find the problem had grown worse, necessitating a further adjournment. The one time the Equality Committee had actually agreed on the nature and scope of a problem, they proposed a solution to Darrow, who in turn formed yet another committee—the Budget Committee—to examine the resource implications of putting the Equality Committee's proposal into practice. The Budget Committee's first meeting was set for sometime in the new year.

With all they'd been through, and with still no changes in sight, the most downtrodden among them had started to exhibit a sharp discontent toward the apathetic and perpetually privileged, a growing number even insinuating the need for a violent revolution of their own. They had, as Billy had heard Jacob once put it, "tripped face first into their own puddle of scorn."

Darrow's transmogrification had been a profound one. Billy had witnessed much of it prior to his escape and incarceration, and George's updates only served to bolster his belief that both the organization and its leader had become hypocritical and hideous. This was no better illustrated than by one of George's anecdotes: A recent reconnaissance team had discovered a fancy jewel on the side of the road—no doubt dropped from the purse, pocket, or pendant of a Bigwig—and had brought it back with them as an offering to Darrow. It was an odd decision, it being a trinket of opulence, and given the group's disdain for the shackles of materialism and luxury. Odder still was Darrow's response, for after taking a good hard look, he decided to hold onto the item for safekeeping. In the days since, Darrow had grown an unhealthy fascination with the glittery object, despite its having no real use or utility except to be intermittently stared at. Yet he'd become fiercely attached, guarding it jealously as a young child might clutch relentlessly to a favorite worn blanket. Darrow seemed transfixed by its power, and had even commanded future mission participants to keep an eye out for similar items.

Billy opened his eyes and looked at his friend. "They all think I'm gone?"

"Everyone," said George.

"Everyone…" repeated Billy, mechanically.

"You need to get outta here…while no one's lookin' for you."

Billy didn't answer.

"I've been thinkin' of leaving myself," said George. "A few already have. Run off and never come back."

Still Billy didn't answer.

"It's awful," said George, through some inflection of distance, "to live in a place like that."

"Awful," repeated Billy.

There was nothing left, thought Billy. He considered what to do next, trying to think of the quickest route out of the area. To play it safe.

Tried but failed.

Instead he thought of his promise: to get them both to safety.

A broken promise.

No, not broken, he thought. *Half broken.*

Sam.

Play it safe.

The city is going to burst!

He'd promised.

"Billy?"

He'd promised.

"I need to get inside," said Billy. By then he was shaking.

"That's crazy."

George explained that their membership had grown "uncountable," despite all the deaths and arrests during Project

Pyromania. "Even getting past the sentries…"

Billy nodded, adding, after a lengthy pause, "You can help me."

Now it was George's turn to fall silent. He kicked at the ground behind the bins.

"How?"

"Volunteer for sentry duty."

"When?"

"Tonight."

Two more kicks at the ground. "And then?"

"Then I slip by you."

"And then?" When Billy was silent, George insisted, "They'll kill you."

Billy finally pulled himself to his feet. He stared at George with a plaintive look and a somber face, as if to say, "If it comes to that…"

It still took several more kicks at the ground before George finally agreed to volunteer for sentry point three, after which Billy slipped quietly away, again hugging the shadows until he found food and water.

Eventually he circled back, cautiously, to an alley with a view of sentry point three. He positioned himself behind a tower of empty milk cartons, the cubes stacked like Lego blocks, then quietly watched the members trickling in and out.

By then it was dark and cold. His breath formed intermittently each time he exhaled.

He'd tended to his thigh as best he could. It still throbbed, but it didn't affect his movements, not if he blocked out the pain. He figured tomorrow would be different, once it had a full night to set in and stiffen up. But that was tomorrow—all that mattered was the next handful of minutes. He tried to concentrate, to think how it might be done.

It would be so much easier if he were still one of them, inside the House, where he could creep up and make it look like an accident, and he quietly conjured up at least nine different ways he could effectively end Darrow by some curious "mishap."

Only now things were exponentially more difficult. He couldn't fall back on that sort of treachery. He'd have to face Darrow head on, and very much in public. The odds were against him. Obscenely so.

He remained there, desolate behind the cartons, where he thought, and he thought, and he thought—until George emerged, good to his word, to relieve sentry point three.

Billy didn't immediately reveal himself. Instead he waited until the moon beckoned midnight. He wanted the House full for his plan, such as it was. Finally he slipped across the street and stepped past George into the darkness, halting just a few feet away.

George looked around and kicked at the ground a few times. Billy knew what was coming, and wasn't the least bit surprised when George offered to go with him.

Too many, thought Billy. Too many times his actions and in-actions had contributed to the deaths of those he cared about. "Hundreds against one or against two, it's not going to matter."

"I guess so."

"You need to get out of here."

George nodded.

"However this goes," said Billy, "it's going to end badly."

"I understand."

"You need to be far away."

Again George nodded, kicking at the ground once more. He told Billy, somewhat sheepishly, that he'd been thinking about going back home. At least if they'd still have him.

"Guess you'll find out," said Billy.

"Guess we'll all find out," said George. He looked around, en-suring they were still alone. "Not so hesitant anymore, are you?"

"I just don't care anymore."

"Sure you do," said George.

Billy didn't respond.

"You know you don't have to do this. Seems like such a waste…"

"But Sam…"

George interrupted him. "But you'd be goin' down there anyway, Sam or no Sam, wouldn't you?"

Billy considered denying it, but found himself nodding in affirmation. Neither mentioned the word "revenge" directly. They danced around it like it was a dirty word. Maybe it was.

But it was more than that—not just revenge, it was rescue. It was responsibility.

It was redemption.

It was a feeling that if he didn't go down there now, then he risked living the rest of his days in dream and regret.

George didn't say anything else, just nodded, then with one last wink of his good eye he parted, stepping quickly from the curb as Billy slunk below to the darkened tunnel.

It was quiet. No signs of a pending train. He crept carefully along the narrow ledge, a few times nearly falling down, his legs numbed by pain and anticipation, his heartbeat quickening as he approached the opening of the tunnel.

Still so quiet. The entrance gaped open, inviting him to enter, as it had all those months before. He accepted, stepped inside the tunnel, felt the familiar rocky surface beneath his feet. By then his anxiety had started to ferment. Step by step it heightened. The gravelly surface felt increasingly bark-like beneath his feet, the air increasingly thin.

He was only halfway through when he spotted someone coming his way. It was too dark to make out the face and too far to turn back.

Step by step, the face drew closer. Formed definition. Somebody? Nobody.

"Hello there, friend," said the stranger.

"Hello," Billy responded curtly. He tried to keep walking but was anchored by this chatty individual.

"Did you enjoy His speech tonight?"

"Darrow knows," said Billy.

"Darrow knows!" repeated the stranger, excitedly.

Billy tried to step past him.

"I don't think I've seen you before," said the stranger.

"No," replied Billy. "I don't think so."

"Have you been here long?"

"A while," said Billy. He cast a look up the tunnel, hoping it would disengage the stranger. It didn't.

"I guess, with so many..."

"Right," said Billy. "Anyway, I have to go. I'm anxious to meet with Darrow."

"Kinda late for a meeting, isn't it?"

"He told me to see him as soon as I got back."

"I see," said the stranger enviously. "Maybe one day I'll also have the chance to meet with Him!"

The reverence sickened Billy, and though his thoughts were unabashedly bloody, he parroted the fawning sentiment to the awestruck minion before him. The young recruit, oblivious to Billy's true motives, went merrily on his way.

Billy traversed the remainder of the inclined tunnel without incident, that is, until he was just about to step into the House of Darrow, when he came face-to-face with Gerry, loitering by the tunnel entrance. He then watched Gerry's mouth curl into a smile. Watched as he hobbled aside, proudly standing usher to justice.

To murder.

To assassination.

To the slaying of mockery!

It was an opportunity Billy wouldn't squander. He whisked past Gerry, then walked briskly to the center of the main platform, stopping almost directly overtop the symbol. Astonished gasps turned quickly to clamor, and those in the subway cars started filing out toward the excitement, just as those in the ghetto began to lift themselves up to the main platform to investigate the source of this late-night commotion. By then Rufus had bounded forward, barking wildly to welcome Billy home, walking still with a noticeable limp. He rushed to Billy's side, nearly knocking him over.

The platform grew crowded and noisy. Billy's anxiety spiked, the branches swaying to the drum of his heartbeat. Branch by branch. Step by step. His mother screamed from below as his airwaves began to constrict. Billy hugged the bark and it pinched his skin.

Focus!

He held his ground atop the symbol as the masses collected around him. He tried to calm himself, felt elated and dizzy. He saw Sam through the crowd with Helena, then looked over to the Wall of Valor to see that "Billy Tabbs" had been unceremoniously scratched away. Sherman's name had been added below, along with a handful of others.

The crowd noise was sufficient to draw Marlon from Darrow's office. He froze once he pierced the crowd, a dumbstruck look on his face. Sherman arrived to his right; a deep scar ran down his left cheek and over his eye. The wound hadn't healed properly and had begun to fester.

The background murmurs grew increasingly loud until Darrow finally made an exultant exit from his office, the members curling away from him to create a path.

"You!" Darrow practically spit the words onto the ground as he sauntered forward. "You dare return to the House of Darrow?"

"I do," answered Billy, with all the confidence he could muster.

Darrow advanced past Marlon and Sherman.

The denizens by then had turned quiet as stone. There wasn't the faintest movement. Even Rufus had heeled to Billy's side. The silence was acute. Painful.

"Then you have a death wish, young one."

Still Billy held his ground. "No death wish," he said, "but death is definitely the reason I've come."

"Oh, is it?" scoffed Darrow.

"It is," Billy replied, barely clinging to composure. "You see, it seems you were right all along, at least about one thing. All this time, I had just needed the right motivation. And now I've found that motivation. So I've come here to kill you, Darrow. And I intend to do it now."

ALL GOOD (& EVIL) THINGS

BILLY FELT RAW, STRIPPED. Felt a wild convergence of emotions that manifested in a faint tremor.

Darrow saw it and pounced. "The young one shakes!" he declared.

Billy stared blankly at Darrow, as if he didn't recognize him. He held that look for an uncomfortable duration, his lips parted slightly and his face immobile.

Again Darrow turned to the gallery. "He is frightened and confused!"

Billy didn't budge. He looked Darrow over, still but for his eyes. He noticed the changes—the few extra pounds, the muscles grown flaccid. "You're wrong."

"The child is—"

"I have a name," interrupted Billy. "And so did she." Billy glanced around, found the House grayer than he remembered. An unpleasantness woven into the fabric. The foulest of smells permeated the air. He seized on it. "The compound has looked better."

He doubly mocked him, and Darrow crinkled his brow. Billy pressed him. "So will you face me yourself, or send in the mob?"

The psychology was apparent, and apparent to all. Still, Billy had confidence in Darrow's ego. Was certain that Darrow wouldn't risk losing face. He was a symbol. A symbol couldn't show fear.

"This young one has found his voice," Darrow chortled, a not-so-subtle reminder of Billy's oft-manifested timidity.

Again Billy scanned the platform, wondering where Lola had taken her last frantic breath, where she had felt the last beat of the weak heart that failed her.

After I failed her.

He stole another quick look at Sam, then drew his eyes back to Darrow. They were only a few feet apart. Marlon and Sherman flanked Darrow a step behind. Nobody stirred. Every breath was held. Only Sam, too young to understand the gravity of the present situation, and Rufus—led gently off to the side by Ears—seemed at peace.

Darrow broke the monotony. "I will enjoy this," he said, his intense anger supplanting his egomaniacal trend of referring to himself in the third person. He started forward, and Billy matched him with small cautious steps backwards, the crowd pulling apart as he did. He could no longer feel the pain in his thigh, or much of anything. The feinting continued this way until Billy had backed all the way to the tunnel opening.

"Why do you continue to back away?" chided Darrow. "Have you not even the courage to back up your own challenge?"

Marlon moved up beside Darrow, with some of the other members now stepping closely behind, as if in a poorly choreographed reenactment of *West Side Story*.

Billy retreated another few steps, now several feet inside the tunnel opening. He ensured he had Darrow's attention, then winked. The wink said, "Come get me!"—and as Billy turned and ran down the tunnel, Darrow obliged, rocks and stones kicking out violently beneath his angry footsteps.

Billy made it to the end of the tunnel and turned to check on his pursuer, surprised to find Darrow barreling in just behind him. Despite the added weight, he was still quick, with strong legs. Billy braced himself and sidestepped the first lunge as Darrow flew past him. Billy swung next, but Darrow recovered quickly and deflected the attack, then struck Billy hard to the side of his head, opening a deep cut over his left ear.

Definitely felt that…

Drops of blood rained down from the open wound and dripped to the rocky surface below. Billy wobbled back from the sting and the disorientation. He felt outmatched in every way imaginable, but he fought through it and jumped into the tracks, immediately running toward the main subway platform.

Darrow jumped down and pursued. Neither had checked to see if a train was coming. Neither was thinking clearly, driven by fear. By rage.

As his feet beat down on the uneven terrain, Billy peeked over his shoulder to find Darrow right on his tail—keeping pace despite his age and girth. Most of the spectators had also jumped down to the tracks or were streaming along the narrow ledge.

Billy's lungs were already on fire, both his thigh and his ear were pounding. He could hear Darrow behind him, the grunts having grown more pronounced, every small noise amplified in the narrow shaft.

Then the grunts faded away. Swept up in the rumble of an approaching train. Billy ran to the opposite ledge and heaved himself to safety. Darrow and all the rest did the same, both ledges now streaming toward the main subway platform.

Seconds later, the train roared by, car after car, trailing noise, wind drag, and fear.

Run. Just run. His thoughts drove him forward past the waiting room and the startled sentry.

The train had now stopped at the main platform up ahead. Billy watched the ants flutter to and fro and saw the train pull away. Watched, as he approached, the ants slowly morph into people.

Then, just as he felt he could run no longer, Billy burst onto the main platform. He ran past a handful of people before careening into a young woman who'd been sipping a late-night latte. It threw her off balance, crashing her beverage to the ground, the contents exploding from the cup and smothering a crumpled dollar bill lying abandoned on the dirty platform floor.

There were fewer than a dozen people scattered about. At first they seemed confused, even mildly amused. Only then came Darrow, huffing and puffing, his face distorted from the run. He stalked Billy behind a man in a tweed jacket. The man started into a run, then the others followed suit as dozens upon dozens of members streamed suddenly in from both ledges, those on the far side jumping down and crossing the subway tracks and swarming back up over the ledge like locusts.

Darrow charged at Billy and took a wild swing, but he was slower this time, and Billy managed to dodge the blow with a quick step back. Darrow launched forward again and sent another wild strike toward Billy's head, grazing his already-wounded ear. Billy avoided a third strike, and before Darrow could recover, launched himself forward and tackled Darrow to the ground.

It had devolved into primal warfare—biting, kicking, gouging. They tussled on the ground for nearly a minute, the members huddled closely around what had become a makeshift ring. Billy's tender thigh hampered him just long enough to allow Darrow to get on top of him and push his face into the ground, scraping his bloody ear along the dirty concrete.

The pain was unbearable.

He bore it.

Then, twisting his body to free one of his legs, he kicked Darrow hard in his gut. The blow pushed Darrow back, the ring shifting with the action. Billy got up and tackled him back to the ground, getting in a few good shots of his own before Darrow bucked him off and to the side. They both got to their feet, chests heaving. Billy was bleeding from his left ear, his thigh screaming, his face red and swollen. One of Darrow's eyes had swelled shut. His nose leaked blood past his lips and onto his chin.

They faced off again, feet apart, circling around one another. They were breathless, each trying to muster enough energy for the next grapple. Neither said a word. They just stared at each other. Swollen bodies. Swollen pride. Looking at Darrow that way made Billy think of the eighth tenet, that no member shall harm any other. There was a time he would have died to uphold the tenets—before Darrow had turned them elastic and meaningless.

The thought gave him life and he dove forward, only to be blocked by Darrow and thrown toward the edge of the platform as the members scurried out of the way. Billy sprung to his feet and tried to center himself but Darrow boxed him out, then pushed Billy back in the same direction. Closer to the ledge.

The members drew in tighter, closing the circle around them. Billy looked for some way out. Darrow in front. Tracks behind.

He felt a faint tremor and knew it was an approaching train. He couldn't tell which side of the tracks, but didn't want to find out.

He tried to run past his opponent but was stymied again and thrown right back to the same spot. The rumble grew louder. Billy peeked and saw it coming: his side. He lunged at Darrow again but it wasn't enough, and Darrow pushed him back with seemingly little effort, this time partially past the edge, his feet skidding out over the side, small bits of dirt whisking down into the tracks. Billy tried to get up, chest heaving, body battered and bloodied.

He got to his feet and took one step forward, then stopped, kneeling down in submission and inhaling deeply.

Darrow seemed surprised by it. He paused as if confused, but only for a moment, then finally lurched forward for the killing blow.

Billy closed his eyes and let his senses go numb, but not too numb to feel the blow that now fell gently upon him.

Lola.

It was a single hit. No more.

Mother.

The lonely strike felt soft, comforting even, and in that instant he recalled so many things—as if that second were a lifetime. He thought not only of Lola, but also of Sam, and of all that had brought him to that point. He thought of his mother, without the screams, or the fear, or the well-intended reach of the firere-tardant yellowy man. And he thought of the old man in the east end, and the girl in the park, and that narrow slice of humanity that had always held him in high regard, and had put Billy's interests on par with their own, ever so briefly, if not even a step or two beyond.

He thought of all these things, and an incalculable set of others, as he let his body fall back to the tracks below. But the fall took longer than he thought, and another second went by, then another, until he finally realized he wasn't falling at all, the strike having been a mere glancing blow to his right shoulder. He opened his eyes to find not Darrow standing before him, but hundreds of wide eyes looking past him and over the edge of the platform. Billy looked two feet ahead of him on the ground and saw the soggy mess of spilled espresso and money framing the skid of Darrow's footprints.

Billy turned around to see Darrow rising to his feet, his head bloodied from his fall into the tracks. Darrow looked up at them with wonder. An expression sparked across his face that may have been remorse but might equally have been defiance. The shrill sound of the advancing train had by then commandeered Billy's ears, yet he could still see Darrow's face, bearing the same deeply penitent look as when Tommy had spoken of their good intentions, and saw, in the distinct quiver of Darrow's lips, three discrete words that would stay with him forever.

The train roared by a moment later to end the chance for fur-ther soliloquy. There was nothing left by the time it passed—only a stain on the tracks, and the memory of a symbol.

The legions of Darrow closed in, pushing Billy aside as an afterthought. They lined up along the edge of the platform and stared into the tracks, at the final resting place of their leader. All were silent but Lizzy—who wailed uncontrollably—and one solitary voice from behind. A voice that remarked, with a solemnity appropriate to the moment, "And now He shall live forever."

Transfixed by the turn of events, none seemed to notice the security guard calling nervously into his radio, or Billy limping quietly away. He somehow made his way back down the subway shaft, where he staggered up the gravelly tunnel and into the compound.

It was shockingly empty. Of the remaining members, most were the ghetto-dwellers, too old or too sick to move. And a few, it seemed, hadn't stirred for some time.

Aside from the infirm, there'd been a malignant apathy from many in the first railcar. More than half of them—those who'd originally been the fittest and strongest of all—hadn't even budged. There they'd remained, abscessed by apathy, choosing instead to have a snack, or to stretch out for a nap while the issue sorted itself out. This included Lyle, who'd managed to sleep through the entire incident; and while a few of them actually had wanted to join their comrades, they'd found their stomachs too large, and their legs too skinny, to follow such a quick procession.

Rufus limped over and started licking Billy's wounds. It hurt, but he let him.

Billy saw Helena and moved to her, asking for The Progeny. Her face contorted, she gave Sam a kiss goodbye, and then passed the little one into Billy's care. He invited Helena to join them. The question was hurried but sincere, and she hurriedly declined. Billy didn't press; just turned to the pair of wide eyes that had set swollen and hopefully upon him.

"Rufus," he said, "we're leaving."

And with that, they retreated through the tunnel, up the subway shaft, and out through the same sentry point that George had left abandoned. Gerry, who'd also stayed back on account of his gimpy leg, hobbled behind as best he could. Several others followed suit, sensing their opportunity, and sensing that the winds had changed.

Minutes later the legions of Darrow filed back into the House like lost souls, with Marlon and Sherman convening in the office to contemplate their next course of action. They hadn't enjoyed their newfound power more than a few minutes before they were forced to calm an uprising among the masses. It had dawned on the group that their leader was dead, and the blank stares had given way to alarm, angst, and frightened chatter. Marlon sent Chester to the crate to shout for order, but his efforts were quickly stymied. Then, moments later, there was the sound of full-blown hysteria.

Marlon and Sherman exited the office to pacify their frightened denizens, only to discover dozens of uniformed men and women funneling through the tunnel and down onto the platform. Dressed in riot gear, and armed with clubs and Tasers, they began to subdue the members, with those who resisted rendered docile through force.

Some resigned themselves to capture and lay down. Others stood together defiantly singing the battle hymn. Meanwhile, Totter tried to talk his way past one of the guards. The majority, however, were in a frenzy, and tried to escape through the lone bottlenecked exit. Marlon himself was one, leading the mass exodus, frantically brushing aside any elders or infirm impeding his dash for freedom. He ran down the gravelly tunnel and nearly made it to the tracks before a well-placed baton cracked him into unconsciousness.

Despite the proliferation of uniformed authority, including a large contingent at the tunnel entrance, they couldn't contain them all. A late surge pushed them back, allowing a handful of members to slip through. Those fortunate enough to elude capture included Sherman, Chet, and Ears. Only they would be the last to escape. The authorities soon refortified their position, securing the House of Darrow and all of its inhabitants within.

They quickly surveyed the area, discovering, among the many horrors, Chester's lifeless body slumped behind the old wooden crate, his jugular slashed open and still oozing blood.

The scene had a heavy feel to it, as did the movement's casket, itself noticeably swelled by the memory of the discarded and the forgotten.

Of the last, the least, and the littlest.

ECSTASY OF MOLD

THE PAVEMENT FOUGHT EACH labored step, indifferent to the plight of its weary passengers. They made it back all the same, to his east end squat with the half-boarded windows and the alleyway replete with graffiti.

Billy peeked inside…Still vacant, after all these months. Soon all three were inside, where Billy laid Sam gently down on the couch, breathing in the familiar stench of mold and mildew. Only now there was something sickly sweet about those smells. They spoke of a different time, a time of innocent destitution.

The water damage didn't matter anymore, nor did the flaked-away brown ceiling, or the walls stained sickly yellow, or the floors shrouded dull and gray from filth. They welcomed him back in concert.

Billy fell exhausted next to Sam, the young one's chest rising and falling gently with each sleeping breath. At that moment Sam appeared not to have a care in the world, but Billy knew better. He knew they had to leave and put the city behind them.

Rufus hobbled over to Billy and lay down on the floor in front of the couch where he almost instantly fell into slumber.

Billy reached down and gently stroked his head. Rufus' paw was still misshapen, but in time he would heal. They all would. In various ways and to various results.

Billy wondered where he might go with this child…with Darrow's child…and no sooner had the question popped into his mind when he found his own answer. He recalled Jacob telling him about his hometown, a place filled with grass and trees and golden wheat fields. A place where the people were fewer and the pace was slower. And he decided in that moment that he would find this place; Jacob had described it well. Billy would find those wheat fields and take Sam there.

And in the days ahead he would often think of Lola, just as he would think of Ash, and Jacob and Tommy, and all the individuals who had inspired him and renewed the purpose in his life. And he would think often of the organization, and of the ecstasies and miseries achieved there, always wondering if he'd engineered its noble failure, and if that were, in fact, any better than an ignoble victory.

And he would ponder Darrow's final words, just as he would ponder whether the sentiment of people would ever change, if their efforts might even start a ripple effect toward progress. The damage they did and the terror they raised may have been, in the grand scheme of things, miniscule in scope; but to Billy and the rest, it was nothing short of revolutionary.

Nothing short of Glorious.

The movement could rise again. Not all of them had been captured, and they'd inspired so many others. And, of course, there was always The Progeny.

But then maybe it wouldn't come to that. Perhaps, after all was said and done, some good would come out of the violence and hypocrisy they had fostered. For when society did finally storm the compound, as Billy knew they would, what would be made of all their sick and suffering in the ghetto? What would be made of their horrid life circumstances? Might something suddenly click? Might someone finally realize what it was all about? And maybe, just maybe, might that information fall into the lap of someone who cared?

Maybe. Only he wouldn't wait to find out, wouldn't wait for the day that people might finally turn their focus to aid over acquisition, love over luxury, compassion past convenience, empathy over exploitation. For the day that society might finally value all lives equally.

Billy would not wait for this fairy tale to come true. And though his weary body was battered and bruised, he'd have plenty of time to lick his wounds in the days to come. They would leave this place, where there was such a profound scarcity of virtue, such a dearth of love that hadn't been bought or paid for. This city, with such rare sacrifice of self to the well-being of others, except when it was cute or convenient or fashionable. It was from this place they would leave, and they would start their journey tomorrow, before it got any colder.

Rufus included.

And as he curled his bruised body around Sam, himself mere moments from sleep, Billy wondered what they might do once they got there. And just before his eyelids became insurmountably heavy, he pledged, when the time allowed, to give the matter more thought.

So he slept, his most restless yet deserved slumber, both burdened and lifted by memory, and by two particular phrases above all, each vying for his last scrap of conscious thought.

Ah, this world.

Ah, the injustice!

D R. LAMBERT?"
It's not until he hears his name called aloud that he realizes how far his thoughts have trailed off. He's been there for an hour now, examining the scene with the wide-eyed fascination of a child.

What a microcosm this was...*They had obviously come to-gether as a makeshift civilization.*

"Just a minute, detective!"

Lambert makes his way back down the tracks, an area ripe with disease and feces. By now he's grown accustomed to the smell.

When the police first stormed the place, they found many sick or emaciated lying about the tracks, and even a few that were still. The bodies of the dead have since been removed, but the foul odor has resisted eviction. They may be gone, but their presence remains.

Lambert takes a few more ginger steps on the rocky surface before something catches his attention.

He directs his flashlight to the ground, kneels down for a better look, then digs the half-buried object out from the rocky terrain and pulls it closer to his eyes. He examines the widget from several angles, then slowly makes his way back toward the caboose.

"What did you find?" asks Meyers, now standing on the plat-form just a few feet away.

Lambert climbs up to join him.

"Nothing, really. Just a rusted bottle cap. I've found them abandoned all over the tracks. This one is from an old Nehi bottle. I used to drink this stuff all the time as a kid. Still do, when I can find it."

"The more things change, I guess..." responds Meyers, his voice trailing off to indifference.

"It's strange, though."

"What's that?"

"I saw some of them in the railcars," said Lambert. "Some were kept clean and polished on the seats. But then there were others wedged down in the cushions or on the floor."

"What's so strange about it?"

"Well, it was as if they collected them. Even valued them a little bit. But then most of them seemed to have been left down in the tracks."

"Bunch of their own were down there, too, though."

"True, but if they'd only..."

Meyers clears his throat.

"Dr. Lambert, please tell me you've got more for the mayor than bottle caps..."

Lambert nods, somewhat sheepishly, before flicking the bottle cap back down into the tracks. It ticks off a few rocks before disappearing somewhere into the darkness.

"So, Dr. Lambert, we've been here for almost an hour...Do you have any preliminary thoughts on what was going on here?"

Lambert doesn't immediately respond. He was struggling with the same question even before Meyers posed it. Has been thinking of nothing else since the moment he was contacted. He still can't fathom what might have drawn them all together this way; what could possibly have caused them to shed their reclusive ways and organize themselves in the manner that they did. What catalyst might have set them on this violent path? He's spent years studying their psychology and living patterns. Nothing fits. Nothing makes sense.

Meyers presses, impatient for some sort of response.

"This wasn't natural though, was it? I mean, it can't really be what it looks like?"

An uncomfortable silence settles in before Lambert speaks again. "It's certainly not like anything I've ever seen before, but I'm sure there was a reason behind all of it. It's a puzzle laid out at our feet. We just have to put the pieces together."

The non-answer exasperates the detective. "Dr. Lambert, felines are your area of expertise! Are you actually suggesting that they might have been *organized?* That this colony of ferals and strays actually moved with a purpose?"

Lambert wishes he could tell him more, wishes that he himself fully understood the circumstances that led to what transpired here over the last several months. Their coming together, their seemingly organized and premeditated attacks. "It's possible..." he responds. "They're highly intelligent beings. They were obviously upset about something."

Lambert considers the resourcefulness it would have taken, not only to secure the food that they had, but to locate so much fresh Nepeta here in the city, evidenced by the dried bits scattered thoroughly about the area.

Visibly frustrated, Meyers strikes up a fresh cigarette, inhales deeply, then exhales an impatient cloud of smoke into the chilly darkness. "The people on the platform said it was quite a spectacle. Said it was like a god damned convention."

Lambert nods, again turning his attention to the wall beside the office, yet again trying to decipher the strange scratchings concentrated in that particular area. They appear to be two separate columns of scrawl, careful but nonsensical scratches—at least to the human eye. Lambert can't help but wonder if there was any meaning behind those claw marks, or if they'd merely turned that particular part of the wall into a surrogate scratching post.

"They said there was a brown-haired tabby front and center," a quick puff, "said he was really fighting for his life."

Lambert responds under his breath, "Maybe they all were," the words falling too softly at his feet for interception.

"Pardon?"

Lambert adjusts his wool cap. "I said maybe they all were," he repeats.

Meyers nods. Another puff. "Looks like they turned on each other real quick."

Lambert doesn't respond.

"Just their nature, I suppose."

Again Lambert doesn't respond.

Meyers turns for the exit. "Well, whatever they were up to, it's gonna be the needle for this lot."

Lambert responds sharply. "You really think that's the answer?"

It's not actually a question, more a shot across the bow; and Meyers doesn't press, sensing Lambert's tone. It's the same smug superiority that Lambert has heard from so many people over the course of his career. The same calcified indifference.

None of them get it.

Many never will.

"We should be going," says Meyers, tentatively.

Lambert doesn't budge, his eyes now lingering on the tracks.

"They're just animals, Dr. Lambert." His voice softer, conciliatory.

Lambert softens his own features in return, curling up a slight smile on his lips, the, "Aren't we all, though," left unsaid.

And with that, each man falls into sustained silence, Meyers flicking the remainder of his cigarette to the compound floor and extinguishing it beneath a twist of his heel, Lambert steeling himself for a return trip down the tracks.

It's just after midnight when they step past the still-leaning flat cap and back into the gravelly tunnel, leaving behind the smell, among others, of stale oil, sulfur, and the promise of better days to come.

Coming (soon?)

The Story of Derek
(Through The Story of Ash)

ACKNOWLEDGMENTS

IF IT TAKES A village to raise a child, I believe it takes nearly as many to raise a novel, and a great deal more antacid.

I WISH TO ACKNOWLEDGE EVERYONE who has supported or inspired me throughout this arduous process, including my family (Robert, Mary, Eric), Michelle Roth—who was supportive beyond words, Meagan Smith, Chris Hanna, Brittany Medeiros, David Dumais, Matthew MacIsaac, The Flying Squirrels— Carolyn Thomas, Sonja Harrison, and Fiona Christie—David D'Iorio, Brian McGuire, John Forrester; all the teachers who believed in and inspired me, specifically Barbara Inman (4th grade, Longfellow Elementary, Portland, Maine), Christine Pittman (10th grade, Chantilly High School, Chantilly, Virginia—where Billy Tabbs was first born), and Naomi Dixon (Grades 10–12, Chantilly High School, Chantilly, Virginia); all those who've been invaluable in editing this book, including Sandy Adelson, Allister Thompson, Michael Kenyon, Sylvia McConnell, Karin Lowachee, Susan Folkins, and Susan Foster; to the writers who inspired me throughout and to which this book pays homage, particularly the legendary George Orwell; and finally to Jay Nadeau and the entire team at Bitingduckpress, who perhaps believed in Billy more than he believed in himself.

THE PHRASE "THE LAST, the least, the littlest" comes from a letter by Cardinal Roger Mahony, Archbishop of Los Angeles: "Any society, any nation, is judged on the basis of how it treats its weakest members—the last, the least, the littlest" (November 12, 1998).

ABOUT THE AUTHOR

An American-Canadian citizen, Michael holds degrees in English, Political Science, and Law. He is employed as a Crown prosecutor in the Greater Toronto Area.

Billy Tabbs (& THE GLORIOUS DARROW) is his debut novel.

Visit www.darrowknows.com

BOOK CLUB AND EDUCATIONAL QUESTIONS

1. What are the major themes of the novel, and what message(s) do you feel the author is trying to convey?

2. What creates class divides? What are the benefits of social classes? What are the disadvantages?

3. Some people believe that we cannot have social and economic equality unless we eliminate classes; others believe that class divides may promote social and economic growth, with the possibility of equality for all. Discuss the two points of view.

4. Describe your view of the ideal society and how it is or is not attainable.

5. If you were a member of the House of Darrow, would you have supported Jacob's or Marlon's approach, and why?

6. Darrow claimed that "Violent indifference earns indifferent violence." Do you agree with that statement? Is violence ever acceptable as a means to an end? Discuss.

7. Describe some of the symbolism in the book, particularly as it relates to:

    a. Class

    b. Animals

    c. Religion

8. Who was to blame for the ultimate failure of the House of Darrow? Explain?

9. Describe some of the literary or pop culture allusions in the book.

10. What gender was Sam? Why do you think so?

11. What do the rail cars represent?

12. What does the water damage to the second rail car represent?

13. What do the tracks represent?

14. What do the widgets represent?

15. What does 'the weed' represent?

16. What does 'the needle' represent?

17. What does Totter represent? What did you make of the theory of Joy Transference? Does it have merit? Why or why not?

18. How old is Darrow? How did you determine his age?

19. What do you think Jacob meant when he told Darrow that "There will always be a man in the tunnels"?

20. Does the revelation strengthen or weaken the novel? If so, how?

21. Does the revelation make the novel more or less satisfying? If so, how?

22. Did your sympathy for the character(s) increase or decrease as a result of the revelation? Why?

23. Did the revelation substantially alter your opinion of any particular event or character, and if so, which one and how?

24. How would you characterize the ending (e.g., happy or sad, hopeful or hopeless)? How does the final scene with Dr. Lambert and Detective Meyers influence your view?

25. At what point in the story (if ever) did you first suspect the true nature of the homeless population? Identify and discuss some of the clues.

26. What, if anything, makes Darrow an admirable character?

27.   How did Darrow change throughout the course of the book, and to what do you attribute the changes?

28.   What, if anything, makes Billy an admirable character?

29.   How would you characterize Darrow? Is he a hero or a villain? Did your view of Darrow change as the story evolved?

30.   How would you characterize Billy? Is he a heroic or tragic figure? What could he have done, if anything, to improve the outcome for the community? What prevented him from doing that?

31.   Jacob and Tommy came from very different backgrounds, but both were devoted (at least for a time) to Darrow. How did their early years contribute to their characters and their views of nonviolence and equality? Would you describe either of them as naïve? Why or why not?

32.   What were Darrow's last words, and what did you take them to mean?

33.   The precise method of Darrow's death had been foreshadowed. Where?

34.   Who was your favorite character, or characters, and why?

35.   Who was your least favorite character, or characters, and why?

36.   How would you characterize Chester (the town crier)? Was he an innocent pawn or a collaborator? Comment on Chester's ultimate fate.

37.   In what ways, if any, do the downtrodden share responsibility for what became of the House of Darrow?

38.   Does Marlon's explanation for Jacob's death ring true? Why or why not?

39.   Which character(s) were you most rooting for? Did your sympathies change over the course of the story? If so, how?

40.   Did your opinion of Rufus change as a result of the revelation, and if so, how?

41.   Did you find any part(s) of the book humorous, and if so, which part(s) were most humorous?

42.   Ash fails to return to the community after Operation Overpass. Did he die or did he survive? Why do you think so?

43.   Billy is hopeful that he was able to save the girl in the blue dress. What suggests that she survived? What suggests that she did not?

44.   Which scene or event stood out most in your mind, and why?

45.   Which was the most difficult scene to read, and why?

46.   Whose death affected you most, and why?

47.   What do you think became of Derek? How does it affect the story that his disappearance remains a mystery?

48.   A few characters, such as Lyle, Neven, and Hannah make only a brief appearance. What is their relevance, if any, to the story?

49.   Do you relate Billy Tabbs to any novels you've previously read, and if so, which ones and how?

50.   Were Darrow's unseen achievements (avenging George, defeating the man in the flat cap, razing the facility) apocryphal or real? Does it matter? How?

51.   Jacob said, "The fabric of our society needs mending." Do you agree or disagree? Why? If you agree, what is the best approach?

52.   Does this book alter your view on the valuation of life or society? If yes, how?

53.   What would a society that values all life equally look like? Is that a desirable goal? Is it possible? Why or why not?

54.   Discuss Detective Meyers' and Dr. Lambert's comments and reactions during the investigation. Which of their views, if either, is more commendable and why?